BEGINNINGS: THE ENDING SERIES ORIGIN STORIES

PREQUEL NOVELLAS 1 - 6

LINDSEY POGUE
LINDSEY FAIRLEIGH

Copyright © 2014 by Lindsey Fairleigh and Lindsey Pogue
All rights reserved.

This book is a work of fiction. All characters, organizations, and events are products of the author's imaginations or are used fictitiously. No reference to any real person, living or dead, is intended or should be inferred.

Cover Design by Molly Phipps
We Got You Covered Book Design

L2 Books
101 W American Canyon Rd. Ste. 508 – 262
American Canyon, CA 94503

978-1-723814-54-9

OTHER NOVELS BY THE LINDSEYS

THE ENDING SERIES

The Ending Beginnings: Omnibus Edition

After The Ending

Into The Fire

Out Of The Ashes

Before The Dawn

World Before: A Collection of Stories

NOVELS BY LINDSEY POGUE

A SARATOGA FALLS LOVE STORY

Whatever It Takes

Nothing But Trouble

Told You So

FORGOTTEN LANDS

Dust And Shadow

Borne of Sand and Scorn

Wither and Ruin (TBR)

Borne of Earth and Ember (TBR)

NOVELS BY LINDSEY FAIRLEIGH

ECHO TRILOGY

Echo in time

Resonance

Time Anomaly

Dissonance

Ricochet Through Time

KAT DUBOIS CHRONICLES

Ink Witch

Outcast

Underground

Soul Eater

Judgement

Afterlife

ATLANTIS LEGACY

Sacrifice of the Sinners

Legacy of the Lost

CARLOS

VOLUME ONE

1

"I can't…I told you," Carlos said, yanking his wrist out of the larger kid's clammy grasp. It wasn't that Carlos was small for his age—quite the opposite, in fact. He was already five-foot-ten and, thanks to the recently wrapped-up football season, nearly 150 pounds, and he was still a few months shy of sixteen. No, the problem was that Julian was just a little bit taller, a whole lot thicker, and really desperate.

Julian raised his hands, running his fingers through his greasy, dirty-blond hair. There was no doubt in Carlos's mind that the kid needed a shower, and based on his pallid coloring and the grayish-purple, bruise-like circles under his eyes, to lay off the Vicodin. Carlos felt the slightest twinge of guilt for being the one who'd supplied Julian with the pills in the first place. Which, as Carlos's older brother had drilled into his head, was exactly why the Hernandez boys only dealt the pills; they never sampled them themselves.

"What am I supposed to do?" Julian practically shouted. He took a lurching step forward, hands outstretched like he might grab the front of Carlos's down jacket.

Carlos side-stepped, easily evading the clumsy maneuver. He

spun around in time to see Julian skitter on a patch of ice and crash into the chain-link fence marking the perimeter of Toppenish High School's snow-covered outfield. Glancing around warily, Carlos backed away, hands in his coat pockets. He hated dealing with this crap at school.

"Next week, man. I should be getting some new stuff this weekend."

Julian's fingers curved into rigid, claw-like hooks clutching at the fence to hold himself upright. Breathing hard, he turned his head so his flushed cheek was squished against the frost-coated metal. A thin crimson trail streaked from just under his right eye down to his chin like a single, bloody tear. It added an extra creep factor to the haunting, almost feverish glint in Julian's eyes.

The final bell releasing them from school for the day had rung a good fifteen minutes ago, and there was no way Carlos's sister, Vanessa, wouldn't guess why he'd been late. She would chew him out the whole ride home for being dumb enough to follow in Jesse's dealing footsteps, then track down their older brother and rip him a new one, too. Carlos started jogging backward toward the student parking lot, where his sister would be waiting for him.

"It's just a few days, Julian," he shouted, tugging his black beanie further over his ears. "You'll survive."

Turning mid-stride, he broke into a run. Each exhale produced a white puff that seemed almost solid enough to grab. He didn't stop until he reached his sister's decades-old, dark green Honda Civic, one of the few cars still sitting in the lot. The temperature was in the low teens, cold even for early December in Toppenish, one of a string of small towns in Central Washington's Yakima Valley, and nobody was eager to linger in a parked car.

Hand tucked inside his sleeve, Carlos popped the passenger door open and ducked inside. He held his hands up to the vents, grateful for the warmth. "Sorry Nessa, I—" When Carlos looked at his sister, the rest of the sentence died on his tongue.

Vanessa was staring vacantly out the windshield, the skin

around her eyes red and puffy, and tears were streaming down her splotchy cheeks.

"Shit..." Carlos reached across the center console and draped his arm over his sister's shoulders, pulling her into the closest approximation to a hug that was possible in the interior of the small car. It was awkward and uncomfortable, but that didn't matter. Vanessa almost never cried. She was barely a year older than Carlos, but he'd only seen her cry a handful of times.

"What is it?" he asked, his voice tight with worry.

Vanessa exhaled a gut-wrenching sob and clutched Carlos's coat. "It's...it's Benny." The baby of their family, Benny was barely two and suffered from a congenital heart condition—the same one that had killed their dad just before Benny had been born.

Benny had come down with a cough and a slight fever the previous afternoon, but their mom had been certain it was just the flu. And she was a nurse; she knew what she was talking about. Of course, influenza could be dangerous to a kid like Benny, which was why their mom had taken Benny to the hospital with her when she'd left for the swing shift the previous night. Just to make sure.

Benny would be fine. He would. He...

Carlos squeezed his eyes shut, holding back tears. There was no use in freaking out before he knew how bad it was. He had to swallow several times before he found his voice. "Is he okay?"

Shaking her head against his shoulder, Vanessa made a low keening sound that was almost too faint to hear.

Carlos felt a single tear escape and inch down his cheek.

"He—he...mom called in the middle of seventh period, but I didn't answer." Vanessa pulled away just enough to meet Carlos's eyes. Hers, a rich chocolate-brown that usually sparkled with laughter—or anger or annoyance—were endless pools of despair. "You know how Mr. Martin is...I *couldn't* check my phone. I didn't know until—" Her chin quivered, and the effort it was taking her to hold back another wave of grief was evident in the hard set of her jaw and the tightness around her blood-shot eyes. "I didn't know until after…when I listened to mom's message that—that—" She took a halting breath. "…that Benny's on life support."

Her words hit Carlos like a punch to the stomach.

Vanessa closed her eyes, shutting out the world. "They don't think he's going to make it." Her voice was high-pitched and small. Carlos knew she wouldn't be able to hold it together for long…if what she was currently doing could even be called holding it together. And she wasn't alone. He was on the brink of breaking down, feeling like someone was shredding his heart while it was still in his chest, but he was determined to maintain the appearance of being strong—at least until he was alone.

"Come on," Carlos said as he released his sister and pulled on the door handle. "Switch with me. I'll drive to the hospital."

Vanessa wiped her cheeks with both hands. Not that it did any good; the tears were still pouring out, if a bit more slowly. "But you don't have your license yet."

He shot her a look that clearly said, "And…?"

Without any further argument, Vanessa exited the car and switched seats with Carlos. As he was releasing the emergency brake, she touched her fingertips to the sleeve covering his forearm. "Hold on. Mom said this flu thing's gotten out of control… said it's becoming a huge outbreak. We're not supposed to go to the hospital—it's bad there. Too many people…" Vanessa shrugged, at a loss for what to do.

Carlos gritted his teeth and narrowed his eyes. "What are they gonna do? Keep us out?" Snorting, he pushed in the clutch and shifted into first gear. He might not have had as much experience driving as Vanessa, but he wasn't a complete amateur. "What about Jesse? Does he know?"

However much Vanessa was bothered by Jesse's chosen "career" and his choice to involve Carlos in what he called "the family business," Carlos knew she still loved Jesse and would want him around during such a hard time. Since their dad's death, Jesse had become the sheltering arms of the family. Helping their mom provide for them was the main reason he'd expanded his illicit business in the first place.

Chewing on her lower lip, Vanessa shook her head. "I called and texted him like a million times, but"—she shrugged—"nothing." She paused for a moment. "He's supposed to be back today, right?"

Carlos nodded as he cautiously navigated his way out of the parking lot and onto the icy street. Jesse had gone down to Cali to meet up with a potential new supplier, and he'd been gone for a little over a week. "He said he'd be back this afternoon at the latest." He glanced at Vanessa, offering a tight-lipped smile. It was a pathetic attempt at reassuring her, but he had to try. "Did you try the house? If he's not home yet, he should be soon."

Out of the corner of his eye, Carlos watched Vanessa touch the screen of her phone and, hands shaking, raise it to her ear. Nobody answered.

2

The parking lots surrounding Yakima Valley Memorial Hospital were overflowing with cars, some parked illegally against curbs, leaving barely enough room for the vehicles around them to vacate their spaces. It was so bad that, as Carlos drove down one of the aisles in the east lot, he had to back out the way he'd come in. To make matters worse, Carlos and Vanessa were hardly the only people in search of a parking spot.

Carlos breathed deeply, fighting the frustration pushing him closer and closer to losing his temper. Anger would be an easier and much more familiar emotion to deal with than the crushing grief he was barely managing to hold at bay. But he resolved to hold it together, whether it was anger, grief, or any other dark emotion that surfaced. For Vanessa. And once they were inside the hospital, for their mom and Benny, too.

"Fuck it," Carlos snapped, tires slipping on the frozen pavement as he changed course, heading instead for the residential streets surrounding the hospital. He found a spot on the street north of the hospital in front of a large, white house. The road hadn't been plowed since the last snow, and chunks of compacted snow and ice crunched under their tires as he drew the car to a stop.

With an anxious sigh, Carlos turned off the car, opened the driver's side door, and stepped out onto the compacted snow. He stuffed his hands into his coat pockets and headed for the sidewalk, where Vanessa awaited him. Before he reached her, the front door of the house they'd parked in front of opened slowly and with an ominous creak. Inhaling, Carlos clenched his jaw, fully expecting some asshole to yell at him about parking in front of his house. He stopped beside his sister and stared at the empty doorway, waiting.

A little girl poked her blonde head around the edge of the door. She was tiny and pale with a cherubic face. She didn't say anything, just watched Carlos and Vanessa, eyes somber.

Vanessa raised her hand and waved to the little girl.

"Are you here to help Nana?" the child asked. "I pushed the button."

Carlos exchanged a look of bafflement with his sister.

"She won't wake up," the little girl said, a tremor in her voice.

Meeting Carlos's eyes apologetically, Vanessa stepped onto the snow-covered lawn and slowly made her way toward the little girl.

Carlos watched his sister walk away from him, then glanced up at the clear blue sky, thinking they really didn't have time for this —they needed to get to Benny and their mom. He huffed once in protest, then followed Vanessa's lead and headed across the lawn.

When Vanessa reached the front porch, she crouched down until she was at the same level as the little girl. Carlos jogged the final few yards to catch up.

The child's trusting, bright blue eyes focused first on Vanessa, then on Carlos.

"What's your name, sweetie?" Vanessa asked. Carlos could tell her warm smile was forced.

The child blinked several times, and a few huge tears spilled from her eyes. "Annie," she told them.

"Well, I'm Nessa, and this"—she nodded toward her brother —"is Carlos."

Annie's gaze shifted to Carlos again, and this time she smiled shyly, despite her tears. Little girls tended to fall head over heels in love with him. His mom always said it was because he had dreamboat eyes and an honest face. He wasn't sure about all that, but the facts remained the same—little girls adored him.

"Where are your parents?" Vanessa asked.

"In heaven," the little girl said softly.

That took both Carlos and Vanessa by surprise, and neither knew what to say for a long moment. Finally, Vanessa managed to gather her wits. "Well...how long has your nana been asleep?" Vanessa asked.

Annie sniffled. "A really long time."

Carlos frowned, but Vanessa maintained her friendly expression. "Did you call 911?"

Shaking her head, Annie held up what looked like a car remote hanging from a nylon cord around her neck. "I pushed Nana's help button." It took Carlos a moment to realize he was looking at a tiny emergency alert device.

Nudging his sister, Carlos asked, "Can I have your phone?" When Vanessa handed it to him, he immediately dialed 911. It rang...and rang...and rang... "Nobody's answering," he muttered.

"Do you want us to come in and check on your nana? Maybe call someone else to come get you?"

"Nessa," Carlos said under his breath, "we don't have time to..."

The look Vanessa turned on him was full of helplessness. She wanted to get to the hospital just as badly as he did. But, she also wouldn't just abandon the little girl.

"Okay," Annie agreed. She opened the door further, and a pungent, rancid odor wafted out of the house—the smell of vomit, and something worse.

Vanessa started coughing, her eyes watering, and Carlos raised the collar of his jacket over his nose and mouth to block the rank odor. How Annie had been able to stand it for any period of time was beyond him. He grabbed Vanessa's arm as they entered the house, stopping her from moving beyond the high-ceilinged entryway. "I'll check on her nana, I guess." He glanced around the entryway. There was a living room to their right, a door, possibly to a closet, to their left, and the way ahead was divided into a hallway leading further into the house and a carpeted stairwell leading to the second floor.

Carlos glanced down at the little girl holding the door open. She was wearing flannel pajamas covered in big brightly colored polka dots, and he thought she couldn't be more than four years old, definitely too young to take care of herself if "Nana" was unable. Vanessa was one step ahead of him.

"I'll look for a cell phone or list of phone numbers…there's got to be someone we can call." She held her hand out for her own phone, which Carlos handed over immediately. "Annie? Where's your nana sleeping?" she asked the little girl.

Annie pointed up the stairs. "In her room."

"Okay, sweetie. Carlos is going to try to wake her up." She took the girl's hand and led her away from the front door, leaving it open so the house could air out a bit. "Can you show me where Nana's phone is?"

"Yeah," Annie said, dragging Vanessa down the hallway toward the back of the house. "She has this one and…"

Carlos watched them until they turned around a corner at the end of the hallway, the little girl's chattering still audible but no longer understandable to his ears. He wasn't overly eager to head upstairs. The odor was nauseating, and if it was coming from Annie's nana, it was going to be a whole lot more unpleasant on the second floor. Dread knotted his stomach.

"C'mon, man, you got this," he said under his breath. He needed to just suck it up and check on the woman so they could finally get to the hospital. Steeling his resolve, Carlos started up the stairs, keeping his hand over his mouth and taking shallow breaths. He passed by countless family photos with hardly a glance.

At the top of the stairs there was a wide landing with four doorways, two on the right, one straight ahead, and one on the left. The two on the right were bedrooms, but with a quick search, Carlos dismissed them as "Nana's" location. They were empty. The doorway ahead lead to a bathroom, which was also empty. It was the doorway on the left, the one with the mostly shut door, through which he was certain he would find Annie's nana.

He hesitated at the door, feeling extremely uncomfortable and a little afraid. What if the woman was awake and thought he was some sort of burglar or was there to hurt her? Scowling, he shook his head, thinking he really needed to grow a pair.

"Ma'am?" Carlos asked as he pushed the door open further. "Are you…" But his words trailed off as he caught sight of her.

She was curled up on her side in a queen-size bed centered against the opposite wall. She was a small, elderly woman with short gray hair and ashen skin. She wasn't just sick; she was dead.

Carlos's stomach lurched, and he gagged. He spun around and rushed into the bathroom, spewing his lunch into the toilet bowl. He broke out in a cold sweat, and his whole body trembled. He'd never seen a dead body, not even his dad's, but he'd always imagined that when he did, it would be dressed in something nice and made-up to look like it was just asleep. That woman didn't look like she was just asleep. Nobody but a young child could mistake the woman in the bedroom for anything but dead.

Carlos stood on shaky legs and stumbled to the bathroom counter. Bowing his head over the sink, he turned on the faucet and splashed cold water on his face and neck. He raised his head and looked at himself in the mirror, but all he could see was the dead old woman, like the image had been burned into his retinas. He felt dirty, all of a sudden, tainted by death. Frantically, he started washing his hands with one of the small, flower-shaped hand soaps in the soap dish beside the sink. He washed his hands until the water was near scalding and his skin was an angry red.

Only after he'd rinsed out his mouth with mouthwash he'd

found in the cabinets under the sink did Carlos emerge from the bathroom. Without looking into the old woman's room, he shut the bedroom door, feeling better once there was a physical barrier between himself and the body. He hoped Annie hadn't spent too much time with her grandma after the woman had passed. The thought was more than a little disturbing.

Carlos wondered what had killed the woman. Had it been the flu, or some other sickness? Shaking his head, he backed away from the door and jogged down the stairs. He'd heard a few reports of people dying from the flu, but hadn't really thought that…well he hadn't really thought much about it at all. At least, he hadn't thought much about it until now.

"Nessa?" he called out as he reached the foot of the stairs. He sounded slightly hoarse, so he cleared his throat and opened his mouth to try again.

"In here," his sister called from somewhere near the back of the house. The kitchen, he realized, as he followed her voice down the hallway. The smell wasn't as bad back there.

He found Vanessa sitting at a built-in kitchen desk, a cordless phone to her ear and a piece of paper in her hand. As he moved closer, he could see that it was covered in neat handwriting. It appeared to be a list, with names and phone numbers squeezed in at odd angles wherever possible. Annie was sitting on the counter of a granite island, watching Vanessa. Her attention shifted to Carlos as he approached.

"Any luck?" he asked his sister, leaning against the doorframe between the hallway and the kitchen.

Pressing her lips together, Vanessa shook her head and lowered the phone from her ear. She pressed the talk button, and heaved a frustrated sigh. "I've had three people answer—one was sick, one was a kid who had no idea what I was talking about, and one was"—she glanced at Annie—"really nasty." She shrugged. "I've left a bunch of messages, too. How about you?"

Carlos shook his head and pushed off the doorframe, aiming

for the little girl. He stopped in front of her, crouching so he could meet her at eye level. "I, um…I'm sorry, Annie, but your nana, well, she's…" He struggled to find the words. How do you tell a little kid someone they love is dead?

Finally, he said. "She's in heaven with your parents."

Tears filled Annie's eyes, and her chin trembled.

"Come on," Carlos said, scooping her up. She wrapped her arms and legs around him and cried, Carlos holding her close the whole time.

3

"Did Mom say anything about cops guarding the place when you talked to her?" Carlos asked his sister, scanning the two hospital entrances he could see from the sidewalk. He was still holding Annie, but the little girl was now bundled up in her winter clothes—a puffy lavender coat, matching purple knit cap and mittens, and pink boots. They hadn't had any luck in finding someone she knew who could take care of her, and leaving her in the house with a dead body wasn't an option.

Vanessa shook her head. "Just that we should stay away."

"I don't think we should take Annie in there." Carlos tucked the girl's head under his chin. Through the glass doors, he could see a thick crowd of people milling around inside the hospital. "I mean, if all those people are sick…I don't know…"

"She was in that house with her nana—if she was gonna get sick, don't you think she would've already?"

Before Carlos could point out that they didn't know if the old woman had even had the flu, Annie said something quietly. It was too muffled for either Vanessa or Carlos to make out clearly.

"Hmmm, sweetie?" Vanessa asked, stepping close and adjusting Annie's faux fur-lined hood.

"I got better." The little girl's voice was small, but clear this time.

Carlos pulled his head back and looked down at her. "You were sick?"

Annie nodded. "Will Nana get better?" Her big blue eyes studied Carlos, seeming to demand answers.

"No, Annie, she won't," Carlos told the girl, hugging her close again. He turned his attention to his sister.

They were standing less than thirty yards from the door, only two rows of parked cars between them and the hospital. They were so close to being with Benny and their mom. So damn close. Yet there was only one way to get inside; they'd have to go through a guard.

As Carlos started to take a step toward the hospital entrance, Vanessa snagged his sleeve, holding him back. "Wait. I don't think…I think we should wait."

"Why? Annie's fine…"

Vanessa pressed her lips together in a thin line and shook her head. "Look, Carlos. Really *look*," she urged. "There's someone guarding the door on the inside too…"

Carlos could see the second cop through the glass. He frowned, not understanding her point.

"If some guy's guarding the door from the inside…" She gave him a meaningful look. "They're not just trying to keep people *out* of the hospital…"

"They're trying to keep them *in*," Carlos finished for her. If she was right, that meant their mom was trapped inside…with countless sick people. His frown deepened to a scowl. "But why would they do that?"

Vanessa shrugged. "Some sort of quarantine maybe?"

Again, Carlos shifted Annie slightly further to his side and held her more tightly. "I think you should try mom again," he told his sister. Vanessa had already called both their mom's cell and the nurse's station in the ICU, where their mom usually worked, several times during the walk to the hospital, but nobody had answered either line, just like nobody had answered their calls to 911 to report the death of Annie's grandma.

Frowning, Vanessa tapped her phone's screen and tucked it between her hood and her ear. Seconds passed, feeling more like minutes, and finally she shook her head. She lowered the phone and tapped the screen again, then returned it to her ear. She chewed her lip while she waited.

"I—yes…hi! Oh thank God!" she blurted, her face filled with a mix of relief and surprise. "This is Vanessa Hernandez, do you—no! Don't hang up! My mom is a nurse there—Eva Hernandez. Do you know her?" She paused. "Is she around? Can I talk to her?" Vanessa met Carlos's eyes, the corners of her mouth turning down. "Why not?"

Carlos kept his increasing anxiety in check by rubbing Annie's back through her thick winter jacket.

"Oh, I—I see." Vanessa cleared her throat, and when she spoke again, her voice was too high, like she was just barely holding back tears. "I'd appreciate that. Thank you."

Carlos watched his sister as she slowly lowered the phone from her ear and carefully returned it to her pocket. She stared at the hospital, at the third floor ICU windows. Finally, her voice dull and lifeless, she said, "Mom's sick." She looked at Carlos, utterly lost. "He doesn't know where she is now, just that she got sick a little before her son—" She raised her hand to her mouth, stifling a sob. "Oh God…Benny's gone. He's gone, Carlos."

Carlos couldn't speak. He feared that if he did, what came out of his mouth wouldn't be words, but a scream of agony…of outrage. This was so incredibly unfair!

Benny was gone.

His mom was sick.

They *had* to get inside.

Carlos felt like his heart was being crushed. His chest heaved with each rapid breath. With shaking hands, he pulled Annie's arms from around his neck and handed her off to Vanessa, then strode toward the officer guarding the hospital's north entrance.

The man was middle aged, and the extra weight he carried around his middle strained the fabric of his dark blue uniform. Despite that, the hard scowl on his weathered face and the way he was resting his hand on the grip of his sidearm as Carlos approached suggested that he was no softie.

With a deep breath and a polite nod, Carlos stopped a half-dozen feet from the officer. He cleared his throat, hoping his voice would be steady when he spoke. "Can I go in there?" With his chin, he indicated the doors behind the other man, then added, "Please. My mom's in there. She's a nurse. And my little brother just…he's in there too."

"Sorry, son. No can do."

Although Carlos wanted to curse in frustration, he smiled, trying his best to look innocent and friendly—harmless. "But—"

The cop shook his head.

His emotions swelled as the reality that he was unable to see his mom set it. The friendly expression melted off Carlos's face, and it was an effort for him not to glare. "Why not? What's going on anyway?"

The older man eyed him skeptically. "You don't know?"

"Obviously not," Carlos mumbled, his patience wearing thin.

The cop narrowed his eyes, apparently taking offense to Carlos's tone, but at least he answered. "The place is under quarantine. No one goes in or out until the CDC folks arrive. We're covering the exits until then." He frowned. "It's been all over the radio and news this afternoon, and schools were supposed to make announcements…"

Carlos shook his head. His school *might* have mentioned it, but he hadn't been in class sixth or seventh period. For what seemed like the millionth time over the past few days, he cursed himself for having dropped his iPhone in a toilet. After Jesse returned with the new drugs and Carlos sold enough, buying a new one was at the top of his list.

"Go home, kid. Your mom'll be safe and sound in here."

Carlos ignored the dismissal. "What's the CDC, anyway?"

"The Center for Disease Control."

"Well, why are they coming here? People get sick all the time."

"Because we have a disease that needs controlling," the officer said, annoyance evident in the sharpness of his tone.

"The flu?" Carlos asked skeptically. "But it's just the *flu*."

"Son, I don't—"

"And what about all the people who have it who aren't in there?" He waved his hand in the general direction of the door before stuffing it back into his pocket.

The cop shifted his feet, making his stance wider, and cleared his throat. "They're highly encouraged to stay in their homes…and out of trouble."

Carlos rolled his eyes and muttered, "Thanks for nothing," completely forgetting to tell the cop about Annie's grandma. He spun around and jogged back to Vanessa and Annie, who'd been watching the exchange. The little girl held out her arms to Carlos as he approached, and Vanessa seemed relieved to hand her over. She was small and fairly light, but so was Vanessa, and Annie was a much easier burden for Carlos to manage than she was for his diminutive sister.

"They won't let us in. C'mon," Carlos said and started walking back toward Annie's house and their car.

"Wait! But what about Benny and Mom?"

"Benny's gone," he snapped, the words tasting sour on his tongue. He heard her footsteps crunching in the snow behind him, then felt a hard smack against the back of his head. His beanie did little to shield his skull from her bony hand. "Ow!" he growled, spinning to face his sister.

She stood with her hands in her coat pockets, somehow managing to look like she had her fists on her hips, but instead of glaring, like he'd expected, she was crying. "I lost Benny, too, okay? I lost him, too."

Recalling what he'd said—Benny's gone—and *how* he'd said it —like a total asshole—his anger quickly dissipated, giving way to his all-encompassing grief. He squeezed his eyes shut. He wouldn't cry. Not yet. "Nessa…I'm sorry. I just…I don't know."

Vanessa held his eyes for a moment longer, almost like she was pleading with him to tell her it was all a mistake…Benny would be fine…everything would be okay. Finally, she averted her eyes and asked, "What'd that cop say?"

Carlos sighed. "You were right—the hospital's on quarantine. These people, the CDC, are apparently on their way to fix everything." He shrugged. "Then Mom'll be able to come home. Until then, nobody goes in or out." A crease formed between his eyebrows. "He said it's all over the news and that school was supposed to announce it or something."

Vanessa's reaction to the cop's information was the same as Carlos's had been—a slow shake of her head. She sniffled. "All they announced was that thing about school being cancelled until after the new year, not—"

"What?" Carlos blurted. There was still another week and a half of school before winter break.

"At the end of seventh period…" Vanessa eyed him accusatorily. "But you didn't hear it because you were skipping, weren't you?"

"Yeah, but I wasn't dealing. It was just because Rosie nee—"

Vanessa threw her hands up in the air. "I don't care about Rosie! You're so stupid sometimes, you know? I mean, with her stupid gangbanger brother…" She shook her head, grief amplifying her anger. "We stay neutral. We don't get caught up in their shit! God, it's bad enough with you and Jesse dealing—"

"I—"

"Shut up," she snapped. "If you'd just go to class, you wouldn't have to do it, you know? You're smart enough—you could get a scholarship, and not have to save up like this, and then we could all get away from this place and live like normal people who *don't* deal drugs and *don't* date people whose families think drive-bys are fun!"

A few months back, there'd been a drive-by a block from their house. Carlos had no desire to get caught up in any gang conflicts, and despite his recent foray into dealing, Jesse had been careful about bringing in drugs that wouldn't step on the toes of any existing gang-affiliated dealings. The Hernandez boys dealt strictly in prescription narcotics, and though Carlos didn't know much about their business beyond his own minimal participation, he knew they were a fairly small fish in an unbelievably enormous ocean. And as far as he could tell, Jesse knew exactly how to keep the bigger fish off their backs.

"I know, but—"

"If you know, then stay away from Rosie! For me and Mom and Benny—" Vanessa's words halted abruptly, and her chin started quivering again.

"Nessa…I'm sorry."

Vanessa looked off to the side and nodded, apparently not trusting her voice. After a long moment, she said, "Let's get back to the car…at least we'll be warmer in there."

"I'm hungry," Annie whined.

"You have cash?" Vanessa asked Carlos.

"Some."

"Let's stop by Mickey D's on the way…get her some warm food."

"And then what?" Carlos asked.

Vanessa raised her eyebrows, clearly unsure. "We go home?"

"What are we supposed to do about—" Carlos flicked his eyes down to Annie.

Vanessa took a deep breath, then continued on her way back toward their car. "Dunno. We'll figure it out when we get home, I guess…"

4

McDonald's, as it turned out, was closed. So was Burger King, Taco Bell, and every other fast food place they passed. Signs proclaiming that each establishment was closed due to the flu were taped to most of their doors and drive-through speakers. The only place that appeared to be open was a gas station near the on-ramp to I-82.

When they pulled up to the pumps, there was one other vehicle stopped, the driver sitting in his locked car while his tank filled. Unlike when they'd been driving *to* the hospital, the streets were almost completely emptied of all but parked cars.

Vanessa turned on the radio and switched it to the AM stations, which Carlos was pretty sure she'd never used. "Someone's got to know what's going on," she said as she fiddled with the tuner.

"I hope so," Carlos said sullenly. "I'll be right back. Lock the doors." He stepped out of the car and shut the door, waiting for the click of the doors locking before he headed toward the tiny convenience store. Which turned out to be locked.

But it wasn't empty. There was a plump, frightened looking woman standing on the other side of the door. "What do you need?" she asked, raising her voice enough to be heard through the glass.

"Gas," Carlos said, responding in kind. He glanced back at his sister's car. "And…do you have any food that's warm?" When the woman shook her head, he asked, "What about sandwiches? Or anything that's real food?"

The woman nodded, then held up one hand and rubbed her thumb and fingers together. She obviously wanted to know Carlos could pay before giving him anything.

He pulled out some cash—three twenties—and held them against the glass. "Milk, too…the smallest one you have, and a bottle of water. And maybe a straw?"

The clerk unlocked the door and pushed it open the tiniest amount, just enough for Carlos to hand her the money. "I'll be right back," she told him, then re-locked the door.

Several minutes later, Carlos returned to the car, carrying a plastic bag filled with a ham and cheddar sandwich, a small bottle of chocolate milk, and a bottle of water that he was pretty sure was the most expensive one the place had, considering it was both fizzy and bottled in France or Italy or some other fancy European country. He filled the fuel tank, then knocked on the passenger's side window.

Vanessa sat in the driver's seat, having switched spots again while he'd been talking to the clerk. She let him into the car, and exhaling a relieved sigh, he settled in the passenger's seat. Even though the car had been off for a good five minutes, it was still a hell of a lot warmer than outside.

He didn't say anything to Annie or his sister as they pulled out of the station. Numbly, he unwrapped the sandwich and handed half to the little girl in the backseat, then twisted the lid off the chocolate milk and stuck the straw in the bottle. He held onto it until the little girl finished eating, then handed the milk to her as well. All he could think about was the sound of the news anchor's voice as she droned on about millions of sick and thousands of dead piling up as a result of the flu. It seemed impossible.

And yet, it was happening.

5

Annie had fallen asleep at some point during the half hour drive from Yakima to their home in Toppenish. The house was small but comfortable, and both their mom and the kids worked hard to keep it tidy, inside and out. The snow-covered lawn surrounding the house was bordered by a waist-high chain-link fence, and the house itself, built in the 1930s, was painted a crisp white with dark green trim. It was one story and just enough house that the Hernandez's didn't go crazy. Being the lone daughter, Vanessa was the only one with her own bedroom. Benny slept—used to sleep—in their mom's room, while Carlos and Jesse shared a room, at least when Jesse was in town. Even then, he usually passed out on the couch in the living room with the murmured voices and shouts from a late-night rerun of some trashy talk show filling the silence.

"You'll carry her in, won't you?" Vanessa asked with a weary glance back at Annie, who'd drooped sideways a bit while she slept. When Carlos nodded, Vanessa proceeded to exit the car as quietly as possible.

Easing the passenger's side door open, Carlos sighed. He was pretty sure he'd never sighed so much in his life. He felt emotionally exhausted and mentally numb. He just wanted to wake up, for this whole nightmare to end. This kind of thing—flu outbreaks that killed thousands, maybe even millions of people—just didn't happen in the United States. It *had* to be a dream, a really awful one.

If only that were true.

He was stepping out of the car when he noticed movement behind their house and froze. The sun had nearly finished slipping behind the hills to the west, and the dusk light made the figure difficult to identify.

Until she stepped out of the shadows. Rosie tentatively raised a hand in greeting.

"Shit," Carlos muttered, offering her a short nod.

Vanessa stepped onto the sidewalk and paused on the curb, following his line of sight. Carlos new the instant she spotted Rosie. His sister folded her arms over her chest and turned a pointed look on Carlos.

He stood, then flipped the passenger seatback forward and ducked into the car to unbuckle Annie's seatbelt. The little girl barely roused as he lifted her out of the car and hugged her tightly. When he again faced his sister, she still had her arms folded and was still glaring at him.

"What? I didn't ask her to come here," he said defensively as he headed toward the chain-link gate. In fact, Carlos had told her multiple times *not* to come to his house, and she'd agreed that was the best plan.

"Well, you can ask her to leave," Vanessa hissed from close behind him.

Carlos glanced over his shoulder at his fuming sister. "Come on…you don't even know why she's here. With everything going on, at least give her a chance to—"

Vanessa held up a hand to stop his words, then huffed past him and pulled out her keys to unlock the front door. Like Carlos, it seemed that Vanessa was finding anger a preferable alternative to soul-crushing sadness.

Carlos stopped at the foot of the porch stairs, listening to his sister mutter to herself while she unlocked the door. Rosie slowly came around the corner of the house, ringing her hands and shooting furtive glances up at Vanessa, who now had the door open and was standing in the doorway, watching with disapproval.

Rosie looked gorgeous, as usual. She was tall—taller than almost all of the other girls at their school—and somehow managed to be both athletic and curvy. She had long, wavy hair that was a brown so dark it was almost black, and equally dark eyes that tilted downward the slightest bit at the outer corners, giving her an eternally sorrowful look. She seemed to be shivering despite her close-fitting down jacket and its fur-lined hood, and worry, or possibly fear, wrinkled her brow.

Carlos wanted to pull her close and comfort her, wanted to kiss her and tell her that he would take care of whatever was bothering her. He desperately wanted to do those things. "We agreed—you shouldn't be here," he said, his voice monotone.

Rosie's lips spread into a weak smile, and she shrugged. "I know, but I didn't know where else to go." She laughed, and it was a desperate, miserable sound. "I overheard Emilio and some of the others…they're being such idiots. I had to get away and, well, I just ended up here." She glanced up at the sky, then at Vanessa, until finally her gaze settled on the back of Annie's head. "Who's that?"

"Don't worry about it," Vanessa snapped. "Both of you get inside before someone sees you. God," she scoffed, "that's all we need."

Carlos studied Rosie for a few seconds longer, searching her face for something—he wasn't sure what—then nodded and turned away. He hurried into the house, eager for its warmth and for the chance to put Annie down. She was small, but he'd been carrying her around for much of the afternoon, and his arms were starting to ache with fatigue.

Vanessa shut and locked the door after they were all inside, then stepped in front of Carlos and held out her arms for Annie. With her slumbering burden, Vanessa headed for the hallway leading to the bedrooms and the home's single bathroom. "I'm gonna give her a bath. She still smells like that place."

Carlos watched his sister round the corner, then turned his attention to Rosie. He felt awkward standing in his living room with her. They spent most of their time together in her car, or in the Tri-Cities at the south end of the valley, where they weren't likely to see anyone they knew. Should he sit on the couch, or in the recliner? Should he turn on the TV? Should he offer her something to drink? "So…"

Rosie started walking around the room, her nervous energy making Carlos that much more uncomfortable. She strode to the fireplace in the center of the far wall, spun and headed for the couch, then turned again and made her way back to the fireplace. She stopped, faced him, and opened her mouth, then shut it again and resumed her pacing.

Her cheeks were more flushed than usual, and had all the shit not just hit the fan, Carlos might have found her fretting cute. But the shit *had* hit the fan, and he had a feeling Rosie was about to fling a few more pieces of shit in that general direction. A horrifying thought struck him—what if she was pregnant? They weren't careless, but they also weren't saints, and not everything they did together included being fully clothed. The more he thought about it, the more certain he became that Rosie was about to ruin his life with two terrifying words.

"I overheard Emilio and Pancho talking a little while ago," Rosie finally said, continuing her pacing. "Pancho's cousin came home after school and found his grandma on the kitchen floor moaning about her hip or something—she's, like, ancient, you know?" She waved her hand dismissively. "Anyway, I guess she fell and broke something, and when Pancho's cousin tried calling 911, nobody answered—ever. He tried for like an hour…okay, maybe for like fifteen minutes," she amended, "before calling Pancho for a ride."

She shook her head in frustration. "But Pancho knew the hospital was closed or whatever so he brought them some drugs for the pain instead and then came straight to my house with this stupid idea, which Emilio went for, of course," she said, putting emphasis on the last two words and rolling her eyes.

"Which was…?" Carlos didn't really care, but he figured it was the right thing to say.

Rosie threw her hands up in the air. "To hit up all the gun stores in the valley and steal, well, everything, and since the cops aren't answering the phone, they think they can get away with it. They're going to store it all at my house and…well, I just couldn't stay there with all this crazy shit going on. I couldn't…" She leaned against the far wall, pressing her hand against her forehead. "God, I'm dizzy."

Suddenly, her flushed cheeks made a lot more sense. "You're sick?"

"I think so," she said, her voice so faint he could barely make out her words.

Concern filled him, but it was quickly overshadowed by a surge of frustration and anger. She was sick. She had the flu virus that had killed Benny and so many others. And she brought it into his home. "Jesus fucking Christ, Rosie…you brought it here?"

Rosie stared at him, wide-eyed and unblinking. Tears welled in her eyes. "Carlos, I'm—I'm…"

Exacerbated beyond his limits, Carlos sat heavily on the couch and rested his head against the couch back. "Benny's…he's dead, and my mom's stuck in the hospital." His voice sounded hollow. He *felt* hollow…numb.

Rosie's hand flew up to her mouth. "Oh God…I'm so—" Eyes

going even wider, she raced into the kitchen, leaned over the sink, and vomited. Repeatedly.

"Really?" Carlos groaned, then stood and headed into the kitchen to see what he could do to help her.

It wasn't much. After nearly twenty minutes of vomiting and dry-heaves, Rosie all but passed out. She would have collapsed onto the linoleum had Carlos not been there to catch her. He dutifully carried her feverish body into the bedroom he sometimes shared with Jesse and set her on his brother's bed. He figured that if Jesse wasn't home by now, he wouldn't be until tomorrow. Besides, if Rosie vomited on Jesse's pillow or comforter, Carlos figured it was the least his brother deserved for abandoning him and Vanessa at such a time.

6

"She won't wake up," Carlos told his sister. They were huddled together on the carpet in front of the muted TV, sharing a fleece blanket and talking in hushed tones. Neither felt especially well, but Carlos knew it wasn't Rosie's fault. They'd likely contracted the virus from Benny, or some kid at school days ago. His stomach knotted, and not only with nausea. He felt bad about how he'd reacted when Rosie admitted to being sick. As soon as she woke up, he intended to apologize.

"Did you shake her?"

Carlos nodded. "It's like she's in a coma or something."

Vanessa shook her head and rolled her eyes. "And now *we* have to take care of her."

Carlos rubbed his temples, wishing his pounding headache would go away and that the room would stop tilting back and forth. "She was scared. She didn't know where else to go." After a brief hesitation, he added, "I wish you'd give her a chance."

Vanessa was quiet for a long time, for so long that Carlos didn't think she was going to respond. "I have to tell you something," she finally blurted.

Carlos drew away slowly, pulling the blanket off his sister's shoulders. "What?"

Vanessa yanked the blanket back up onto her shoulders and stared at the stats scrolling across the TV screen, reporting the death toll by country. "Back when we were Freshmen, me and Rosie…we were close." She eyed Carlos. "You don't remember?"

"Sort of…not really," Carlos admitted. "So what happened?"

Again, Vanessa took a long time to answer. "Rosie and me… we went to a party, and Jesse was there, and Rosie had a huge crush on him, being the big, cool Senior and all, and she and Jesse…" Vanessa hesitated.

"She and Jesse, *what*?"

"I walked in on them in the bathroom and, you know…they were together. Like *that*. After I'd specifically told her not to…"

Carlos's brain felt sluggish as it processed what his sister was telling him. "Jesse…and Rosie."

"Mmhmm."

"Were together."

"Yeah."

"Like that."

Vanessa inhaled. "Yep."

"Fuck," Carlos breathed. He suddenly felt sicker. Dirty. Disgusted. "I can't believe she—we…what a bitch!"

"Yep."

Carlos rubbed his hand over his face, gathering his chaotic thoughts. His stomach lurched. "I think I'm gonna puke."

"Oh, believe me, I know," Vanessa said. "It's not like I—"

Carlos slapped his hand over his mouth and lurched to his feet. Just as Rosie had done, he rushed into the kitchen and vomited into the sink. He retched into the metal basin over and over again until his legs gave out and he collapsed onto his knees on the white and blue linoleum, huddling over the large bowl Vanessa thrust at him. Eventually, he sank onto his side and passed out.

7

Carlos woke to someone trying to poke needles into his eyeballs, cheeks, and forehead. But they felt too blunt to be needles. He thought they could be nails, or maybe sticks?

"I'm hungry," a tiny voice said.

They weren't needles or nails, Carlos realized, but fingers.

"I'm hungry," the voice whined.

Groaning, Carlos flopped onto his back. Whatever he was laying on was cold and a little sticky. And there was a rank odor in the air, as though someone had vomited, possibly on him.

He opened his eyes to see an expectant Annie, and sat up slowly. Glancing down at the front of his hoodie, he realized he'd been right. Someone had vomited on him—likely *him*.

"Where's Nessa?" he asked, his voice raspy. His mouth tasted like crap mixed with rotting dead animal…not that he knew what either tasted like, but he could imagine.

Annie pointed, and Carlos followed the direction of her tiny arm with massive apprehension. His sister was curled up in the corner of the kitchen, the small wastebasket from the bathroom a few feet away from her.

With immense horror, Carlos recognized a second, less intense but equally foul scent under the overwhelming cloud of vomit. He'd smelled something similar once before, when he'd been standing in the bedroom doorway at Annie's house, staring at a dead woman.

He clambered across the kitchen floor, every joint and muscle aching. He slipped when his knee landed in an unnoticed patch of sick, but he didn't care in the least. Vanessa was…dead.

But she couldn't be. Not her. Not like Benny. He was frantic, panicked under the intensity of his denial. She *couldn't* be dead.

He scooped his sister up, pulling her upper half onto his knees and only remotely noticing Annie snuggling between them. Vanessa wasn't cold, but warm. Hot even. And breathing. And groaning.

She wasn't dead!

"Nessa!" Carlos cried, squeezing and shaking his sister at the same time. "Nessa! Wake up!" He shook her again, more intensely, but again, all he earned was a groan. Letting her lay back down on the floor, he looked around the kitchen. What could he use to wake her?

What could he use?

What could he use?

What the hell could he use?

His eyes landed on the sink, which he vividly remembered puking into. But…tap water tended to be ice cold this time of year, and a splash of that would wake the dead. Or the almost dead.

With a grunt, he used the wall to steady himself as he rose to a hunched standing position. He lurched across the kitchen to the sink, the world seeming to spin around him. He was so incredibly dizzy, and his legs felt boneless and shaky.

When he reached the sink, he leaned his elbows on the edge and turned on the faucet, avoiding looking at the contents of the basin. Through the east-facing window behind the sink, he could see the first sliver of the sun as it started to rise. He frowned, surprised he'd slept through the whole night when he felt so crappy…and had been sleeping on the cold, hard kitchen floor.

He flipped the switch on the wall beside the window, bringing the garbage disposal to life. That, at least, sped up the process of clearing out the sink. He reached for a half-full glass on the counter to the right, dumped out the room temperature water, and refilled it with frigid water from the tap. He drank the whole glass down greedily, then filled it again.

But when he turned to start his way back across the kitchen, a surprisingly daunting task, he realized how much of an idiot he was being. Vanessa was sick, and if she—or him, for that matter—was to have any chance of recovering instead of ending up like Annie's grandma and Benny, then she needed rest. She needed to sleep as much as possible so her body could heal itself. She didn't need him splashing her with ice-cold water.

Carlos turned back to the sink, setting the glass on the counter and shutting off both the disposal and the faucet. He glanced down at Annie, who was still sitting on the floor beside Vanessa.

"You went to sleep on the floor for a long time," she told him, her lower lip sticking out like she might burst into tears at any moment. "I'm scared."

Carlos's lips spread into a weak smile, and he raised a shoulder, hoping to look nonchalant. "Sometimes I like to change it up, sleep in the kitchen…" He shook his head. Even a four-year-old could see through that lie, or maybe *especially* a four-year-old.

"Can I have some juice?"

"Sure." Carlos trundled over to the fridge and took out a plastic jug of OJ. He retrieved a small plastic cup from the overhead cabinet beside the fridge and, hands trembling, somehow managed to fill it without spilling. "Here you go," he said, holding the cup out to the little girl.

Annie rose to her feet and trotted over to him, accepting the orange juice eagerly.

Carlos returned the jug to the fridge and exchanged it for a bag of plain bagels from the middle shelf. He felt weak and half-starved, as though he hadn't eaten anything in days. He practically tore open the bag and shoved the first bagel into his mouth, consuming nearly a quarter of it in one bite. Once he'd finished that bagel, he pulled out two more and split them in half, sticking them in the four-slot toaster.

"D'you like peanut butter?" he asked the little girl, who was watching him with wide, somber eyes while she drank her juice.

She nodded.

"Cool," he said, grateful that preparing her breakfast would be as easy as slapping some peanut butter on a toasted bagel. He wasn't sure he had the energy for much else. The bagel he'd already scarfed down seemed to be helping, along with the water, but what he really needed was to sleep somewhere more comfortable than the kitchen floor, possibly for the rest of the day. As his eyes landed on his sister, he figured she could use a change of scenery as well.

Carlos worked his head from side to side, stretching his neck with several sharp cracks, then pushed off the edge of the counter. He didn't have the strength to carry Vanessa anywhere, but he managed to drag her as gently as possible into the living room. He placed a throw pillow from the couch under her head and covered her with the fleece blanket they'd been sharing the previous night.

Out of the corner of his eye, he caught sight of an open, apparently empty box of cereal and a handful of discarded granola bar wrappers strewn about on the floor in front of the TV. He looked at Annie, who had followed him into the living room and was sitting cross-legged on the floor at Vanessa's feet, holding the cup of juice in both hands.

"Did you eat all that?" Carlos asked the little girl, surprised, despite the evidence, when she nodded. "Last night? You ate all of that…last night?"

Annie shook her head. "Yesterday." The single word was as shocking as stepping into an ice-cold shower.

Frantically, Carlos searched for Vanessa's phone. He found it on the end table beside the couch, but the battery appeared to be dead. Luckily, his family had chargers plugged in to an outlet in pretty much every room of the house, including the one behind the end table. He plugged in the phone and stared at the screen while it powered up. It seemed to take forever.

Once it was booted up, all Carlos could do was stare at the date. For at least a minute, he just stared. He couldn't believe it. It didn't seem possible. He'd passed out on Friday night, but the display claimed it was Sunday morning. How the hell had he lost an entire day?

He glanced at the granola bar wrappers, then remembered the faint odor he'd noticed when he'd first awoken. He'd thought it was Vanessa, had thought she was…

"Rosie," he whispered. He dropped the phone and stumbled down the hallway to his and Jesse's bedroom, falling to his knees beside Jesse's bed.

Rosie hadn't vomited in her sleep like he and Vanessa had done. Her eyes were closed, her face relaxed, peaceful.

"Rosie?" Carlos touched a hand to her pale cheek and drew back almost immediately. She was cold. And the smell—it was faint, but it was stronger in the bedroom than it had been in the kitchen. "Rosie…Oh God, Rosie…" Carlos bowed his head, and for the first time since his dad's death, for the first time in years, he truly cried.

"I'm so sorry," he whispered, "so sorry." He regretted the last thoughts he'd had about her, the last thing he'd said about her. He didn't care about whatever had happened between her and his brother. He didn't care. He could forgive her for not telling him. He *would* forgive her if she would just wake up. "Please, Rosie…wake up…"

"Are you sad?" a tiny voice asked from the doorway.

Carlos raised his head and wiped his face free of tears. He cleared his throat roughly. "Yeah, Annie, I am."

Her quick, faint footsteps marked her progress as she entered the room. She wriggled under his arm, crawled onto his lap, and wrapped her little arms around his neck. "Nana says hugs are the best medicine if you're sad."

Carlos clutched at the little girl, drawing comfort from her presence.

They sat like that for a few minutes, until Annie broke the silence. "Can I have something to eat now?"

Carlos laughed. It was a hollow sound, but at least it was something. He set Annie on her feet. "Yeah. Why don't you go check on Nessa, and I'll be out in a minute, okay?"

Annie nodded and left the room.

Once she was gone, Carlos turned his attention back to Rosie. He'd really liked her—a lot. For a little while, he thought he might have even loved her, but the news Vanessa had shared had shattered that illusion. Still, seeing her like this, knowing she was gone, made his heart ache intensely. It wasn't fair. She didn't deserve this. None of them did.

"Goodbye, Rosie," he said, swallowing several times to hold in the renewed urge to cry. He shook his head, denying his weakness, and started wrapping the comforter around her body, hoping it would at least contain the stench for a while. When he rolled her over to wrap her more fully in the blanket, her body felt stiff. He didn't know enough about bodies to know what that meant about how long she'd been gone, but from biology class, he was fairly sure she hadn't just died. Plus, she was cold.

Feeling somewhat numb, Carlos returned to the kitchen and washed his hands. His motions were robotic as he spread peanut butter on the toasted bagels for him and Annie. They ate on the couch, watching Vanessa sleep. To Carlos, the food tasted like cardboard, but it was what his body needed.

When he was finished, he lay down on the couch with Annie snuggling in beside him. "How 'bout a nap?" he asked quietly.

"I'm not sleepy," Annie said, following the statement up with an enormous yawn.

"Yeah, me either."

Within seconds, they were both fast asleep.

8

Carlos woke to the sound of screaming. Terrified, blood-curdling screaming. He shot upright, a quick glance around telling him he was on the couch in the living room. Vanessa. She was the person screaming. Down the hallway, in one of the bedrooms.

Scrambling to his feet, Carlos skittered around the corner into the hallway and burst through the open doorway into his and Jesse's room. He nearly trampled Annie, who was standing in the middle of the room, wide-eyed and trembling, on the verge of a full-blown meltdown. Vanessa stood beside Jesse's bed, no longer screaming, but staring in horror at what she'd found wrapped inside the comforter. Or rather, *who* she'd found.

Carlos scooped Annie up, and she latched on to him like a child-sized barnacle. He strode to Jesse's bedside and flipped the comforter back over Rosie's face. It was grayer, making her somehow seem more dead than she'd appeared when he'd first found her.

"That—that's Rosie," Vanessa said, pointing at the comforter. "In a blanket. She—she's dead. She's *dead*, Carlos, in our house. She's dead and…what if someone finds her? What if the police come?" She started wringing her hands. "Oh God. Oh dear God." Her wide, horrified eyes latched on to Carlos. "Oh my God, Carlos. Rosie's *dead*!"

"I know, Nessa," Carlos said, shifting Annie a little to the side so he could hold her with one arm and wrap the other around his sister. He led her back out to the living room and settled her on the couch.

"What if Emilio comes looking for her? She's dead, and—and…he'll kill you, Carlos! He'll *kill* you! We have to call the police…but what if they still don't answer?" She stood abruptly. "We should bury her. But…the ground's frozen…" She slowly sank back down to the couch and looked at Carlos. "What do we do?"

Carlos somehow managed to unlatch Annie's limbs from around his neck and waist, and set her on the couch beside Vanessa. "Take care of Annie. She's probably hungry. The monster's *always* hungry," Carlos added dryly. "I'll move R—the body out to the shed, then I'm showering."

"Good…that's good. You stink," Vanessa told him, then sniffed her shoulder and added, "So do I."

By mid-afternoon, only the living were left in the house, and everyone was cleanly scrubbed of all remnants of illness. They were sitting at the dining room table, Annie curled up on Vanessa's lap, staring at the radio they'd moved to the table from the kitchen. It was the radio their mom used when cooking, at least on those rare nights she was actually home to cook.

Carlos stretched in his chair. He still felt a little achy and weaker than usual, but he was alive, as were his sister and Annie. That was better than most people could say.

This will be this station's final broadcast...

Carlos paid close attention to the message he'd already listened to twice. They couldn't get a television signal, but all of the radio stations seemed to be playing the same thing on a loop.

...The President of the United States of America sent out the following message a few minutes ago. To all who are listening, I wish you luck.

...static...

Our country is at war. Humanity is at war, yet our enemy is not one we can fight openly. Our enemy has swept through every nation, attacking discretely, killing indiscriminately. We lost thousands before we even knew we were under attack. Many have already fallen, and many more will fall. But we cannot give up the fight.

Over the past century, through technological achievements, we made our world smaller. We made the time it takes to communicate across oceans instantaneous, and the time it takes to travel those same routes nearly as fast. We made our world smaller, and in doing so, we sowed the seeds of our own destruction: a global pandemic.

I regret to tell you that as of midnight on the 10th of December, over eighty percent of the world's population has reported or is assumed dead. It is estimated that the death toll will continue to climb. This news is devastating, I know, but all is not lost.

Some of us are surviving. This is how we will fight our enemy—by not giving up, by being resilient and resourceful, by surviving. We are not a species that will go out quietly, so I task those of you who are still alive with one essential purpose: live.

Survive.

Thrive.

If you believe in a higher power, ask for guidance. If you don't, believe in your fellow man. You, the survivors, have the chance to start over, to build anew. Learn from our mistakes. Let the world remain big.

And most importantly, live.

God bless you, my beloved citizens of this great nation. God bless you, and goodnight.

…static…

This will be this station's final broadcast...

Carlos clicked off the radio and sat back in his chair.

Vanessa sniffled and wiped a stray tear from her cheek.

"That was last night," Carlos said. "Do you think they're still alive…wherever they are?"

"Who knows," Vanessa said, shaking her head. "So what should we do now"—she held up her phone—"because alternating between calling Mom, Jesse, the hospital, and the police is getting us nowhere, and—"

Carlos did a double take at the phone's screen and snatched the device out of his sister's hand. He flipped it around and held it up in front of her face. "You've got a text!"

Vanessa's face lit up. "It must be Jesse…or Mom!"

Carlos swiped his thumb across the screen to unlock it, and the display immediately blacked out. "What the f—" Glancing down at Annie, he amended his exclamation with, "heck." He pressed the power button. Nothing. "It just turned off."

Vanessa frowned and reached for the phone. "That's weird… the battery was like half full." She stood and set Annie on the floor, then crossed the room to the charger behind the end table. "Maybe I was wrong about the battery," she said as she plugged in the phone and pressed the power button. "Maybe it just needs to charge, or be reset, or—" She looked at Carlos. "Did you see any of the message?"

Clenching his jaw, he shook his head. Abruptly, he stood, his chair tipping back precariously on two legs.

"What are you doing?"

"Changing into warmer clothes. I think we should go back to the hospital…to get Mom." Carlos started toward his room.

Vanessa followed close behind him. "Wait. We should think this through, you know. Make sure we're ready for—"

"And what if Mom needs help right now? I'm not going to just sit around. We should be doing something!"

"I know, but—"

Carlos spun in the bedroom doorway, furious and fully aware

that his anger was misplaced. He didn't care. He was freaked out and so close to breaking. "But *what*?"

Vanessa took a step back at hearing the harshness in his tone. "I'm scared," she said, barely loud enough for Carlos to hear.

Exhaling heavily, he retreated a few steps into his room. "Yeah…me too."

9

They were just reaching the outskirts of their small town, Vanessa at the wheel, when Carlos grabbed Vanessa's nearest wrist. Her hand had been on the gearshift, but slipped off under the force of Carlos's grip. "Stop."

She shot her brother a confused glance. "Wha—"

"Just stop!" he urged. When the car came to a halt, he pointed through the windshield to the last house on the right side of the street, where the residential area gave way to fields of snow and orchards of dormant apple trees. It was about a quarter of a mile away. "Someone just came out of that house." It was late enough in the afternoon that it was hard to make out much about the person, other than that they were standing on the porch and wearing light colors.

Vanessa stared at the survivor, blinked, then turned thoughtful eyes on Carlos.

"D'you think we should try to talk to them?" he asked, frowning. It was the first living person they'd seen, outside of themselves, in nearly two full days.

Nodding, Vanessa said, "Yeah, okay…but from the car," and started inching the Civic forward as slowly as possible.

"Nessa?"

"Yeah?"

"At this rate we won't get there 'til tomorrow."

Vanessa exhaled, adding a touch of a nervous laugh. The look she flashed his way was slightly apologetic. "I didn't want to spook 'em." She pressed down on the gas pedal, and soon they were slowing to a stop in front of the house.

A young woman stood on the porch of the house in a long, plain cotton nightgown and robe. She cradled a bundled-up baby in her arms and, with a placid smile, nodded in greeting at their car across a well-kept white picket fence. For some reason, it seemed odd to see another person, though the outbreak had really only grown out of control a couple days ago.

"A mommy and a baby!" Annie squealed happily from the backseat.

As the woman descended the porch stairs and started across the yard toward their car, Carlos looked at his sister, eyebrows raised. "So…"

"Maybe we should just go. I mean, what if—"

"What? She pulls a gun on us?" Carlos asked dubiously. He shrugged a shoulder and started to roll down the window. "She might know something we don't…we've got to at least ask."

Vanessa's eyes were filled with worry, but she nodded. He rolled down the window two-thirds of the way and watched the woman pass through the short gate. She stopped in the middle of the sidewalk, several feet away from their car, and hunched over a little to better see through the lowered window.

Carlos raised his hand to wave. "Uh…hi."

"Hello there." The woman's face spread into a warm smile. She was pale and tired looking, and appeared to be in her early twenties. "Would you like to come inside?" Her smile widened as she caught sight of Annie in the backseat. "I see you have a little one, too."

"Uh…actually, we were wondering if you've heard any—"

The woman looked down at her baby, murmuring, "Shhh…" She glanced at Carlos, her eyes crinkled at the corners. "Sorry. She can be a bit fussy."

"It's cool," Carlos said, unnerved. The baby hadn't made a noise.

The corner of the blanket tucked around the baby's head flopped down, and Carlos was given his first look at the baby's face. He recoiled and instantly started rolling up the window. He hadn't heard the baby make a sound because it *couldn't* make a sound.

Apparently Vanessa had caught a glimpse of the baby as well, or maybe she was just responding to Carlos's sudden reaction, because she stepped on the gas a little too enthusiastically. The tires spun on the slick road for a second or two before catching. The car skidded a little to the side, and then they were off…away from that *thing*.

"Was it"—Vanessa's eyes flicked up to the rearview mirror—"dead?" She whispered the word like it was something tainted, evil.

"Yeah…like, a lot." Carlos looked into the side mirror, watching the woman. She was still standing on the sidewalk before the open gate, holding her dead baby, a small smile on her face. A shiver crept up Carlos's spine, and he felt a renewed sense of nausea. "Do you think…should we have tried to help her?" Carlos asked tentatively.

Vanessa scoffed. "That chick was crazy…"

Carlos stifled some of his rising panic and cleared his throat. "This is *all* crazy." At this point, he felt like *he* was crazy.

10

"Holy sh—"

Vanessa shushed Carlos, hitting his arm with the back of her hand. "Language. Annie…"

"Yeah, but look at that!" He pointed through the windshield at a thick pillar of black smoke. Originating somewhere northwest of the freeway in the heart of Yakima, it had come into view as they'd passed through the gap carved in Ahtanum Ridge by the Yakima River. "That's in the middle of the city." He felt the blood drain from his face. The hospital was in the middle of the city. "What if it's—"

"Don't say it," Vanessa said, shaking her head. "Don't you dare say it."

But as Vanessa exited the abandoned highway and headed west into the equally abandoned streets of Yakima toward the hospital, their worst fears came true.

"How?" Carlos's voice was barely a rasp as Vanessa brought the car to a halt about a block from the hospital. "How's this possible?" he gasped, pushing the passenger door open and practically leaping out of the car. He stumbled up the street a few steps, then stopped and stared at the blackened, burning mass that had once been the hospital, the place where his mom *worked*. It was more smoke than flames, making Carlos think he was witnessing the tail end of whatever had happened. His mom…she'd been in there, unless…

With a renewed sense of purpose, Carlos ran back to the car. Vanessa was staring out the windshield, tears streaming down her splotchy cheeks.

"Mom must've gotten out," Carlos told his sister, desperate for her to believe him. If she believed him, maybe he could, too. "She had to have…before it…she *had* to. We have to find her!"

Vanessa was hugging herself and rocking back and forth the faintest amount. She shook her head. "Carlos," she said, her voice wobbling. "She was sick…"

"We got better…who's to say she didn't, too?"

"Carlos—"

"She would have gone to her car," Carlos told his sister, not hearing her protests. "She could be home right now. She could have gone the back way. We wouldn't have passed her." He suddenly felt giddy and a little sick with nervous excitement. "We just have to look in the parking lot. If we don't see her car, we'll know she's okay."

Vanessa exhaled heavily, hope mixed with the uncertainty on her face. Part of her, even if it was a small part, believed he was right, that their mom was okay.

Until they found their mom's sedan parked in its usual spot. Vanessa pulled up behind it, and Carlos jumped out and raced to the driver's side door of his mom's car, sure he would find her or some sign of her inside. He just needed some indicator that she hadn't been in the hospital when the fire started. This close to the blackened ruins, the stench of all that was burning was overwhelming, but he couldn't tear himself away from the driver's side window. It was as though if he stared at it long enough, his mom would appear.

In a daze of horror and despair, he felt a tug on his arm. He let

Vanessa pull him back to the car, let her push him down onto the passenger seat. She didn't waste any time in driving away from that place, from their mom.

Shame welled within Carlos as he stared at Vanessa. He was her brother. *He* was supposed to be the strong one…was supposed to take care of her. But he couldn't. He just couldn't. He lowered his face into his hands, and for the second time that day, he cried.

11

Vanessa drove home on highway 97, following a route Carlos and his family had always called "the back way." They didn't talk—not about the fire or their mom or anything else. Only the sound of Annie's wails filled the car. She'd been crying hysterically in the backseat ever since they'd sped away from the hospital.

When, after minutes of coaxing on Carlos's part, she showed no signs that her ear-piercing meltdown was winding down, he unbuckled her seatbelt and pulled her into the front seat. Hugging the little girl close and patting her back, he told his sister, "Don't crash."

A heart-wrenching whine escaped from Vanessa, and nodding, she wiped her cheek with the side of her thumb.

They parked in front of their house shortly after sunset and hurriedly locked themselves inside the safety of its familiar walls. Annie was asleep in Carlos's arms, as she'd been for the last fifteen minutes. He was just setting her on the couch in the dark living room, Vanessa gathering up the blanket from the floor to settle it over the slumbering child, when he heard the ominous, metallic chk-chk.

He and Vanessa froze and exchanged a look of terror. Adrenaline flooded his bloodstream.

With the click of a light switch, the overhead light flared to life.

"Carlos? Nessa?"

Carlos spun around and stared in shock at the man standing in the entrance to the hallway. It was Jesse. Carlos watched as Jesse tucked a pistol in the back waistband of his jeans, a look of relief on his brother's face that had to mirror his own.

Unable to find any words, Carlos lurched toward his brother, embracing him with as much strength as he could muster. He released him a few seconds later, giving Vanessa a turn to greet Jesse as well.

"Didn't you get my messages?" Jesse asked as he patted Vanessa's back.

Carlos shook his head. The message on Vanessa's phone might have been from him, but it didn't matter now. "We tried you like a million times. You never answered."

Jesse rested his chin on top of Vanessa's head. "I was driving. Didn't have service most of the time…" He shifted his focus to Annie, who was curled up in a ball on the couch, sound asleep. "Who's the kid?"

"Annie," Vanessa told him as she pulled away. She moved to the couch to sit beside the sleeping child. "We found her a few days ago. Her mom was…well, you know."

"Yeah," Jesse said somberly. "I know."

Something in Carlos's chest clenched. This reunion was about to become very depressing. "I've, uh, got some bad news."

"You mean Benny? Mom told me he was sick a few days ago." Sadness clouded his face. "I just figured, with everything…"

"That's not all, man." Carlos brought a hand up to rub his temples. He squeezed his eyes shut, unable to look at his brother's face, unwilling to watch his reaction, while he told him. "We just came from the hospital." Carlos had to fight back tears. He refused to cry in front of his brother. He was done with crying. Reluctantly, he opened his eyes. "There was a fire at the hospital, and we're pretty sure Mom was still inside..." Carlos wanted to believe there was still a chance that she'd made it out, still a chance that she'd recovered and they would see her again. He wanted to believe that...desperately.

"Jesus..." Jesse sank onto the arm of the couch. "I thought, maybe...since I survived, you all might, too." He scrubbed his hand over his face, then started rubbing the back of his neck. "At least you guys are alright."

"Barely," Carlos muttered, feeling a spark of irritation at his brother. Jesse should have been there to help with all this end-of-the-world shit. "Where've you been?"

With a sigh, Jesse moved to the recliner opposite the couch. He told them what had happened over the past week, how when he'd been passing by Lake Tahoe on his way to meet with one of his suppliers, he'd become too ill to continue driving and pulled off into what appeared to be an empty campground at the south end of the lake. He'd awoken to find a woman—her name was Mandy—tapping on his window. She'd taken him to her one-room cabin by the lake and looked after him until he returned to health.

Jesse leaned forward to rest his elbows on his knees. "Mandy's gathering survivors. Last night, when I left, there were already about twenty people camped out around her cabin...everyone working together, taking care of each other." He laced his fingers together and offered a close-lipped smile to Carlos and Vanessa, who were sitting next to each other on the couch. "But I had to check on you guys and Mom, and bring you down there, you know...if you survived too."

"Why?" Vanessa asked. "Wouldn't it be easier just to stay here?"

Jesse's mouth curved into a considering frown. "Easier... maybe, for now. But it's a whole lot safer down there.

Carlos bumped his sister's shoulder with his own. When she

looked at him, her eyes full of uncertainty, he said, "I think we should stick around here for a week or two…look for Mom and stuff, just in case." His sorrow rose, and he had to clear his throat to keep his voice steady. "Then we figure out what to do…maybe go down there? What matters is that we stick together, right?"

Vanessa looked into his eyes with such intensity that it felt like she was seeing inside him, examining his soul. Finally, she nodded. "We stick together."

Carlos felt a tug on his opposite sleeve. He glanced down to find Annie staring up at him, bleary-eyed from crying and sleep. "I'm hungry," she whined.

He exhaled in a weary, breathy laugh. "Of course you are."

This concludes the first installment of *The Ending Beginnings*. Carlos is also a supporting character in the full-length novels, *After The Ending* and *Into The Fire.*

MANDY

VOLUME TWO

1

PRESENT DAY

Mandy trudged through the snow toward the sole parked car. Despite the substantial amount of weight she'd gained over the last decade, she still loved walking around the campground. *Her* campground. With Lake Tahoe on one side and the snow all around, she could almost lose herself to the beauty of the winter wonderland. She could almost forget everything she'd done over the past 22 years.

She laughed. It was a harsh sound, at odds with the soft white puffs of air that marked it. She'd hurt a lot of people, not that they'd minded. The more she thought about it, the clearer the truth became; even if she could erase the past—forget it, or even do it over—she wouldn't. Every single act of wretched devotion she'd enticed out of her followers had shaped her into what she was. A queen. A goddess. The most adored person who'd ever lived. Who wouldn't want that?

The car had pulled into the small parking lot of the picnic area the previous evening. It was a newish, black Honda Civic with muck from the slushy roads crusted to its lower half. When one of Mandy's followers had pointed it out, Mandy opted to wait and see if the driver, a man who appeared to be the only occupant, would emerge. He didn't, indicating he was probably sick and would likely die. It was the virus, of course. Even though she'd known it was coming, Mandy still found the sheer, devastating volume of death caused by the virus awe-inspiring.

Against the odds, the driver had yet to perish. It had been nearly twenty hours since he'd parked, and the last person to check on him—Kevin, one of her followers who'd been with her the longest—said he was still breathing. He'd vomited all over himself, but he wasn't dead. It looked like he would be one of the few to survive. Whether he would be one of the chosen few or the tainted others was yet to be determined.

Mandy approached the driver's side of the car and bent down to peer through the window. The man was slumped against the door, his face turned away from her. But yes, despite the pervasive below freezing chill and the vomit coating the front of his jacket, she could see the steady rise and fall of the driver's chest. Kevin had been correct. He was alive.

Mandy stood beside the car for a few minutes and studied the unconscious man. After a while, she figured it was safe enough and raised one plump arm to wave for Jen and Cole, two of her most valuable companions, to join her.

"Well, what do you think—chosen or tainted?" Mandy asked the slender young woman.

Jen crunched a few steps closer and removed her right glove. She pressed her hand against the window so the glass was the only thing between her skin and the driver's dark hair. Closing her eyes, she wore a look of deep concentration and held her breath for a protracted moment. Finally, she exhaled and opened her eyes, focusing on Mandy. "It's too soon to say for sure, but I think he's chosen."

Mandy nodded. "Good enough for me." Again, she raised her arm and waved two more of her followers over—the strapping young men she'd acquired during the last set recruitment trials five months ago—and watched as they approached. She really was quite pleased they were both among the chosen; they were quite attractive. "Move him to one of the cots in my cabin," she told them as they neared. "Clean him up and make sure he's warm. You know the drill."

"Of course," the taller of the two said. He reached for the door handle and pulled, but it was locked.

His companion looked to Mandy. "Do you want us to break a window?"

Mandy sighed and shouldered them out of the way. They may have been strapping, young, and easy on the eyes, but these two weren't the brightest of her followers. Mandy crouched low enough that the driver would see her face when he woke and looked out the window. It wasn't a comfortable position, considering the bulk her leg muscles had to hold up, so she didn't waste any time. She knocked on the glass.

The driver started awake, sitting up straight in his seat and turning his face to the window. He was young, in his early twenties, and his skin was a tan that complimented his dark hair and warm brown eyes. He was quite average-looking, and at the same time, his hard-featured face was the most shocking, remarkable thing Mandy had seen in a very long time.

Her breath caught. "My God," she whispered.

Cole sidled up beside her and peeked through the window. "Is that—it's not possible. Is that—"

"If you say *his* name, I'll kill you." Mandy turned her livid gaze on him, daring him. Though his value was unquestionable, he was also one of the few people who could be in her presence and *not* adore her. He was also the one who made her into what she was. Queen. Goddess.

Monster.

She despised him almost as much as she needed him. If those scales ever tipped just enough in the other direction, she really *would* kill him.

2

22 YEARS AGO

Mandy tapped the eraser of her pencil on the kitchen table while she stared at the classifieds from last Sunday's paper. It was nearly a week old, but she'd yet to throw it away; instead, as she milled around her small apartment during her three days off, she found herself staring at the same advertisement over and over again. It seemed too good to be true.

TAKE CONTROL OF YOUR LIFE!
This is your chance to become the person you're supposed to be.
Contact us to see if you're eligible to take part in
THE FULFILLMENT STUDY, an experimental program designed to help YOU discover and achieve your full potential. Spots are limited - CALL TODAY!

Sitting back in her chair, Mandy adjusted the elastic waistband of her leggings a little higher. She glanced down at her belly and blew out an exasperated breath. No matter how determined she was to lose the weight, she couldn't get herself to stick to any kind of diet or exercise routine for longer than a week. Not that it mattered anyway…

Ever since elementary school, Mandy had been "the chubby girl." Her mom, who Mandy was pretty sure had never worn anything larger than a size six, used to tell Mandy she would grow out of it. Once puberty hit, her mom used to say, once Mandy went through a growth spurt, then she would slim right down. Apparently puberty had missed *that* memo.

Mandy went through middle and high school as "that shy girl, you know—the chubby one," and her senior yearbook was chock-full of impersonal well-wishes like "Stay sweet!" and "Good luck next year!" and the dreaded "Have a great summer!" She was eighteen years old and had never had a real boyfriend. Hell, she'd never even kissed a boy outside of one game of truth or dare played at sixth grade camp, and that had only been a peck.

Mandy desperately wanted to be somebody's girlfriend. With all the love she'd been storing up all her life, she thought she had the potential to be a fabulous girlfriend. She just wanted somebody to love her—somebody who didn't love her by default like her mom and her mom's best friend, Sherry. Again, she glanced down at the ad.

The address listed was in Reno, just a couple-hour drive from Auburn, her hometown in northeastern California. Maybe, just maybe, it was time for Mandy to take charge, to grab life by the horns, to seize the day, to…

She sighed. Who was she kidding. She'd never been a go-getter —thus her eternal state of *blah*. She had all the determination of a wet mop, or maybe just a dry mop. After all, a wet mop was preparing to *do* something.

Reaching for another glazed old-fashioned donut—her third of the morning—she pondered her pathetic existence, thinking that at least she would always have fried dough.

"Go ahead and take a seat. We'll call your name when we're ready for you," Mandy told the mother and son standing before her section of the reception desk. She'd been working as a part-time receptionist at Riverside Dental, Auburn's largest dental clinic, for the past seven months. It wasn't her dream job, but then, she didn't really have a dream job.

As the duo headed for the partially enclosed waiting area, Mandy swiveled in her chair to face the wall of alphabetized and color-coded files. Sherry—her mom's closest friend who just happened to be the head receptionist and reason Mandy even had this job—handed her the folder containing the boy's dental records.

"You know, Sugar Plum"—Sherry loved using the nickname she'd given Mandy years ago, when Mandy had been a little girl obsessed with *The Nutcracker*—"You've got a really nice voice. Have you ever thought of doing voice acting, you know, like for animated movies and books on tape and stuff like that? I know how much you love to read…"

Mandy sighed. "I don't know Sher…I wouldn't even know where to begin." She stood just enough to place the file in the tray on the counter for the next available dental hygienist to pick up.

Sherry sat in the office chair beside Mandy and clicked her computer mouse, refreshing the appointment calendar on her monitor. She scanned the info quickly, then turned her chair so she was facing Mandy. Her eyebrows drew together as she took a deep breath. "Do you remember when you were little and you used to write those plays about…what was her name?"

Mandy considered pretending she didn't know what Sherry was talking about, but she was perfectly aware that if she did that, Sherry would persist in trying to jog her memory all afternoon. "Jacqueline," Mandy admitted. Better to get it over with than be pestered for the next three hours.

"That's right! You'd pretend to be Jacqueline the Great, treasure hunter extraordinaire…and you'd write such fantastic adventures for you and Fuzzy"—Fuzzball, Fuzzy for short, had been Mandy's oh-so-cleverly named cat—"in the Amazon and Egypt and, well, all over the place really. And then you'd perform them for us, and…" Smiling, Sherry shook her head. She reached out and gathered Mandy's hand into both of hers. "I guess what I'm trying to say is—you were happy then, Sugar Plum." She raised her eyebrows, her expression filling with concern, and shook her head. "But are you happy now?"

Tears welled in Mandy's eyes, and she couldn't manage to look away from Sherry's face. Mandy damned Sherry for her impeccably awful timing, then damned herself for being mad at the other woman for having the audacity to care about her enough to broach the subject. Which only nudged her closer to an all-out breakdown.

The sound of a masculine throat-clearing finally drew the attention of both of them. Dr. Keith Slater, the clinic's founder and lead dentist, stood on the other side of the counter, eyeing them cautiously. He was a tall, slender man in his early sixties who could easily be described as a silver fox. That he was a widower only solidified his status as the most eligible bachelor to the single, middle-aged women—and some of the younger women—of Auburn.

"Am I interrupting, ladies?"

Mandy cleared her throat, but it was Sherry who answered first. "No, Keith"—she blushed—"Dr. Slater."

"Alright then…" The dentist offered Mandy a brief nod, then shifted his focus to Sherry. "Would you mind staying late this evening? I have a few new processes I'd like to go over with you —to help the office run more smoothly."

"I, um, yes. Of course," Sherry said.

"Great." With another nod Mandy's way, Dr. Slater retreated back down the hallway that led to the exam rooms.

Mandy held her breath, waiting until he was out of sight before she exhaled in wave of hushed giggles. "I have a few processes I'd like to go over with you," she said, repeating the dentist's words suggestively.

Sherry swatted Mandy's arm. "Oh hush, you!"

Despite her lack of experience with men, Mandy could tell something was going on between those two. She was happy for Sherry, who was like a second mother to her. Sherry had carried a torch for Dr. Slater for as long as Mandy could remember. But wedged in beside that happiness was envy. A whole damn lot of it.

It wasn't that Mandy cared about Dr. Slater; it was that she wanted what was developing between him and Sherry to happen to her. She wanted to meet someone who made her stomach flutter with giddiness, and who had the same reaction to her.

She was suddenly resolved. She was done with being miserable. She would call the number in the ad. She would achieve her full potential...whatever that meant.

Mandy sat in her gently used Chevy pickup, and stared at the entrance to *PANBO BIOTECH*, the company running the *Fulfillment Study*. It was located in a business park on the west side of Reno along with dozens of other engineering, technology, and biotech companies. The whole complex was one story, sprawling, and boxy, and all of the buildings were coated in gray and white stucco. It definitely didn't look grand or life-changing by pretty much anyone's definition.

After a quick peek in the rearview mirror to make sure nothing had gone awry with her makeup, Mandy grabbed her leather mini-backpack off the passenger seat, opened the door, and hopped out of the truck. She'd worn her most flattering jeans and an oversized sweater that, to her eyes, disguised most of her pudge. She really wanted to make a good first impression. She was desperate to change her life, and the fact that the study had been advertised in *her* newspaper only a few days ago, when her dissatisfaction with life had reached an all-time high, seemed almost serendipitous. It was like someone, some higher power, was looking out for her, directing her toward the path to…

Mandy shook her head and shut the truck door, knowing full well she was being silly. She shot a quick glance up at the sky. Nobody—not God or guardian angels or anything like that—had stepped in during her previous eighteen years of miserable loneliness and mediocrity, and she doubted any such beings had decided to step in now.

No, this was coincidence, Mandy was certain. The idea actually made her feel better, as though she'd already taken her future into her hands by being brave enough to call the number in the ad in the first place. She was done with waiting around for someone to save her; she had to save herself.

Taking a deep breath, Mandy felt a sly smile curve her lips as she took her first step toward her future. She'd never felt more confident.

She hadn't parked far from the entrance to *PANBO BIOTECH*, but by the time she reached the glass door, familiar self-doubt had weaseled its way into her mind. What if she wasn't good enough? What if the people running the study didn't want her?

The door swung outward before Mandy could reach for the handle. A man, maybe a few years older than her and dressed in khakis and a light blue polo shirt, stood just inside the threshold, holding the door open. She could see the edge of a black tattoo peeking out from his collar and from his right sleeve. He was taller than Mandy—not that that was difficult when she barely reached five and a half feet—but not overly tall, and slender with dark hair, tan skin, and hard features. She wouldn't have called him handsome, but there was something about his eyes, almost like he knew a secret that he would share with only her, that made him instantly appealing.

"Amanda Samuelson?" he asked, his voice smooth and deep.

"I—" She had to clear her throat. "Yes. I am." She smiled hesitantly. "But everyone calls me Mandy."

The man returned her smile, and his face transformed, becoming open and appealing. He held out his hand. "Victor Ramirez." There it was again, that sparkle in his eyes, the suggestion that maybe, just maybe, he'd let her in on his secret. "Call me Vic."

Mandy accepted his hand, consciously making her grip firm. "It's, um, nice to meet you." She held his eyes for a moment longer, then glanced down at the blue-gray carpet. Her cheeks heated, and she cursed herself for blushing.

Victor withdrew his hand. "Well, come in." He turned away from the door and stepped further into a waiting room. Mandy followed.

There were a dozen or so gray padded chairs set up around the perimeter of the room. The far side of the space was partitioned off by a reception desk that was occupied by a woman with short, permed brown hair. She was typing on a keyboard, only looking away from her monitor long enough to meet Mandy's eyes and offer a curt nod in greeting.

Victor held out his arm, indicating that she should take a seat. "You're one of nineteen candidates were testing today, but—lucky you—you're the only one here at the moment." He offered her a charming smile. "You'll have our full attention."

Suppressing a giggle, Mandy sat in one of the chairs set against the wall to her left. As she looked around the room, she wondered if she would have felt more or less awkward had there been any other "candidates" there to wait with her.

"There are some magazines," Victor said, pointing to the three small tables interspersed with the chairs. "Hopefully there's something you like. We'll get you processed in no time." With that, he turned and headed down a hallway beside the reception desk.

Mandy reached across the chair on her right to search through a short stack of magazines. She settled for the third from the top—

last month's edition of *National Geographic*—in lieu of the standard fashion and entertainment magazines sandwiching it. There were otters on the cover. Mandy had always liked otters.

She'd just settled back in her chair and had opened the magazine when the receptionist called her name.

"I need you to fill out these forms, please, Miss Samuelson." She held out a clipboard layered with at least ten sheets of paper.

"Oh…yes, of course." Mandy set aside her magazine and quickly retrieved the clipboard, then settled back in her chair to fill out the paperwork. She had to provide background information, such as education and employment history, medical history, both personal and family, and answer a two-sided questionnaire asking why she was interested in the study and what she hoped to gain from it, among other things. The final few sheets included a waiver and a confidentiality agreement. She wasn't allowed to tell anyone about her participation in the study; if she broke the agreement, her potential participation would be terminated.

There was no way she would risk that. Her lips were sealed.

About fifteen minutes in to the paperwork, Victor reemerged from the hallway and headed straight for the glass door. Mandy could see someone else approaching from the other side. It was a tall, skinny man with a ponytail who looked to be in his late thirties or early forties.

Mandy couldn't believe Victor's perfect timing, and surprising herself, she said as much to him. She wasn't sure where her new boldness was coming from, but she hoped it never went away. Talking to strangers—men in particular—definitely wasn't one of her strong suits.

Victor caught her eye before opening the door for the newcomer and nodded to the wall opposite Mandy. "I was watching from the office right there."

"Oh…got it." Feeling too warm and little silly, Mandy returned her attention to her paperwork…or, at least, most of her attention. She listened as Victor welcomed the new candidate, a man named

Carl Matthews. She felt a swell of satisfaction that their interaction wasn't as long or friendly as her and Victor's had been. Not that it had been *super* long or friendly, but still…

In under a minute, Carl was also seated and filling out paperwork. The only words he and Mandy exchanged were a quick "Hi" and "Hello."

Again, Victor disappeared down the hallway, but he reemerged a few minutes later, just as Mandy was signing the confidentiality agreement. He stopped in the mouth of the hallway, and when Mandy looked up from her paperwork, he smiled. "We're ready for you. Follow me."

Standing, Mandy glanced down at the clipboard, then held it out, unsure what to do with it. "Uh…"

"Go ahead and bring it with you. If you have any questions about any of it, you can ask me."

"Um…okay." Mandy started across the waiting room. As she neared him, Victor turned and led her down the hallway. They passed several closed doors and finally stopped at the last one on the left.

After Victor opened the door, Mandy followed him into the room, surprised by how large it was. She'd been expecting a small office about the size of an exam room, but this was roughly the size of a classroom. Instead of desks and chalkboards, there was a long, evenly partitioned table that looked like it wouldn't be out of place in a library, and counters and cupboards lined the walls.

"This is our collections lab, where we collect the samples we need to do DNA analyses of candidates."

Mandy looked around curiously. In her eagerness to make a change in her life, she hadn't actually asked for any details on the study. She had no clue as to *how* it might help her "fulfill her potential." That her DNA would be analyzed was curious, to say the least. "What does that mean, exactly? What do you need? And why?" Realizing she'd more or less blurted her questions, Mandy stared down at her feet. "Sorry." Her cheeks were flaming, again.

Victor touched Mandy's shoulder gently. "No worries. I told you to ask questions." He let go and motioned toward the first section of the table. "Take a seat." When she did, he sat opposite her. "We're looking for a specific DNA marker—it's only present in a very small minority of the population, but it's required for participation in the study. It's what makes it possible for participants to…well, to sort of evolve into better versions of themselves."

Evolve. Mandy liked the sound of that. She was *so* ready to evolve.

"As for what I'll need, I'll just take a sample of your blood and do a buccal swab."

Mandy shook her head. "Buccal swab?"

Tearing open one of the few items on the table between them, a paper wrapper a little shorter than a ruler, Victor pulled out what appeared to be a long cotton swab. "It's just a sample of the cells from the inside of your cheek."

"And that'll tell you if I have this, um, marker?"

Victor nodded. "Open up," he said, opening his own mouth to demonstrate.

Mandy did as instructed, feeling like a gaping buffoon. She tried not to breathe too much while Victor rubbed the inside of both of her cheeks with the cottony end of the swab. She was surprised by how long it took—a good 30 seconds on each side.

"Why do you need a blood sample if that"—Mandy pointed to the swab, which Victor was sticking into a plastic test tube—"tells you all about my DNA?"

"Well, the blood tells us a bunch of things about you, like whether or not you have any vitamin deficiencies or other ailments…basically whether or not you're healthy. But mostly it's just a backup in case something goes wrong with this thing." He held up the plastic test tube and secured a cap on the open end.

Mandy frowned. "And if there's something wrong with me, like a deficiency or something…?" Because it would be just her luck to be disqualified for having high cholesterol or because she didn't eat enough broccoli.

Victor held his hand out on the table, palm up. "Your arm, please." Once Mandy's arm was extended and he had a gentle grip on her wrist, he explained, "If you're a viable candidate, meaning you carry the marker in your DNA, then we'll make sure you get all the health care you need to be as healthy as possible...and if you're not, we'll give you the information so *you* can take care of any health issues we uncover."

"Wow. That's really nice of you," Mandy said.

Victor shrugged. "We do what we can. Are you squeamish about blood?"

"I don't like it, if that's what you mean." She didn't tell him that the last time she'd really seen her own blood, when she'd been chopping onions for her mom's French onion soup and the knife had slipped, cutting fairly deeply into her index finger, she'd almost passed out.

"Look up at the ceiling." Victor squeezed her wrist. "I'll be done in no time."

He didn't lie. Mandy felt him wipe something cool and damp over the skin at the crook of her elbow, quickly followed by a sharp prick of pain. A few seconds later, she felt a cotton ball being pressed against the minuscule puncture. Victor's fingers were warm on her skin, and his touch was light enough to give rise to goose bumps.

"All done," he said. "How was I?"

Mandy lowered her gaze from the ceiling tiles and stared into the honey-brown depths of Victor's eyes. "Great." She cleared her throat and gave him a tight-lipped smile. "I mean, not bad. Didn't hurt a bit. You're really good at this." She felt a sad little pang of longing when Victor withdrew his fingers. Guys didn't touch her very often, and guys who looked at her with a mischievous twinkle in their eyes *never* touched her.

"Thanks. So...you're all done." He paused for a moment. "I

can't really answer any specifics until you're a confirmed participant in the study, but do you have any questions?"

About a million. Mandy thought about it for a few seconds. "Does this study make that big of a difference for people?" She looked down at the table. "I mean…what if you don't have that much potential to begin with?" She hated how piteous she sounded, but she couldn't help it.

"Everyone has more potential than they give themselves credit for."

Mandy met his eyes.

"Take me, for example," Victor said, pointing to his chest. "Everyone I grew up with thought I'd spend my life behind bars. *I* thought I'd spend my life behind bars." Chuckling, he shook his head. "Not behind any bars, am I? I couldn't see it back then, but I had the potential to be a part of something"—he looked around the room, then returned his gaze to Mandy's—"to change lives." He leaned forward, resting his forearms on the edge of the table. "Giving up—that's the only guaranteed path to failure."

Mandy held her breath for a few seconds, then let it out in a soft laugh. "Wow…you could be a motivational speaker." She gave a half-hearted fist pump. "Go get 'em. You can do it. Ra. Ra. Ra."

"Now you're just making fun of me."

Again, Mandy laughed. "Maybe a little." She'd never felt so comfortable talking to a guy as she did at that moment with Victor. She never wanted it to end.

A hint of concern dampened the spark of mischief in Victor's eyes. He shot a quick glance back over his shoulder, then stood. "Why don't I walk you out? Make sure you get to your car safely."

"Oh, um, okay," Mandy said, standing as well. She followed Victor back up the hallway, watched him drop off her clipboard with the receptionist, then walked with him out to the parking lot. "I'm that blue truck right there," she said, pointing to her truck, which was parked in the nearest row of spaces.

"Great." Victor walked by her side to her vehicle, glancing

back at the building every few steps. "Listen," he said once they reached her Chevy. He stuck his hands into the front pockets of his khakis and shifted his feet. "You'll hear from us in a few weeks, once we've had time to analyze your samples, but, well…"

Mandy's heart rate seemed to double, triple even. Was he going to ask her out on a date? She really, *really* wanted him to ask her out.

"…you seem like a really nice person, and—"

"Vic?" an unfamiliar male voice called from the way they had come. Mandy turned in time to see a tall, slender man striding across the parking lot toward them. "Victor!" He was wearing gray slacks and a white button down shirt, and few people would argue that his was a very handsome face.

"Shit…thought he was still at lunch," Victor said under his breath. He met Mandy's eyes. "Sorry."

Mandy had no idea what he was apologizing for.

The unfamiliar man stopped a few feet away from them. "You forgot to introduce me," he said to Victor.

"Right. Sorry, Cole." Victor looked at Mandy. "Amanda Samuelson"—he motioned toward the other man—"this is Dr. Cole Michaels, the director of the study. You'll be working closely with him if you qualify to participate."

"Oh. Hi." Mandy extended her hand. "It's nice to meet you."

"And you," Dr. Michaels said. The moment his hand touched hers, she felt slightly dizzy and her thoughts seemed sluggish. "I trust that you'll hold to the confidentiality agreement and tell nobody about your potential participation in this study?"

"Of course," Mandy managed to mumble. When the doctor released her hand, her wits returned to full-strength, but she had little recollection of what had just happened, other than an odd sense that she'd forgotten something.

"I like to make it a point to meet all of our potential participants…put another friendly face to the study, and all that," Dr. Michaels said.

"That's, um, very kind of you." Mandy looked at Victor, then at the doctor. "I should be going. It takes a couple hours to get back home, and my mom'll be worried if I'm late for dinner—we eat together every Thursday night…" Realizing she was babbling, she let her words trail off.

"Yes, well…we wouldn't want that, would we, Vic?"

Victor shook his head.

"Drive safe, Amanda." The doctor gave a quick nod, then turned and walked back to the building.

"Good luck," Victor said with a small smile and an apology in his eyes. Without another word, he turned and followed his boss.

3

PRESENT DAY

The driver lay on one of a half-dozen cots set up in Mandy's one-room cabin. Shortly after waking in his car, he'd passed out again. Cole, who'd supervised the clean-up of the young man and given him a quick medical exam, had claimed they hadn't found a wallet on him, though that easily could have been a lie.

Regardless, Mandy didn't know his name or where he was from or why he looked so much like a ghost from her past. She was, however, certain of one thing about him, which just happened to be the most important thing—he was assuredly one of the chosen. She would keep him. And until he woke and could tell her his name, in her mind, at least, she would call him Vic.

4

22 YEARS AGO

Mandy grabbed the telephone off her nightstand just as it started its fourth shrill ring. "Hello?"

It had been nearly three weeks since her brief trip to Reno to see if she qualified for the *Fulfillment Study*. She felt like she was wearing blinders, but for all of her efforts to convince herself otherwise, she was certain that the study was the only sure-fire way to improve her life, to reach her true potential…whatever that may be.

Which was precisely the problem. She didn't know her potential and was relying on someone else to enlighten her…possibly Dr. Michaels, or maybe even Victor. After all, it was the latter of the two she couldn't get out of her head.

But neither Victor nor Dr. Michaels nor the permed receptionist was on the phone. "Hey there, Sugar Plum." It was Sherry.

Mandy's heart sank. She needed to know if she was in or out so she could get on with her life.

"Would you mind covering my shift on Friday?" Sherry giggled. "Keith asked me to go with him to a dental conference up in Washington."

"That depends—are you going as his receptionist or as his date? Wait, do people do that…take dates to dental conferences?"

"I'm not going to the actual conference, you goof—just up to Seattle to stay with him. He's going to take me to the Space Needle!" Sherry's obvious excitement rubbed off on Mandy, just a little.

"Well, if he's taking you the Space Needle, then of course I'll fill in for you." Mandy rolled her eyes—not at Sherry and her budding relationship with the dentist, but at her own nonexistent plans. It wasn't like she had anything going on anyway.

"Thanks so much, Sugar Plum! See you in a few hours."

They said their goodbyes and Mandy hung up. She hoisted herself off the edge of her bed and, dragging her feet, made her way to the studio apartment's only bathroom to shower and get ready for work. It was Monday, she had four days of work ahead to keep her busy and at least part of her mind off the study—and Victor—while she waited to hear back.

"You seem distracted," Sherry told Mandy. It was the mid-afternoon lull, and both were busy at their own computers, double-checking appointments to make sure none of the dentists were overbooked. "Penny for your thoughts…"

Sighing heavily, Mandy tossed a quick glance at the older woman. "Oh, I don't know. I guess I've been thinking about what you said…you know, about me being unhappy and all that." Mandy shrugged, gave up on scheduling for the moment, and swiveled her chair so she was facing Sherry. "I've been thinking about what I can do…what changes I can make."

Sherry turned her chair as well, placing her hands on the top of her thighs with a soft patting noise. "You have no idea how happy that makes me! You should check out the programs at the JC. You've saved up enough by now to take a class or two, and I'm sure your mom'll help out"—she grinned—"and so will your Aunt Sherry!"

"Oh, gosh, Sher…you don't have to do that." Mandy fought a flush of embarrassment. From the burn in her neck and cheeks, it was a futile effort. In all honesty, Mandy had plenty of money to attend the JC, especially if she continued working part-time at Riverside Dental. It was an entirely different issue that kept holding her back. Again, she sighed.

She was afraid. Meeting people and making new friends had always been hard for her, especially the part where she had to talk to complete strangers, and she was fairly certain that being able to talk to people she didn't know was somewhat essential to doing well in college. Call it a hunch.

Sherry reached across the several foot distance separating them and patted Mandy's knee. "Don't worry a bit about it. I want to help." She shook her head and laughed a soft, humorless laugh. "God knows I don't have my own children to spend anything on, so…" With a sad, wistful smile, she turned back to her computer and selected a time block on the screen. "Uh-oh, Dr. Lee is double booked tomorrow at 11:15. Hmmm…"

Mandy turned back to her own computer screen just as a visitor opened one of the double glass doors a few paces away from the reception desk. Her heart practically skipped a beat…or three. Victor walked through the doorway and into the dental office—*her* dental office.

Mandy stood so abruptly that her chair was propelled backward with enough force that it bumped into the wall of color-coded and filed folders behind her. "Vic! What are you doing here?"

Victor, who'd been scanning the reception and waiting areas, turned his attention to Mandy. "I'm here to get my teeth cleaned?"

The laugh that bubbled out of Mandy was a little shrill. "You are not!" she said breathily. "We don't take walk-ins, and you don't have an appointment, so…"

Victor held up his hands in surrender. "You got me there." He flashed a mischievous smile, the always-present hint of a secret that might be shared glittering in his brown eyes. "I'm here to see you."

Mandy's heart raced as she considered that Victor might really be interested in her. Her fretting over what her DNA results would reveal had only been overshadowed by one thing during her weeks of waiting—daydreams of Victor and what might have happened had Dr. Michaels not interrupted their conversation in the parking lot. Would he have asked her out? Would he have kissed her right there? Would he have pulled her into the truck bed and…

She shook her head. Of course he wouldn't have done *that*. And now she was blushing, again.

Victor leaned his elbows on the counter. "Do you have a break coming up? Maybe we can grab a coffee?"

"Yes!" Sherry said with way too much enthusiasm. "In fact, her shift ends in a few minutes—you can have her for the rest of the day!"

Looking over her shoulder, Mandy started to ask Sherry what the heck she was talking about; her shift didn't end for a few *hours*, not minutes. But she only managed to get out, "What are you—" before she finally understood. She snapped her mouth shut and plastered on a smile. It wasn't difficult. She was giddy with excitement. "Thank you," she mouthed, then turned her attention back to Victor. "Yeah, um, just let me grab my things and we can go, um, wherever, I guess…"

"Cool. I'll wait out front."

In a few minutes, after Sherry had given her the quickest and least-detailed third degree in the history of girl talk, Mandy was walking with Victor toward his car, a maroon Toyota Camry that looked brand new.

"You hungry or just want coffee?" he asked.

Mandy stood by the passenger side of the car while Victor unlocked it from the other side. "Well, that depends. Is this about the study, or…"

"Or…?" Victor raised his head and met her eyes, his eyebrows raised.

"Nothing." Mandy glanced down at the pavement. This whole embarrassed, clamming up issue she had every time she spoke to a guy was exactly the reason she had so little—as in *none*—experience dating.

"Hop in," Victor said as he ducked inside the car.

Mandy did so, and as soon as she shut her door and buckled her seat belt, Victor handed her a manila envelope. She stared at it for a moment, disappointed. The envelope definitely indicated Victor's visit was business, not pleasure.

"Congrats, Mandy."

With those two words, Mandy's disappointment was forgotten completely. "I passed?" She looked from the envelope to Victor, and back down at the envelope. "I mean, I'm a viable candidate?"

"That you are." Victor turned in the driver's seat as much as he could to face her fully. "You're one of the exceptional few, and what you're about to experience"—he shook his head and laughed softly—"is the chance of a lifetime."

Mandy's heart was racing, and she couldn't hold back the smile that spread across her face, wide and joyous. She didn't want to. This was her ticket to happiness. "What's next? How soon can I start?"

Victor pointed to the envelope. "Along with the info packet explaining what'll happen over the next few months once you begin the study, there's also several packs of a vitamin supplement you'll need to take every day to prepare. Once you've taken all three doses, you'll be able to start with—"

Before he even had a chance to finish, Mandy was opening the envelope and fishing out one of the vitamin packs. She held the small, square package up and read the medical mumbo-jumbo on the wrapper. Despite her best efforts, it remained gibberish to her.

She glanced at Victor. "It's safe?"

"As a daily vitamin," he said.

Shaking the packet, Mandy noted aloud, "It's a powder."

"It is."

Mandy retrieved the plastic water bottle she brought to work every day and unscrewed the lid. There was about an inch of water left at the bottom, just enough to dissolve the powder and gulp it down, taking the first step toward her future…toward being a better version of herself. "Bottoms up." She chugged the whole thing down in two big gulps. It tasted bitter and a little tangy, with the barest hint of orange attempting—and failing—to mask the flavor.

"Ugh! It tastes like"—she frowned sheepishly—"well, like crushed up vitamins, I guess." She finished with a one shoulder shrug. "What now? You deliver the good news, then head back to Reno?"

A smile flashed across Victor's face, there and gone in an instant. "Actually, I thought you might want to celebrate. How about dinner?"

"Like a date?" Mandy said without meaning to. She felt flustered, her thoughts suddenly muddled. "I didn't mean to say that!" She slapped her hand over her mouth, her eyes going wide. She hadn't meant to say *that* either. Her tongue started to feel swollen and slightly numb, and a tingling sensation began in her fingers and toes, spreading quickly to her hands and feet, then further up her limbs. Her hand fell away from her mouth, despite her best efforts to keep it there.

"Vic," she tried to say, but it came out as more of a mumbled, "Vmm."

She could no longer move her arms or legs, and her head lolled to the side. Blackness crept in from the edges of her vision, closing in quickly. Had he…had he drugged her?

He had. Victor had drugged her!

"Welcome to the Program," he said. It was the last thing Mandy heard before she lost consciousness.

5

PRESENT DAY

Mandy sat at the small wooden table in her one-room cabin, opposite the six cots. Three were occupied with recovering "chosen" and three were empty. But Mandy only had eyes for one of the occupants—the nameless driver. She watched him from the table, alternating between taking sips of coffee from a stainless steel thermos and munching on biscotti one of her followers had made that morning.

Even passed out cold, the familiar stranger reminded her of Vic. Part of her mind had already started to think of him *as* Vic, not just as someone who looked like him. It didn't bother the illogical portion of her brain that this man was about the same age as Vic had been some 22 years ago.

He would be awake soon. Thoughts whirled around in Mandy's mind.

What would she say to him?

Would she ask for his real name?

Would he be like Vic in other ways?

What if…

"It's not him, you know," Cole said.

Mandy jumped in her chair, dropping the piece of biscotti she'd been about to bite into. She slowly turned toward the doorway, glaring.

"You do know that, don't you?" Cole stepped further into the cabin, stopping before the wood stove in the center. He held his hands out to soak up some warmth from the fire. "He has no tattoos, and he's far too young. I suppose it's not impossible that he's—"

"Shut up, Cole." Her voice was scathing.

Cole glanced back at Mandy for the briefest moment, then returned his attention to the stove. "Temper, temper. It'll be your downfall one day…that, or your desperate need to be loved. One or the other…"

"Shut up!" Trembling with rage, Mandy stood. "You forget—without me, your plan is useless. Without me, *you're* useless."

Cole turned around, facing Mandy fully. A nasty sneer twisted his handsome face. "Perhaps…but that's still not Vic."

6

22 YEARS AGO

Beep…beep. Beep…beep. Beep…beep.

Mandy groaned and tried to swallow, but her mouth was so dry that she ended up coughing instead. Dazedly, she opened her eyes and blinked several times, processing her surroundings. She was in a white room and seemed to be lying down. The room's walls were all bare except for the one to the right of her. That wall was inset with a huge mirror from corner to corner. There were two doors in adjacent walls, and she could see what appeared to be a simple white dresser beyond her feet.

Looking down at herself, she discovered that she was tucked into a hospital bed, though she had no recollection of how or why she would be in one. She felt odd—muddle-headed and sort of tingly all over, as though her nervous system was just booting back up. There was a pulse sensor pinching her right index finger, and an IV had been stuck into the back of the same hand.

Again she scanned the room. "Hello?" she whispered, not because she was afraid, but because it was all she could manage without some water to moisten her throat. Her mind was too fuzzy for fear. "Hello?"

A door opened in the wall opposite the foot of the bed, and Mandy raised her head as much as she could to see who was entering the room. It was a tall white man. He was incredibly good looking and somewhat familiar. After a few moments, Mandy's sluggish mind placed him. Dr. Michaels…from the study.

Like fog clearing ever so slowly, she remembered what had happened before she'd lost consciousness.

She'd been at work.

Victor had showed up unexpectedly.

He'd given her the good news—she was a viable candidate for the study.

She'd taken a vitamin powder. *Not* a vitamin powder, but some sort of drug…a sedative.

Victor.

"Vic…did this…drugged me," she rasped, both telling Dr. Michaels and solidifying the fact in her own mind. Finally, fear started to bloom, speeding up her heartbeat and quickening her breaths.

"He retrieved you, yes," the doctor said. "How are you feeling? Any discomfort?"

"What am I doing here?" Mandy asked, ignoring his pseudo-kindness.

Victor had drugged her and brought her…somewhere. She had no clue where she was, but she *did* know that Victor had brought her to this man. You didn't have someone drugged and "retrieved" because you wanted to give them an all-inclusive spa treatment.

Mandy felt like the biggest idiot in the world. The ad had seemed too good to be true because it *was* too good to be true. She tried to move, to get out of bed, to do something, but she found she still had little control over her limbs.

"That's the paralytic your feeling," Dr. Michaels said, confirming her suspicions about being drugged. He tapped the IV bag hanging a few feet from the side of the bed. "It's mild, but mixed with the right sedative, it's just enough to keep you calm and safe from hurting yourself or others."

"I don't understand." Why would she hurt herself or anyone else—besides the doctor or Victor.

"I know," Dr. Cole said as he pulled a chair made of white plastic and stainless steel to her bedside. As far as Mandy could tell, it was the only chair in the room. He sat and leaned his elbows on his knees. "I'll explain everything once you've recovered, but for now"—he reached out, capturing her left hand, and a numbness clouded her mind—"you must listen carefully. You will not remember this part of our conversation, will you?"

"No," Mandy said, her voice faint. She didn't know why she'd said it, other than she knew it was the truth. She could *feel* that it was the truth.

"Good. Whatever happens to you over the next few days, whatever changes you experience due to the treatment, you will never use your new abilities against me. You will always listen to me and do as I say, won't you?"

Mandy mumbled an affirmative.

"Good." Dr. Michaels released her hand, and the semblance of clarity returned, though for the life of her, Mandy couldn't recall why the doctor had taken her hand in the first place. "I'm going to increase the sedative so you can sleep. Depending on their nature, the changes can be a bit uncomfortable for some people. No point in making you suffer."

Her fear spiked. He was going to knock her out again. Not yet. She couldn't let him do it yet. She needed to stall him. Maybe then the drugs would wear off enough that she could move and do something—escape or call for help. "Water? Can I have some water?"

"Next time you wake up," the doctor told her. "But don't worry…we've got you on fluids."

Mandy might have snorted or rolled her eyes, had she not been more terrified than she'd ever been in her entire life. Whether or not she was on fluids was the least of her worries.

She watched, unable to object, as the doctor injected the additional sedative into her IV.

Faster than she'd expected, her eyelids drooped, and the world faded away.

Mandy awoke to the sound of a door shutting. She blinked several times before she was able to focus on the man approaching her bedside. Victor. Her heart plummeted as she realized she was still in the white room with the mirrored wall; it hadn't been just a dream…a nightmare.

Victor stopped by her bedside, and Mandy's heart rate doubled. She gripped the sheets in her clenching fists as best she could with the IV still stuck in the back of her hand and the pulse sensor on her index finger. At least the tingling in her limbs had faded almost completely. If she needed to fling herself out of the bed and away from him, or possibly to hit him, she thought she *might* be able to manage.

With frantic urgency, she searched the side of the bed for buttons or a remote that might raise the top portion of the mattress so she would be somewhat upright. She was unsuccessful.

Victor apparently took pity on her, because he reached down, found the remote dangling over the edge of the bed, and set it beside her hand. "It's this one," he said, pushing the triangular shaped button at the top.

The upper portion of the bed rose gradually until Mandy was sitting up, more or less. She didn't say thank you, instead opting to glare.

Nonplussed, Victor held out a disposable drink cup with a lid and straw. "It's water—*just* water," he explained when Mandy showed no signs of accepting the cup. "Thought you might be thirsty."

Begrudgingly, she took it, but in the back of her mind, she couldn't help but think of the last time she'd consumed something given to her by him. Thirst overshadowed her caution. She sipped from the straw, and the cool water felt incredibly soothing as it washed down her dry throat.

"Listen, Mandy..." Victor sat in the chair that had been occupied by Dr. Michaels the last time Mandy had been awake. "I'm really sorry about—"

Mandy turned her head on the pillow so she was facing away from him. "How long have I been here?" Her voice was small, barely more than a whisper.

Victor sighed. "About a day and a half."

She looked at him sharply. "My Mom'll be freaking out! She'll call the police. They'll be looking for me...they'll find me." But even as she said it, a cold, almost nauseating feeling settled in her belly. She hadn't told anyone about the study. The newspaper with the ad in the classifieds wasn't even in her apartment anymore.

She was so damn screwed, unless...

Mandy remembered learning about Stockholm Syndrome in the psychology class she'd taken her senior year. She'd learned about another syndrome, one that was similar, but opposite; instead of the captive becoming sympathetic and loyal to the captor, it's the captor who begins to, in some cases, genuinely care about the well-being of the captive. Lime...Limo...Lima Syndrome. That was it—Lima Syndrome. Victor already seemed to feel bad, possibly even guilty, about having abducted her; would it be that difficult for her to make him care enough to free her?

Victor took a deep breath. "I know you must hate me, but I did try to warn you...before..." He paused, then added, "He was supposed to be gone for another half-hour, and I was going to destroy your samples and paperwork before he got back, but..." He shrugged. Mandy knew the rest. Dr. Michaels had returned early, and tracked them down in the parking lot. But she didn't have time or energy to waste thinking about what could have been, not right now.

If she was going to do this, to foster some sort of Lima Syndrome effect, she'd have to make it convincing and honest, and telling Victor she didn't hate him so soon after the drugging and kidnapping would be easily seen as the ridiculous lie it was. She did hate him, she was certain…and Dr. Michaels and whoever else was involved with the so-called "Fulfillment Study." But she also hated herself for being so weak and gullible and stupid and just plain-old pathetic.

Mandy made herself smile, just a little, and meet Victor's eyes. "I'd hate you less if you told me what the heck's going on…" She looked around the room, then focused on the expansive mirror. "Is someone watching from the other side? Where are we anyway? And what are you going to do to me?" Genuine tears welled in her eyes, and her voice trembled. "Are you going to hurt me?"

Victor rested his elbows on his knees, much as the doctor had done, but Victor didn't reach for her hand. A tiny voice in the far recesses of her mind wondered why Dr. Michaels had done that in the first place. Not that it mattered now.

"You know, I wasn't lying when I told you your DNA contained the marker we needed"—he winced—"and *that* was pretty much the only thing I didn't lie about." He took another deep breath, exhaling heavily. "The, uh, 'Fulfillment Study' doesn't actually exist. It's the cover we use to draw in potential candidates for the Program." Before Mandy could ask what program he was talking about, he added, "Which doesn't have a name, so don't bother asking. It's just the 'Program.'"

"The program," Mandy said. "That's what you call *what*, exactly?"

With his third deep breath, Victor sat back in his chair. He slouched down as though he were exhausted, and shrugged. "I don't know who runs it, someone way above Michaels, but the whole point of the thing is to find people whose DNA can be altered"—he held up his right hand, his thumb and index finger almost pinching the air—"just a touch." A humorless laugh shook his body. "You'd be surprised how much that tiny modification can change someone."

"What are you—" Mandy started to snap, but she stopped herself and made her tone less waspish. "I don't understand what you're saying. You guys are doing something to me—to my DNA?"

Victor flicked his hand in the direction of the IV stand. "It's already done. Your DNA's been altered. You'll, uh, start to notice the changes soon."

Mandy felt her throat tighten. "What kind of changes?" Was she going to grow tentacles out of her ears, or maybe sprout an extra head?

"Honestly, it's different for everyone. Some people develop the ability to talk to others in their heads, or to move things with their minds, or to catch glimpses of what's going to happen in the future—"

"That's, like, telepathy and telekinesis, and what…precognition? Those are"—Mandy shook her head in disbelief—"that's like comic book stuff—superpowers, and…" She laughed shrilly. She was losing it. Victor obviously already had, and now she was too. "That stuff's not real!"

Victor raised his left hand and made a "come here" motion to the mirror. Mandy realized there really was someone on the other side, watching her. The idea thoroughly creeped her out.

A tall, athletically built woman with straight blonde hair held back by a scrunchie strode into the room. "Demo time?" She raised her eyebrows as a wide, eager grin spread across her face.

Victor shifted his attention from Mandy to the other woman. "It's all you, Cas."

Cas rubbed her hands together, then caught Mandy's eye briefly before looking at a tiny, gray plastic waste basket in the corner of the room, near the other door. She pointed at the receptacle and slowly raised her finger. As she moved, so did the waste basket. It floated about a foot off the linoleum floor for several seconds…until Cas started humming. As her tune picked up speed, the trash can started hopping around in the air, almost like it was dancing to her song.

"That's not—" Mandy cleared her suddenly hoarse throat and shook her head back and forth. "That's not possible. It's a trick. There's a string or magnets or something."

Cas sighed and lowered her hand. The waste basket settled back on the floor. "Just once, it'd be awesome if someone just said, 'Oh, hey, that's cool!'"—she cocked her head to the side and looked at Mandy—"You know?"

"Uh…" Mandy had no clue how to respond. When Cas raised her left hand and Mandy's long hair started floating around her head, she momentarily lost the ability to speak altogether.

Cas narrowed her eyes and pointed at the water cup with her other hand. She made a flicking motion toward the ceiling, and the straw shot out of the lid, bounced off the ceiling, and landed on the bed beside Mandy's right calf.

Eyes wide with a mix of shock and terror, Mandy opened her mouth. What came out was a barely discernible shriek. "Get out! Get out get out get out get out! GET OUT!" She squeezed her eyes shut, holding back tears. This wasn't real. It was so incredibly *not real*.

She was losing it. No, she'd already lost it. Her sanity was gone. Gone. Gone. Gone.

When she heard the door open and close, she pried her eyes open and looked to her bedside, expecting to find Victor still sitting there. Instead, he was halfway to the door, apparently planning to follow Cas out.

"Wait," Mandy whispered. "Victor—Vic…don't leave." A soft sob bubbled up from her chest. She felt like she was suffocating. She took rapid gulps of air, but couldn't seem to get enough. She was being crushed under the weight of her insanity. She didn't want to be alone with her madness. "Please don't leave me," she whimpered.

The side of the bed dipped as Victor sat on the edge. "I'm sorry, Mandy. I really am." Gently, he gathered her into his arms and held her while she cried.

7

PRESENT DAY

"Who are you? Where am I?" the man who looked so much like Vic asked. He sat up slowly, looking around the cabin.

Mandy had moved a chair to the side of his cot when he'd started stirring, and had her followers move the other two recovering chosen out of the cabin. She wanted to be alone with him. As she leaned forward, the chair creaked under her shifting weight. "I'm Mandy." She smiled reassuringly. "You were sick. You passed out in your car, and I found you. I've been taking care of you."

He returned her smile, and she knew—could see it in his eyes—that she had him. He leaned back against the wall beside the cot. "I remember…I remember pulling off the road and parking…in a campground?"

Mandy nodded. "Yes, your car's still there. I moved you to my cabin so you'd be more comfortable. It's too cold outside—you would have frozen to death if I'd left you in your car."

He patted his jeans pockets then met her eyes. "My phone…?"

She had it, or rather, Cole did, but she wasn't ready to let him know that yet. "It must still be in your car. We can get it later, when you're stronger." The virus hadn't had a chance to spread fully and wipe out the unworthy yet, and she didn't want him running off after his sick friends or family to God-knows-where—not when her curiosity regarding his resemblance to Vic was unsated. And if it wasn't just a random resemblance, if he was, through some freakish coincidence, related to Vic, she would make sure the past didn't repeat itself. She would keep this one.

Mandy rested her hand on his shin; she could feel the warmth of his skin through the jeans. "I have some soup on the stove. Why don't you have some, then rest a bit more?"

He nodded. "Sounds good."

With another smile, Mandy stood and started for the stove. She paused and looked back at him. "By the way, what's your name?"

"Jesse. Jesse Hernandez." He ran the fingers of one hand through his disheveled dark hair. The gesture was so reminiscent of Vic that it stole Mandy's breath. But deep down, she felt disappointed. Vic's last name was Ramirez, not Hernandez. Maybe it *was* just a random resemblance.

Stifling her disappointment, she turned away and continued to the stove. "We'll have you up and about in no time."

"Thanks, really. I owe you."

Mandy felt an eager grin spread across her face. She knew *exactly* how he would repay her.

8

22 YEARS AGO

Mandy was propped up in her hospital bed, arms crossed over her chest. She was grateful they'd removed the ceaselessly beeping machines, but she still felt like a prisoner. "I want to *leave*. Why is that so hard for you to get?"

Dr. Michaels sat calmly in the chair at her bedside. "I understand perfectly."

"So I can go home?"

With a slow shake of his head, Dr. Michaels vanquished Mandy's rising hope. He smiled. "You're stuck with us. Now, your wrist please. I need to check your pulse."

Mandy huffed and thrust her left arm at the doctor. As soon as his fingers touched her skin, numbness clouded her mind.

"You will not remember this. You are not to use whatever new abilities you develop against me, and you will always listen to me and do as I say. Am I clear?"

"Mmhmm," Mandy mumbled.

"And you can thank Vic for this little favor—not that you'll remember..." He cleared his throat and took a deep breath. "You are content to be here...happy, even, aren't you?"

"Yes." The word was faint, barely more than a whisper.

"Excellent." Dr. Michaels released Mandy's wrist.

Blinking, Mandy felt like she was waking from a daydream. "I'm sorry…did you say something?" She shook her head and laughed softly. "Must've zoned out." She rolled her eyes. "Mandy the space cadet…"

"Nothing important." The doctor returned her smile. His breathing was slightly labored, which seemed odd. He rubbed his hands together briskly as he stood, then retrieved a clipboard from a wall pocket by the room's only exit and turned to face her. "We're going to go through a series of questions to see if we can narrow down how exactly the treatment has changed you. Someone will go over these with you every day until we've identified your new ability…or abilities."

Mandy raised and lowered her shoulders in a complacent shrug. "Sounds good."

The doctor reclaimed his seat. "Have you noticed objects moving seemingly of their own accord?"

"Nope—well, when Cas was in here…" She shivered, remembering the shock of witnessing such a thing with her own eyes. It still didn't seem real, but at least remembering the way the little trash can had hovered no longer frightened her.

"Have you heard people say things, but when asked, they claim not to have said anything?"

Mandy shook her head.

"Have you…"

The questions went on and on for nearly twenty minutes. By the time Dr. Michaels was finished, a large man wearing green scrubs knocked on the door and then entered the room. He wore a severe, almost standoffish expression and was carrying a tray of food—a roast beef and cheddar sandwich, a small bowl of potato salad, an even smaller bowl of chocolate pudding, a bottle of water, and a diet Coke.

"Well, I'll leave you to your lunch." The doctor stood and moved out away from the bed.

"Okay. Thanks," Mandy said vaguely as the other man set the tray on the movable bed table. She offered him a shy smile. "Thanks. I love chocolate pudding."

To her surprise, he returned the smile. "You're welcome." He turned to walk back to the door, which Dr. Michaels was holding open, a thoughtful frown on his face.

"Wait," Mandy said when the man who'd brought her lunch was halfway to the door. "What's your name?"

He looked back at her, still smiling. "Kevin." He raised his eyebrows. "You?"

"Mandy."

Kevin acknowledged the exchange with a slight bow of his head. "I've got a good feeling about you."

Before Mandy could ask him what he meant, he left her alone with her lunch. The doctor followed him out.

For three days, Mandy had three different people—all doctors, according to the names they gave her—quiz her on her potential physical and mental "Abilities" with a capital "A". Apparently it was the accepted term for the genetic changes brought on by the treatment. Despite the doctors' varying levels of aloofness at the start of their sessions, she'd managed to end each interview with chatty, friendly conversation. She and the sole female doctor had even ended up giggling about how hot Dr. Michaels was.

A few of the people she mentally considered orderlies, though she didn't actually know their job titles, had brought her things to occupy her time. When she wasn't being interviewed, she walked around her room, played cards or checkers with whoever was around, or when she was alone, played solitaire or read.

She'd quickly found it in her heart to forgive Victor. After all, she *was* happy with her situation at the Program; she could hardly be angry with him for bringing her there. He'd taken to eating his meals with her, and promised to take her out of her room and show her around the facility once they had her Ability nailed down. Talking to him was easy, and Mandy loved how quickly their friendship was developing. She thought it was even possible that soon it might progress into something more.

Overall, she was comfortable…utterly content. She'd never had such an easy time talking to people. She liked everyone she'd met so far and had even started to make friends with Cas.

And then there was Dr. Michaels. At the moment, he was sitting beside her bed, giving her the developing Abilities interview for his second time.

Mandy sat atop the bed, cross-legged and bored. She was pretty sure she had the whole list of questions memorized. Dr. Michaels was the one person she'd encountered while she'd been with the Program whom she hadn't formed any kind of connection or friendly rapport with…despite having several interactions every day. She figured there must be a grouch in every group, and Dr. Michaels was it for the Program.

"Have you become injured and noticed that your body healed at an increased rate?" the doctor asked.

Mandy held up her right hand, showing off the slight bruising on the back where the IV had been inserted into her skin. "Obviously not…"

"Have you—"

"Nope," Mandy said. Still holding up her hand she started ticking off items with her fingers as she spoke. "And no…no… definitely not…I don't think that's physically possible…no…I wish…no…"

Setting his pen on the clipboard, Dr. Michaels raised his hands in submission. "Okay, I get it. No change." He frowned. "Whatever it is, it must be a subtle Ability—either that or it's just taking a long time to develop."

"Or it's so weak that it's useless. Or maybe I'll never develop any Ability…then I could go home…"

"And return to your riveting life as a lonely receptionist whose only standing social engagement is her weekly dinner with her mother?" the doctor finished for her.

"Hey! That's not—I do other stuff!"

"You know that I've had your mind read. Wishing to do things and actually doing them are *not* the same thing."

Mandy opened her mouth to argue, but snapped it shut without saying anything. Because he was right. She couldn't remember the last time she'd done something with a friend. Her evenings and days off were filled with watching TV, and the highlight of her week *was* Thursday night dinners at her mom's house. Sometimes Sherry came too, and it was a real party—or what Mandy thought of as a party. Pitifully, she'd never actually been to a *real* party, not one that didn't include colorful paper hats and cakes decorated with cartoon characters.

With a heavy sigh, Dr. Michaels leaned forward. "I'm sorry. That was rude. Friends?" He extended his hand.

Reluctantly, Mandy accepted his apology and shook his hand. As soon as their palms touched, her mind grew fuzzy.

"You won't remember this. You'll never use your new Abilities against me, whatever they may be, you'll always listen to me and do as I say, and you're happy to be here, correct?"

"Yes," Mandy said quietly.

"Good." Dr. Michaels released her hand, and she blinked several times. His face looked paler than it had before.

"Are you feeling okay?"

"What?" The doctor seemed taken aback. "Yes, I'm fine. Just overextending myself a bit, I think." He turned his left wrist to check his watch. "It's about time for—"

With a short rap of his knuckles on the door, Kevin entered the room, lunch tray in hand. "Good news, Mandy. It's a chocolate pudding day," he said cheerfully. "I got you an extra bowl." He winked at her as he set the tray on the bed.

"Awesome!" Mandy gave him a high five. "Checkers rematch later?"

"Wouldn't miss it for the world." Wearing a broad grin, Kevin strode out of the room and shut the door.

Dr. Michaels stared at the door, then slowly turned his head to look at Mandy, who was digging into her mac and cheese.

"What?" she asked around a mouthful.

"A few days ago, when you first met Kevin, he was friendly to you. He's never friendly to me…"

Swallowing, Mandy shrugged. "You can be kind of a jerk… maybe that's the problem." Her eyes widened as she registered the verbal vomit that had just spewed out of her mouth. She raised one shoulder and smiled sheepishly. "Sorry."

The doctor's eyes narrowed. "You're a social misfit."

Mandy raised her eyebrows. "I take back my apology." She nodded to herself and continued eating.

"You *don't* make friends easily."

"I guess people around here are just friendly…"

"No, they're not."

Dr. Michaels stared at Mandy for such a long time that she grew uncomfortable. She set her fork down and met his eyes. "What?"

"Tell me the name of each person you've befriended here."

Mandy took a deep, exasperated breath. She really just wanted to eat her lunch…especially her two bowls of chocolate pudding. Instead, she crossed her arms over her chest and started listing everyone she'd interacted with while she'd been at the program, including Victor, Kevin, Cas, the other doctors…everyone *except* Dr. Michaels.

"It must have something to do with your Abilities," the doctor mused.

"What? Like I can't make friends on my own? Like I need some mutated superpower to make people like me?"

"Exactly," he said thoughtfully. Without warning, he stood and bounded to the door, tossing it open and thrusting the upper half of his body out into a hallway Mandy had only ever seen but never actually been in—at least not while conscious. She'd been in the facility for nearly a week, but her exploring had been limited to her room and the tiny but practical en suite bathroom.

"Hey! You-er…Carson, or Carlton…yes, you!" Dr. Michaels shouted. "Come here." A moment later, the doctor said, "Yes, *right now*!"

He walked back into the room, and a few seconds later, another man, tall and wiry with graying hair and wearing dark blue coveralls, entered and shut the door.

"Have you two met?" Dr. Michaels asked the newcomer.

Both Mandy and the stranger shook their heads.

"Perfect. Mandy, this is…" Staring at the other man, Dr. Michaels let the introduction hang expectantly.

Hesitantly, the man answered, "Ch-Charlie."

"Charlie," the doctor repeated with a nod. He looked at Mandy. "Charlie, this is Mandy."

Charlie stayed by the door but raised his hand and waved, and Mandy smiled in greeting.

Dr. Michaels returned to Mandy's bedside and turned to face Charlie. He beckoned for the other man to join them. "C'mon, don't be shy." As Charlie did as instructed, the doctor asked, "What do you think of Mandy?"

Charlie stopped at the foot of the bed. "Uh…she seems nice. Real nice actually, like someone who'd be easy to talk to." He smiled at Mandy and shrugged, as though he didn't know why he felt that way.

Mandy started to wonder if Dr. Michaels wasn't entirely wrong about his theory. She couldn't think of any other reason Charlie would feel that way about her.

"She does, doesn't she. Describe her to me," the doctor prompted.

Tilting his head to the side, Charlie studied Mandy for a long, uncomfortable moment, then blinked repeatedly and returned his attention to Dr. Michaels. He stuck his hands into his pants pockets. "She's very…I don't know how to describe it. There's just something about her. She's—I just feel really good about her." He looked down at his feet. "She's perfect."

Mandy's mouth fell open.

"And you're certain you've never met her before."

"Nope. I mean, yep. Never met."

Dr. Michaels's eyes narrowed in thought and he brought his fist up to his face, pressing the side of his curled index finger against lips. A few seconds later, he lowered his hand. "One last question, then you can get back to work." He paused, the silence expectant. "What would you do for Mandy?"

Charlie's expression turned rapturous. "Anything."

9

PRESENT DAY

"It's my mom," Jesse said, his cell phone pressed against his ear. He and Mandy were standing by his car. "My baby brother's in the hospital." He shook his head while he continued to listen to the message, his expression horror-struck. "She says it's a virus—a *pandemic*—and tons of people are dying." He frowned, and then all of the color drained from his face. "She's sick, too."

Mandy touched his shoulder. "I didn't want to tell you until you were feeling better, but…it's gotten pretty bad out there. While you were recovering…" She shook her head, trying to appear sympathetic. "You should call her back."

Jesse did as she suggested, but the conversation between him and his mother was brief. When he hung up, desperation to be with his family practically oozed from his pores.

Mandy refused to make the same mistake with Jesse as she'd made with Victor. "I'm your family now. You'll be safe with me… and happy, won't you?" She slipped an arm around him, giving him a side hug.

Jesse nodded, but his eyes held a plea. Apparently he hadn't been around her long enough for his devotion to her to become as all-encompassing as she'd hoped. Her Ability affected everyone at a different pace, but she'd hoped he would succumb to her power more quickly.

Fighting back a scowl, Mandy stood on her tip-toes and brushed a soft kiss against his lips. "I'll take care of you."

"I'm betting on it," Cole said. It was the second time he'd startled Mandy in as many days. Before Mandy could stop him, Cole had hold of Jesse's wrist, and Jesse's expression grew distant, almost vacant. "You will leave and check on your family."

"No!" Mandy gasped, but it was too late. Cole's power, though less expansive, was more concentrated than Mandy's, and commands given using his Ability overrode her followers' devotion to her. Her blood boiled. "Take it back!"

Cole narrowed his eyes. "But you will return...with any members of your family who survive. And when you return, if you don't see me alive and healthy at Mandy's side, you will kill her or die trying, won't you?"

"Yes," Jesse whispered.

Letting go, Cole turned a wicked grin on Mandy. "That's good for at least a month."

Mandy's hands balled into fists, her nails digging into her palms. "How dare you," she snarled.

Cole raised his eyebrows. "How dare I? Quite easily, dearest, and quite necessarily, I think. I needed insurance. Now I have it."

10

22 YEARS AGO

Mandy spent the afternoon after Dr. Cole identified her Ability restlessly—she paced around the room, then reorganized her wardrobe of gray sweatpants and sweatshirts, gray t-shirts, sports bras, cotton undies, and plain white socks in the lone dresser. She'd been wearing essentially the same thing ever since waking in that room, though she always changed in the bathroom. There was no way to tell if anyone might be watching from the other side of the mirror, and she'd yet to find any cameras in the bathroom.

When Kevin showed up around three o'clock, a box of checkers in hand, she sent him away. She couldn't stand that he'd only befriended her because she'd developed a freakish superpower that made people like her, even love her, if the rapturous way Charlie had been staring at her by the time he'd left was any clue. She didn't mean to do it. She didn't want to make people feel things they wouldn't feel naturally.

Mandy shivered. She felt dirty, as though she'd been mentally raping the minds of everyone around her. She'd done it, and she'd enjoyed it...before she'd known *what* she was doing. It had been nice to be popular for once in her life.

She spent a good half hour in the shower, trying to wash away the guilt of what she'd unknowingly been doing to everyone who crossed paths with her. She scrubbed herself with a soapy washcloth until her skin was an angry red before finally turning off the steaming water.

She spent another ten minutes brushing her hair with meticulous care. When people complimented her, it was usually on her hair. Her eyes were a murky hazel color, and though her complexion wasn't bad, her features were plain. But her hair, a rich chestnut brown, was thick with a gentle wave, and it reached the bottom of her shoulder blades. It had always been her best feature. She even took the time to pluck her eyebrows using the tweezers that were in the grooming kit she'd been provided.

By the time she emerged from the bathroom, skin clean and still a little raw, sporting a fresh pair of sweatpants and a t-shirt, Vic was waiting in the chair beside her bed. Two trays of food had been set on the movable bed table. As had become their routine, he was there to eat dinner with her. Tonight's menu appeared to include country-fried chicken, mashed potatoes, gravy, and green beans, and there was a small bowl of berry cobbler. A carafe of white wine had been placed on the bedside table.

Mandy stopped in the doorway between the bedroom and bathroom and leaned her shoulder against the door frame. The revelation that all of her other budding relationships were more or less fabricated was painful, but the idea that Victor only liked her because her Ability *made* him was agonizing. She stared at the floor near the foot of the bed. "Vic…"

He started to stand. "I know what you're going to say—"

"You should go."

He paused halfway up, his hands still on the armrests. "What?"

Mandy finally raised her eyes to his, and his part-hurt, part-baffled expression nearly made her lose her nerve. Nearly. "Go away and…just stay away from me." She turned so her back was against the door frame and, taking a deep breath, wrapped her arms around her middle. Her voice trembled when she spoke next. "Please, Vic…just go."

Victor rose the rest of the way and wasted no time in crossing the room to stand in the doorway with her. It was a tight fit, leaving only a few inches between them. "No." He rubbed her upper arms. "Why would you say that?"

"Because I—I…" Again, Mandy forced herself to meet his warm brown eyes. "Being around me is bad. My Ability—I make people do things—feel things. I'm *bad,* Vic." Her words lost coherency as she let out a faint sob. "I'm bad."

"That's crazy talk," Victor said, shaking his head and smiling reassuringly. "You're the nicest, sweetest, most innocent person I've ever met."

Mandy stared at him, pleading with her eyes. "You don't understand. I make people—" She shook her head in frustration, and as she did, an idea struck her. He didn't believe her…well, she could show him. Then he would see. Then he would understand. "What would you do if I told you to kiss me?" she whispered.

A hint of a frown curved down Victor's mouth, though it was quickly washed away by a sly grin. His eyes sparkled as he leaned in slowly, drawing out the moment.

Mandy's heart was racing as excitement and guilt fought an epic battle inside her. She placed her hand on Victor's chest. "No, don't. You don't have to…"

"What if I want to?" Victor's face was so close to Mandy's that she could feel his breath as he spoke, smell the faint scent of coffee and peppermint.

"Um…"

When Victor's lips touched hers, butterflies burst into being in her stomach, washing away the mild nausea that had been building since she'd emerged from the bathroom to discover she wasn't alone. It was her first real kiss. She opened to him, letting him in as he pressed the front of his body against hers.

She relaxed back against the door frame, but wasn't sure what she should be doing with her hands. It was supposed to be a magical moment, wasn't it—one that banished coherent thought? But all Mandy could think about was that her hands felt odd wherever she rested them on Victor, whether on his shoulders or behind his neck.

It was a short kiss. Their tongues had barely touched before Victor broke the contact between their lips. He pulled the lower half of his face away from Mandy's while resting his forehead against hers.

"See," he said, smiling just a little. "Wanted to."

Which reminded Mandy why, despite desperately wanting him to kiss her again, she felt sick about the whole thing. "But you *didn't* want to—not really. That's what I mean. It's my thing, my Ability or whatever you want to call it. I *make* people want to please me." After a moment she added, "whether I want to or not…"

Victor chuckled. "Making people want to please you—imagine the fun you could have with that…"

"But it's wrong!" Mandy persisted. "You didn't actually want to kiss me. I *made* you want to."

"No, you didn't—"

"I did!"

Victor pulled away further, so their eyes were about a foot apart, and placed his hands on either side of her face. "Listen to me. You didn't make me feel anything that I wouldn't have felt on my own. You *can't*. That's *my* Ability. I'm like the anti-Ability guy."

Mandy blinked. "What?"

"Nobody's special skills work on me"—he dropped his hands and shrugged one shoulder, offering up a lopsided smile—"unless Cas decides to chuck a pencil at me or something like that."

She furrowed her brow. "So you're not desperate to do whatever I want?"

Victor's smile widened to a grin. "I never said that."

Mandy chewed on her bottom lip while she considered the implications of his revelation. "So…you like me anyway?"

"Is that so hard to believe?"

"Well, I'm just not used to…you know…um, guys, um, liking me." After a brief hesitation, she added, "Why *do* you like me?" She cringed as she finished speaking, realizing she sounded like an insecure middle school girl talking to her crush—possibly in note form. She *was* insecure, but that was beyond the point.

"Honestly?"

Mandy nodded.

"Your innocence is addictive."

Mandy frowned. That wasn't really the glowing endorsement she'd been hoping for.

With a sigh, Victor leaned back against the opposite side of the door frame. "You said you were a bad person—well I really am. My innocence died a long time ago and…" He took a deep breath. "I've done a lot that I'm ashamed of. The Program is a second chance for me, and being around you, well, that just makes the whole second chance thing seem that much more real." He ran his hands through his hair, making it stand up haphazardly. It was a relaxed, charming look on Victor. "When I'm around you, all that shit I did before doesn't matter because *you're* there with all your innocence and trust and…" He exhaled in a laugh and gave her a lopsided smile. "I'm totally botching this, huh?"

Slowly, Mandy shook her head. She straightened and pushed off the door frame, closing the distance between them. This time, when their lips touched, thought fled her mind completely.

"Do it!" Dr. Michaels practically snarled.

Mandy stared at the woman sitting on the floor in the middle of the room. "But—but…it's mean!"

Now that they had a pretty good idea of what she could do,

Ability-wise, she was allowed to leave her room. She, the doctor, and a woman named Kathy were in a room across the hall from Mandy's. It was sparsely furnished, with only a long, gray table, a couple of chairs, and a plastic box about the size of a steamer trunk with tiny holes cut in the top and sides. Mandy and the doctor were sitting in the chairs with Kathy standing on the opposite side of the table.

"It won't be like on the video," he said. "Her desire to please you should override her fear of snakes."

Thinking of the video, Mandy shivered. The poor woman had screamed like she was being flayed alive when the lid had been taken off the box and a giant snake had slithered out. Mandy didn't know much about snakes, but the sheer size of the thing was enough to trigger a fear of snakes she hadn't previously been aware of.

Frowning, she turned her attention away from Kathy, whose earlier bout of fear had abated and was now sitting as calmly as possible, to Dr. Michaels. "I don't want to. You shouldn't make me do this. This doesn't please me."

Much to her surprise, the doctor didn't give under the press of her power. He simply returned her stare and said, "Do it."

Suspicious, Mandy narrowed her eyes. "It doesn't work on you. Why not?"

Dr. Michaels raised his eyebrows but didn't answer.

"Are you like Vic, you know, where Abilities just don't affect you?" Mandy asked.

Nodding, the doctor took a moment to truly respond. "You could say that. Now"—he flicked his eyes toward Kathy—"please proceed. I think you'll feel better once you see her reaction—or lack of reaction—to the snake."

"Fine," Mandy grumbled. She, too, shifted her attention to the other woman. "Kathy, It would make me very happy if you opened the box."

The doctor glanced at Mandy. "And…"

"And picked up what's inside," Mandy added reluctantly. Her palms were sweaty, and her chest felt tight, like she couldn't get enough air. She felt like *she* was the one unsnapping the little hinges securing the container's lid.

When Kathy reached into the box, she displayed no outward signs of the terror Mandy knew she should be feeling. Mandy was pretty sure that she, herself, was experiencing more of a reaction to what Kathy was doing than Kathy was. As the heavy, undulating creature was lifted out of the box, Mandy had to stifle a scream.

"How do you feel, Kathy?" Dr. Michaels asked.

"Fine—happy, actually." Kathy smiled and looked at Mandy as the snake's tail coiled around her waist. "I'm just glad I can do something to please you."

"Um, yeah…thanks." But Mandy definitely didn't feel very pleased. The whole situation was just too weird. Kathy clearly wasn't afraid at all, almost like she'd been cured of her fear. The possibility that that's exactly what had happened made Mandy think; if her Ability could do things like this—help people—maybe it wasn't such a bad thing. "I'd like you to put the snake back, Kathy." Out of the corner of her eye, she could see Dr. Michaels frowning, but she didn't care. He had his results. He'd been right. She could end the stupid test.

Mandy watched as Kathy returned the creature to the box and secured the lid. Kathy's lack of fear was almost miraculous.

"Thank you. You may return to your regular duties," Dr. Michaels told Kathy. "Please let Vic know we'd like to see Charlie next.

"Of course," Kathy said as she made her way to the door. She left without another word.

Seconds later, Victor opened the door and dragged in an oversized foot locker. Charlie followed him in, wearing his usual dark blue coveralls. Victor caught Mandy's eye, but instead of seeing playful mischief in his expression, she found a furrowed brow and a slight frown. He was concerned…for her? The thought prompted her own frown.

Victor left the container in the middle of the room, exchanging it for the box holding the snake. With one more glance Mandy's way, he left the room and shut the door.

"You suffer from severe claustrophobia, am I correct, Charlie?" Dr. Michaels asked.

With a smile at Mandy, Charlie nodded.

Dr. Michaels looked at Mandy. "Tell him to open the foot locker and get inside."

"What? No!"

With a heavy sigh, Dr. Michaels said, "Do we really have to go through this again? He'll be fine. Happy even, I expect."

For several seconds, Mandy alternated from looking at one man to the other. "Well…if you're certain." But she knew he wasn't certain. That was why they were doing these experiments in the first place—to see how extensive Mandy's effect on people was. And still, knowing that, she said, "Charlie, I'd like you to open the foot locker and get inside."

Charlie's smile widened as he nodded. "Anything for you, Mandy. Anything."

Mandy would've been lying to herself if hearing that phrase didn't make her feel a little happy. Nobody had ever been eager to do things for her, aside from her mom and Sherry, but even their love hadn't compared to this all-out devotion. It was thrilling… intoxicating, even.

"Good. Now tell him to shut the lid."

This time, Mandy didn't argue. She felt a pang of guilt about that, but it faded quickly. After all, she, too, was curious about the extent of her Ability. "Charlie, I'd like you to shut the lid."

He did so eagerly.

"Now what?" Mandy asked without looking away from the box. "How long are you going to make him stay in there?"

Dr. Michaels touched the fingertips of his right hand against his chest. "Me? I'm not the one who convinced him to shut himself in there."

Mandy rolled her eyes. "Yes, yes, you're very clever. I'm awed by your cleverness," she said dryly. "Can *I* let him out now?"

"No. I think we'll leave him in there for a bit. Why don't you go see what Vic's up to?"

Mandy felt her eyes bulge. "You seriously want me to leave him in there? Why?"

"To see if the effect lasts after you're gone…and if it does, for how long."

"But—but…how will you know if it wears off?"

Dr. Michaels stood and rounded the table. He stopped in front of the foot locker and slid a lock in place. "I'd assume he'll start making a bit of a fuss."

"But that's torture!"

"It's an experiment. It's science."

"You're a monster!"

"If you weren't already exhausting me…" There was a warning in his voice Mandy didn't understand.

"I won't do this anymore. I won't participate in your sick *experiments*!" She spat the last word like it was a particularly foul curse, stood, and stormed to the door.

"You'll change your mind," Dr. Michaels said.

Hand on the doorknob, Mandy looked back at him over her shoulder. "I won't."

"Whatever you say."

Mandy huffed in irritation and yanked the door open, slamming it as hard as possible on her way out.

The hallway wasn't empty. Victor was leaning against the opposite wall, arms crossed over his chest. He eyed her for the briefest moment, then pushed off the wall. "How 'bout a walk?"

"Ugh! If I have to stare at these stupid walls for a minute longer, I'm going to scream." She'd yet to see a window, other than the two-way mirrors that had been built in to many of the rooms. She hadn't seen the outside world in days and was pretty sure the whole facility was underground—either that or she'd been spending all of her time in the center of an enormous building.

"C'mon." Victor snagged her hand and started leading her up the stark hallway. "I'll take you topside. Get you some sunshine."

"For real?" Mandy picked up the pace until she was the one leading Victor. Not that she knew the way to get the heck out of there. "I can go outside? I'm allowed to?"

"If you're with me." Victor flashed her a broad grin. "I'm special."

Mandy snorted. "Yeah…keep telling yourself that."

Mandy had been right; the Program facility was underground. It actually lay underneath a sprawling Spanish-style villa. It wasn't Mandy's taste in architecture or decor, but that didn't keep her from noting that the place had to cost a fortune, especially with the secret facility that had been built beneath it.

The grounds surrounding the villa consisted of expansive lawns, palms of various sizes, exotic, brightly colored flowers, and an enormous infinity pool that sparkled all the way to the edge of a sharp drop off. Beyond, the high desert landscape was remote… barren. There wasn't another building in sight.

"Where are we?" Mandy asked as she stared out beyond the pool.

"Just outside Reno—you can actually see the city from the other side of the house."

"This is crazy, you know?" Mandy scanned the estate and grounds. "Who lives like this? And who has a super-secret underground facility filled with people who have super-secret superpowers? It's just…crazy." Somewhere in the back of her mind, Mandy also thought it was pretty cool. *She* was part of something so incredible. She never would have guessed such a thing was possible, especially not for her.

Victor reclaimed her hand. "C'mon…I want to show you something." He led her around the pool and started down the steep incline. Scrubby vegetation covered the hillside and the valley below as far as the eye could see. In the distance, jagged, snowless mountains cut into the horizon.

When the incline finally gave way to flatter ground, Victor released Mandy's hand and motioned toward a small boulder. "Sit, please."

Mandy did as requested, keeping her eyes on Victor. "So… what's up? I mean, the scenery's, uh, cool and all, but I'm betting that's not why you dragged me out here." Though, regardless of the reason, she was glad he had.

"There's some stuff I've got to tell you." He started walking back and forth a few paces in front of her.

Mandy clasped her hands together and squished them between her knees in an effort to keep herself from fidgeting. "Vic…you're making me nervous. What's going on?"

Victor stopped pacing and looked at Mandy so intensely she felt like he was seeing inside her, examining her soul. "The Program—Michaels—you being here…" He shook his head, clearly frustrated. "None of it's what you think. I mean, c'mon… you should hate me for what I did to you. You should hate that you're trapped here. You should hate everything about this place, but you don't."

Mandy stood and took a step toward Victor, but stopped when he held a hand up. "Vic…I don't hate it here. I've never felt more, I don't know, important…significant…*something*." She fidgeted with the hem of her t-shirt. "I *like* being here. I'm kind of glad you did what you did. I mean, if I weren't here, if I hadn't been one of the few people who had the DNA thing that made me eligible for all this, I'd be…just me. Nothing. My whole life has been pointless moments of nothing sandwiched between more nothing. I was miserable. Now I'm not. Don't you see?"

Victor took two steps, closing the distance between them, and squeezed her upper arms. "I see perfectly. That's the problem—I see what you can't. All of that stuff you just said, that's just your mind justifying—filling in the blanks. It's coming up with reasons for why you *have* to be happy here. You're being forced to like it, just like all of those people in there are forced to think they love you."

With those words, Mandy felt as stunned as if she'd just been slapped. She wrenched herself free of his hold. "It's part of who I am now," she snapped. "I mean, if I was some gorgeous, tall bombshell with curves only in the right places and a perfect little nose, people falling all over themselves to make me happy would be just fine. But because the reason they're doing it is something inside me and not how I look, it's not okay? They love me because of *me,* Vic." She pointed to herself. "These changes, this Ability, it's a part of me as much as any lingerie model's huge boobs are."

"Mandy…" Victor held out his hands to her, imploring. "I didn't mean—" He ran his fingers through his hair and made a frustrated growling noise. "*I* care about you as much as any of those people back there." He threw his hands up in frustration. "God, Mandy, ever since I met you, I felt like maybe, just maybe, I can be a better person. That's how you make me feel, not because of any superhuman hoodoo whatever, but because of *you*, because of who you are."

Mandy stared, shocked. "What are you say—"

"I'm falling in love with you," Victor said, sounding relieved to finally tell her. "I love you, and I hate what's happening to you here…what Michaels's doing to you." He muttered something that sounded like, "What he's already done to you."

Mandy had to swallow several times and clear her throat before she could speak. "I—I think I love you, too." She almost couldn't believe she had the nerve to say it aloud.

Victor laughed softly. "Don't sound so sure about it."

Stepping closer to him, Mandy tilted her head back and looked up into his eyes. "You said I can't see what's really going on"—she offered a small half-smile—"so tell me."

Placing his hands on either side of Mandy's face, Victor returned her half-hearted smile. "Michaels's Ability is that he can control people."

Frowning, Mandy shook her head. "I don't know what you mean."

"Mind control. He can make people do things. He's not the most powerful one with an Ability like that, but it's why he's in charge here." Victor rested his forehead against Mandy's. "If someone doesn't want to do something, he can *make* them. If someone's doing something that could hurt the Program, he can *make* them stop. His control's not perfect…it wears off pretty quickly, and using it tires him out, but…" Victor sighed. "You know your Ability hasn't been working on him, right."

"Yeah," Mandy said, her voice tiny.

"Well, that's because he told you not to use it on him."

Mandy shook her head the smallest amount. "But…I can't control it. I can't, like, turn it off or anything, so how could that work?"

Victor shrugged and started rubbing his hands up and down Mandy's arms. "Must be subconscious or…I don't know. But his command's working, right?"

Mandy bit her lip and nodded.

"That's why. He's probably commanded you to do or not do other stuff, like to listen to him and always do what he says…stuff like that." After a moment of hesitation, Victor added, "And I'll totally understand if you're pissed at me about this, but you were just so unhappy at the beginning…" He sighed. "I asked Cole to command you to be happy here." He laughed, a short, bitter sound. "It's probably the only reason you don't hate my guts."

Mandy touched her hand to the side of his face. "Remember when Cas showed me what she could do, and I freaked out?"

"Yeah…"

"Well, I was really, *really* unhappy then, and I didn't hate your guts." Mandy smiled, warm and genuine. "You comforted me… and I wanted you to. I meant what I said about my life being crappy before. I was miserable, Vic. I hated myself. Now, well, I don't. It's like I matter now. People can't help but notice me."

"What if we left? Just ran away?" Victor pulled his face away from hers and raised his eyebrows. "Would you?"

Mandy felt a rush of excitement. She could be this new, improved version of herself with Victor by her side, but away from all of Dr. Michaels's craziness. "Now?"

"No. Soon." He flicked his eyes up the hillside toward the estate. "There's surveillance all over the place. We need a way to disable it…" A thoughtful frown turned the corners of his mouth downward and narrowed his eyes. "There's someone who should be able to help us. Her Ability allows her to, er, manipulate electricity, but she's on loan to another facility right now. She should be back in a few weeks though." He looked into Mandy's eyes with such intensity that he stole her breath. "Can you wait that long? You'll have to put up with Michaels and his experiments, which won't be pleasant…"

"It's fine. I can deal with him." She smiled reassuringly. "Just so long as it's only a few weeks."

"Promise," Victor said, and then his lips were on hers and he was stealing her breath in a completely different way.

11

PRESENT DAY

Mandy stared at the radio. It was the morning after Jesse left, and her mind had been so snarled with thoughts of him that she'd hardly been able to sleep. What if something happened to him while he was away? What if he never returned? These first few days after the new beginning would be the most dangerous, when the tainted were numerous because they'd yet to start picking each other off.

No, instead of thinking *more* about that, she stared at the radio and listened to the President speak.

Our country is at war. Humanity is at war, yet our enemy is not one we can fight openly. Our enemy has swept through every nation, attacking discretely, killing indiscriminately. We lost thousands before we even knew we were under attack. Many have already fallen, and many more will fall. But we cannot give up the fight.

Over the past century, through technological achievements, we made our world smaller. We made the time it takes to communicate across oceans instantaneous, and the time it takes to travel those same routes nearly as fast. We made our world smaller, and in doing so, we sowed the seeds of our own destruction: a global pandemic.

I regret to tell you that as of midnight on the 10th of December, over eighty percent of the world's population has reported or is assumed dead. It is estimated that the death toll will continue to climb. This news is devastating, I know, but all is not lost.

Some of us are surviving. This is how we will fight our enemy—by not giving up, by being resilient and resourceful, by surviving. We are not a species that will go out quietly, so I task those of you who are still alive with one essential purpose: live.

Survive.

Thrive.

If you believe in a higher power, ask for guidance. If you don't, believe in your fellow man. You, the survivors, have the chance to start over, to build anew. Learn from our mistakes. Let the world remain big.

And most importantly, live.

God bless you, my beloved citizens of this great nation. God bless you, and goodnight.

Humanity *would* build anew, and as she and Cole had planned, they—or maybe just Mandy, depending on how long it took Cole to slip up—would be the ones to lead this new, evolved species of man toward a brighter future. It would be glorious.

"Do you love me?" Mandy asked Kevin. They were in her cabin, alone, Mandy sitting at the table in a chair turned toward the wood stove and Kevin standing a few feet away from her.

He dropped to his knees before her. "More than anything."

"Would you die for me?"

"Yes. Do you want me to?"

Smiling, Mandy placed her hand against his cheek. "Not today, my dear friend."

Kevin returned her smile, and she knew that had she asked him to, he would have taken his own life right then and there. Of her followers, he'd been around her longer than almost anyone else, and the effects her Ability had on people multiplied the longer they were in her presence. Unfortunately, that also seemed to sap him of his personality, leaving him a servile, devoted mannequin. But at least he loved her. He would always have that.

"Are you sad?" Kevin slipped his hands under her long skirt and traced his fingertips over her swollen ankles. "Do you want me to make you feel better?"

Mandy sighed. "No, Kevin, that's not what I'm in the mood for right now." After a moment of thought, she let a sly grin curve her lips. "Why don't you fetch one of those pretty young men—no, both of them. I think it's about time I broke them in."

Kevin stood immediately, eager to do as she bid. He was *always* eager to do as she bid. Everyone was. Except for Cole… and Vic. But Vic was long gone.

Minutes passed with Mandy lost in thoughts of things that happened over two decades ago. When Kevin returned with the two young men who'd helped transfer Jesse from his car to the cabin, she stood and shrugged off her robe.

She looked first at one of the young men, then at the other. "Tell me, my pretties—do you love me?"

12

22 YEARS AGO

Days passed, turning into weeks. They were the oddest two weeks of Mandy's life. She was happy, both because Dr. Michaels commanded her to be and because she knew that her and Victor's escape was close at hand.

With each new experiment she and Dr. Michaels conducted, she felt a twisted combination of guilt and exhilaration. While the test with Charlie and the oversized foot locker had proved that her effect wore off after she was a certain distance away—he'd apparently begun screaming a few minutes after Mandy left the room—her Ability seemed to be gaining strength with each passing day.

The reach of her power expanded in spurts, but the devotion of those around her intensified at a steady rate. People wouldn't just face their fears with joy if she told them doing so would make her happy; they would even hurt themselves or others, and they would be ecstatic about doing it. Mandy had never felt so confident, so sure of herself, but at the same time she was sickened by the fact that people were getting physically hurt.

But it was all in the name of getting away from Dr. Michaels. She could manage for a little while longer.

"Good morning, Mandy," Dr. Michaels said as she entered the small cafeteria where everyone took their meals. "Come. Sit."

Mandy did as requested without question. Now that she knew about the doctor's commands, she noticed the warring desires within her—the desire to do every little thing he said and the desire to tell him to go screw himself. Everything would be so much easier if he'd just forget to give her his daily "don't use your Ability on me" command. If he was as devoted to her as everyone else was, she and Victor could stroll right out of the facility. By the time they were so far away that the others were out of range of her influence, she and Victor would have a generous head start.

Unfortunately, Dr. Michaels *never* forgot. A fact that was evident by the lack of an effect she had on him.

As soon as Mandy sat opposite him at his small square table, he reached across the tabletop. Before his fingers latched around her wrist, she did the one thing she shouldn't have done—she flinched. It was the first time in two weeks that she'd been unable to mask her aversion to his touch. She had to consciously force herself not to pull away, at least until the mental fog clouded her mind.

Dr. Michaels raised his eyebrows. "You don't want me to touch you—tell me why."

"I don't want you to control my mind," Mandy said, little more than a mumble.

"Who told you I can do that? Tell me."

"Vic."

"Tell me what else Vic said when he told you what I could do."

"He said you commanded me to be happy to be here and not to use my Ability on you. He said your power's not that strong. He said we would leave together, because he loves me."

"Leave? Explain."

"We're waiting until someone returns who can knock out the power, then we're going to run away together."

"How romantic," Dr. Michaels said. "You will listen to me and do as I say, you won't use your Ability on me, and you will be content with your place here, correct?"

"Yes."

"You will forget this conversation." He released Mandy's wrist, and she blinked as her mind cleared. Dr. Michaels was breathing harder than usual, and his cheeks were flushed.

Mandy had come to recognize such moments of foggy-mindedness as remnants of the doctor using his mind control on her. She hated that she couldn't do anything about it—hated that she couldn't react, that she had to pretend to be the ignorant young woman she'd been when she'd first woken up in the facility over a month ago.

"Aren't you going to eat?" Dr. Michaels asked.

"I—" Mandy cleared her throat, feeling a little sick. "I'm not hungry." She stood abruptly. "I'll wait for you back in my room… assuming you have more experiments planned for today."

Dr. Michaels nodded. "I do. I shouldn't be more than an hour. Today's will be quite enlightening. We're going to see just how much pain the subject can inflict upon himself before his devotion to you is overridden by the body's physiological responses and innate drive to survive."

Mandy gritted her teeth. "Great…" Turning, she wandered from the cafeteria. She actually did return to her room, but only for a short while.

Victor showed up a few minutes after she did, full of barely contained excitement. He bounded across the room and took her into his arms, swinging her around before planting a very steamy kiss on her lips. He pulled away, twining their fingers together, and dragged her to the door. "C'mon. Let's go for a walk."

"Vic…"

"You've got time. And trust me, this is worth it."

They were aboveground and out of the villa in under a minute. They crossed the lawn, passed by the pool, and descended the slope to the desert valley below at a near-jog.

"Vic," Mandy said, laughing and breathing hard. "What is it?"

He turned to face her, his grin ecstatic. He captured both of her hands in his. "Dana's back—the woman who can control electricity. This is it. We're getting out!"

Mandy covered her mouth with one of her hands and blinked rapidly, holding back tears of joy. It wasn't that she was unhappy with her current situation—according to what Victor had told her about the command the doctor kept giving her to be happy, she literally couldn't be—but she was so excited to start a life with Victor. They'd have to keep under the radar for pretty much the rest of their lives, but with her Ability, she didn't think it would be too difficult. She just wanted to be with Victor, someone who genuinely loved her, and who she loved back. Pure, manipulation-free love.

"When? When can we do it? When can we go?"

"Soon," Victor told her, stepping close and kissing her soundly. "This afternoon maybe. I have to convince Dana, but I've always been good and convincing people to do things they have no interest in doing."

"You're going to make her—you're not going to hurt her, are you?" Mandy asked, surprised that the thought upset her. She'd been making people hurt themselves and others all week, so why did it bother her that Victor might have to do the same thing, especially when the result would be their freedom? She shrugged it off. "Never mind. Do what you need to do." She glanced over her shoulder at the steep hill up to the estate. "I've got to get back. *He's* going to be looking for me soon."

"Do what he wants, but I promise you, Mandy, this'll be the last time you have to bend to that psycho's will." He kissed her one last time, a sweet, gentle brush of his lips against hers, then together, they started back up the hillside.

"Very nicely done, Mandy," Dr. Michaels told her, patting her back. "Think of his loss as a great victory for us. Now we know their devotion to you is stronger than the most basic human instinct —the need to survive. Amazing, really. I've never seen the like." He squeezed her shoulder. "You and I will do great things together."

But…what had she done? Mandy shook her head, denying the truth of what she was seeing. Charlie. Quiet, shy Charlie who was terrified of enclosed spaces and stared at his feet when he spoke to Mandy.

Dead.

He lay on the floor, a bloody heap of sliced flesh and broken bones. He'd died wearing an enraptured smile. The ghastly grin was locked in place. Mandy thought it might haunt her dreams for the rest of her life. She'd done this. She'd tortured him, then killed him through the power of her words alone. Maybe Dr. Michaels had *made* her obey him through some command she couldn't remember, but she'd still been the one to give the instructions. She'd been the one to push Charlie, telling him to hurt himself more and more, and he'd done so eagerly—ecstatically, even. Until he'd lost so much blood that his heart simply stopped beating.

"Why don't you return to your room. Rest." Dr. Michaels guided her to the door. "Good job, Mandy. Very good job."

"Thank you," she said numbly. She left the room and returned to her own in a state of shocked disbelief. She felt hollow, empty. What would Victor say when he found out what she'd done? There was no forgiveness for something like this. He loved her innocence —well, that was gone.

Mandy wasn't sure how much time passed while she sat on the edge of her bed and stared at the wall. An hour, maybe more. Eventually, there was a knock on the door, and when it opened, she was surprised to find Dr. Michaels entering her room. She'd been expecting Victor. Been waiting for the power to go out. Been waiting to escape this place and everything she'd done there.

But, deep down, she knew she could never escape from the memories of what she'd done. Charlie had been happy to die for her. He'd died happy. For her. Because she told him to.

Dr. Michaels wore a somber expression as he entered the room. He pulled the lone chair to her bedside and sat, leaving less than a foot between their knees. "I'm afraid I have some rather upsetting news."

Mandy doubted that any news could make her any more upset than she already was. "What?" she asked quietly.

"It's Vic…he's gone. He took off this afternoon after…well, you know."

Mandy stared at the doctor. "What?" She shook her head vehemently. "That's not possible. We were supposed to—he was supposed to…" Tears spilled from her eyes and streaked down her cheeks. "He loves me…he wouldn't leave me. He *loves* me."

"He's gone, Mandy." Dr. Michaels set a piece of notebook paper on her lap. She was fairly certain the handwriting was Vic's. "He left this for you in his room."

Blinking rapidly, Mandy wiped the tears from her cheeks. She took a deep breath, then started to read.

Dear Mandy,

I'm sorry, but we can't be together. I heard about what you did to Charlie. I could never love someone who could do that to another person. I'm leaving. You'll never see me again. I'm sorry.

Vic

"I don't understand." Mandy looked up from the heartbreaking note to Dr. Michaels's clear blue eyes. "He said he loved me."

"He was mistaken, Mandy. Don't you see?" Dr. Michaels reached up and brushed the backs of his fingers over Mandy's splotchy cheek. The familiar numbness filled her mind. "We love you more than he ever could. You know that, don't you?"

"Yes," she whispered.

"Tell me you love me."

"I love you."

"*Feel* that you love me more than you've ever loved another person," Dr. Michaels said. He retracted his hand.

Mandy blinked, staring at the doctor in wonder. It was as though she was seeing him for the first time. He'd always been handsome to her, but now there was something else. She almost…*loved* him. She would do anything for him.

13

PRESENT DAY

"Why do you do that to yourself?" Cole asked Mandy as she polished off her sixth scone of the morning. He was sitting across from her at the table in her cabin.

Mandy stared at him while she finished chewing, then licked her fingers. "Why don't you stop me? *Command* me not to."

Cole laughed. It was a cold, spine-tingling sound. "These games—aren't we beyond them?"

Mandy cocked her head to the side. "That day you commanded me to love you—did you forget to make me forget, or was that on purpose…just another one of your mind-games?"

The smile Cole gave her was chilling. "Does it matter?"

Licking a smear of raspberry jam off her thumb, Mandy shrugged. "Did you know, back then, that one day I'd hate you more than I needed you?"

"Ah, my dear girl..." Cole sighed. "You love power more than you hate me—were you to get rid of me, you'd regret it in time." Again, he smiled, but it was a mocking expression. "Alone, you're a spider, waiting in her net to capture her unwitting victims, but with me, you're a queen, able to send out your obedient little worker bees to snag more devotees than you'd ever attain otherwise." He shook his head and laughed softly. "Between the spider and the queen bee, tell me which is worshipped and which is alone?"

He was right, and it made her hate him that much more. His mind control made it possible for her followers to leave the several-mile reach of her Ability for weeks at a time without her fearing they wouldn't return. She and her followers were essentially hamstrung without him.

But he needed her as much as she needed him. Without her, he could only control a handful of people, and his grand plans required so much more. He would draw their followers in, and she would keep them there. In time, once the virus had run its course and the chaff—the unworthy and tainted—were separated from the wheat, she and Cole would draw in and rule over the survivors.

Mandy stretched her arms over her head and yawned, pretending to be bored. "Do you ever wonder how our little arrangement might have worked out if we actually liked each other?"

"No."

Mandy scowled.

"I do, however, wonder how our little arrangement might have worked out if you hadn't built up such strong resistance to my commands. And on that note"—he reached across the table and captured her wrist—"You will neither use your Ability on me nor will you do anything to hinder my ability to give you commands." He'd learned to add the second part after she'd tried to stab him nearly twenty years ago when he'd attempted to give his regular commands. She couldn't stop him from using his Ability, couldn't even purposely move out of his reach, but her consolation was that those two commands sapped his Ability for several days.

Nobody else had built up a resistance to Cole's mind control like Mandy had; of course, he hadn't used it on anyone else as much as he'd used it on her. But then, he hadn't needed to use anyone as much as he needed to use her. Without her Ability, he was just a two-bit mind-control lackey to whoever was really calling the shots. *That* was the only person Mandy viewed as a worthy competitor, and she had big plans to take them down once the virus ran its course and her army of followers was large enough.

Mandy rubbed her wrist irritably. If they were airing their dirty laundry, she figured it was the perfect time to finally ask the question that had been on her mind for years. Until Jesse showed up in her life, she hadn't wanted to know the answer. Now, she needed to know. "Vic didn't leave, did he?"

"What makes you say that?"

Mandy waved a hand dismissively. "You killed him."

Cole shook his head.

Leaning into the table, Mandy snarled, "You're lying!" Her breaths came in heaves. "He loved me."

"He did." Cole squinted and frowned as though he was considering something carefully. "At least, I believe he did. He certainly didn't enjoy writing that little farewell note. But…he loved his freedom more."

Mandy placed her hands on the table, palms down. "What did you do?"

"He was in prison—a life sentence for murder. I offered him a chance to start over, and he joined the Program, but then he had to go and fall for *you*." Cole wet his lips and leaned forward. "It's your fault, really…"

Mandy's eyes narrowed to a glare.

"You see, I know you don't remember this, but I made you tell me about his plans to whisk you away"—Cole made a fluttering motion with his hand—"and I couldn't have that." He clasped his hands together on the table and shrugged. "I gave him a choice. Either I'd turn him in to the authorities and he'd return to a life behind bars, or I'd give him a new identity—a new life, the true second chance he'd always wanted—and let him go free."

Mandy felt like a crushing weight had been lifted off her chest.

Vic hadn't been killed, and he hadn't voluntarily abandoned her; he'd been forced to leave. And he'd been given a new identity. Was it possible that he was still alive?

She gripped the edge of the table so hard that her nails dug into the wood. "What was it?"

"Sorry? I don't follow…"

"His name—you said you gave him a new identity," she said through gritted teeth. "What was it?"

Cole's lips spread into a wide, vicious grin. "Jesse…Jesse Hernandez. Based on the resemblance, I'd guess your new boyfriend is his son."

Shocked, Mandy shot to her feet, but before she could respond, a woman barged into the cabin.

"Pardon the intrusion," the newcomer said, bowing her head. It was Mary, who'd been among the chosen for over a decade. She was quite elderly, but her age didn't lessen the usefulness of her Ability. She could sense people within a certain proximity, and beyond that, tell whether they were chosen, tainted, or one of doomed, normal people.

Mandy turned her hostile glare on the woman. "What is it?"

"Four approach. The one who left—Jesse—is among them."

"And the rest," Mandy asked, excitement tempering her rage.

"Two are chosen."

"And the other?"

"Tainted."

This concludes the second installment of *The Ending Beginnings.* Mandy is also a supporting character in the full-length novel, *After The Ending,*

VANESSA

VOLUME THREE

1

. . . The death toll will continue to climb. This news is devastating, I know, but all is not lost. Some of us are surviving. This is how we will fight our enemy—by not giving up, by being resilient and resourceful, by surviving. We are not a species that will go out quietly, so I task those of you who are still alive with one essential purpose: live.

Survive.

Thrive.

If you believe in a higher power...

The President's broadcast continued to replay in Vanessa's head as she stared out her living room window, her legs folded beneath her. It had been six days since she'd first heard it...six days since her older brother, Jesse, had returned...six days since she'd discovered the devastating fate of the hospital where their mom had been working when the virus claimed her; it was now little more than a smoldering husk. Vanessa had lost count of how many times she'd listened to the broadcast, but it had been enough that she didn't even need the radio to hear it anymore. At the moment, the words were so vivid, so clear, that she could almost believe she really *was* hearing them.

She glanced back at the dining room table, where the radio sat, and confirmed that it was turned off. The President's voice faded away, and Vanessa breathed out heavily. It had just been her imagination. With a shake of her head and a soft laugh, she settled back on her heels and returned her attention to the window.

You're lying to yourself, chica—you did *hear it...*

Vanessa started and spun around on her knees so she could see the rest of the room. That voice. She couldn't have heard *that* voice. It was impossible. Rosie...*she* was dead...and had been for a week.

Vanessa scanned the living room, her eyes moving from the couch to the hallway and from the kitchen to the dining room. Nobody was there. Annie, the little girl she and her younger brother, Carlos, had found in a house alone with her dead grandmother a week ago, was still napping in Vanessa's bedroom. Carlos and Jesse were up in Yakima, searching around the hospital for any sign of their mom; though they assumed the worst, they still didn't know for sure if she'd perished in the hospital, either from the virus or from the fire. Vanessa wasn't expecting them back for another hour or two.

You're all alone. Like just you could protect Annie? You're helpless without your brothers, pendeja...

Slowly, Vanessa stood and took a few steps toward the end table beside the couch, where she'd set Jesse's pistol just after her brothers had left. The moment her fingers curled around the cold metal grip, she felt some of her tension ease. With trembling arms, she raised the gun so it was aimed directly in front of her.

"Rosie?" Terror constricted her throat, making her voice raspy.

You and Annie should have gone with them, you know? If something happens to them—if they don't come back...you know you can't protect her on your own...

"Stop it!" Vanessa shrieked. Her hands started shaking so

intensely that the gun was making a faint clacking noise. "You're dead!"

Am I? That's right—Carlos stuck me in the shed. But...you're hearing me right now. Maybe you should make sure I'm still there...

Doubt, followed closely by the bone-deep chill of fear, washed through Vanessa. But…it couldn't be Rosie. There had to be somebody else in the house, playing a trick on her.

She eased her way across the room toward the hallway that lead to the bedrooms. When she reached the doorway to her room and peeked inside, she found Annie snuggled under the covers on the bed, fast asleep. To Vanessa's ears, her own heartbeat sounded like the relentless beating of a tribal drum as she checked the two other bedrooms, the bathroom, and finally, the kitchen. Empty, all of them.

Do you think I'm, like, a zombie? Or a ghost? Or you could just be crazy, you know...

Vanessa shook her head as though Rosie's voice were an annoying fly that could be shooed away with a sharp movement. There had to be a logical explanation; one that didn't involve walking corpses, being haunted, or insanity. There was one guaranteed way to eliminate the first option.

Swallowing hard, Vanessa adjusted her grip on the gun. It was still extended in front of her, like its presence alone would repel any danger. Just point it and shoot; don't think too hard. That's what Jesse had told her before he and Carlos left that morning. Her palms were sweaty, but her grip felt solid. She could protect Annie. She could.

Vanessa took a deep breath, and on her exhale, she started toward the sliding door in the dining room. Beyond it lay the patio and backyard…and the shed, Rosie's tomb.

She slipped her feet into a pair of men's snow boots that were sitting beside the door but didn't bother with searching for her jacket, and when she slid the door open, the icy air buffeted her skin. With another deep breath, she stepped out onto the snow-covered patio. She crunched her way to the yard easily enough, but with each step closer to the shed, fear eroded more and more of her resolve. Rosie's body had to be out there. It just *had* to be. Bodies didn't simply get up and walk away.

And dead people don't talk, right?

"Shut up!" Part of Vanessa hoped the body wasn't there. Part of her hoped they'd been wrong, that Rosie hadn't actually been dead and now she was better. It was the only reasonable explanation.

Is it? 'Cause I've been in the shed for days. It's like ten degrees at night…

"Shut up! Shut up! Shut up!" Vanessa hissed.

I'm dead, and you know it. Maybe if you hadn't abandoned me…

Vanessa reached the shed and tucked her hand into her sleeve before grasping the frozen, metal handle. "You were sick…"

So was Carlos, but he survived…'cause you took better care of him.

"That's not fair! I was sick, too!" Vanessa wasn't sure why she was responding to the voice, but she couldn't seem to stop herself. It felt natural. When someone spoke to her, it was her general habit to respond. Except there wasn't actually anyone else there to respond to.

And now you're not, and neither is Carlos. Did you want me to die? Did you hate me that much? Carlos really cared about me, you know. Is that why you did this to me?

"No!" Vanessa twisted the handle and yanked the door open. "I didn't—"

Her eyes landed on the shed floor, and then she frantically scanned the rest of the shed. It looked as it always did in the winter—gardening tools tidily organized along the back wall, plastic and ceramic pots arranged on the shelves on the left side, and two snow shovels propped up against the right wall near the door. And no blanket-wrapped body. There wasn't even a blanket.

That's odd, huh? And now Annie's all alone inside. Unless, you know, I'm in there with her...

"Oh God, no," Vanessa whispered. Stomach twisting, she rushed back across the yard and into the house, not stopping until she reached her bedroom. Her *empty* bedroom. "Oh my God... ohmygod ohmygod ohmygod..."

At feeling something touch her hip, Vanessa screamed. She spun around and lurched backward into the room, tripping over the too-large boots that were still on her feet. The gun slipped from her grasp as she landed on the carpet. It bounced once, barely, and skittered under the edge of the bed.

"Nessa?" Annie said. "You were gone. Where'd you go?"

Breathing hard, Vanessa rolled onto her back and raised her head so she could see the little girl standing in the doorway. Annie's blonde hair was mussed from sleep, and she was missing a sock, but other than that, she looked fine. Vanessa wasn't sure what state she'd expected to find the little girl in, but she'd been so sure it would be horrendous and would involve a no-longer-deceased Rosie. Yet here Annie was, absolutely fine.

Vanessa closed her eyes for a moment. Annie was okay. Rosie wasn't here. Rosie was gone—somewhere—but not here. Surprising herself, Vanessa started to laugh. It was a shrill, somewhat hysterical sound. Remotely, she felt Annie plop down on the floor by her hip.

Vanessa knew she was being ridiculous. One of her brothers must have moved the body. Rosie's voice was all in her head. She might be losing her mind, but at least it was unlikely that there was a dead Rosie shambling around, searching for little girls to snack on.

"Nessa?" Annie tugged on the hem of Vanessa's sweatshirt. "Nessa?"

Vanessa's laughter quickly died out as she sat up and looked at Annie. "Sorry, sweetie. What's up?"

"Somebody's coming."

Vanessa cocked her head to the side and narrowed her eyes. "I'm sorry—what?"

Annie blinked several times. "The voices said that somebody's coming."

Vanessa was momentarily stunned. Seconds passed, then she reached for the little girl, grasping her shoulders gently. "What voices? What did they say?" She sounded eager, insistent. What would it mean if Annie had heard Rosie too?

Annie shrugged. "Lots of things."

"And who—"

Someone started pounding on the front door. Vanessa's heart rate doubled, and slowly, she registered what Annie said "the voices" had told her: *somebody's coming.*

Vanessa sucked in a breath. "You knew. How—" She shook her head. There was no time. She scrambled closer to the bed, reaching for the gun, then turned back to Annie. "Who is it? Do you know that, too? Is it Carlos and Jesse? My mom?"

Eyes wide, Annie shook her head.

The pounding on the door suddenly stopped, and Vanessa's blood seemed to turn to ice. Would whoever it was go around to the back of the house? Had she shut the sliding door? She'd been so panicked when she'd been rushing back into the house to check on Annie…she couldn't remember.

Don't think so…

"Shit. Shit. Shit!" Vanessa hissed, cursing both her stupidity and the return of Rosie's haunting voice. She squeezed Annie's shoulders. "Stay here. Do *not* come out unless I tell you to, okay?" She looked into Annie's bright blue eyes and waited for the little girl to nod. Her face mirrored Vanessa's own terrified expression, but there was nothing Vanessa could do to comfort her. "Not a peep," Vanessa said before standing and heading for the bedroom door. Once she was standing in the hallway, she shut the door as quietly as possible, took a deep breath, and listened.

Another breath. No noises.

Another breath. Nothing.

She inhaled.

And heard the floor creak in the dining room. Someone else was in the house.

Somebody's coming.

2

Vanessa opened her mouth, ready to tell whoever was in her house to get the hell out before she shot them. Because she *would* shoot them. She was sure. Pretty sure.

Or you could stay real *quiet and hope whoever this cabrón is just goes away, you know? I thought you were supposed to be all clever and shit...*

Begrudgingly, Vanessa admitted that Rosie—or Rosie's *voice* —had a point. But was it a valid point? Frozen by indecision, Vanessa continued to stand in the middle of the hallway, breathing as quietly as possible.

There were noises coming from the kitchen—metal clattering and glass clinking and shattering.

"Where the hell are you?" someone called from the kitchen. "You better get your ass out here before I destroy your whole house!" It was a male voice, strained and teetering on the edge between a rumbling baritone and an adolescent whine. "Little shit-stain of a—you said *next week*!"

Before Vanessa could decide what to do—stand and fight or run and hide—a large teenage boy stepped out of the kitchen, stopping in the junction between the living room and hallway. He scanned the living room, then turned his attention up the hallway. His eyes narrowed as he finally noticed Vanessa.

Stand and fight, chica. Decision made. Now do *something!*

Vanessa gulped. She had *no* idea what to do. In fact, she was fairly certain she'd never felt less sure of what to do in her entire life.

The intruder looked somewhat familiar, but Vanessa couldn't quite place him. He was clearly a teen, so she figured he went to school with her but was possibly in a lower grade.

"Who are you?" the boy snapped.

Uhhh…who the hell are you, *guy?*

Vanessa squeezed her eyes shut for a fraction of a second, attempting to block Rosie's voice. It was distracting, to say the least, and she really couldn't afford any distractions at the moment. She swallowed, then cleared her throat and glared at the intruder. He didn't seem to notice the gun dangling from her hand at her side, so she eased it behind her back, not wanting to reveal all her cards just yet.

"Who *the fuck* are you?" the boy repeated. He was breathing hard, and blinking in odd increments. His head twitched to the side. "ANSWER ME!"

Vanessa jumped at his shout. "V—Vanessa. I li—live here." Her voice was small and shaky. "Wha—what do you w—w—want?"

The boy sneered. "C—C—C—C—Carlos," he said, clearly mocking her terror-induced stutter. He laughed roughly and twitched again. "Where's the little fucktard?"

Julian! That's his name! I think he's one of Carlos's little druggie customers. Maybe he's looking for a fix or something…

Right. Julian. Vanessa remembered him now—vaguely. She took a deep breath. "He's, um, not here."

"You're lying." Julian's voice only increased in hostility.

Vanessa shook her head vehemently, shooting a furtive glance toward the closed bedroom door. Annie was doing such a good job of staying quiet. Vanessa just wished she'd told her to hide somewhere—in the closet, or under the bed, or…anywhere. If Julian went in there…

You could tell him Carlos died. Then maybe he'll leave us alone.

Vanessa frowned. "He—he got sick and—and died." Internally, she tried to convince herself that she would have said the same thing even if Rosie's voice hadn't suggested it.

"Where's he keep the stuff?"

"The *stuff*?"

"The drugs, bitch. Where're the drugs?"

Again, Vanessa shook her head. "I don't know. They don't—"

"Stop *lying*!" Julian lurched toward her.

Instinctively, Vanessa thrust the pistol out in front of her, aiming it at the teenage boy barreling toward her. Julian froze mid-step, arms extended. A few more paces and he would've been on her.

Vanessa backed away slowly and focused on keeping her hands steady. She wasn't very successful. "I'll shoot you! I will!"

With another compulsive head twitch, Julian took a single, tiny step forward. "You're going to shoot me?" He smiled and raised his eyebrows. "*Kill* me?"

"I…" Vanessa took another step backward.

Tilting his chin down, Julian started humming the tune to "Ring Around the Rosie." It was eerie as hell and more than a little unsettling, especially considering Vanessa's uninvited mental guest. He kept humming until he reached the final line and murmured, "Ashes…ashes…we all fall down." The sickly grin melted off his face, and he took a step.

"Stop!" Vanessa shrieked. "I'll shoot you. I'll do it!"

"Do it," Julian said as he took another step closer to her.

Vanessa continued to back away. She couldn't risk a glance behind her, but she knew she didn't have much room left before her back would be against the door to her mom's room.

"Do it."

"Stop."

"Do. It."

Vanessa's back touched the door, and she swallowed a yelp.

With small, achingly slow steps, Julian kept coming.

Vanessa couldn't tear her eyes away from his face. His pupils were dilated to the point that his irises were almost entirely blacked-out, and beads of sweat were streaming down his forehead and cheeks despite the chill pervading the house from the open sliding door.

A low, vicious growl started behind him.

Julian paused, eyes narrowed.

Risking a glance past him, Vanessa was beyond surprised to find a huge Pit Bull, poised to strike. Its stance and mien fell somewhere between very-pissed-off and I'm-going-to-rip-your-throat-out. Or rather, *Julian's* throat. The dog's eyes never left Vanessa's would-be attacker.

What the—

Another warning rumble joined the Pit's, and with the click of nails on linoleum floor, another enormous dog—some sort of long-haired mountain dog—trotted out of the kitchen. A small terrier with curly white hair trailed the larger dog. All three beasts' lips were retracted, and the larger dogs' long canines looked more than sharp enough to tear through human flesh.

Slowly, Julian turned his head to look back at the dogs.

Ducking into your mom's room might be a good choice right about now...

"Mmhmm," Vanessa squeaked as she took her left hand off the gun and reached behind herself to search for the doorknob. When her fingers found it, she twisted, practically falling into the room when the door opened. She scrambled to slam it shut. Trembling, she pressed in the lock and stared at the door. She could still hear the dogs' growls through the wood. They seemed to be growing louder, transforming into something more akin to a rabid snarl.

Don't forget about Annie...

Vanessa spun around and lunged across the bed to the nearest window. A hoarse, agonized scream pierced her eardrums as she fumbled with the latch. She managed to get it unlocked and raised the window right before the door crashed inward.

A bloody, tangled mass of human and dog fell into the room, writhing and emitting the most horrifying, animalistic sounds punctuated by the tearing of flesh.

Gagging, Vanessa hurled herself through the open window. Once she was outside, she righted herself and clawed at the bottom pane so desperately that the nail on her middle finger snapped backward, tearing off halfway down the nail bed. She barely felt it.

By the time she slammed the window shut, she was panting, and she didn't think her heart had ever beaten so quickly. But she'd made it out. Lurching to something resembling a sprint, she rounded the corner of the house and trampled the shrubbery blocking the way to her own bedroom window. She knocked on the glass.

"Annie! It's Nessa...unlock the window!" She needed to get the little girl out of the house. She could still hear the sounds of the dogs mauling Julian, muffled as they were by the house's walls and windows.

A tiny hand pushed aside the purple curtains Vanessa had made last year, and Annie's face appeared in the window. Tears streaked down her chubby cheeks, and her eyes were wide with terror.

Vanessa pointed to the latch. "Remember what Carlos showed you? Unlock it, sweetie." She balled her hand into a fist and lowered it to her side so Annie wouldn't see how badly she was shaking. Her stomach lurched, and she had to swallow back rising bile. Taking a deep breath, she held it.

Annie screwed up her face and reached up to unlock the window. It seemed to take forever.

Vanessa exhaled heavily as she helped the little girl push the lower half of the window up. She reached into the house and hooked her hands under Annie's armpits. Vanessa was a small woman, and it wasn't easy, but she managed to pull the five-year-old through the open window.

She held Annie, hugging her tightly, and started stumbling away from the house.

So…where are we going?

3

Breathing hard and shaking from the combined effects of adrenaline and cold, Vanessa moved as quickly as she could with a five-year-old hanging onto her for dear life. They'd fled from her home without a backward glance, leaving the back door wide open and a mauled—presumably dead—teenage boy in her mom's bedroom. And then there were the man-eating attack dogs…who she was pretty sure just saved her life.

Could this day get any freakier?

Vanessa ignored the voice. Looking around, she realized she'd carried Annie nearly three blocks already. She slowed to a stop, and panting, shifted Annie so the little girl was propped on her hip. They needed a place to hide, where Vanessa could gather her thoughts and figure out what to do until Carlos and Jesse returned. Because if her brothers returned to find Vanessa and Annie gone and the house in the gory state she'd left it in, they would lose it completely.

At least you know they care…

Vanessa was standing near the end of a block of single-story houses surrounded by chain-link fences in various states of disrepair. She knew a few of the people who lived—*had* lived—in the neighborhood, and based on how psycho the few survivors she and her brothers had crossed paths with the past week were acting, Vanessa wasn't overly eager to go find out if anyone had survived. If she remembered correctly, she was fairly certain that the house on the corner had been for sale for the past month or two. If it had still been on the market when the virus struck, she figured it was probably her best bet for a safe, temporary hideout.

Still breathing hard from her several-block run, she speed-walked to the end of the block, careful to keep a wary eye on the houses, trees, bushes, and anywhere else around her where someone might be lying in wait, poised to ambush them.

Annie sniffled and raised her head from the crook of Vanessa's neck. "Where're we going, Nessa?"

"Shhh…somewhere safe," Vanessa said softly.

When they reached the house, Vanessa felt a tiny stab of victory at seeing the small, red and white *FOR SALE BY OWNER* sign that was sticking up proudly from the lawn. She walked around the perimeter of the house, making sure there were no signs that the place might already be occupied—by persons alive *or* dead—and was relieved to find no broken windows and no unlocked doors. It appeared absolutely untouched. Perfect.

So what…you're going to break a window or something? With what…your fist?

Vanessa stopped behind the one-story house and stared at it for a moment. Narrowing her eyes, she scanned the snow for tell-tale lumps indicating a rock or solid chunk of ice she could use.

Out of nowhere, Annie giggled. She immediately started squirming and repeating, "Down! Down! Down!"

Vanessa adjusted her hold on the little girl, doing everything in her power to keep her off the ground. "I'm not putting you down! You don't have any shoes."

"Dowwwwwwwwwn!" She whined…loudly. At this rate, Vanessa feared everyone left alive—sane or crazy—would be aware of their presence within seconds.

"Okay, okay." Hesitantly, she lowered Annie to the snow-covered ground, fully intending to pick her back up as soon as possible. She *really* didn't want Annie to get frostbitten toes just because Vanessa had given in to her whining.

As soon as Annie's feet touched the snow, she started running back the way they'd come, making a sound that was more of an excited squeal than laughter. It wasn't much of an improvement over the impossibly loud whine.

"Annie!" Vanessa hurried after her, the oversized boots slowing her down. "Annie! Stop!" And then she caught sight of *them*, racing up the street, heading straight for Annie.

The dogs.

4

Vanessa gave up all pretense of laying low. "ANNIE!" Her ear-splitting shout echoed off the apparently vacant houses along the street as she chased after the little girl.

She caught up to her quarry a few seconds before the dogs and scooped Annie up, swinging her around to place her own body between Annie and the dogs' blood-soaked snouts. Their barks reverberated off the houses of the abandoned neighborhood in mockery of Vanessa's earlier shouts.

"Nessa!" Annie screamed. "NO!"

One of the bigger dogs crashed into Vanessa from behind, its paws pressing against her upper back. She grunted and barely managed to twist mid-fall so she would land on her shoulder rather than on Annie.

Black sparks exploded in her vision as soon as her head slammed into the snowy sidewalk. Vanessa blinked, and despite her best efforts, her grip on Annie slackened.

Blink.

Annie's face was so close, cheeks reddened by the cold and eyes wide with shock.

Blink…blink.

Annie's face blurred, and the world dimmed. Rosie's face, pale and gaunt, appeared beside Annie's, staring down at Vanessa with vacant, glazed-over eyes.

Vanessa's eyelids drooped shut one last time. This time they didn't reopen. As consciousness drifted in and out like the ebb and flow of the tide, she heard a whimpering sound.

Annie?

No. The dogs...

5

Awareness returned to Vanessa slowly. She felt like she'd dropped off the face of the earth—simply stopped *being*—for some unknown period of time, and she was just now returning to existence. And it wasn't a comfortable existence. It was cold and wet…

Because you passed out in the snow…

…and hard…

…on the frozen-ass sidewalk…

…and painful…

…and hit your head.

…and really high-pitched.

I think that might *be Annie…*

Annie…

The dogs…

Groaning, Vanessa tried to sit up. Her ability to think was waking up about as slowly as her ability to move. Annie was crying—was she hurt? Had the dogs attacked her? Her mind was a tangle of thoughts too slippery to hold onto for very long.

With another groan, Vanessa tried wiggling first her toes, then her fingers. Feeling adventurous, she even tried shifting her arms and legs.

"Nessa?" Annie said, her tiny voice tear-laden. Vanessa felt a tug on the shoulder of her sweatshirt. "Nessa," Annie sobbed. "Wake up, Nessa. Wake up…"

Vanessa coughed, and with one final, heartfelt groan, opened her eyes. The mid-day sun shone exuberantly in the clear winter sky, its rays stabbing into Vanessa's retinas. Such skull-drilling effort deserved an encore groan, which Vanessa supplied easily.

Annie gave another tug on Vanessa's sweatshirt. The little girl's fingers dug into Vanessa's flesh; they were remarkably strong for fingers belonging to a five-year-old, especially for fingers that had to be nearly frozen.

"Hey…" Vanessa brought her arm up to pet the little girl's blonde head, and bit her lower lip to keep from whimpering. The more clear-headed she became, the more her body ached from the cold. Each joint felt brittle, like it might shatter into a thousand shards if she moved too quickly.

Annie scrambled on top of Vanessa, hugging her torso with her small arms and legs and burying her face in Vanessa's neck. If anything, she was crying even harder now.

Gingerly and with a whole lot of effort considering the small person who was more or less lying on her, Vanessa curled up to a sitting position. She wrapped her arms around Annie, holding her close and multiplying their warmth, and murmured soothing nonsensical sounds. She wasn't sure how she was going to manage standing up, especially considering that her lower half was still numb from the frozen ground.

Bet it's gonna hurt…

In her post-passing-out stupor, Vanessa had completely forgotten about Rosie's voice. Haunting her. Rosie…

Vanessa vaguely remembered seeing the dead teen's face just before losing consciousness, looking gaunt, with hollowed cheeks and vacant eyes. Had Rosie really been there? Or had it just been a trick of the mind? A hallucination?

Like I'm gonna tell you...

Vanessa sighed, feeling more irritated than freaked out. Whatever Rosie was *now* was as much of a pain in the ass as she'd been in real life. Reluctantly, Vanessa pulled her arm away from Annie to leverage herself up...and froze, staring at her palm. It was stained red—she rubbed her fingers together—and it was sticky.

It could be blood...

Blood? On her hand? She glanced at the top of Annie's head, at the smears of crimson and carmine staining her pale hair.

Blood...in Annie's hair? Vanessa placed her hands on Annie's tiny shoulders and pushed her away so she could see her face. "Are you hurt? Did the dogs bite you?"

Annie blinked at Vanessa a few times, then shook her head.

Vanessa quickly examined as much of Annie as she could see. Her pajamas, hands, hair, and face were all covered with smears of blood ranging from the brightest red to a rusty brown, but Vanessa couldn't find any other signs that the girl was injured. It was almost as though the dogs had rubbed their bloody snouts all over her, but hadn't actually taken a bite.

"Rosie..." Was it possible that Rosie had really been there? Had she *saved* them?

Vanessa shot a quick glance around, then stared into Annie's big blue eyes. "Was Rosie here? Did she scare the dogs away?"

Sniffling, Annie stuck out her lower lip—more of a thoughtful expression than a pout—and shrugged.

"Was *anyone* else here?"

Again, Annie shook her head.

"And the dogs didn't hurt you? Where'd they go?"

She was more than a little surprised when Annie shifted on her lap to point over Vanessa's shoulder. She was pointing to the corner house they'd been planning to break into. Sure enough, the three dogs—a muscle-packed Pit, an enormous, shaggy mountain dog, and a scruffy little white terrier—were all pacing in the yard by the side of the house. Their eyes were locked on Vanessa and Annie.

WTF?

Vanessa lumbered to her feet as quickly as she could, which, in all reality, wasn't very quickly. She set Annie on the snow, aware that the little girl's bare feet must be so cold they were nearly falling off. But if Vanessa had tried to pick her up right then, her increasingly achy knees would have given out immediately. As it was, her own body weight was almost too much to hold. Watching the dogs, she stretched, trying to regain some strength and range of motion.

She could see the dogs' paw prints in the snow, punctuated by a few bright spots of blood, and tracked the trail back to where she and Annie were on the sidewalk. There was a halo of trampled snow surrounding them and trail of paw prints leading back down the street toward her house. Vanessa frowned.

It's weird, you know—the way they showed up at your casa and only attacked Julian. And now they're, like, watching over you guys. Hmmm...

If tackling Vanessa to the ground and knocking her out had been an accident, then it almost seemed like the dogs *were* protecting her and Annie. Vanessa shook her head. None of that mattered at the moment. She and Annie needed to get warm, and fast. They'd been outside in the freezing cold, wearing far too little for far too long. And assuming the dogs weren't a threat to them, there was only one place Vanessa was absolutely certain could provide heat and warm water and the possibility of safety...and a shredded teenage boy.

Keeping the dogs in sight, Vanessa picked up a shivering Annie and started back down the sidewalk, heading home. She crossed her fingers. With any luck, Carlos and Jesse would already be there.

6

They weren't. Or rather, the dark green SUV Jesse had driven from California wasn't in front of the house when Vanessa rounded the block, bringing their home into view. With dread that seeped deep into her bones, Vanessa did *not* want to enter that place without her brothers. She stood on the sidewalk in front of the house, afraid to enter her own home.

Aren't you afraid of like losing your toes? Or Annie losing her *toes...*

"Of course, but—" Snapping her mouth shut, she clenched her jaw, refusing to carry on a conversation with a disembodied voice.

Annie whimpered. They were both shivering, but it wasn't Vanessa's discomfort that forced her into action; it was the feeling of Annie trembling in her arms, the sound of her little teeth chattering. Vanessa squared her shoulders, hugged Annie more tightly, and stomped through the chain-link gate leading into the yard. With one hand on the back of Annie's head, she pressed the little girl's face against her shoulder.

"Close your eyes, sweetie, okay?" Because the last thing she needed to do to the five-year-old girl was traumatize her with visions of a mutilated human body.

She rounded the side of the house and paused on the patio, staring at the open sliding door.

What if he's not dead? You think he could be waiting in there for you? Think you could, you know, actually shoot him this time?

Vanessa took a few seconds to think back on what she'd seen of the dog attack before she'd bailed. They'd been ripping Julian apart, she was certain. Even if he wasn't all the way dead, he had to be incapacitated and on the verge of death.

Shit or get off the pot, Ness...

Vanessa held in her inappropriate, knee-jerk reaction to laugh. She and Rosie had picked that particular phrase up from Rosie's dad when they were in sixth grade, requisitioning it as their own. Hearing it said now—in Rosie's voice—brought back memories of the time before their falling out, and for the first time since she'd heard the voice in the house, Vanessa didn't feel afraid or panicked or annoyed. She felt comforted. She felt like, somehow, the Rosie she'd been friends with years ago was really there with her, not just keeping her company but possibly even looking out for her.

Like I'm a freaking guardian angel or something? Me, chica? Me*? You can't be serious...*

That was exactly what Vanessa was thinking, and Rosie's response only solidified her theory. It was just such a Rosie-ish thing to say. A tiny smile touched Vanessa's lips.

Resolutely, she stepped into the house, shifting Annie to her left hip so she could slide the door shut. She breathed through her mouth, not wanting to find out what a shredded human body smelled like. As she passed through the kitchen, she hoped the carnage was contained within the bounds of her mom's room and hadn't bled into the hallway.

Vanessa paused before stepping through the doorway that led from the kitchen into the hall. Looking down at the floor, she took a deep breath, then moved through the opening. She kept her eyes averted until she'd made it into the bathroom and shut the door. She set Annie next to the sink on the countertop and crossed the rest of the way to the tub to start running the hot water. Considering that she and Annie were quite thoroughly chilled to the core, a hot soak in the bathtub seemed like the most effective way to stave off potential hypothermia.

Holding her fingers under the faucet to test the temperature, Vanessa looked back at Annie. The dogs had left her covered with smudges and smears of Julian's blood, and with a quick glance down at herself, Vanessa found similar bloodstains. A change of clothes was definitely in order for both of them.

Minutes later, she and Annie were both scrubbing themselves clean in a bathtub full of luke-warm water that felt burning hot. Two piles of clean, dry clothes awaited them on the counter, but Vanessa thought it would take at least three tubs of water before they'd be clean enough for anything to touch their skin but more soap and water.

Each time she drained the tub, she refilled it with noticeably warmer water, letting their bodies grow accustomed to the temperature increase. Annie stopped shivering during the second load of warm water, but her eyes were open wider than usual, making her look shell-shocked.

Like you don't look the same?

Vanessa nodded thoughtfully. They'd all been through so much, but Vanessa couldn't imagine being a little girl and having to deal with the aftermath of the virus and losing pretty much everything. It was hard enough as a young woman.

She turned the knob, shutting off the steaming stream as the waterline neared the top of the tub for the fourth time, then pulled her knees up and hugged her legs. Annie mimicked her at the other end of the bathtub, resting her chin on her bent knees. There was no sign of injury on her tiny body. The dogs really hadn't hurt her while Vanessa had been unconscious. It just didn't make sense.

She studied the little girl, but despite how long Vanessa stared at her, Annie just looked like a normal, adorable five-year-old. "Annie?"

Her big, blue eyes blinked. Silently, Annie returned Vanessa's stare.

"What happened with the dogs?"

Annie's chin trembled. "They didn't want to hurt you. They said they were sorry."

Vanessa frowned. "They…were *sorry*?"

Annie pushed her lip out into a pout and looked down at the water. "That's what they told me."

"I…" Vanessa shook her head, confused. "I'm not sure what you mean. How did they tell you that?"

Annie shrugged. "They just told me…like when they told me somebody was coming and the mean man got here."

Vanessa's heartbeat sped up as she processed what Annie was saying. The dogs had *spoken* to her. In her mind. But that was impossible.

Really? You're one to talk, chica…

Moving her hand absently through the water, Vanessa considered Rosie's words. If she was hearing a dead person's voice in *her* mind, then Annie sharing some sort of telepathic connection with those dogs didn't seem quite so impossible. And, if she really could talk to them—and they could talk to her—it would banish any lingering doubt that Rosie's voice wasn't just in her head, but that the deceased teen was talking to her from the great beyond. Vanessa wasn't going insane; she could *actually* talk to the dead.

She let out a relieved breath.

Annie drew Vanessa's attention with a single word. "Car."

"I'm sorry…what?"

"There's a car coming." She blinked her big blue eyes at Vanessa. "*They* told me."

The dogs, right. Vanessa stood abruptly and stepped out of the tub to hastily dry off. She wrapped a towel around herself, then helped Annie out onto the linoleum as well. "Is it my brothers?"

Annie nodded. "Think so."

"Where are the dogs now?" Vanessa wrapped the second towel

around Annie's shoulders and started to pull on her own clothes as quickly as possible.

"Outside. They're guarding us."

"Shit—I mean, shoot." She tugged up her long underwear, quickly followed by a pair of jeans. "Can you tell them not to attack Carlos and Jesse?"

Annie giggled. "They wouldn't do that! They're my friends."

Her friends...that's so *weird...*

"I know, seriously..."

As Vanessa was pulling a fresh hoodie over her head, she heard the sound of a car engine outside. It was the final confirmation she needed. It was real. Annie could talk to dogs, and Vanessa could talk to dead people—or *one* dead person. It was *all* real.

To make things even better, her brothers were finally home.

7

There was a sudden knock on the bathroom door. Vanessa froze, her right foot raised as she pulled on a sock. She hadn't heard either the front door or the back slider open. How had her brothers entered the house so quietly?

"Nessa, honey? Are you in there?"

Vanessa's heart leapt, and her breath caught in her throat. "Mom?" Sock dangling halfway off her foot, she lunged at the door as her mom knocked again. Her mom…was alive. She was *alive*! Vanessa had been certain she would never see her mom's warm hazel eyes again, never smell her faint lilac and freesia scent, never be held in her comforting arms. She'd been certain her mom had died in the hospital fire, if the virus hadn't taken her life earlier.

"Mom!" Yanking the door open, Vanessa felt her muscles trembling with barely contained elation. She was fully prepared to launch herself into her mom's waiting arms.

Except nobody was standing on the other side of the door. The hallway was empty of all but a faint meaty scent.

Before she could stop herself, Vanessa's eyes darted to the right, seeking out the doorway to her mom's room. The door itself had been torn off its hinges and had settled haphazardly against her mom's bed, and the splatters of blood and bright pink and crimson chunks of shredded flesh added an extra grotesque touch.

"Mom?"

You think maybe she went into her room to get some clothes?

Rosie sounded as doubtful as Vanessa felt. Despite her overwhelming desire to figure out where her mom had gone, Vanessa couldn't bring herself to actually move any closer to that room…to Julian's savaged body. Besides the fleshy bits stuck to the door, the only other part of him she could see was a white sneaker, streaked with blood.

What if she didn't hear you and when she saw Julian's body, she, like, went out to get your brothers or something because she thought you were hurt and hiding somewhere? They could all be looking for you right now…

Nodding, Vanessa felt her rising panic recede. "She went outside…they're looking for me…that's it." Vanessa turned back to the bathroom, helped Annie finish getting dressed as quickly as possible, and took hold of the little girl's hand. "Close your eyes." She rushed out of the room, down the hallway, and toward the front door. She was almost to the door when it opened from the outside.

Carlos walked into the house, head hanging as he scanned the living room, and Jesse followed close on his heel.

Vanessa strained her neck to see around her brothers. Unlike her, they were fairly large people, easily fitting the bill as "strapping young men," and therefore blocked her view through the doorway very effectively. Once they were both inside, Jesse shut the door.

Their mom hadn't followed them in.

"Where is she? Where'd she go?"

"Why don't you sit down, Nessa?" Jesse took hold of her elbow and led her back a few feet, guiding her down onto the couch. Annie scooted off to the side, snuggling between Vanessa and the arm of the couch while Jesse lowered himself onto one knee on the floor in front of them. "You see, we found—"

"Where's Mom?" Vanessa interrupted, thoroughly confused.

With his back partially to them and head still hanging low, Carlos rubbed his hands over his face. He made a sniffling noise, then cleared his throat. Finally, he turned to face the rest of his family. When Vanessa saw his bloodshot, red-rimmed eyes, her confusion multiplied.

"*Where's* Mom?" she repeated more forcefully.

"She's gone, Nessa." Carlos met her stare briefly, and the weight of the sorrow contained within the brown depths of his eyes nearly stopped her heart. "She's really gone."

"But...but..." Vanessa had heard her knocking on the bathroom door. She'd heard her voice. Hadn't she?

Maybe she's a ghost, like me, and she's finally found you?

The possibility was both crushing and a relief, a combination that was unsettling to the point of being a little nauseating.

But...what about the knocking?

Vanessa shoved the detail aside as unimportant. "Mom's g—gone?" Talk about dropping from the highest high to the lowest low, only to settle somewhere in the middle. Vanessa looked from Carlos to Jesse and back. "How do you know? Did you find her—her body?"

Carlos shook his head, but it was Jesse who answered. "There was a list taped to one of the doors—it's in part of the hospital that the fire didn't damage much. There were names...thousands of names."

"Deceased," Carlos said, his voice hollow. "Written at the top in red like we'd miss it otherwise."

So...if someone wrote her name on a list, that means she died before the fire, right? At least she didn't get burned alive...

How such a morbid notion could be a comfort was beyond Vanessa's comprehension, but it *was* a comfort. "I heard her." Vanessa's mind felt tangled, like all of her thoughts and feeling were meshing together, becoming indistinguishable. "And Rosie. Where'd you move her?"

Jesse and Carlos exchanged a look. "Uh…what?"

"Rosie…and Julian's in Mom's room. There were dogs…"

Carlos strode toward the hallway. "Julian's in the—" He halted in the entrance and covered his mouth with his hand. He turned and looked at Vanessa, his eyes surrounded by too much white. "What the hell happened?"

Again, Vanessa looked at each of her brothers, then pulled Annie closer to her. She cleared her throat. "Annie was napping, and I went outside to check on Rosie."

"Why?" Carlos's voice was harsh.

Vanessa swallowed a few times, giving herself a moment to wade through her tangled thoughts. "I, um, heard something." She shook her head, not sure why she wasn't telling them about hearing Rosie, only that she couldn't bring herself to explain it. "When I went out to the shed and found Rosie gone, I had a momentary freak out and rushed back into the house. Then Julian was at the door, and—"

Jesse squeezed her elbow. "What do you mean, Rosie's *gone*?"

"'Cause you, um, moved her…?"

"No," Carlos said. "We didn't."

8

Vanessa stared through the shed door, mouth hanging open in shock. Rosie's body was on the shed's plastic floor, wrapped in the comforter that used to be on Jesse's bed, exactly where Carlos had put it a week ago.

Jesse stood beside her, their shoulders almost touching. Carlos was inside with Annie, packing their things. What with finding out about their mom's passing and with the soon-to-be-reeking dead body—and parts—littering their mom's bedroom floor and walls, the three Hernandez kids had agreed that it was time to leave.

"But—but…she wasn't there!" Vanessa was positive that the shed had been empty when she'd checked earlier.

Are you absolutely *sure?*

As she heard Rosie's voice, her view of the shed altered.

It was empty.

Rosie's body was there.

Empty.

Bundled-up body.

Rosie's body flickered in and out of existence, over and over again.

That's so weird…

Vanessa raised her hands to her face, pressing her palms against her eyes. She didn't understand what was happening to her. Was she wrong? Was it all in her mind? Was she going insane? But there was still Annie and the dogs…

Be careful…who knows what they'll do if they think you're crazy like that lady with the baby…

"I—I guess I was wrong." Vanessa shook her head, unwilling to share her fears of her burgeoning insanity with her brother.

Nice one.

"Shut up!" Vanessa hissed.

"What?"

Vanessa glanced at her brother and felt the color drain from her cheeks. "Nothing." A nervous laugh bubbled up from her chest. "Just talking to myself." *Not* to imaginary dead people.

Right…keep telling yourself that.

"I, uh, thought Carlos put her behind the shed, not *inside* it." She shrugged, trying to appear unconcerned. "Guess I looked in the wrong spot, that's all."

Jesse studied Vanessa for a moment longer, prompting her to shift her feet and tuck her hair behind her ear self-consciously. "C'mon, Sis." He draped an arm over her shoulders and used his free hand to shut the shed door, locking Rosie's body in a plastic tomb with gardening tools as her eternal companions. "Let's get our shit together so we can hit the road."

Hunching her shoulders and hugging her middle, Vanessa trudged along beside her brother back to the home they'd lived in their entire lives. "You really think that place in Tahoe is our best bet?" She didn't actually care where they went, so long as it was far away from here. She just wanted to talk about something that might take her mind off the reality of what was happening to her.

You think you can leave me behind, don't you? Like, getting far away will shut me up or something? I don't think so…

Vanessa squeezed her eyes shut. Rosie had an uncanny way of picking up on the thoughts she was trying her hardest to ignore.

As she stepped through the sliding glass door ahead of her brother, the waning warmth of their house wrapped around her. The electricity had finally stopped working shortly after her brothers returned; they were all surprised it lasted that long. At least their water heater was fueled by natural gas, allowing the boys to take one last hot shower before they left for good. Who knew when they might get to take another.

Vanessa walked through the kitchen, part of the way down the hall, and headed toward her bedroom, avoiding looking at the sheet her brothers had taped up over their mom's bedroom doorway, hiding Julian's body. She paused to look into the bedroom her brothers shared. Carlos and Annie were in the room, Annie sitting on the bed, watching Carlos fill a few gym bags, a backpack, and a duffel bag with essentials. As Vanessa stood in the doorway, Carlos added their dad's watch and old manual camera to whatever other personal items he'd already loaded into the backpack.

Carlos paused while stuffing handfuls of white socks into the largest bag and glanced Vanessa's way. "I left mom's duffel and your backpack on your bed. Let me know if you need more space." He pointed to one of the gym bags; it was dark gray with bright pink lining. Vanessa had never seen it before. "We stopped by that thrift shop next to the hospital on our way back—Annie's good to go." He shifted his arm to the left, motioning toward the other gym bag. That one she recognized—it had been their dad's. "I've got towels and shampoo and soap and stuff, too, so don't waste space on that."

"Thanks." Vanessa offered him and Annie a weak smile before turning and heading into her own room.

She would have thought that condensing the material goods she'd acquired during her seventeen years of life should have taken a really long time. But in reality, she had the duffel bag filled to the brim with clothing and her backpack loaded with only those items most important to her—a photo album, a diary, a few of her favorite books, the stuffed dinosaur she'd had since she was a baby

—in the time it took Jesse to disappear into the bathroom, shower, and emerge scrubbed and ready to go.

After zipping up both bags, Vanessa walked around her bedroom, feeling like a stranger in the familiar space. She picked up an item here and there—a small, lacquered jewelry box filled with all of her favorite earrings, a movie ticket stub, one of the porcelain angels her dad used to get her each year on her birthday. She wrapped the last in a t-shirt and added it to the keepsakes in her backpack.

Again, Vanessa zipped up the pack. She shrugged it onto her shoulder, then lifted the hefty duffel bag and walked out of her room, grateful that, for once, Rosie's voice was leaving her alone.

9

"NOOOOO!" Annie's wail was like iron nails being driven into Vanessa's eardrums. "My doggies! MY DOGGIES!" But Annie's epic tantrum wasn't what was keeping the Hernandezes from leaving Toppenish without the three dogs.

The mountain dog, Pit Bull, and diminutive white Terrier were blocking their path. Vanessa and her brothers couldn't get to the SUV without going through the dogs, and based on the bared, glistening teeth, that wasn't going to be easy…or healthy.

Maybe if you threw, I don't know, bacon or something it would distract them?

Vanessa ignored Rosie's unhelpful suggestion. If she'd had any bacon at all, they would have eaten it already. As things stood, they'd whittled their food supply down to the graham crackers, peanut butter, jelly, canned fruit, and boxed cereal they were bringing with them.

"Annie!" Vanessa shook the girl's tiny hand. "We need to leave! Tell them to let us by."

Annie's only response was to magnify the level of hysteria contained within her by screaming and crying. If there were still any sane people left living on their street—or on any of the streets nearby—they'd certainly think Annie was being mutilated by savages.

"I'm sick of this bullshit." Jesse dropped one of the bags he'd been carrying and reached behind him, pulling his handgun from the waistband of his jeans.

You've got to stop him! Think about it—the dogs can keep watch at night, you know. You guys can't afford not *to take them with you.*

Vanessa's nostrils flared, and she gritted her teeth. "Jesse! Wait!" She took a few quick steps toward the car, placing herself between Jesse and the dogs. "If Annie can talk to them—and she can, I swear—then they could be useful." She looked back and forth from Jesse to Carlos, imploring with her eyes. "Think about it"—she nearly cringed as she realized she'd repeated Rosie's words—"we'll have guard dogs we can trust completely because Annie can freaking *talk* to them. I don't think we can afford to not take them with us."

Jesse's sharp glare shifted from Vanessa to the dogs, and his eyes narrowed. He clearly didn't trust them or Annie's ability to communicate with them. But when his eyes once again landed on Vanessa, they softened, and it was clear that he trusted her.

For now…

Jesse stuffed the gun into his waistband and nodded. "Fine. They can come with us. But if one of them pisses in the car, they're all gone."

Relieved, Vanessa exhaled heavily and squeezed Annie's hand. "Does that work for the doggies?"

Annie looked up at her, her big blue eyes still shining with tears despite the smile making deep dimples on either side of her mouth. She gave a divisive nod. "Yep!"

The dogs backed down almost instantaneously. They sat on the snowy sidewalk by the SUV, whimpering and wagging their tails as they waited for Vanessa and her brothers to let them into the vehicle. Vanessa skirted around the Pit Bull, recalling how effectively she'd been bulled over and knocked out by it only a few hours earlier. She had the massive headache to prove it.

You know they were just trying to protect Annie…

"Like I would've hurt her?"

"What, Nessa?" Carlos asked while he loaded bags into the back of the SUV.

"Nothing." Inside, Vanessa cursed herself. If there was one thing she needed to stop doing, it was responding to Rosie's voice, because Rosie wasn't real.

Rosie was dead.

10

From her vantage point behind the driver's seat, Vanessa stared out the window into the pale morning light. She and her brothers had been alternating drivers for the past ten hours, and it was Jesse who currently had the wheel. Carlos was sitting in the front passenger seat, discussing with Jesse whether or not they should stop at the next gas station to attempt to stock up on food.

Against the odds—especially considering that all of the gas stations seemed to have been drained dry of fuel—gas wasn't something Vanessa and her brothers had needed to worry about. They'd had fairly good luck finding cars parked at rest stops with plenty of fuel to siphon into the SUV's gas tank. Some of those cars had apparently been abandoned, and some most definitely hadn't.

Vanessa wrapped her arms around her middle and shivered. She could just imagine what it must have been like for the people in *those* cars. They would have been feeling ill, pulled off into the rest stop for a nap, then never recovered enough to continue on their way. Never recovered enough to make it home. They'd died alone, covered in their own vomit and excrement. Gross as that was to imagine, it was the dying alone part that troubled Vanessa the most. Had her mom died alone?

She worked at the hospital—she probably had tons of friends around her when she, you know...

Vanessa tensed but continued to stare out the window, watching a small flock of sheep. They were only a few hours away from their destination at the south end of Lake Tahoe, and she'd gone almost the entire drive without hearing Rosie's voice. Her hopes that it had just been a phase—that she'd gotten over whatever psychotic break had caused her to hear Rosie's voice in the first place—evaporated.

You're ignoring me?

Vanessa clenched her jaw and rolled her eyes. It wasn't like she could respond with her brothers, Annie, and the dogs crammed into the SUV with her—not to mention all their stuff packed in behind the backseat. The space was so cramped that someone was bound to notice her chatting with empty air. Taking a deep breath, she shut her eyes.

You are! You're ignoring me! That's messed up...

Vanessa opened her eyes and focused on her breaths and the ever-changing view out the window. They were driving along a two-lane highway surrounded by pastureland and, beyond that, mountains, distant and barren on the left and just out of reach and dusted with snow on the right. The sheep were gone, replaced by a half-dozen fenced-in horses, then untended land, then cows and more sheep.

At feeling a tap on her arm, Vanessa turned her head to ask Annie, who was sitting on the opposite end of the middle row of seats, what she needed. Immediately, Vanessa flinched, shrinking back against the car door. Annie wasn't the person she found staring back at her. No, the eyes that met hers weren't bright and blue and still filled with wonder despite everything they'd seen; they were dark, sunken, and dull, and they were way too close to her.

Rosie.

Freaking Rosie was sitting right there in the middle seat between Vanessa and Annie.

And Rosie didn't take her eyes off Vanessa for one second. She arched an eyebrow, and the corresponding corner of her graying, too-pale lips quirked upward.

All Vanessa could do was gape at the obviously dead teenage girl sitting beside her. The nails of her left hand dug into the faux-leather padding on the inside of the door.

With a heavy, dramatic sigh, Rosie broke eye contact. She glanced down, looking herself over, then met Vanessa's eyes. *"Does this outfit make me look dead?"* But it wasn't the outfit that made Rosie look dead. It was the blueish-gray, bloodless skin…the sunken cheeks…the dead cast to her eyes.

"You're not real," Vanessa said without meaning to. She heard the hushed conversation between her brothers cut off, and figuring they must have heard her, she held her breath.

"Nessa?" Carlos had turned around in his seat to look back at her, the little white Terrier snoozing on his lap. The two bigger dogs were behind Vanessa and Annie, sharing the third row of seats. Carlos studied her, looked at Annie, then returned his attention to Vanessa. "Who're you talking to?"

Rosie nudged Vanessa's arm with her elbow. *"Tell him you were talking to me. See what he says."* She cackled. *"He's gonna be like—what the fu—"*

Vanessa shot Rosie a horrified look. "No!" She cringed immediately after voicing that single word. She shouldn't have responded, but with Rosie actually sitting there, real as her brothers to Vanessa's eyes—if a little on the dead side—it was almost impossible *not* to react to her as though she were really there.

"I could be real." Rosie scoffed and pointed her thumb at Annie and then at the dogs behind them. *"I mean, c'mon…"*

Vanessa opened her mouth to respond, but caught herself before she actually spoke. She looked at Carlos, whose face was etched with a mixture of worry and confusion. "I, um, think I was talking in my sleep. I'm just really tired and apparently that makes me act like a crazy person."

Rosie laughed. *"Or...maybe you* are *a crazy person."* To add an extra fringe to Vanessa's already frayed nerves, Rosie started humming "Ring Around the Rosie." Aside from sounding creepy as hell all on its own, hearing Rosie hum that song brought back some disturbing memories, and not just of Julian singing it right before his insides were ripped out.

The last school project Vanessa and Rosie had worked on together had been about that song. They'd been Freshman, and their world history teacher had tasked them with musical sleuthing. They had to discover the historical significance of an assigned song, "Ring Around the Rosie" in their case. Rumors abounded that it was originally about the Black Death—making Rosie's singing of the song eerily apropos at the moment—but Vanessa and Rosie had discovered nothing conclusive. Rosie had decided that the only way to truly understand the song was to act it out via interpretive dance, leading to a night of sore cheeks and aching abs from laughing hysterically for far too long. Two weeks later, Vanessa had stumbled upon Rosie and Jesse hooking up in a bathroom at a party. Their friendship immediately crumbled.

Rosie stopped humming and shook her head. *"I never got why that made you so pissy."*

"I'm fine, really," Vanessa told Carlos. Only once he'd returned to facing forward did she turn a scathing glare on Rosie. But deep down, even Vanessa wasn't sure why it had bothered her so much. She'd known Rosie had a thing for Jesse, and she'd known Rosie was a horrid flirt. But back then, Jesse had been running with a bad crowd, and Vanessa had warned Rosie to stay away from him. And Rosie had ignored her.

"So what...you thought I betrayed you or something?" Rosie rolled her eyes. *"God, that was* forever *ago. Can't we just forget about it and be friends again?"*

Vanessa might have considered it had Rosie not been an invisible, likely imaginary walking corpse.

"That's racist!" Rosie frowned. *"Or…you know what I mean! Just 'cause I'm dead doesn't mean I don't have feelings."* She crossed her arms, pouting.

Chilly realization washed over Vanessa. Rosie was responding to her thoughts—*had been* responding to her thoughts since the beginning.

"Ding ding ding," Rosie said, laughing. *"Ten points to you"*—she poked Vanessa's arm—*"girl interrupted. I don't know how you didn't notice."*

Feeling numb, Vanessa turned to stare out the window. She stared for unknown minutes, not really seeing anything in the dawn light.

"Nessa?"

Startled, Vanessa looked at Carlos, who had once again turned in his seat to face her. "Yeah?"

"We're just gonna drive through. Should be a little over an hour 'til we get there, but Jesse says they have food and stuff, so we don't need to stop for that." Carlos raised his eyebrows in question. "You good with that?"

"Does wittle Nessa need a potty bweak?" Rosie said in her most annoying baby voice. She could be such a little…

Vanessa smiled at her brother. "I'm good with that." She just hoped he didn't notice the sharp slap she'd landed on Rosie's thigh with the back of her hand.

No such luck. Carlos's eyes flicked down to her hand.

Vanessa forced her lips to remain curved in what she hoped looked like a carefree smile and raised her shoulders just a bit. "Thought I saw a bug."

Rosie snorted.

"You sure you're feeling okay?" Carlos's eyebrows were drawn together, a clear broadcast of his concern.

No. She was absolutely positive that she was *not* feeling okay.

Arguing with a dead teenager who looked, sounded, and felt just as real as her very real brother was about as far from okay as possible.

"Yep." Vanessa flashed Carlos one more tight smile. "I'm fine."

11

"So...this is it?" Carlos was alternating between looking out the windshield and the passenger-side window as Jesse drove along the snow-covered road. "It's really, uh, woodsy."

Vanessa—and Rosie—were doing pretty much the exact same thing, looking out the nearest windows to examine their surroundings. For the most part, all Vanessa could see was an endless sea of snow and tall pine trees on either side of the car. The snow-covered road stretched out in a gentle curve ahead and behind them, and Vanessa had yet to spot any sign of a campground or other people, which was what Jesse had described.

"It's creepy, no?" Rosie leaned in closer, nudging Vanessa's shoulder. *"I can't decide if seeing some strange place all abandoned is worse than seeing our own home like that."*

Vanessa nodded slowly but didn't look away from her window.

"Shouldn't there be, I don't know, like some sign of all these 'people' J's been talking about?" A shiver crawled up Vanessa's spine as Rosie spoke; whether it was caused by the haunting absence of people or the unsettling sensation of Rosie leaning into her to get a better view out the window, she didn't know.

They'd passed through the small resort town of South Lake

Tahoe with its packed parking lots and hulking lodges that were, based on all the cars, equally packed with dead bodies. Recalling the body she'd seen hanging by its neck over the edge of a fourth-story balcony, swaying in the wind and leeched of color by the freezing temperature, Vanessa realized her unease stemmed far more from the disturbing sight than from Rosie. In comparison, the tactile reminder of Rosie's presence—imaginary or not—was surprisingly soothing.

Someone squeezed Vanessa's shoulder, and she instantly stiffened. The only bodies occupying the backseat were the two bigger dogs, emitting occasional barks, sniffs, and whines. Dogs didn't have hands, and they certainly couldn't squeeze shoulders.

Holding her breath, Vanessa craned her neck to look down at her shoulder. The hand resting there was slender and pale. It gave another gentled squeeze, then pulled away.

"Don't worry, sweetie. We'll be here with you no matter what. We won't let you end up like that man," her mom said.

Vanessa exhaled a faint whimper and shut her eyes as tightly as possible, more to block the tears that were suddenly welling in her eyes than to avoid seeing her mom. On the contrary, she desperately wanted to see her mom.

Vanessa turned in a rush, her fingers latching onto the top of the seatback like talons, and when she finally laid eyes on the woman sitting directly behind her, the tears broke free. She slapped her hand over her mouth to muffle her sudden, uncontainable need to sob.

Her mom. Was sitting *right there.*

She needed her mom so badly right now…would continue to need her forever. She didn't think she'd be able to survive without her.

Her mom smiled a comforting, familiar smile that looked a little out of place on her gaunt face. *"You won't have to, sweetie. I'll be here whenever you need me."*

"Shit!" Carlos shouted.

Turning to face forward, Vanessa dredged her mind for some excuse that would reasonably explain why she was acting so weird. But Carlos wasn't looking at her, wasn't swearing because of her, and concern wasn't etching his youthful face. As far as Vanessa could tell, Annie was the only one who'd noticed her seemingly random fit of tears at all. The little girl was staring at Vanessa, her big blue eyes keen with curiosity.

Jesse brought the car to a skidding halt. Apparently there were things other than Vanessa's erratic behavior to pay attention to. One of Carlos's hands was on the dash, the other was extended in front of him, pointing to the woods off to the left of the car. He shifted from staring out the window to staring in shock at Jesse. "Did you see them? They just appeared…like, they came out of freaking nowhere!"

Vanessa followed the direction of Carlos's outstretched arm and sucked in a surprised breath. Standing among the trees not more than few feet from the road were at least a dozen people. They were all wearing heavy winter clothing…all except for one woman.

Slowly, she stepped onto the paved shoulder, a slender middle-aged man on one side of her and a hulking man with long, dark hair pulled back into a low ponytail on the other. Or rather, he would have appeared hulking had he not been standing beside the woman. She was truly enormous—obese even—wearing what appeared to be a heavy, fur-lined robe made of a fabric that looked to be both insulating and luxurious over some sort of long gown.

Vanessa also spotted an old woman, far too aged and frail to be out tromping around in the snowy woods. Everyone else was too concealed within their winter outerwear to display any notable distinguishing features. And the way they were all standing out there, spread out between the trees, with only the three of them approaching the car, was just…

"Creepy. As. Hell," Rosie said.

Movement from the driver's seat momentarily captured Vanessa's attention. Jesse had bowed his head; he no longer showed any interest in the eerie scene beyond the windshield. His breathing was quicker than usual, sounding almost labored.

"Jesse, man—what's up?" Carlos asked.

The older of Vanessa's brothers simply sat in his seat, his head drooped and each inhale and exhale clearly audible.

When Vanessa felt a persistent poking on her arm, she turned to hiss a quiet "Not right now!" at Rosie, but instead found herself looking at Annie. The words died on her tongue. "What is it, sweetie?"

Annie's tiny, chubby features broke into an ecstatic grin. "I made new friends!" She was pointing out the window on her side of the SUV. She was clearly pointing into the woods to the right of the road, but Vanessa couldn't see any movement, let alone anything that might qualify as another of Annie's "friends." At first.

Dark shapes slinked among the forest's concealing shadows. They neared the road in a haphazard zigzag, uncountable and indistinguishable from the spots of darkness they used as cover.

The Pit Bull Annie had named Pepper—an ode to his short black-speckled-white coat—stood abruptly and nearly pressed his nose to the passenger side window, fogging up the glass with each breath. A low, ominous growl rumbled in his barrel chest. Pepper, apparently, wasn't as instantly fond of Annie's new friends as she was.

With a wary glance at the Pit, Vanessa reached across Rosie's lap to pat Annie's knee. "That's, uh, great."

Annie beamed, then returned her attention back to the window.

Vanessa looked at her brothers in the front seats in time to see Jesse handing his pistol to Carlos. "Just do it!" her older brother demanded.

"No way in hell," Carlos returned, equally adamant. Whatever words they'd exchanged while Vanessa had been preoccupied by Annie and the fluidly moving shadows were obviously important.

"We're not leaving you to—to…Jesus, Jesse! Why didn't you say something before? If what you're saying is true…" Carlos stared at Jesse for a long moment, then shook his head. "No. No way in hell."

"Uh…this is not good," Rosie whispered.

Vanessa's mom gave her shoulder another supportive squeeze. *"Maybe it would be best if we all just drove away right now. We can survive as a family. We don't need these people, whoever they are."*

Vanessa studied her brothers, first one, then the other. "What are you guys talking about?"

Jesse shot a look over his seatback. His eyes were wild, filled with all the panic of a trapped, injured animal. "I can't," he said, his voice strained. "I can't—JUST GO!" Without warning, he lurched to his left. The driver's door burst open, and he rolled out of the SUV.

"Jesse!" Vanessa reached for him instinctively, but grasped only air.

12

Instead of obeying Jesse and sliding over the center console to sit in the driver's seat, Carlos shoved open his own door and leapt out of the car. Vanessa watched confused and frozen by her brothers' startling behavior. She watched Jesse straighten in the snow, watched the play of emotions dance across his face as he looked back and realized Carlos hadn't listened, watched the utter devastation wash over him, slumping his shoulders and bowing his neck.

"What's going on?" Rosie's voice was laced with panic.

"It's alright, girls," Vanessa's mom said, her voice steady. *"Let's just stay calm. And sweetie"*—she touched the back of Vanessa's head—*"you might want to move up to the driver's seat... just in case."*

"But..." Vanessa looked from her mom to Rosie and Annie, then back out the windshield. "We can't just leave them! Why would we..." Her words trailed off as she watched the scene outside of the car.

"Nessa," Annie said softly, her voice pitched higher than usual.

The trio of approaching strangers had stopped. About halfway between the front of the car and the trio, Jesse was standing absolutely still, his hands raised to head-height.

"But this is a safe place," Rosie whispered frantically. *"He said we'd be safe here..."*

Directly in front of the car, Carlos stood, feet spread shoulder-width apart, both arms extended in front of him, aiming the pistol. It took Vanessa only a brief scan of the strangers to understand why.

The middle-aged man had produced his own weapon, a shotgun, and had it trained on Jesse.

As Vanessa watched, Jesse started shaking his head. "I did what you said—I came back," he shouted. "It's done, okay? It's done. Just...just let them go. You can do whatever you want with me—use that mind control shit—I don't care. Just, please, let them leave!"

"No! Bring the tainted one to us!" the middle-aged man yelled. "Do it!"

Jesse shook his head more emphatically, lowering one arm to wave it behind him in an jerky shooing motion.

"I think that's for us...a signal to leave," Vanessa's mom said.

"And abandon them?" Rosie squeaked.

Vanessa still sat behind the driver's seat, unable to move. She didn't understand what was happening. This was supposed to be Jesse's "safe place." Why would he try so hard to convince them to drive hundreds of miles, only to risk getting shot so they could turn around and drive away?

"Get them out of here," Jesse ordered, looking at Carlos with such urgency that Vanessa's already racing heart actually sped up a little more. "They'll kill her!"

Shaking his head, Carlos started backing toward the SUV.

"I wouldn't, son." The middle-aged man was speaking to Carlos, but his gun remained steadily aimed at Jesse. He took a step. Then another. Slowly, he was closing the distance between himself and Carlos. "The tainted ones are dangerous—driven mad by the virus. Surely you must have noticed."

"Don't let him get close enough to touch you, Carlos. He can get into your mind, make you do things," Jesse warned. "Just turn and run. Get them out of here!"

"She'll turn on you eventually," the man said.

"Stop! Just stop!" Carlos emphasized his words with pointed shakes of his gun. "I'll shoot you!"

"Will you?" The man stopped a half-dozen paces from Carlos. "Mandy?" he asked over his shoulder. "Perhaps you can convince this young man?"

The large, robed woman trundled forward, but Vanessa never found out what she might have said or done. Carlos spun around and made run for the open driver's door. Seemingly of its own volition, it slammed shut before he reached it. He tugged on the handle, but the door wouldn't open.

BOOM.

At the sound of the shotgun firing, Carlos ducked out of Vanessa's view.

"NO!" Mandy wailed. She lurched forward a few final steps, trying to catch Jesse as he crumbled to the snow. A crimson patch blossomed as his blood melted the snow around him.

He'd been shot. Jesse had been shot.

"You have to do *something!"* Rosie insisted.

But Vanessa couldn't think of a single thing she should or could be doing at that moment. She couldn't *think* period. Jesse. Had been shot.

Mandy rose over Jesse's body, menacing in her enormity. "Cole…" Her voice was low, filled with warning. She glanced back at the large man who'd been at her side. "Kevin—disarm Cole. *Hurt* him."

The middle-aged man who had to be "Cole" tsked. "You've still got one of Vic's precious little boys to use as a plaything." His vulturine eyes were fixed on Carlos. "I'd rethink sicking your lapdog on me. I *will* shoot this one, too."

"And I'll kill you!" Mandy snarled.

Cole shrugged. "It was bound to happen eventually. At least I'll know your misery is secure."

Mandy's face twisted into an ugly mask of rage, but she raised her right hand and signaled for the large man—Kevin—to wait.

"Wonderful," Cole mused. "Now, you"—he looked past Carlos, his eyes focusing on Vanessa—"get out of the car and bring the whining brat, or I'll shoot your *other* brother."

Vanessa felt like her mouth was filled with sand. She shook her head, numb on the inside. Shouldn't she have been crying? Or screaming? Annie was doing both, quite enthusiastically. But like those of her mom and Rosie, Vanessa's face was locked in a mask of horror and disbelief, and she was silent. Completely silent.

Jesse. Shot. Not moving.

Dead?

Rosie was the first to break their spell of shock. She shook Vanessa's arm. *"You can't let him kill Carlos, too!"*

Vanessa nodded numbly. Rosie was right, of course. She couldn't let that happen. That would be…no, she couldn't let that happen. But as she reached for the door handle, her mom placed one hand on her shoulder. *"No, sweetie. You can't risk your life and Annie's…what if they kill you and Carlos both? That madman's already taken one of my children; I won't let him take all of them."*

Vanessa froze, her fingers gripping the cool metal handle.

"No!" Rosie wailed. *"You can't* not *do anything. You have to help him!"*

Her mom's grip tightened on her shoulder. *"Look at Annie."*

Vanessa did as instructed. The five-year-old was bawling, the three dogs huddled around her, low growls rumbling in their chests.

"Do you want her to end up like me?" Vanessa's mom's voice was harsh.

Vanessa looked back at her and drew in a sharp breath. Her mom no longer looked like the pale, semi-gaunt version she'd come to expect, but was covered in a layer of charred, still-smoking skin. Her face was unrecognizable, barely human.

"Do you want her to die?"

"No," Vanessa breathed. There was no way she would risk bringing Annie out of the car with her—not that the dogs would let her.

Amid Carlos's protests and before Rosie could talk her out of it, Vanessa pulled on the handle and shoved the door open. She stepped out onto the snow-covered road, hugging herself and shivering, and stared into Cole's cool, uncaring eyes. "What do you want?"

Cole's eyes narrowed. He'd told Vanessa to "bring the whining brat" with her, and she'd disregarded his demand. His irritation was obvious, but he didn't say anything about her defiance. Instead, without taking his eyes off Carlos and Vanessa, he waved at the people who were still standing among the trees on the left side of the road. "Come here, Mary. Tell me if she's the one."

It was the old woman who responded to his command. She hobbled out onto the road, the snow making her already slow movements almost painstaking. When Mary reached Cole's side, her dull eyes fixed on Vanessa, washing her in an odd, tingly sensation.

Rosie linked her arm with Vanessa's. *"What's she looking for?"*

"God only knows," her mom said, wrapping an arm around Vanessa's shoulders. *"God and* these people,*"* she amended, her voice giving away only a sliver of how much she loathed "these people."

Vanessa stared at Jesse's motionless body, and the rapidly melting patch of crimson snow spreading out beneath and around him. There was so much blood. She stifled the urge to run to him, to shake him until he woke. She wouldn't risk doing something so rash that could lead to losing her other brother, too.

"There's too much blood, sweetie—I don't think Jesse's ever going to wake." Vanessa's mom sounded desolate, but resolute. Jesse was gone.

Jesse…her brother…

Vanessa scanned the faces of the strangers standing out in the winter afternoon with her, finally landing on Cole's. This man—*these people*—killed her brother. Her shock was wearing off, replaced with white-hot, center-of-the-sun rage. "WHAT DO YOU WANT?"

Nobody answered.

Mary's eerily tangible stare released Vanessa, and the old woman turned to Cole. She gave one quick nod, then started her way through the snow back to the others standing among the pines.

Cole's lips spread into a humorless smile, and without warning, he swung the shotgun in Vanessa's direction.

There was the sharp crack of gunfire at the exact moment that a body slammed into Vanessa's back. She lunged to the ground, barely managing to break her fall with her hands before face-planting in the snow. She heard shouting—Cole, Carlos, and others—but had no clue whether it was her brother who had fired the gun or the murderous stranger.

Whoever had tackled her to the ground was doing a really good job of keeping her there, lying on her back and using all of their weight to hold her down. She raised her head as much as she could with her attacker settled on her back and looked around wildly. Her eyes landed on four enormous, gray paws, attached to the strong, black-ticked-gray legs of a huge dog just a few feet away.

"That's not a dog," Rosie said.

"I'm fairly certain it's a wolf," her mom offered.

A wolf? As the possibility sank in, Vanessa realized there was a very distinct panting noise coming from the being who'd tackled her, who was still planted firmly on her back. It wasn't a *who*, she realized, but a *what.*

"A wolf's on your back!" Rosie sounded more excited than worried for Vanessa's safety. *"A freaking* wolf *is on you, and it's not trying to rip your throat out!"*

The dark gray wolf standing beside Vanessa started slinking forward, toward Cole and her brother.

"Nessa! Get Annie the hell out of here!" Carlos shouted.

The wolf on Vanessa's back eased off her and settled on its haunches beside her, letting her push herself up onto her hands and knees. She finally had a clear view of her brother. Carlos was grappling with Cole near the car. He seemed to have the upper hand, until Kevin lurched toward them and seized Carlos by the shoulders.

"Ha!" Cole shouted as he managed to wrap a hand around the front of Carlos's neck. "Stop fighting."

To Vanessa's horror, Carlos obeyed. His limbs relaxed, and he sat in the snow, partially held upright by Kevin and doing nothing to even *try* to break Cole's hold on his neck.

"Very good," Cole said.

As she watched them, Cole retrieved Jesse's pistol from the ground and handed it to Carlos.

"That's odd," her mom said. *"Why would he give Carlos his gun back?"*

Without removing his hand from Carlos's neck or his eyes from Carlos's face, Cole said, "Shoot her." He was so focused on Vanessa's brother that he didn't seem to notice one of the wolves edging closer to them.

Carlos squeezed his eyes shut, his gun hand shaking. "Nessa—run!"

"Wh-what?" Vanessa stammered, certain that Carlos would *never* shoot her.

"I can't—I have to do what he says! I can't—I have to—" Carlos's eyes snapped open, wide with horror. He raised the gun.

Crack.

Vanessa was so shocked by the muzzle flash that she almost didn't feel it at first. Almost.

A burning spot of pain radiating from her left shoulder. She glanced down to see that the sleeve of her winter coat was torn at the crux of her shoulder, revealing a thin streak of raw flesh where the bullet had skimmed her.

He'd shot her.

Carlos, her own brother, had shot her.

"We've got to go now, sweetie," her mom said, tugging on her arm.

At her insistence, Vanessa climbed to her feet. The air was filled with the sound of low, reverberating growls and vicious snarls as more creatures emerged from the woods on the right side of the road. Some looked like wolves, while others looked like Huskies, and others, still, appeared to be a mix of the two.

They padded closer to the humans in a manner very uncharacteristic to wolves' usual, avoid-humans-at-all-costs instincts.

"It's got to be Annie," Rosie said as she tugged on Vanessa's sleeve. *"C'mon! We've got to get her out of here before that psycho makes Carlos try again. His aim might not be so bad next time..."*

"She's right, sweetie. We've got to go!"

Vanessa hesitated for a moment, exchanging the briefest of glances with her brother. His eyes were tortured, but she could see him losing the battle between his will and Cole's. "Go," he mouthed just as his gun hand started shaking again.

Vanessa sprinted around the back of the car, her wolf attacker-protector close by her side. At the crack of gunfire, she ducked behind the illusory safety of the SUV's back end and crawled the rest of the way to the rear passenger door.

As soon as she opened it, the Terrier and mountain dog leapt from the interior and started prowling around her, while the Pit Bull remained inside on the seat beside a shrieking Annie, blocking her from the view of the people on the other side of the car.

"Shh…shh…shhh, sweetie," Vanessa murmured as she tried, hands shaking, to unbuckle Annie's seatbelt. It took ages, but the latch eventually clicked, and Vanessa tore the hysterical little girl out of the car. She hugged her close and ran toward the woods, the several inches of snow slowing her pace. More of the wolves and dogs surrounded them, running alongside Vanessa, a living, breathing, snarling barrier of fur, teeth, and claws.

As one, Vanessa and the pack dove deeper into the relative safety of the woods and away from the homicidal strangers.

Away from danger.

Away from the only family Vanessa had left.

"You have me, sweetie," her mom said, and in Vanessa's peripheral vision, she could see her mom running beside her.

"And me." Rosie nudged Vanessa's elbow with her own. *"We'll never leave you."*

13

CARLOS

One Month Later

Carlos sat beside his mistress's chair, dressed only in loose-fitting linen trousers, utterly content that she'd chosen him to be one of her favorites today. The man who sat on the floor on the opposite side of the chair was new, but he seemed to bring Carlos's mistress joy, so he was glad the newcomer was there. They both ran their hands over her skin, savoring the chance to touch her.

Carlos lived for the moments when he was touching her. When he was one of her chosen…her favorites…her "pretties." He'd never loved anyone as much as he loved her. In fact, Carlos was fairly certain that if he ever strayed too far from her side, he would die of heartbreak. Of longing. Of need.

His life was now divided into two time periods: Mandy and before Mandy. As far as he could remember, "before" had been a time of misery and loneliness. His life had been empty, but now it was full of *her*, his queen…his goddess. He hoped that tonight would be one of the nights she chose to keep her pretties with her to please her in any way she desired.

"We are the Prophets of the New World," Mandy said in chorus with Mary and Cole. Carlos wished the other two would shut up so he could listen to the perfection that was Mandy's voice all on its own. Mary's voice was scratchy with age, and Cole's voice grated for the simple sake that it was Cole's.

Only Carlos's deep-seeded hatred for Cole ever managed to shake the all-encompassing peaceful euphoria he felt in Mandy's presence.

"We have foreseen your arrival and desire you to join the followers of the One True Religion. With us, you will find safety, and above all else, peace. We welcome you." It was the greeting the prophets recited to all newcomers. This group was just one more in a long string of survivors who would assuredly join Mandy's followers.

Carlos felt a twinge of jealousy as he risked a glance at the man who seemed to be their leader. Would he become another of his mistress's favorites? Would Carlos have to share her with one more man? The leader was tall and muscular with short, dark hair, brilliant blue eyes, and chiseled features. It seemed likely that Mandy would want to keep him.

"We would like to stay with you and your people for a few more nights," the leader said, sounding confident and a bit formal. "But then we really should continue on our way."

Carlos stiffened in shock. They would leave? Nobody but the tainted *ever* left, and they usually departed *the world*...permanently. Carlos felt Mandy's pillowy flesh tremble under his fingers. She'd obviously found the idea of these people leaving as surprising as Carlos, and she wasn't pleased about it. Carlos felt instant and unquenchable hatred toward them—the man—for upsetting his mistress. He stroked her arm in an effort to soothe her, and to remind her that she still had him. She didn't need anyone else.

After introducing herself and the other prophets, Mandy told the leader, "You are more than welcome to stay with us for as long as you like. Let us dismiss this talk of leave-taking until you've seen everything we have to offer." There was a throaty note to her voice that told Carlos she was definitely anticipating adding the leader to her favorites.

"Prophets," the leader said, "do you mind if I speak with my people for a moment? Your kind offer is very persuasive." At least now he was behaving more rationally and less likely to displease Carlos's mistress.

Carlos focused all of his attention on Mandy, on soothing her irritation with gentle strokes of his hands, while the leader drew his people around him and spoke with them quietly.

Though she appeared outwardly calm, the tension radiating from Mandy's body let Carlos know she was nearing the end of her patience. "What is your decision, Jason?"

At hearing the name, Carlos recalled Jen and Mark describing the leader—Jason—and his group to Mandy early that morning. Carlos hadn't cared enough about the man to note his name at the time, but now his odd behavior made him stand out. Jason.

"We'll stay indefinitely, of course," Jason said.

Carlos could feel the tension seep out of Mandy's body. "Very well. Everyone may leave—except you," she said to Jason. "And my pretties, of course." Mandy patted the shoulder of the man on the other side of the chair, spawning another spike of jealousy in Carlos. At least she hadn't sent him away with the others.

"Why is that stringy little thing still here? Send her away." The annoyance sharpening Mandy's otherwise velvety tone drew Carlos's attention back to Jason. To Carlos's surprise, Jason wasn't alone.

A petite young woman with extremely red hair, extremely pale skin, and quite a few freckles, stood by Jason's side, holding his hand. A large German Shepherd sat on her other side.

Jason's eyes bulged. "Oh…great Prophet…she's harmless, and

she's only comfortable when I'm around. Besides, you can say anything around her and she won't hear a word."

Carlos frowned. Did Jason mean that the little red-haired woman was deaf? He studied her, intrigued. Something about her reminded him of his sister. It wasn't that they shared any resemblance aside from both being small and female, but it was as though their slight stature combined with an almost visible inner strength made them the same in a way beyond mere physical appearance.

Suddenly, Mandy stood and flung Carlos's and the other man's hands off her. Carlos felt a sharp sting of shame. She didn't want him touching her. He'd failed her. He hung his head, filled with self-loathing, and racked his brain for some way to prove to his mistress that he was worthy.

"I said, send her away. If you refuse, my pretties will kill her." Mandy motioned for Carlos and the other man to attack the red-haired woman.

This. This was what Carlos had been hoping for—a sign of what might please his mistress. Eagerly, he drew the long-bladed knife that he always stowed in the back waistband of his pants when he was on duty as one of Mandy's chosen pretties and prowled toward the little woman.

"Over my dead fucking body," Jason said in chorus with a growl from the German Shepherd. Faster than Carlos had thought possible, Jason drew a pistol from the holster on his hip and aimed it at Mandy.

"Jason, wait!" the woman shrieked. "What if—"

Hearing her voice made Carlos feel a little regretful about what he was about to do, but the joy he was sure to feel in knowing he'd pleased his mistress washed it away. He always felt joy in carrying out her will, whether it meant hurting or even killing others, or simply giving her pleasure. Carlos pushed any lingering doubt out of his mind and continued on toward his target.

He was so close, almost within his blade's reach, when the crack of gunfire resounded within the temple.

He froze, then spun around to watch Mandy's body collapse in a massive heap of limp, fatty flesh. There was a moment of utter confusion, when his brain was firing competing signals in response to her death—horror and elation, loss and relief—before he was filled with wave after wave of uncontainable rage. If he didn't find a way to expel it, he was sure he would explode from the sheer force of the emotion.

The things she'd done…the things she'd made him do, and not just pleasing her or hurting and killing strangers.

She—her man, Cole—had killed his brother.

They'd made him shoot Vanessa, his beloved sister.

Mandy and Cole had torn his emotions, his free will, away from him.

Mandy had destroyed his soul.

With a howl, Carlos launched himself at Mandy's lifeless body. The moment the long, dangerously sharp blade of his knife sank into her soft flesh, he felt a much needed emotional release. The hatred and rage flowed out of him through his knife, seeping into her. But it wasn't enough.

Withdrawing the knife, Carlos flexed his muscles to stab deeper. Harder. He did it again.

And again.

And again.

Until, finally, he was free.

This concludes the third installment of *The Ending Beginnings*. Carlos, Mandy, and Vanessa are also supporting characters throughout The Ending Series: (1) *After The Ending,* (2) *Into The Fire*, and (3) *Out Of The Ashes* (August 2014).

JAKE

VOLUME FOUR

1

Jake hunched over a small dining room table, his head resting in his hands. His house was too quiet. He'd been sitting there for hours, oblivious to the sound of the incessant tapping of his foot against the hardwood floor. Not even his churning stomach distracted him from his festering thoughts, burdened with indecision and doubt.

Lifting his head, Jake scanned the front of the house, uncertain how it had come to this—him up in the middle of the night with a feeling of dread looming over him…dread that he would make the wrong decision…a decision he might regret for the rest of his life.

The house was dark and quiet, a combination Jake would have welcomed a few days ago but was now unsettling. The bluish haze of dawn filtered in through the barely cracked blinds, casting shadows through the small, conjoined kitchen to his right that was still in disarray from him rushing around over the last 48 hours. The adjacent living room to his left was stark, and with the exception of the twinkling, rainbow lights on the Christmas tree in the furthest corner, it looked like it had been forgotten. There was no noise save for the sound of his own breathing and the occasional creak of the house settling. For the first time, Jake *felt* utterly alone.

How many hours had he been sitting there, wasting time? According to the glowing, red numbers on the microwave above the old, tan stove, more than four hours had passed since he'd sat down to think. Four hours, and he still wasn't sure what to do.

Jake shook his head, dispelling the urge to close his eyes and sleep. Why hadn't the damn doctor returned his calls? Hadn't he been clear with the receptionist? And he'd left several voicemails in the last 24 hours alone. It had been four days since Dr. Bishop told them Becca's illness was a simple flu that needed to run its course, four days since he'd prescribed ample rest and copious amounts of fluids, and in those four days, Becca had only worsened. She'd become sleep deprived and delusional and had lost her appetite…she was completely convinced her vivid dreams of blood and death and torture were real.

It wasn't the goddamn flu, or a simple fever…his sister was losing her mind.

The longer Jake sat there, the more exhausted he became, and he struggled to stay focused. Straightening, he scrubbed his hands over his face and stared at the cordless phone in its cradle on the tile counter beside the refrigerator. With the doctor nonresponsive and his sister's hysterical pleas to avoid the hospital at all costs, Jake could only think of one other possibility:

Gabe, Jake's best friend. He knew people, and if there was ever a time to call in a favor, now—when Jake felt more desperate than ever—was that time.

Jake rose from his chair, its legs scraping against the worn hardwood as he scooted it back. Muscles feeling leaden and sluggish, he took two steps toward the phone. He reached for the receiver, pressed TALK, brought the cool plastic to his ear, and paused. There was no dial tone.

Hanging up, he tried again. Still nothing.

Frustrated, Jake hung up the phone and took a few wavering

steps into the living room toward the L-shaped sectional situated beneath the picture window. Becca's purse was on the arm of the sofa, and he hoped her cell phone was inside.

He dumped the contents of his sister's purse onto the couch cushion. A pink-cased cell phone, among an array of other items, landed on the worn leather with a soft plop. Jake paid little attention to the contents rolling in between the cushions, instead fumbling to turn on the phone.

Luckily, the cell illuminated to life, and a picture of Cooper, their Husky, lying on his back with his tongue hanging from his open mouth, filled the screen. Impatiently, Jake scanned through the icons, searching for the phone function. Finally finding it, he typed in Gabe's cell number. There was a reason Jake didn't have a cell phone—they were expensive, easy to break, and after shattering one and losing another, he'd decided they weren't all that important.

With a deep, controlled inhale, Jake pressed CALL and waited with bated breath for his friend to answer.

Gabe had been distant since losing his little sister, Lizzy. Jake hadn't spoken to him in months, not since Gabe had last come over for Becca's birthday dinner. Jake had walked in the front door after a long day of wrenching on trucks over at the fire station to find Gabe sitting at the dining room table, drinking a beer and chopping tomatoes. As usual, Becca had been chatting his ear off and hounding him for whatever life updates he would surrender. Gabe had filled them in on his non-existent love life and the mysterious, female doctor friend he'd made at work.

She was the reason Jake was trying to reach Gabe—Jake just hoped she was still around.

"Come on," he mouthed, tapping his index finger against the back of the phone. He hoped to God that Gabe was still a morning person, though it *was* early, even for him. Jake wondered if the guy ever regretted working for the military; the confidentiality around his contracted research projects at Peterson Air Force Base made him seem illusive, even to Jake, who was more like family than just a friend.

Jake was about to hang up when Gabe finally answered. "Becca?" His friend's voice rang with surprise and more than a hint of worry. "Is everything okay?"

Hesitating, Jake steeled himself before answering. Articulating the severity of the situation proved more difficult than he'd thought it would be. "It's me."

There was a heavy silence before Gabe said, "What's wrong?"

A mixture of relief and fear made it difficult for Jake to speak, and he had to clear his throat in order to get the words out. "She's really sick."

"What do you mean, *sick*? Sick *how*?"

Pushing Becca's purse clutter to one side of the couch, Jake sat down, some of the items sliding into the impression around him. He took a deep, shaking breath and scrubbed his three-day-old beard, fighting to stay awake. "The doctor said it was just the flu, but it's—it's different. She's seeing things…she swears they're real." Jake paused, not wanting to scare Gabe, but his own fear outweighed his concern. "I can't get ahold of the doctor, and Becca freaks out when I try to take her to the hospital." Jake cleared his throat again, wishing he could crawl out of the dark hole he felt himself falling into. Gabe might be his only hope. "Would that doctor friend of yours be able to see her? Or, do you know anyone else who might be able to help—"

A loud crash and angry growl rumbled through the phone.

"Gabe?" Jake asked carefully. "Everything okay?"

"No, it's not," he breathed. Rustling preceded the sound of Gabe's ragged breathing.

Jake frowned. Was Gabe running? "I didn't mean to scare you, man. I just…I didn't know who else—"

"This wasn't supposed to—I'll be there as soon as I can." Without another word, Gabe disconnected the call, leaving Jake to stare at the screen until it dimmed.

He wasn't sure what had just happened. He'd expected Gabe to be worried about Becca—she was like a sister to him—but there'd been something off in his voice.

Leaning back against the couch, Jake cringed. The growing soreness in his neck and shoulders was making it increasingly difficult to move. He wanted to stretch out on the longer portion of the sectional that backed up to the entry, pull the folded blanket hanging on the back over himself, and fall asleep. But that would require him to move. Postponing any movement, Jake remained where he was, staring into the shadows around the living room.

After experiencing a childhood he would rather forget and spending his young adulthood getting into trouble, Jake had finally manned up, started taking proper care of his sister, and bought them a place to call home. It was small and a fixer-upper, but it was theirs all the same. In the year and a half that they'd lived there, he'd felt more content than ever before, happy even. Taking a job as a mechanic at the Colorado Springs Fire Department provided him a steady income and routine, something he hadn't realized he'd really wanted until recently.

Jake eyed the antique desk pushed up against the opposite wall. It was cluttered with loose papers and notepads, and Becca's medical textbooks were stacked to one side. She was happier, too—she could work on her sculptures and go to nursing school. They didn't have to depend on other people anymore.

Jake looked down the hallway. The light beneath her door had been on all night, but not even the slightest noise had come from her room for hours. Cooper's belly rose and fell with each breath as he slept soundly outside her door. Jake hoped Becca was finally asleep too.

Exhaling, he leaned back and stared up at the popcorn ceiling. His heart constricted as he grappled with the possibility that his sister might never be the same carefree, whirlwind of a woman he'd been devoted to his entire life. He couldn't help but wonder if what was happening to her was some suppressed reaction to

Lizzy's death a few years back. Lizzy and Becca had been best friends from the moment they'd met—the very day Jake and Becca had moved in with Gabe and Lizzy's family, the McLaughlins—until the day Lizzy lost her battle with leukemia. Jake also considered that what was happening to Becca might have something to do with their mom. Jake hated that Becca had been the one to find her dead of a drug overdose. He should've forced her to talk to someone about it, but then again, he should've done a lot of things differently.

As Jake's eyelids grew heavier and exhaustion made his mind even more useless, he let his thoughts drift into oblivion. Despite it all, at least he felt a little better knowing that Gabe was on his way. *He* would be able to help.

2

Pounding.

An incessant pounding stirred Jake from a deep sleep. Someone was pounding on the front door.

"Jake." It sounded like Gabe's voice, muffled by the door. "Open up." There was more pounding, followed by another, "Jake, open up!"

Cooper rose from his curled position outside of Becca's room and scurried over to the front door, his tail wagging languidly as he sniffed the wood like he could smell Gabe from the other side. The Husky whimpered excitedly.

"When are you gonna learn how to open the door, huh?" Jake asked his dog dryly.

Cooper cocked his head to the side. His tail wagged a bit more enthusiastically, but as expected, he didn't open the door.

With a groan, Jake stretched before he climbed to his feet, his body protesting every movement. Although he was fully dressed in gray sweatpants and a navy blue, long-sleeved shirt, a chill raked over his body, a dizzy spell quickly following as he straightened.

The pounding at the door continued. "Jake, everything alright in there?"

"Yeah," he grumbled and shuffled over to the entry. He was feeling worse than before he'd fallen asleep. Unlocking the deadbolt, Jake slowly opened the door. He was temporarily blinded by the morning sunlight gleaming off the snow-covered yard.

Gabe strode purposefully into the house, looking haggard. His eyes scanned the living room as he reached down, absently petting Cooper, then focused on Jake. "You look like shit." As usual, Gabe didn't waste any time with pleasantries.

"So do you," Jake retorted and closed the door behind his friend. Regardless of his appearance, relief nudged its way into his tense shoulders. He instantly felt better knowing Gabe was there to help.

"So," Gabe said, letting the impending question linger. "How is she?" He ran his hands through loose, blond hair that was longer than Jake had ever seen it, and when he leaned against the back of the couch, he let out a heavy sigh.

"She's asleep, I think…I didn't tell her you were coming," Jake admitted. His friend's harried appearance made him feel guilty that he'd caused the guy so much panic and worry. "I should've called you sooner," he said in apology.

Gabe rubbed the back of his neck and glanced at Becca's bedroom door. "You might change your mind about that."

"Why?"

"Never mind," Gabe rasped as he exhaled. "You should probably wake her up."

Jake noticed that Gabe's collared shirt looked too rumpled to have been freshly donned. "When was the last time you got any sleep?"

Gabe shook his head and shoved his hands into his pockets. "It's been a while. You?"

Jake's looked at the clock on the microwave. Three hours had passed since their phone call. "I dozed off while I was waiting for you."

"Yeah, uh…sorry about that. Something came up." Gabe's eyes darted away from Jake's.

"Are you alright, man?" Jake asked.

"I've just got a lot on my mind." Gabe cleared his throat. "We should probably hurry."

Jake nodded, not wanting to waste any more time, and lumbered toward his sister's room. He hesitated and turned back to Gabe. "What's our plan? I need to tell her *something*."

Gabe's eyebrows drew together, and he shook his head. "I don't know, I—I've got to ask her a question, then we'll know what we need to do."

Sleep had made Jake's muscles ache more acutely, and he was too distracted by the void settling inside him to ask questions or argue. He closed the distance to his sister's bedroom door, fighting to stay upright as a wave of nausea nearly knocked him on his ass. He braced himself against the wall in the dimly lit hallway and took a long, deep, steadying breath.

"You alright?" Gabe asked skeptically.

Jake nodded. "Becca," he said quietly through her door. He rapped his knuckles lightly on the hollow wood. She didn't answer, and there was no noise to indicate movement inside her room. He knocked again, more loudly this time, the simple movement painful. "Becca."

Fierce concern flared to life when she remained silent. "Becca," he nearly yelled and reached for the doorknob. Hearing a stifled sob on the other side, he paused.

After a long second, the door creaked open. Stale, slightly sour air drifted toward him, making his stomach churn. His sister stood in the doorway, ghost-like in her nightgown. No matter what they'd been through over the past few days, nothing prepared him for what he saw staring back at him.

Her usually striking violet eyes were dull and gray, and dark circles surrounded them. Her tanned features were ashen, and her once round cheeks seemed sunken. Seeing her like this, a haunting shadow of herself, was heart wrenching.

Her desk lamp illuminated the room behind her. Everything was in disarray; her bed was unmade, tissues covering the balled-up blankets and scattered around the carpet surrounding it. Medical text books were strewn out on her side table and all over the floor.

"Morning," she rasped. Although a weak smile spread across her lips, Jake honed in on her red, swollen eyes and the stray wisps of damp, dark brown hair matted to the sides of her face.

Reaching out, he took her hand in his and was pleasantly surprised to notice how cool her skin felt. "Your fever's gone?" He put the back of his other hand to her forehead. Becca was small compared to him, only around five feet six inches, but she seemed smaller and weaker than he was used to.

"I think so."

Jake smiled at her. "That's good."

"I don't feel sick anymore," she said quietly. "At least not that kind of sick." Becca's eyes blurred with unshed tears as she searched her brother's face for something.

His momentary relief dwindled. "But you're still having the dreams?"

A tear slid down her cheek. "They're not dreams, Jake." Her voice was only a whisper. "They're real…they're going to happen. I don't know how to explain it. I can just…*feel* it."

Involuntarily, Jake winced. A sharp pain lanced through his back.

Gabe cleared his throat in the kitchen or possibly living room, and Jake didn't miss the way Becca's eyes widened, fear filling their violet-gray depths.

"Is Gabe here?"

Jake nodded, wincing again as another pain shot through his temple.

"It's happening," she said. She straightened and wiped the rogue tear from her cheek.

"What?" Jake could barely register what she was saying. "What's happening?" He exhaled, trying to expel the pain pervading his body. "Come on, he's waiting." He tugged at her hand gently. "We're going to see if he can help you."

Jake thought he saw Becca cringe before she shook her head.

He didn't want to force her, but he was running out of patience. "Don't you think it's at least worth a shot?"

"He can't help me."

The certainty in her voice disturbed him, and another wave of chills made him shudder. "You don't know that, Becca," he said, his eyes pleading. "Please." He glanced toward the living room. "Let him at least try."

After a moment's consideration, Becca took her brother's outstretched hand. "No one can help," she muttered, and her emotionless surrender nearly broke his heart.

As they moved slowly into the living room, Jake tightened his hold on her hand but said nothing. The old, hardwood floor protested with a creak beneath Jake's heavy footsteps, while Becca's rubber-soled slippers dragged sluggishly across the scuffed oak.

"Wait," she said, her voice still a raspy whisper. Becca pulled Jake toward her and peered up at him, brow furrowed. "I need to tell you something, Jake. It's important."

He eyed her nervously, waiting.

"There's something you—"

A crash came from the kitchen.

Jake glanced into the living room, where he expected to see Gabe, only he wasn't there. "Just a sec," he said and squeezed her hand reassuringly as he turned toward the living room. But before he could encourage her forward again, Becca stumbled into him and wrapped her arms around his neck.

"I love you," she croaked. "You're the best brother in the whole world."

At her words, a strange sense of sorrow filled him, and Jake felt an emptiness he didn't understand. He could feel her trembling, and he wrapped his arms around her protectively. "I love you, too."

Becca took a long, uneven breath before she pulled away from him, hesitant. Her tear-streaked face was just as composed as before, but her violet irises were suddenly brighter, burning with intensity. Something about the look in her eyes brought him a sense of inexplicable peace amidst an impending disquiet, and everything inside him stilled; he felt like he was standing in the eye of a storm.

"Becca, I'm—"

The front door was flung open. "Your ten minutes are up," a gruff voice said, and Cooper's angry barking immediately followed.

"I need more time," Gabe said from the kitchen.

Jake stepped into the living room, wondering who the hell had the nerve to barge into his house.

Gabe was standing by the dining room table, his chest heaving as he pointed at an armed soldier who was standing in the front doorway. "Wait outside!"

"What the hell's going on?" Jake asked. His eyes darted between Gabe and the soldier.

Becca squeezed his hand again. "It's alright, Jake. This is supposed to happen," she said.

Gabe turned to Jake and Becca, his eyebrows rising perceptibly as he took in Becca's mussed hair and wrinkled, white nightgown. "What's supposed to 'happen'?" he asked, flashing a warning glare at the soldier before refocusing on his friends. "What is it, Becca? What did you see?"

Jake didn't like the urgency and what sounded like comprehension in his friend's tone. He also didn't like the way Gabe's pale blue eyes zeroed in on Becca, the two of them seeming to have a silent, private exchange.

Adrenalin pumping through him, Jake scowled at the soldier

standing just inside the doorway, glaring at them. "What the hell's going on? Why is he here?"

Gabe ignored him. "Becca," he said. "I'm going to ask you something, and I need you to think carefully before you answer." His eyes darted to Jake and then back to her. "These dreams… you're sure they're more than that?"

"You know they are," she said sadly.

Jake's eyes shifted between them. "What am I missing?" He could feel sweat beading on the back of his neck, and his heart rate quickened. He grabbed onto the back of the couch, trying to hold himself up. "What the hell—"

Two more soldiers, carrying assault rifles at the ready, rushed into the house, bypassing Gabe completely when he tried to get in front of them. Stunned by the fact that there were three men with loaded guns in his home, Jake barely registered his sister heading into the kitchen or Cooper getting shoved outside by Gabe.

"You were supposed to *wait outside*," Gabe seethed as he shut the front door and glowered around at the three soldiers.

They stopped in front of Jake, who was barely holding himself up at the end of the couch.

"What are they doing in my house, Gabe?" Jake asked through gritted teeth. This was not what he needed right now. What he needed was to pass out for a day or two, not to have three armed soldiers stomping around his home, menacing rifles in their hands.

A young, freckle-faced soldier took a step closer to Jake. "Is he the one we came for?"

Had he been feeling even an ounce better, Jake would've had to fight the urge to rip the rifle out of the man's grasp despite the consequences. Instead, he scowled at Gabe.

"Dr. McLaughlin?" the soldier prompted, his eyes still zeroed in on Jake. "Is this the one we came for?" The young soldier's eyes narrowed as he appraised Jake.

"No," Becca said as she reappeared from the kitchen. "It's me." Her voice was small and detached.

"Becca," Jake growled in warning, taking a step toward her.

"She's the one," Gabe confirmed.

Jake's eyes shot to Gabe, whose features were strained in discomfort. "What the hell are they talking about?" Jake stepped in front of his sister, facing his unwelcome guests. "Get out," he ordered, his gaze pinning the closest soldier in place. His head began to spin, and his nausea worsened, his mouth watering and his muscles weakening by the second. "Gabe, get them out of my fucking house!"

The three soldiers took a step closer to Jake, their hands audibly tightening around their rifles.

"You have to let us take her," Gabe said, meeting Jake's judging glare. "She's—it's protocol."

"Fuck your protocol!" Jake backed up, his mind reeling as he tried to formulate a plan. "You're not taking her anywhere…"

"What other choice do you have, Jake?" Gabe nearly shouted. "Look at her…and look at you." He pointed between Jake and Becca. "You heard what she said—what she's *seen*. She needs help. *I* can help her." Gabe's eyes were pleading, but as much as Jake wanted to trust his oldest friend, the weapons now aimed at him were difficult to ignore. "There's nothing else you can do for her," Gabe said. "You can barely even stand. You're sick, Jake. You need to rest. Let me take care of Becca. I'll protect her until… I'll protect her. I promise."

Jake felt Becca's cool, delicate hand wrap around his wrist. "Jake," she said faintly. With a sudden, grave sense of panic, he turned. His sister stood beside him, her eyes imploring and filled with apology.

His mouth went dry as he recognized her resolve to do something irrational, and he suddenly felt desperate. "Gabe promised they won't hurt you." Jake didn't even know what he was saying. He didn't trust the soldiers, but whatever Becca was going to do was worse; he could see it in the remorseful gleam that lit her eyes.

Becca blinked up at him as if it were just the two of them in the room—no cursing Gabe or barking dog outside, no guns loaded, ready and waiting, and no soldiers inching their way closer to them. Her lips parted into a tight smile, and she pulled her hands out from behind her back.

Her fingers were wrapped tightly around the handle of a long, silver kitchen knife.

Jake was stunned—unable to think or move.

Without hesitation, she thrust the blade into her abdomen, angling it up toward her heart. She wobbled a moment, Jake staring at her dumbly before she fell into a crumpled heap on the floor. A mixture of pain and relief twisted her features.

"Becca!" Jake shouted, horrified. He fell to his knees beside his sister's shaking body; tears flooded his eyes, and panic suffused his thoughts. "Gabe, call someone! Call for help!" The amount of blood soaking through her white gown only heightened his panic. "Why would you—" His hands hovered around the knife's handle, but he left it in, afraid he'd lose her more quickly if he removed it. "What the hell were you thinking, Bec?" he said. He watched in a paralyzing shock as the life quickly faded from his sister's eyes. His blood turned cold as her skin paled.

The seconds felt like minutes as it grew more difficult for Becca to swallow. "Jake," she gurgled, her teeth colored with blood.

He glanced over his shoulder at Gabe who was frozen in terror. "Do something!"

"J-Jake," Becca said again.

"Hold on, Becca," he pleaded, wiping her tear-dampened hair from her face. "Hold on." He braced his forehead against hers. "Why the hell did you do that?" He tried to be strong, to keep himself together, but there was too much blood…so much blood. She was…she was *dying*.

Jake couldn't breathe. He couldn't think. Trying to swallow the lump in his throat, he fought with reality. His little sister would *not* die in his arms!

Squeezing her eyes shut, Becca seemed to be summoning what remained of her strength. "You need…to know…" She choked and swallowed thickly. "She'll…she'll die because of you…"

Jake shook his head, his eyes flooded with tears. "What?" There was a commotion behind him, but he couldn't look away from Becca. "You're not making any sense."

"The woman," she continued. "The woman…with the black hair…and teal eyes…" She swallowed again with more difficulty and tried to smile. "You'll…you'll save her, Jake…"

His head felt like it was splitting in two.

Becca's smile fell. "But she'll die…because…of you…" Her eyes trained on his wild, amber ones.

"Becca, you're not—"

"You have to leave…you have to," she muttered stubbornly, her eyes filled with tears. "Promise me…"As she struggled to say her last words, her trembling lessened and her choking ceased.

Jake dropped his forehead to hers again, his body quaking with quiet sobs as he clenched the blood-stained fabric of her nightgown in his hands, his arms tight around her. "No," he pleaded. "Please no." He pushed her hair away from her face. "Becca?"

Jake cried out, his fury and pain filling the room. Putting his large, burning palm over her bloodied face, Jake gently closed his sister's vacant eyes.

Behind him, Gabe was shouting, and Cooper was barking incessantly from outside.

Jake squeezed his eyes shut, trying to block out the noise. "Get out," he begged, sick to his stomach with grief as he cried into his sister's hair. The faint scent of her peach shampoo lingered, only solidifying his despair.

Heavy footsteps grew nearer.

"Jake, I'm—" But whatever else Gabe said was lost on him.

There was an explosion of pain and then everything went black.

3

The warm August Indiana breeze brushed across his face, and the scent of dried grass and summertime filled his nose. Jake had grown used to the smell of the country, and he didn't want to leave.

Eleven years old with a head of spikey, brown hair, he stood in front of Joe, who was leaning against a rusted pickup parked beside a dilapidated garage. They'd spent the entire summer working on muscle cars, lawnmowers, and tractors together—an entire summer of greasy breakfasts, fence repairs, and iced tea breaks on the front porch of the farmhouse.

"Are you listening to me, son?" Joe said, the old man's green eyes crinkled easily at the corners, gleaming with emotion. Even the wrinkles around his mouth quivered as he tried to keep his voice level and his expression neutral. "I can't take care of you kids anymore...they've found you a better home, a family for you to live with. They've got kids your own age."

Jake shook his head. "But we want to stay with you, Joe." He searched the old man's face, hoping he'd change his mind. "We like it here. Becca's finally talking again, and—" Jake cleared his throat, the desperate, high pitch in his voice foreign to him.

"It's not right for a couple of kids to be living with an old hermit," Joe croaked. He swallowed thickly, his Adam's apple barely noticeable beneath the scruffy, loose skin of his neck. "We knew this day would come eventually, son. We knew this situation was only temporary."

"But—"

"Son," Joe said sternly. "They won't let you stay here, even if I felt I could take proper care of you." His face softened as a silent tear streamed down the boy's cheek. "You need schoolin'," he added quickly. "You need a family and kids your own age to be around." Joe stared down at his hands, absently turning the silver wedding band around his finger. "I won't be around for much longer, and then you'll be alone again."

Jake never cried. Not in the year since he and Becca had lived with Joe, their former neighbor who had become the father they'd never had. He hadn't cried from fear or sadness the day he and Becca found their mom dead. But now, the only adult in the world he'd ever truly cared about was sending them away. Years of loneliness and resentment bubbled up inside him, and he couldn't contain his emotions any longer. He let out a single, choked sob.

"Did you hear me, son?" Joe reached out and placed his hand on Jake's shoulder, squeezing it gently.

Jake nodded. Ashamed of himself for being so weak, he roughly wiped the tears from his eyes.

"It's okay to be sad, son." The old man took a step forward and leaned down.

When Jake looked back up at him, Joe's imploring eyes fixed on his.

"If I could have it any other way, I would...but it's just not right. Your sister's only five, she needs someone who can take proper care of her."

"I'm *taking care of her," Jake said, his chest heaving with each faltering breath.*

With a sympathetic smile, Joe cleared his throat. "I know you are." He patted the boy's shoulder. "You're doing a fine job, too, but, she needs a family. You *need a family."*

Across the yard, the farmhouse's screen door swung open, and Jake turned around to see his sister standing in the front doorway. She glanced around sleepily.

Using the sleeve of his shirt, Jake swiped the wetness from his cheeks again. He didn't want Becca to see him upset.

Joe bent down, his eyes full of suspicion. "Promise me you'll be good for the McLaughlin's, Jake. They're good people."

Too easily, Jake nodded, and the old man eyed him warily, all too familiar with the boy's protective instincts and innate distrust in people, no matter the blank expression blanketing his face.

"Promise me," Joe said evenly. "Promise me you'll give them a chance before you do something stupid...and remember your sister deserves a real family."

Jake nodded again.

"I want you to say it," he demanded. "Look at me, and promise."

"Jake?" Becca stepped out onto the porch, the screen door slamming shut behind her as she searched the dirt lot for him. Her dark hair was rumpled from her nap, and she was squinting into the sunlight. "Jake?"

"We're over here by the tractor, darlin'," Joe said gruffly, raising his hand with a single wave.

When Becca saw them, she slowly plodded over, her raggedy doll hanging from underneath her little arm, its limbs flopping with each step.

Unable to lie to the old man's face, and refusing to deny his sister the chance of having a family, Jake squeezed his eyes shut and quickly searched for a partial truth. Maybe Becca would like Colorado, and maybe she would like the McLaughlin family.

Reticent, Jake glanced up at Joe and nodded. "I"—his lips pressed together in a slight grimace—"I promise I'll give them a chance."

Joe's features relaxed. "Thank you, son." He reached his wrinkly, shaking hand into his pocket, pulling out his favorite pocket knife. "Here," he said, offering it to the eleven-year-old on his palm.

Jake's eyes widened, and he took a step closer, eyeing the knife Joe used for one reason or another every single day.

"I want you to have it," Joe said, inching his palm closer.

Jake could only stare at the closed knife, picturing the worn, wooden handle in Joe's shaky fingers as he cut through zip ties and used it to open boxes of car parts like Jake had seen him do over a hundred times. "But you've had it since the war," he said dumbly. "It's your favorite..."

Joe nodded. "That's why I want you to have it. It's a good knife. It might come in handy someday."

In awe, Jake reached for it. He'd never really received a gift before. Becca made him paper dolls and drew him pictures sometimes, but he'd never been given anything so important...so meaningful. So, Jake was surprised and his feelings hurt when Joe snatched it away.

Jake's wounded, brown eyes met Joe's scrutinizing green ones.

The old man straightened and hooked both thumbs around his suspenders. A playful grin tugged at his lips. "Now, don't get any crazy ideas with this, son. It's for protection...or if you find yourself in a sticky spot. Don't abuse it. Don't be careless."

Jake blinked rapidly and shook his head. "I—I won't."

Apparently satisfied, Joe proffered the knife once more, and timidly, Jake accepted it. The knife was warm from being in Joe's hand, the handle smooth from years of use.

Becca sidled up beside them. "What're you doing?" she asked as she glanced between them. She yawned and hugged her doll tighter against her.

"We're about to go finish up the small block," Joe said, rumpling her mussed hair. He turned and strode toward the garage. "Come on, the sun'll set soon."

Jake watched Becca follow Joe automatically, scuffing her untied tennis shoes in the gravel behind him. "Can I hold up that lamp thing again?"

"Only if you make me some of the sweet sun tea you're so good at brewing for me. It's gonna be a hot one tomorrow."

"Alright," she agreed. "But you have to save some for Jake this time."

Joe laughed. "You've got yourself a deal, darlin'."

Jake exhaled a steadying breath, stared once more at the knife, and shoved it deep into his pocket. His fingers rubbed the worn handle once more before letting go, and he followed the two of them inside the garage.

"Alright, time to get started," Joe announced, handing her the light to shine under the hood. "This ol' Ford is gonna purr when we're finished with her. Just you watch. She might even place at the fair."

"How do you know the car's a girl?" Becca asked, sounding equally fascinated and confused.

Jake couldn't help but smile. At least he'd always have his sister.

Jake woke with a splitting headache, vaguely aware of the smell of pine trees and the feel of the cold floor beneath him. He peeled his eyes open and immediately regretted it. Bright morning light filtered in through a window behind him, and his headache worsened as he lifted his head.

With quaking muscles, he struggled to his knees, squinting as he took in his surroundings. A pathetic Christmas tree was nestled against the wall to his left, the lights still aglow, and an antique secretary's desk was situated against the wall in front of him. It was his sister's desk.

He was lying on his living room floor.

Shaking the fog from his mind, Jake climbed to his feet. A

groan accompanied each stiff movement as his aching muscles stretched and flexed for the first time in what felt like days.

Ringing blared in his skull, and he rubbed his temples vigorously. "Jesus," he muttered. The noise turned grating as his mind started to focus, like nails on a chalkboard. It seemed to be emanating from the hallway. Just as Jake registered that it was probably Cooper shut inside one of the bedrooms, his curiosity and plan to let him out vanished.

Blood and vomit covered the floor. Covered *him*.

Becca.

A rainstorm of memories flooded his mind, drowning the heat from his body. He remembered the remorse in Becca's eyes and the way she'd hesitated to leave her room. An image of her lifeless body on the floor right where he was standing made his hands tremble, and it became difficult to breathe. Jake pivoted around, his eyes searching the living room frantically.

"Becca!" The weight of what had happened plummeted to the pit of his stomach, making him nauseous all over again. "Becca!" He hoped more than expected she would answer.

She—her body—was gone; she'd been on the floor, in his arms…dying. Now she was gone.

Jake ignored the shooting pains racking his body as he lunged to the front door and yanked it open. The brisk Rocky Mountain air assaulted his skin, and the sun glared off the snow, temporarily blinding him. Had there been any footsteps or tire tracks, they were long gone, hidden beneath the fresh, white blanket of winter. There were no military vehicles or soldiers waiting for him outside of his house, and other than the blood on the living room floor, there was no sign of Becca.

Slightly disoriented, Jake searched the rest of the house, flinging open doors and calling out for Gabe and Becca. He refused to believe events had happened as he remembered them.

Swinging the garage door open, Jake found his Jeep parked in the garage as usual. The backyard was desolate, just as it had been since the first snowfall, and the kitchen was just as he'd left it—glasses half-filled with water cluttered the tile countertop, and bowls of uneaten soup still filled the sink, the soup that Becca hadn't eaten.

Jake jogged through the living room and into the hall, flinging Becca's bedroom door open as he stepped through the threshold; it, too, was empty, as was the bathroom. Finally, he stopped in front of his own bedroom, the only shut door left in the house. Cooper whined from the other side.

Cracking the door open, Jake was promptly assailed by an excited Cooper, his paws digging into Jake's arms and chest. A stinky, wet tongue lapped at his face, and the sound of a happy tail thumped against the doorframe. Cooper whimpered and yelped, and although Jake was relieved his dog was unharmed, he couldn't share in his enthusiasm.

Jake stroked Cooper's head absently, wondering what exactly had happened and why Gabe would've taken his sister's body. Was it because she was sick? But Jake had been sick, too. Was it to get rid of the evidence? But there was still blood everywhere, and Jake was still alive…

An image of Becca's inscrutable expression the moment she'd opened her bedroom door haunted him. She'd known something he didn't…understood something he was ignorant of. Her features had been softened with acceptance…but acceptance of what? She couldn't have possibly known all of *that* would happen…

Any remaining hope that the memories had been a horrible dream quickly faded as the sting of reality set in, and Jake's pulse quickened. He nudged Cooper down to the floor and staggered back to the edge of the mattress just as his legs gave out. The burn of regret brought tears to his eyes, and the foul taste of misery made it difficult to swallow. He wasn't sure how long he sat there, lost…hopeless…grieving.

Becca had been trying to tell him something, but he hadn't listened. Her eyes had been set with a determination that would haunt him for the rest of his life, and he would never understand why.

Jake shook his head. He'd been too blinded by the false hope that he could fix her—by his mistaken belief in Gabe—to listen to what she was trying to say. If he hadn't called Gabe, none of this would've happened. Becca might still be sick, but at least she'd still be alive. What had he done? And what was he supposed to do now?

His eyes burned, and his heart ached. His stomach twisted into a painfully tight knot as reality hit him all over again. Becca was dead…she was *gone*. Jake groaned, the sound almost a whimper, as he ran both hands over his stubble-covered face. How had everything come to this?

Gabe, he remembered. He'd called Gabe because he'd trusted him. Gabe—those men—had been the reason she'd killed herself…it was *Gabe's* fault.

Jake clung to his rage, unwilling to let remorse break him down into a complete heap of despondency. Why would Gabe do this to them…to Becca? Why the hell had he brought soldiers and guns at all?

Jake stepped out of his room and into the hallway, unsure where his feet were taking him. He shuffled into the living room, peering around a space filled with painful memories. She was gone. Forever. "You son of a bitch!"

Cooper skirted out of Jake's path as Jake stormed back into his bedroom and switched on the light. Everything was just as it should be—his bed perfectly made, his end table with only a single book, *The Count of Monte Cristo*, a digital clock, and his wallet sitting on it, his laundry folded in the laundry basket at the foot of his bed…

A sloppily-written note was taped to the glass door of the old display case standing between the closet and the bed. The display case housed ammo, a shotgun and two pistols—weapons he could've used to protect his sister. Guilt sprouted anew as Jake stepped up to read the note.

Please don't do anything stupid, Jake. She's gone. If you're smart, you'll leave Colorado.

I'm sorry, brother.

-G

Jake rammed his fist through the glass door, the puncturing of his skin and the warmth of the blood a welcome distraction from his misery. Chockfull of purpose and unwilling to stop and think, Jake pulled his 12-gauge shotgun and two handguns from the cabinet and tossed them onto his bed. He needed to find Becca's body, needed to say goodbye…and he needed answers. He *needed* to find Gabe.

As Jake tossed boxes of ammunition onto his bed, his mind became saturated with poisonous memories of the past, memories that only hardened his resolve. He flashed back to the weekends spent at the shooting range with James and Gabe, the father and son who'd taken Jake and Becca in and treated them as part of their family. Gabe had come to Jake right before high school graduation, torn between a career in science and a career in law. He had trusted Jake to help him decide; he'd wanted his friend's help and advice.

The memories stung, and Jake fought the urge to smash something else.

Grabbing a small duffel bag from his closet, he filled it with all the ammunition he had. After zipping the bag shut, he barreled into the bathroom to clean the vomit and blood from his body. Pulling off his blood-stained shirt, Jake shrugged on a clean, long-sleeved thermal, a pair of jeans, and his work boots before he whistled for Cooper and headed for the garage.

Just as Jake reached for the door handle, he stopped, and his bags dropped to the floor with a thud. Turning around, he back-tracked to his sister's bedroom, once again stepping over the blood stain in the living room and continuing down the hall. Her bedroom door was still open from his frantic search, but this time, he stopped in the doorway and took a deep breath.

The room was a mess, exactly the way she'd left it. Her bed, situated in the corner where one white and one burgundy wall met, was disheveled—the pillows strewn and her white comforter balled up into a pile at the foot of it. Only a few of her books were actually in the bookcase beside her bed, and many of her clothes were scattered across the floor.

Chest tightening, Jake steeled himself and stepped into her room. He searched the wicker laundry basket for her favorite jeans, a few seconds later finding what he'd been searching for—the pocket knife he'd given to Becca the night of her prom—"for protection," he'd told her. He'd never asked for it back. He'd wanted her to keep it in case she would ever need it.

The thought that he'd let things get so bad made him sick. And every time an image of her violet eyes flashed in his mind, he wanted to hurt Gabe…wanted to hunt him down and *kill* him.

He squeezed the pocketknife tightly, thankful he'd not forgotten it, snatched a photo of him and Becca off her bulletin board, and headed out of the house.

4

Jake's Jeep rumbled to life in the garage, and when country music blared from his speakers, he felt an acute loneliness. His severe dislike of Becca's beloved twangy, depressing music didn't matter anymore. Part of him wanted to listen to it, to remember how Becca would sing along out-of-tune when one of her favorite Reba songs came on, and how she'd sing the same chorus over-and-over for days when one would get stuck in her head. The slightly torn beauty magazine lying haphazardly on the floor on the passenger side didn't help alleviate his encroaching loneliness either.

Cooper looked down at the magazine from his spot in the passenger seat and then back up and Jake. The Husky's fluffy tail thumped against the door a couple times, but the confused way Cooper looked at him made Jake wondered if the dog had any idea that his walking buddy was gone forever. When Cooper whimpered amidst the intermittent static and guitar strums coming through the speakers, Jake couldn't stand to listen to it a moment longer.

Reaching forward, Jake turned off the stereo and shifted the Wrangler into reverse. He backed out of the garage and circled the

1950s ranch house, trying not to dwell on Becca's snow-covered garden boxes on the back porch or the metal sculpture she'd been assembling outside the garage before the first snowfall.

He pulled out onto snow-dusted Highway 24, heading for Colorado Springs. If Jake hadn't been driving so hard and dangerously fast along the windy mountain road, he would have wondered why there were absolutely no other cars on the road and why very few of the homes had smoke coming from their chimneys, which was practically necessary in the dead of winter.

"You have to leave this place, Jake."

He shook his head, dispelling Becca's words. Of all things, why would she say that to him?

When Jake rounded the corner near the Main Street intersection, he eased his foot off the gas. On the left side of the road, a black Mercedes sedan was completely smashed against an F-250 pickup truck. While the truck, front wheels up on the curb, showed little damage, steam radiated from the sedan's steepled hood.

By the looks of it, the accident had happened only seconds before Jake had shown up. A woman climbed out of the Benz, staggering and clearly injured. Blood trickled from her nose and her right ear, and her head shook slowly as she took in the wreckage.

The truck driver jumped down from the F-250 a few seconds later. He had a bloody nose, but it was the ferocious expression on the man's face that was disconcerting.

"Keep driving," Jake told himself. He had his own shit to deal with. But as he watched the irate man storm toward the woman and reach out and strike her across the face, Jake slammed on the breaks.

"Shit." He killed the engine and opened the driver's side door. Fumbling to remove a pistol from the duffel on the backseat, Jake watched as the woman stumbled backward, shrieking. She cowered as the man stepped closer, gesturing emphatically and cursing so vehemently Jake could almost hear him amidst his hurried movement inside of the Jeep.

Fingers finding the cool metal of his pistol, Jake opened the door, climbed outside, and tucked his gun into the back of his jeans. Cooper whined from the passenger seat, and Jake looked him directly in the eyes. "Stay." Cooper whined again, but Jake closed the door and hurried toward the accident.

"Hey!" he called out, interrupting the man's shouted curses. Jake's boots crunched over several inches of snow as he broke into a jog, worried that if he didn't hurry the man would hit the sobbing woman again. "What the fuck's wrong with you, man?" He peeled his eyes away from the tatted-up bastard long enough to scan the woman's face and jogging suit for more blood.

The forty-something man righted himself from his looming position, his glare focusing on Jake and his mouth pulled into a snarl. "Mind your own business, asshole!" His face had a filmy sheen to it, and he pointed at Jake with his left index finger. "This is between me and this bitch who hit my truck."

Instead of minding his own business as suggested, Jake took a step forward. "Just keep your hands off her, and we won't have any problems."

The truck driver shook his head and laughed bitterly. "Alright," he said, scratching the back of his head before throwing both of his hands up in the air. "Alright, you win." The man turned on his heel and stomped back toward his truck.

"Asshole," Jake muttered, and he crouched down to the woman, who was quivering on the ground. "Are you alright, ma'am?" Her lips were chapped, her hair was greasy and matted in the back, and her clothes looked as if they hadn't been changed in days. Catching the unmistakable scent of vomit, Jake took a step backward.

Had she been driving drunk, and that was the cause of the crash? Or was she just sick?

Frowning, Jake extended his hand to the woman. "Can you stand up?"

She was muttering to herself, shooting furtive glances around as though she couldn't remember where she was or how she'd gotten there.

"Ma'am, can you understand me?" Jake worried that her sweat-covered skin and the black circles around her eyes were more than a concussion. "What's your name?"

"It's…I…um…"

"…this God damn, mother fucking—" Jake could hear the truck driver grumbling in his truck.

"Did either of you call the police?" Jake called out. He kept his eyes trained on the woman's dilated pupils. "She needs medical attention."

As if the woman suddenly noticed Jake for the first time, she focused on him, her bright blue eyes boring into his, and she shook her head. Like an egg cracking, the woman went from dazed, confused, and a little frightened to hysterical. "Oh my God!" She began screaming and lurched to her feet, scrambling in the direction of her car. She tripped, falling down in the snow. Crawling to her feet again, she resumed screaming, her shrieks turning to choking sobs and coughing spasms that forced her to her knees.

"Jesus, Lady," Jake mumbled. She clearly wasn't stable.

"This bitch nearly kills me with her fancy fucking car that she doesn't know how to drive," the truck driver bellowed from behind Jake. "Then you show up…"

Jake pivoted around to shut the guy up just as the driver hit him in the face with a baseball bat. Jake's jaw sang in acute, searing pain that spread up the side of his face as he spun and fell to the snow.

"You should have left it alone," the man grumbled.

With his head and vision pulsating, Jake reached for the pistol in his waistband with one hand and flipped himself over with the other…just in time for another head-splitting blow from the bat. A ringing sound filled his ears, and everything went black.

Seconds passed, or possibly minutes, and when Jake finally came to, it was just in time to register the click of his pistol's safety and the echo of a bullet discharging into the still morning. He felt a burning pain in his shoulder, and with another gunshot, an explosion of fire in his chest.

Jake lay motionless in the snow as everything around him swirled away to nothing—his vision fading in and out, his hearing tunneled. But the distant, blood-curdling screams were more disconcerting than Jake's awareness of his own impending death.

Paralyzed and numb from cold and blood loss, Jake stared up into the gray sky, focusing on Cooper's distant barking instead of the woman's ear-piercing screams. Although Jake didn't have the ability to fight back or flee, he did have the ability to regret getting out of his Jeep, for not wearing warmer clothes, and for not driving straight to Peterson.

Now Jake would never have answers…he'd never get to hurt Gabe the way Gabe had hurt him.

As the cold and darkness swallowed him, Jake cursed himself for a lot of things.

5

A dusting of something soft and cold stung Jake's cheeks, making his eyes flit open. Body aching from the cold, he strained to move and grimaced; his lips—nearly frozen—were cracked and stinging like a dozen paper cuts marred their surface. Muffled barking resounded in the distance, and stiffly, he sat up and turned to see Cooper's outline inside the Jeep, which was still parked on the side of the road. The dog pawed at the window impatiently, his gray and white fur almost glowing in the light of the street lamp above.

Remembering the wild-eyed truck driver—the gunshots…the pain—Jake straightened in a surge of panic. How the hell was he alive? His head craned around as he searched the darkness. The Mercedes was still parked haphazardly a few yards to his left. It was half-covered in a layer of snow that twinkled in the moonlight, and the hood was crushed like an aluminum can.

In a moment of clarity, Jake's heartbeat quickened, and his hands flew to his chest. He'd been shot, twice from what he remembered. Unzipping the front of his jacket, he reached inside, tentatively smoothing his hand over his thermal shirt as he gazed down. The fabric was crusted with dried blood, but other than a dull, internal aching, he didn't feel any pain. Probably because he was freezing to death, he thought. But as his fingers brushed over what felt like gravel beneath his shirt, he froze.

"What the—" He pulled up the hem of his shirt to get a look at his chest, and a small, roundish piece of metal fell into the snow on his lap. His fingers fumbled around in the frozen flakes for only a few seconds before he gave up, unable to feel anything anyway.

Absently, Jake's hand rubbed the planes of muscle on his chest, searching for a wound. Had he not been shot at all? Had he imagined the whole thing? That wasn't possible. The wrecked sedan to his left, and the blood crusting his shirt indicated otherwise.

He searched the fabric for a bullet hole, but after a few seconds gave up. He needed to get warm. Jake ventured to move his legs, palming his jaw with one hand as he remembered the truck driver hitting him with a baseball bat. He looked out at the snowy landscape, searching for his attacker, but the truck was gone.

What the hell had happened? He'd heard the gunshot, he'd *felt* the pain, and yet here he was, alive, and completely confused.

It was too cold to gauge how badly he was actually injured, and a quick scan of the area confirmed what he'd already expected—his gun was either covered somewhere under the snow, or it was gone.

Awkwardly, Jake climbed to his feet and stretched. He wiggled his toes, his worry increasing when he couldn't feel them.

Cooper started barking enthusiastically, and Jake felt a twinge of relief at seeing his four-legged friend apparently unharmed. He figured it didn't really matter what had happened during the hours he'd been unconscious, so long as he and Cooper were alive.

Shaking from the cold, he was about to turn and head for the Jeep when he noticed a mound in the snow beside the sedan's driver's side door. Jake remembered the poor woman's screams. He assumed her body lay beneath the snow, but enough snow had fallen that he couldn't tell for sure. Unwilling to tolerate the cold any longer, he headed for the Jeep, needing to defrost and to assess his wounds.

On feet he couldn't feel, Jake limped to the Jeep and yanked open the driver's side door. Cooper leaped to the ground and jumped up onto Jake, knocking him back on his heels.

"Hey, buddy," Jake said. Cooper's tongue was hot against his face and neck, and Jake struggled to keep them both upright; he couldn't help but wonder how many of his toes and fingers were frostbitten, but he lacked the energy to care and chuckled at the dog's excitement. He patted Cooper's furry head and lovingly tugged on his silken ears. "Sorry about that," he said, hating that the poor guy had been locked inside the Jeep for who knew how many hours. Jake wondered how it was possible that he was still alive if he'd been lying unconscious in the snow for just as long.

He sighed, dumbfounded. The last couple days had been so impossibly confusing and exhausting, he didn't bother trying to wrap his mind around it right now.

A gust of wind raked over his chilled body. "Alright," Jake grumbled, rubbing the dog's head once more before pointing to the trees lining the side of the road. "Go do your business."

Cooper needed no further commands and trotted off into the darkness.

It was a chore to climb into the Jeep, but even with his body numb and aching from the cold, Jake managed to lift himself inside and close the door. Thankfully, his keys were still in the ignition. He closed his eyes, grateful that the crazed truck driver had been smart enough not to come near his Jeep with Cooper closed up inside. That meant the rest of his guns were still in his bag in the backseat.

Jake reached for the key in the ignition, turned it, and felt a warming sense of relief when the engine roared to life, minutes passing before the heater warmed and his entire body began to sting and unthaw.

If the man hadn't shot Jake, what *had* happened? Had the

driver missed him somehow and the bullet only grazed him? Jake raised his hand to his jaw. It was still tender, but nothing felt broken. And his shoulder and chest *were* aching, if only slightly.

Whatever had happened, the truck driver was clearly crazy. He'd attempted to murder Jake and had probably taken the rest of his anger out on the poor woman.

Jake eyed the mound in the snow. Deep down he knew she was dead. Even if the truck driver hadn't beaten her to death, the cold on top of her wounds would have been enough to kill her. But the cold hadn't killed *him*, and nothing had been what it appeared since the moment Becca fell ill. He felt a nagging need to check on the woman, regardless of what he expected he would find.

Reaching to his duffel in the backseat, Jake winced as he withdrew the other pistol from the bag and checked it to make sure it was loaded. He slipped his hand between his seat and the door, feeling metal against his fingertips, and pulled out his four-cell Maglight. All he needed now, besides maybe a drink and some rest, was a better jacket, which he hoped he had in the back of the Jeep. With a resolute sigh, he opened the door and climbed out, leaving the heater on full blast.

The snow falling more steadily now, Jake hurried to the back of his Jeep as quickly as his tense body was able. He opened the tailgate and breathed a sigh of relief. His heavy, greasy work jacket lay in a heap behind the backseat. Body protesting, Jake shrugged his jacket on, closed the hatch, and headed toward the Mercedes.

The car's driver-side door was open, and the contents of the woman's purse were strewn out on the passenger seat.

Jake paused. A car seat was buckled in the back, and he felt a little bit worse. She had kids.

Crouching beside her body, Jake examined the portion of her face that was devoid of snow. She was battered, and if he could guess was the rest of her face looked like, she was probably beaten beyond recognition. Her body was curled in the fetal position; she'd died, cowering.

His hand tightened on the flashlight. Why the hell had the driver done this? What could the poor woman possibly have done for him to want to beat the life out of her? Jake took the woman's icy, blue-tinged wrist in his hand and checked it for a pulse. Just like he's assumed, there wasn't one.

Cooper trotted back from his exploration of the wooded area along the road, sniffing around the Benz and exploring the scene.

"Come here, Coop," Jake called, not comfortable with the dog sniffing around a dead body.

He glanced into the back of the sedan at the car seat belted in. He needed to contact the authorities—the woman's family needed to know what had happened to her. Standing, he quickly scanned through the rest of the car's interior with his flashlight. A cell phone lay amidst the contents of the woman's purse strewn out on the passenger seat. Snatching it up, he shoved it into his pocket and trudged back toward the Jeep.

As he passed the impression in the snow where he'd lain, Jake stopped. Curiosity made him want to find the object that had fallen from his shirt. He needed to *see* it. As he fumbled around in the slush, he felt something solid against his fingertips. Angling the light beam to the tiny object he held in his hand, Jake recoiled. It really *was* a bullet.

Stupefied that he *had* been shot yet had no wounds as far as he could tell, Jake examined the bullet. It just didn't make sense. Shoving it into the pocket of his jeans, he rose to his feet. "What the hell," he rasped and continued toward the Jeep, questions looping through his mind: How long had he been unconscious? How was he still alive?

What the hell was going on?

6

After holding his hands in front of the heater vents for a couple of minutes, Jake pulled the phone from his pocket and turned it on. The screen brightened, and a photo of a young girl—a toddler with blonde hair, pigtails, and a wide, toothy grin—illuminated the display. With a sigh, he looked at the stereo, surprised to see it was only 7:30. It felt like a year had passed since he'd woken up on the floor in his living room. Shaking his head, he dialed 911. The line rang, and Jake felt an unexpected sense of relief.

Gazing out at the road, he thought it strange that he hadn't seen any commuters, any cars at all actually, and that no one had stopped to check the accident for any injured people. As the phone continued to ring, his relief diminished. Why was no one answering?

Jake hung up and tried again. There was still no answer.

Dropping the phone into his lap, Jake weighed his options. He was exhausted and wanted the comfort of his home. Except…that wasn't exactly right. He wanted the comfort his home had once brought him, but Becca had died there, and it would be too disturbing to return now.

Jake rubbed the back of his neck and leaned his head back against the headrest. He could drive into town, to the hospital. He could get himself checked out and report what had happened before heading to Peterson. He'd been sick enough that it was probably a good idea for him to see a doctor anyway, and then someone would know they needed to come collect the woman's body and follow up with her family. He could at least do that much.

Pressing CALL again, Jake wedged the phone between his shoulder and his ear, using his right hand to put the Jeep in gear before pulling back onto the road. Cooper jumped into the backseat, letting out a heavy exhale as he curled up.

The phone continued to ring.

"Answer the damn phone," Jake grumbled as he took a right before pulling onto I-25. Aside from a few cars parked on the side of the road, the interstate was deserted.

Ring.

Exhausted and trying not to yell into the phone, Jake let out a deep breath and gritted his teeth, watching the road for any signs of life. Where the hell *was* everyone? Noticing a Civic parked in the middle of the interstate, Jake switched lanes. He eyed the Civic as he passed, the fogged-up windows making it so he couldn't see if anyone was inside. Something definitely wasn't right.

The phone resting against his ear continued to ring without an answer. "Pick up the damn phone! Jesus…" Jake tossed it onto the passenger seat. He was getting tired of everything being so damn difficult.

Slowing, he took the exit toward St. Francis Medical Center, the off ramp providing an ample view of Colorado Springs. The city that stretched out before him was glowing with lights and billboards as usual, but there was no movement—no evening traffic or holiday shoppers hustling down the sidewalks to get out of the snow. The city looked lifeless.

Jake eased into downtown and slowed the Jeep, creeping down

the street. A handful of sporadically parked vehicles cluttered the street; head lights illuminating the cars in front of them and the outlines of people unmoving inside.

Looking around more carefully, Jake noticed that the city was looted. Some storefront windows were smashed, garbage littered the gutters and sidewalks, and lights were flickering inside some of the shops while smoke curled out of others through the broken windows and open doors. A small group of people rushed down the sidewalk, bags hoisted over their shoulders and items piled in their arms, but Jake had the feeling those weren't gifts they were clinging to. They held tightly to one another, anxiously peering around as they dashed into an apartment building, out of sight… into safety.

Had a war started he hadn't heard about? Was Peterson under attack? Jake looked up into the sky, half expecting to see a comet trail or fighter planes or a purple, Gozilla-looking space monster trampling through the city.

Cooper jumped into the front seat, his ears perked forward and his head cocked to the side as he looked around.

Jake stopped in front of a drugstore. "I dunno, Coop…"

An older man, bundled in a down jacket and scarf, came jogging around the corner of the block.

"Hey," Jake called, rolling down his window.

The man kept jogging.

"Excuse me, sir!" he tried again.

The gray-haired man jumped, startled. His wild eyes met Jake's.

"What the hell happened?" Jake nodded curtly, his eyes skimming the street. The man looked like he might run away before answering, so he added, "I just got into town."

The old man scowled at him, incredulous. "Turn on your radio," was all he said, and then he continued jogging past the drugstore before he disappeared into the shadows.

As Jake started to roll up the window, he paused. The city was completely quiet. He'd been in Colorado Springs for work just the other day, and he'd taken Becca to the doctor right after that…how could so much have changed in so little time? Finishing rolling up the window, he wondered how long he'd been unconscious on his living room floor.

Tapping the phone's screen back to life, Jake squinted at the sudden brightness of the display before he could focus on the time and date. It was December 13, three days after he'd called Gabe, which meant he'd been lying on the floor of his house for two days and lying in the snow most of another.

Jake peered around, wondering what could've happened in a few days that would've resulted in this. Whatever it was, it was going to make his horrible week even worse. He needed to figure out what the hell was going on.

"Time to get out of here, Coop." Jake glanced around at what he could see of the city, still in disbelief that Colorado Springs, the military mecca and "best city to live in," had been eerily looted and nearly abandoned.

With clammy hands, he steered the Jeep around a few cars and continued crawling down the road. Feeling both eagerness and trepidation, Jake reached for the radio and turned it on.

Static. He scanned through one station after the other, finding nothing but static on every station.

7

As Jake focused on getting to the hospital only a few more blocks away, he pushed SEEK and let the stereo scan for a clear channel. Driving with caution, he slowed at red lights and stop signs, but didn't actually stop. There was no reason to.

Jake spotted a police car patrolling the street ahead of him and headed toward it. Just as he accelerated, a garbled voice broke up the static on the radio.

This is a looped recording.

Jake turned right onto a deserted residential street, momentarily forgetting about the police car as he pulled the Jeep to the side of the road and parked beneath a street lamp.

...we received this message from White House officials a few hours ago. The President is in lockdown in an underground location with her family and a few members of the Cabinet.

Idly, Jake stroked Cooper's thick, soft fur as the President's voice, calm but severe, emanated from the speakers.

Our country is at war. Humanity is at war, yet our enemy is not one we can fight openly. Our enemy has swept through every nation, attacking discreetly, killing indiscriminately. We lost thousands before we even knew we were under attack. Many have already fallen, and many more will fall. But we cannot give up the fight.

Over the past century, through technological achievements, we made our world smaller. We made the time it takes to communicate across oceans instantaneous, and the time it takes to travel those same routes nearly as fast. We made our world smaller, and in doing so, we sowed the seeds of our own destruction: a global pandemic.

I regret to tell you that as of midnight on the 10th of December, over eighty percent of the world's population has reported or is assumed dead. It is estimated that the death toll will continue to climb. This news is devastating, I know, but all is not lost.

Some of us are surviving. This is how we will fight our enemy—by not giving up, by being resilient and resourceful, by surviving. We are not a species that will go out quietly, so I task those of you who are still alive with one essential purpose: live.

Survive.

Thrive.

If you believe in a higher power, ask for guidance. If you don't, believe in your fellow man. You, the survivors, have the chance to start over, to build anew. Learn from our mistakes. Let the world remain big.

And most importantly, live.

God bless you, my beloved citizens of this great nation. God bless you, and goodnight.

There was another moment of static and then the garbled voice returned, repeating the same message.

A pandemic?

Becca had been sick. She'd seen things, more like she was losing her mind than dying of some sort of virus. He compared the Becca he grew up with—the fun, outgoing and outspoken sister he'd been taking care of his whole life—with the withdrawn, reflective recluse that had taken her own life at the end. Had she gone mad with some sort of fever? The truck driver who shot him had clearly lost his mind…and the woman in the Mercedes had reeked of vomit and filth. Fear bit at the back of Jake's neck making him shiver.

Pushing SEEK again, Jake hoped to get more answers; he hoped to hear something that would make more sense, something that would answer his questions.

There was only static on some stations and the same looped recording on a few others.

Tired of being a step behind, Jake pounded his fist against the dashboard. "Damn it!"

Looking up and out the window, he tried to gauge where he'd parked. He pulled back onto the road and noticed a ghostly figure appear from the shadows to the right of the Jeep. A person… walking slowly down the sidewalk in Jake's direction. Increasing his speed, Jake drove toward the figure, but instead of stopping to ask questions, he continued past. It was an old man, probably in his seventies, hobbling down the street in a hospital gown. All that accompanied the old man was an IV stand on wheels that kept getting caught up in the snow and bursts of white breath each time he rapidly exhaled.

"Shit." Jake was no longer convinced going to the hospital was an option, especially with eighty percent of the world's population dead or dying from a pandemic he knew nothing about. He tried to understand—to grasp the facts and ignore his reeling thoughts, afraid he'd lose focus if he allowed himself to consider the possibilities. He eyed the old man in his rearview mirror as he shuffled out of sight. There was no way Jake would chance getting stuck in a building filled with sick people.

And what about Gabe? He hadn't looked sick, at least not the same way the truck driver or Becca had. But maybe…

A stomach-turning realization washed over Jake. *He* had been sick. How much longer until *he* became crazed? Despite his uncertainties, indifference and exhaustion kept him calm. He needed rest if he was going to care what happened to him next.

The sound of a revving car engine startled him, and an old, red Cadillac sped around the corner ahead, sliding on a patch of ice before fishtailing. With a shattering crash, the horn of the car blared, and the front end crumpled against the trunk of an oak tree.

"Jesus!" Jake instinctively jumped out of the Jeep and froze. He clutched the side of the door, searching for movement inside of the Cadillac. Shrill screams came from the back of the car—a kid's scream. Wanting to take no further chances, Jake pulled his shotgun out of his duffel and snatched up his flashlight. After he checked to see if the shotgun was loaded, he approached the old car, Cooper trotting beside him.

Glancing down at the Husky, Jake held out his palm, commanding Cooper to stay while Jake continued to creep forward, the shotgun clutched in his hand as he peered into the front and then the back of the car. A small boy, about five years old, sat wailing in the backseat, his face and knee bloodied like they'd made contact during the crash. Aside from the blood and the tears streaming down his cheeks, it looked like his seatbelt had saved his life.

"It's alright, kid." Jake said, unsure how to calm a screaming child. He continued toward the driver's seat to find a man splayed out over the steering wheel, his face covered in blood. *He* wasn't wearing a seatbelt.

"Sir?" With his flashlight, Jake eyed the man's clothes the best he could. They appeared to be clean, no vomit stains, which Jake thought a good sign. Although he wasn't sure if the man was just stupid for speeding on an icy road, or careless for doing so with his kid in the car, Jake couldn't leave the boy in there or leave the father to die…assuming he was even still alive. "Sir, can you hear me?" Jake took the man's wrist in his hand to check for a pulse. It was weak, but it was there.

The boy was still screaming in the back.

"Son, it'll be okay," Jake said. "Sir," he started, unsure if the man could hear him at all, "I'm going to remove your son from the car. I want to make sure his injuries aren't worse than they look." Jake moved around to the other side of the Cadillac.

Resting the shotgun against the car's quarter panel and sticking his flashlight in his pocket, Jake opened the back door. Cooper, apparently unwilling to listen, nudged his way in, curious.

"Back, Coop." Jake unfastened the screaming kid from his restraints. His forehead was bleeding and his body trembling.

"What hurts?" Jake asked, unsure if trying to comfort the kid was a bad idea.

The little boy's body convulsed as he sniffled and choked on his own sobs, but in spite of his hysterics, he pointed to his head.

"Calm down, kid." Jake clicked his flashlight back on and quickly appraised the rest of the boy's body as the kid sat, helplessly staring over at his father, his feet dangling from the seat as he continued to sniffle. "I think you'll be alright." Looking back to the man up front, Jake wondered what to do with a screaming kid and an unconscious father.

Cooper squeezed his way in again, sniffing and nuzzling up to the boy. Since the kid's cries seemed to lessen with Cooper around, Jake left him with the boy while he grabbed the shotgun and returned to the front of the car. "Sir?"

Jake had no idea if the man would live even if he could find help, but he needed to try, for the kid's sake.

Jake spun around as he tried to figure out exactly where in town he was. He couldn't be more than a mile or so outside of downtown. He'd been distracted, lost in swirling thoughts, but he couldn't have gone too far off the main road. Regardless, the hospital was no longer an option.

Rubbing his hands over his face, he wondered how long it would take him to get to his work. The fire station he worked at was stocked with medical supplies, and one of the EMTs might even be able to help…if any of them were still alive.

As Jake turned back toward the Cadillac, the flashlight illuminated a sign, a corner of it mauled by the car. PINE SPRINGS

HOSPITAL. He scanned the yard behind the sign. A wrought iron fence stretched out around the perimeter, the main gate open and leading to a longish driveway where a two-story, brick building rose at the end.

Jake had never heard of Pine Springs Hospital. It looked small, but he hoped he would find someone inside who could at least help the kid.

"Daddy…" The kid began wailing again, Cooper's presence no longer curbing the boy's fear. "D…daddy…" Each cry was followed by hiccupping sobs.

Jake couldn't take the kid in with him, he'd only slow him down and distract him. But if the dad died, Jake was certain the kid would too.

Going around to the other side of the car again, Jake crouched in front of the boy. "Kid," he said softly. "Can you stop crying for a minute?"

The boy continued to wail, completely ignoring Jake. "Da… daddy…" He started coughing, but that only momentarily detoured his hysteria.

Jake pulled the kid into his arms and up against his chest. He patted his back uncomfortably. The gesture was foreign and felt contrived, but Jake couldn't leave the boy behind and alone in a looted city with sick people running around while he was sobbing —a beacon for danger.

"Shhh," he murmured as softly as he could. "It's alright." The kid took a few ragged, but wail-free breaths, and Jake hoped that meant he was calming down a bit.

Cooper whimpered at his feet, piquing the boy's interest, and he looked down to investigate.

"His name's Cooper," Jake offered, wondering if his only option was to leave Cooper outside to watch over the boy while he went into Pine Springs Hospital.

The Husky whimpered again, sitting on the snowy ground but inching his way closer to Jake…to the boy's outstretched palm.

"You like him, huh?" Jake asked the boy, thankful he was no longer sobbing.

The boy's features softened, and he nodded and sniffled as he continued to stare down at the dog.

"What's your name, kid?"

"Kyle," the boy said absently, and he leaned forward in Jake's hold.

Rising from his haunches, Cooper stepped closer, smelling Kyle's fingers before he began to lick the boy's hand. Although Cooper tended to like kids more than Jake did, he'd never seen the dog so interested in one before…unless the child had food.

Jake looked at the interior of the car. A bag was crumpled on the seat next to where the boy had been sitting, potato chips strewn all over the place.

"Hmmm." Jake looked back at Kyle who was smiling, despite his tears. "Chips are his favorite," he said dryly. "How did you know?"

Kyle continued to sniffle but watched Cooper continue to enthusiastically lick his fingers.

"Kyle," Jake cleared his throat. "You're daddy's sick and needs some medicine."

Leaving his hand outstretched, the boy peered back at Jake, his eyes wide with fear.

"I can help him," Jake said. "I can help your dad, but I need you to do something for me." Jake glanced at Cooper, who was patiently waiting beside him for a command. "I need to get a nurse or a doctor who can help him." When the boy said nothing, Jake continued, "We're going to go inside that building," he ventured tentatively, unsure how the kid would respond. "I'm going to find someone to help him, but you have to come with me."

Kyle started screaming again. "Nooo!"

"I need you to come with Cooper and me so we can keep you safe…I need you to watch over Coop for me, Kyle."

Kyle began wriggling in his arms, and Jake didn't have the

time to deal with that. "Okay," he said, setting the boy back down on the asphalt and watching him crawl back into the car. "Fine." He ran his hand over his face and sighed, frustration and nerves amplifying his exhaustion. "Fine." He looked down at Cooper, who was staring up at him.

"Coop, you're staying here with Kyle." Jake waited for the hair on the back of his neck to rise with alarm at the idea, but it didn't. He waited for his instincts to tell him he was being an idiot and should pack up his dog and get the hell out of there, but his inner voice was so distant, Jake ignored it.

"You have to stay with Cooper," Jake told Kyle. "And you have to stay in the car…and you have to stop crying." He didn't want the kid drawing unwanted attention while he was away. "Please, kid. You've gotta stop crying. Your daddy needs to rest, and you're going to wake him up by making so much noise. You want him to get better, don't you?"

Kyle looked between the seats at his dad, his chin quivering, but he seemed to be keeping it together.

"Okay, good." Jake stared at the hospital. An expansive lawn and oak trees surrounded what he could see, but the road was a straight shot to the main entrance. Most of the lights in the building were off, but a few still glowed. A good sign, Jake hoped.

He met Cooper's eyes, his tail swinging casually back and forth, and his head cocked to the side quizzically. Jake hoped that if Cooper ran into any trouble he'd come find him.

"Watch him, Coop." Jake leaned over and reclaimed the shotgun leaning against the Cadillac. "Alright, Kyle. You're in charge while I run inside. Stay in the car," he said firmly. "Watch over your dad."

The boy sniffed and looked up at him.

"I'll be right back."

Infuriatingly, Kyle started to cry again, and without wasting any more time, Jake went to the Jeep, shoved a few more rounds into his coat pockets, and jogged toward the hospital. He was going to find some help, and then he and Cooper were getting the hell out of there.

This concludes the fourth installment of *The Ending Beginnings.* Jake is also a supporting character throughout The Ending Series: (1) *After The Ending,* (2) *Into The Fire*, and (3) *Out Of The Ashes* (August 2014).

CLARA

VOLUME FIVE

1

Without taking her eyes from her book, Clara reached for her chocolate milk, which was sitting on the laminate cafeteria table beside her tattered backpack. Lips pursed around the straw and her feet bouncing with happy anticipation, she took two long pulls of the rich, cold liquid until her straw made a slurping sound, and she set the empty carton back down on the table. All of the other students were out in the quad, fussing about their homework or gushing about boys or complaining about the teachers they didn't like, but Clara had better things to do. She ignored the ceaseless giggling and chatter as it trickled in through the open cafeteria doors and lost herself in her book.

"It was very late; yet the little mermaid could not take her eyes from the ship, or from the beautiful prince." She read each line with more passion and longing than was probably natural for a thirteen-year-old girl, but she couldn't help it. Fairy tales...Prince Charming...happily ever afters...she loved it all. "He is certainly sailing above," she read softly. "He on whom my wishes depend, and in whose hands I should like to place the happiness of my life."

Clara thought about Patrick, about his dreamy black hair and his light brown eyes, which always seemed to be saying more than his words ever did.

She sighed and kept reading. "I will venture all for him, and to win an immortal soul..."

Clara smiled as she devoured line after line, every word resonating in her soul, giving her hope that there was another life out there, a life different from the one she had with her mom—a better, easier life.

After another sigh, she stretched her legs out under the table, wiggling her toes in her holey converse and crossing her legs at the ankles, and settled in for a few more pages before the bell rang, signaling the end of lunch.

"'But if you take away my voice,' said the little mermaid, 'what is left for me?' 'Your beautiful form,' said the witch. 'Your graceful walk and your expressive eyes. Surely with these you can enchain a man's heart.'"

Clara paused and wrinkled her nose. Your form? Your graceful walk? *That didn't seem right. It sounded too much like something her mom would say.*

With a shrug, she pushed her glasses up higher on the bridge of her nose and continued reading. The little mermaid was so passionate, so sure about the prince. Clara longed for the day when she felt that way for someone. Or rather, she longed for the day when someone *felt that way about* her...

Daydreams of Patrick flitted into her mind, and she closed her eyes, imagining what it would feel like to run her hand over his spikey hair. He seemed so mysterious. He was *popular and seemingly untouchable, so she guessed that had something to do with it. But there was also the way he looked at her sometimes, his gaze lingering a little too long and his mouth curving into that tiny smirk he seemed to reserve for her alone. Clara was pretty sure he thought about her...at least more than not at all.*

And there was that one time at the bus stop, when they'd been waiting under the awning to stay out of the rain. She could never forget the feeling of his soft skin, still tanned from a summer of baseball games played under the afternoon sun, as his arm had brushed against hers. Although she'd been freezing all day because she'd forgotten a coat, it had only taken that one moment, that single, fleeting contact, for her incessant shivers to seem completely worth it.

Clara giggled. Maybe Patrick was her soul mate, her happily ever after; he just didn't know it yet. But as quickly as the thought fluttered into her mind, it fluttered away.

"Men are pigs, Clara Bear." *Her mom's voice was grating in her mind.* "They're only as good as the size of their wallet." *Like sand in a windstorm, all of Clara's whimsical thoughts of* her *Prince Charming blew away. Her mom clearly didn't believe fairy tales, but then again, Clara often thought her mom was just an uneducated hussy. At least, that's what she'd heard other people say about her...when they weren't saying* worse *things.*

The older Clara was, the more she heard and the more she understood. Part of her knew thinking mean things about her own mom was wrong, but she couldn't help it. Eye rolling and hateful thoughts had become the norm for Clara when she was around her mom.

"Love is for blind fools, Clara Bear, and blind fools deserve whatever comes to them."

Clara wondered if her mom had ever been in love. From the sound of it, Clara thought probably not. She knew her own dad was nothing more than a handsome face passing through town; her mom had said as much herself.

Clara resituated herself on the bench of the lunch table. The sound of squeaky soles on the polished floor behind her drew her attention away from her book. Pushing her glasses up on the bridge of her nose, she looked over her shoulder at the cafeteria entrance. Patrick was heading her way.

"Hey," he said, stopping at the end of the cafeteria table.

"Um...hey." Clara smiled dumbly, her eyes darting to her

beat-up lunch pail, the same Care Bears one she'd been forced to use since elementary school. She shoved it into her backpack.

"You working on Mrs. Larson's homework already?" He hoisted his backpack up onto his shoulder and pointed to the open book lying on the table in front of Clara.

"Oh"—she held up the book of Hans Christian Andersen's fairy tales—"yeah. Just trying to get a head start on the book report." Although it was partially true, she really loved fairy tales, even if these versions were darker than the ones she was familiar with.

Patrick smirked. "We still have, like, three weeks."

Clara shrugged. She refused to tell him she had nothing else to do. "I think I might be going on vacation next week," she lied. "I don't want to fall behind." Clara couldn't bear for Patrick, the boy of her dreams, her very own Prince Charming—even if he didn't know it yet—to learn how boring and lonely she was. "Have you started yet?"

He shook his head, his smirk turning into a smile. His eyes flicked down to her book. "Any of it any good?"

Clara couldn't hold back the grin that engulfed her face. "The one I'm reading now is pretty good," she said, not wanting to go so far as to admit she was enthralled with The Little Mermaid. "But I love fairy tales, so…"

Patrick eyed her for a moment, then took a step closer. "Cool. Maybe there'll be a story in there that I'll like."

Clara wondered why he'd stopped to talk to her, but didn't have the guts to ask. "Maybe."

"So…where are you going on vacation?"

"Oh, umm, I'm not sure…somewhere with my mom's boyfriend, I think."

Snickering and cackling broke into the stillness of the cafeteria behind her, and Clara and Patrick both started. Her heart began to race. No. Please, *she silently begged.* Not now…

Patrick peered over her head, his eyes narrowing. "What's so funny?"

Clara squeezed her eyes shut, wishing Joanna Rossi, with her long black hair and crystal blue eyes, would just disappear already...forever. She was the most horrid girl at school and seemed to love torturing Clara more than anything else.

"She's not going on vacation," Joanna spat. "She's such *a liar." Her voice grew closer with the sound of each footstep until she finally stepped around the lunch table and planted herself beside Patrick. She looped her arm through his, and her friends strutted up to the other end of the table to watch, like perched vultures waiting to pick away at what was left of Clara once Joanna was finished.*

Why didn't Patrick push Joanna away? Why wouldn't he at least pull his arm out of hers? They weren't together, *were they?*

Joanna's eyes zeroed in on Clara. "You're so *pathetic. We all know your mom can't afford to take you anywhere. She can't even buy you new shoes." Dropping Patrick's arm, Joanna took a step forward and leaned down on the lunch table. "My mom said* your *mom sucked all the men in Bristow dry, so unless you're moving somewhere else so she can find* new *rich men to suck dry, you're full of crap."*

After another wave of boisterous laughter from her friends at the opposite end of the table, Joanna curled her lip and reached for Clara's backpack. "Have you ever even gone *on a vacation before?" As if she were holding a slimy worm, Joanna took the open flap of Clara's pack between her fingers, pinky raised in disgust as she inspected the ratty state of the bag. Letting go, she wiped her hand on her pants.*

"Yes, I have." Clara snatched her backpack away from the evil witch, her skin flush as she scrambled to zip it up.

"Liar," Joanna muttered.

Before Clara's eyes began to blur with unshed tears, she grabbed her book, hugging it against her chest and left the remnants of her lunch on the table. "You'll eat your words when I'm not here next week!" she screeched before running out of the cafeteria, down the hall, and into the bathroom, slamming the door shut behind her.

The bathroom smelled of mold, soggy paper towels, and toilet water, but Clara didn't mind. She couldn't bear seeing Patrick again, not after he'd witnessed her utter humiliation.

Clara's hands began shaking as her anger and embarrassment combined, resulting in the tears streaking down her cheeks. No one *made her cry—not her mom, not her mom's horrible boyfriends, not other students' mean comments—and Clara* hated *that Joanna, of all people, had been the one to provoke the sudden onslaught.*

Her horror quickly hardened into seething hatred. "Stupid bitch."

But deep down, Clara knew it wasn't just Joanna she was angry at. This was her mom's fault. Bristow was one of the smallest cities in Oklahoma, so of course, everyone would know how horrible her mom was. No matter what her mom told herself and others, she wasn't special or entitled to anything in any *way—she was pathetic, and she was dragging Clara down with her.*

If her mom had been normal, Clara knew she wouldn't have to worry about stupid girls like Joanna; they'd have nothing to hold over her. Clara knew that, even though she was a little scrawny for her age and poor, she was pretty, or at least, she thought she could be if she tried. All she needed was a different past and newer clothes. If she had those things, she *would be the one laughing at the others,* she *would be the one tormenting Joanna.*

As Clara opened her book, she tilted it toward the dim, florescent light and began reading. With each word of hope, love, and happily ever after, she swore to herself that she would never ever *be the butt of anyone's jokes again.* Ever.

And she'd do whatever was necessary to make sure of it.

2

"Earth to Clara..." Beth waved her scarred hand in front of Clara's face.

Clara blinked herself back to the present, her mind a bit foggy and her head aching.

"What were you thinking about?" Beth blew her wild, black bangs out of her face. Her short hair swayed as she tilted her head to the side, and her wide, curious eyes and shy smile made her seem pitiably innocent. "Are you okay?"

Clara brushed the meek woman's concerns away. "I'm fine. I just have a headache." It didn't matter that she'd woken a few hours earlier from a solid night's sleep or that she'd eaten a hearty breakfast. It didn't matter that Clara was sitting in a drab room with the blinds drawn over the barred windows or that no one was yelling or making obscene amounts of noise. In fact, all she could hear was the quiet humming of the incandescent lights shining overhead, mingled with the whispers of the three other women sitting around her. Regardless of all of that, her head still ached, and she still felt bleary-eyed and muddled.

Clara pulled her long, blonde hair out of its ponytail, letting it fall around her shoulders. As she took the ends of her hair between her fingers, she brushed them against her palm and stared down at the embroidered buffalo on the front of her University of Colorado sweatshirt. She didn't like thinking about her past and wasn't sure why she'd started to now. Most likely, her reminiscing stemmed from therapy sessions like the one she was about to start, which encouraged her to "dig deep" and "try to understand where the anger came from." She sneered.

So much had changed for Clara during the summer between middle and high school; *she* had changed. After a complete makeover, she'd started freshman year at Bristow High with a completely new persona—no more glasses or hiding behind old, holey clothes, no more cowering, and no more innocence. Clara had decided to use her mom's absence and frivolousness to her advantage by raiding her closet for posh, new clothes and by using her makeup and hair products just enough for Clara to accentuate what she already had.

The hands of the clock on the wall ticked, and Clara peered up at its white face. Their session was supposed to have started ten minutes ago; Dr. Mallory was *never* late. All Clara wanted was for group to be over already so she could crawl back into bed and sleep until the dull thumping in her head went away and the lead in her limbs dissipated. But the two hour session had yet to begin.

With a sigh, she shifted in the padded chair, positioned a little bit outside of a circle of mostly empty chairs. She pulled her sock-covered feet underneath her and rested her elbow on the arm of the chair, her forehead cradled perfectly in her palm…so perfect that she thought she just might fall asleep.

The sound of the hydraulic metal door swinging open, followed by the muffled sound of hurried footsteps, told her Dr. Mallory had finally arrived. She would have to wait for her nap.

"Sorry to keep you waiting, ladies. It seems that a few of our group members will not be joining us for today's session. Many of them are in bed with the flu, so it'll just be the five of us today."

Glancing around at the circle of chairs, Clara was happy to see that four of them were empty and even happier that they would remain that way. It was her day to speak, and the less people to ask her questions, the better.

"Okay," Dr. Mallory said, opening his briefcase and settling into his chair. "Shall we get started?"

He was actually pretty cute for a doctor. His hair was blond and always combed back away from his face. He was professional and young, too, and much better than Dr. White, who stomped through the halls, always smelling of smoke and his eyes yellowed with age. Dr. Presley was the only female doctor, but anyone under her supervision was screwed. From what Clara had heard, she was a heartless bitch. It made sense; she was beautiful and had a judgment about every movement her patients made, about every thought they had. Clara was glad she'd dodged *that* bullet.

"Let's check in, ladies." Dr. Mallory sat back, his warm brown eyes sweeping over his four patients. "I'll start." He cleared his throat. "I've had a very busy morning. With so many of the staff out sick with this flu that's going around, I've been putting in some late hours, and quite frankly, it was difficult for me to get out of bed this morning. But…" he let out a deep sigh. "Here I am. I'm sorry to see that so many members of our group are also ill. But, I guess there's nothing we can do except to focus on staying healthy in other ways."

Clara felt Dr. Mallory's eyes on her, and she met them with a bored glare. He definitely hadn't forgotten that it was her turn to share today.

"Dr. Mallory," Beth squeaked. Although Clara often chastised her for being so pitifully innocent, Beth was the sweetest, gentlest person Clara had ever met, and regardless of how annoying that was at times, Clara kind of liked her. At least, more than she liked the other women.

"Yes?" Dr. Mallory crossed his legs. "What is it, Beth?"

"I—I um…I think that I might be getting sick, too. But, I don't know for sure." She looked down at her fingers as she picked at them. Her nails were short and scabbed from being bitten too close to the quick. "I mean, I'm trying to get better, but I feel sick."

"What makes you think you're sick, Beth? Do you have a fever? Have you been to see Nurse Hadly?"

"Well…well, no I haven't. But I know what's wrong with me."

With a unanimous groan, everyone settled in to listen to all the reasons why she was sick…again.

"You always think something's wrong with you," Alicia blurted and rolled her eyes as she smacked her gum. Clara wanted to slap her mouth shut to spare everyone the maddening sound of her disgusting molestation of the wad of gum for the next couple of hours.

Alicia was a tall, pale woman with a buzzed head and green eyes that Clara had once thought were pretty…before she'd actually met the bitch. One of Alicia's many infuriating qualities was a compulsive need to always have something in her mouth—anything counted—and since gum was the only thing the staff would allow at all times, she had to make each piece last as long as possible.

"Alicia," Dr. Mallory said. "Let Beth speak. You'll get your turn soon enough."

"I don't need a turn," she mouthed off. "I'm just saying…the idiot always thinks something's wrong with her."

"No name calling, Alicia." Dr. Mallory rubbed his temple. "You know the rules."

"But there *is* something wrong this time," Beth whined.

"And what do you think is wrong with you?" Dr. Mallory was all patience and mock concern.

For some reason, Beth's gaze darted to Clara before landing back on the doctor. "Well, I've been feeling dizzy and nauseous lately. I'm pretty sure I'm getting the flu…just like the others."

"Alright, Beth, why don't you go see Nurse Hadly after our

session today...how does that sound? I'm sure she can give you something that'll make you feel better."

Everyone but Beth knew it wasn't flu meds Dr. Hadly would administer to her.

As they continued around the room, checking in about their day and how they were doing since their last session a week before, Samantha chimed in. She was a short, gangly young woman with a bright smile but often down-trodden eyes. She told them about her sleepless nights, that her nightmares had been growing increasingly worse instead of getting better. It was nothing new.

And of course, when it was actually Alicia's turn, she complained about everything that had irritated her during the last twenty-four hours. The list was very long and, though it included all the whining and commotion from some of the other patients getting sick, she complained most about the sound of the squeaking wheel on the laundry cart echoing through the hall at night when Devon was making his rounds.

"I don't get any sleep because of it. Do you know what that does to my nerves? It's like you people are *trying* to make me crazy. I can't even eat without someone coughing on my food. Between all the crying and sniffling, it's like I'm living with a bunch of goddamn kindergarteners." Her eyes were wide and bloodshot, and Clara had half a mind to throw the water bottle sitting on the floor beside her chair at the woman's gaunt face. Alicia was just as ridiculous as Beth, she was just too pissed off all the time to realize it. As the woman griped on, Clara thought of Joanna once more.

"Steven Quick," Principal Sheppard called out. A scrawny, freckle-faced boy walked up to the gray-haired woman and accepted his middle school graduation certificate, smiling as he turned toward the photographer.

Clara stood in line, ecstatic that she was about to receive her own graduation certificate. After today, she would never have to set foot on her middle school campus again. And with any luck, Joanna would be going to a different high school, and Clara would never have to see the girl's smug face again. Clara was actually proud of herself for making it through the school year relatively unscathed. She'd survived the most torturous years of her life—maybe not with as much dignity as she would've liked, but at least she'd survived.

"Anita Quincy," the principal's voice droned over the loud-speaker.

Clara allowed herself a satisfied grin. Anita's dress wasn't nearly as pretty as hers was. Clara's mom had splurged and bought her a new summer dress to wear for the ceremony. Clara assumed it was because her mostly absent mom felt bad for not attending, but Clara hadn't wanted her there anyway; she would only have been an added embarrassment. It was intimidating enough looking out at a sea of over a hundred faces—proud parents, older siblings, and beaming teachers. She didn't want to see her mom's face out there as well, pretending to be someone she wasn't—a loving mother—when really she was the town whore.

"Oops," Joanna said, bumping into Clara.

Clara turned around, the color draining from her face as she considered what scheme Joanna might try to play on their final day of school.

But to Clara's surprise, Joanna offered her an apologetic smile and shrugged. "Sorry, I tripped."

Clara's eyes narrowed on her before she turned around. She hated the fact that the person she loathed most in the world had to stand beside her in the graduation line.

"Kevin Raymond," the principal called.

Joanna tapped Clara's shoulder. "Psst..."

Clara glanced behind her. "Leave me alone, Joanna."

"Look...I just want to apologize for being so horrible to you

this year," she whispered. "I've been going through some crap at home and...well, the point is, I'm sorry."

Clara searched Joanna's eyes, waiting for the evil gleam to overshadow the unexpected softness.

"I shouldn't have taken it out on you."

"Why are you telling me this now?" Clara asked, skeptical and more hopeful than she knew was probably wise.

Joanna shrugged again. "I just don't want to go into high school being enemies." She smiled. "I guess I was sort of hoping we could be, you know, friends." Joanna looked down at her feet then out at the crowd...anywhere but at Clara.

"Are you being serious?" Clara asked, turning around completely.

Joanna's head cocked to the side. "Of course I am, silly." She nudged Clara's shoulder with her own. "Why would I go to all this trouble if I wasn't?"

A tiny smile tugged at Clara's lips, and she was just about to agree to be Joanna's friend when she heard her name over the loudspeaker.

"Clara Reynolds."

Beaming and filled with a new sense of hope, Clara stepped up to the hunched-over woman on the small, creaky stage. She barely registered the snickers behind her as she accepted her certificate. In twenty minutes, the years of hell Joanna had put her through would be a distant memory.

"Congratulations," Principal Sheppard said. Clara gazed out at the sea of faces, realizing that some of the people in the crowd were wearing strange expressions.

"Oh dear," Clara heard Principal Sheppard mutter as Clara registered the muffled laughter in the line of students waiting to walk across the stage. "Clara, dear," Principal Sheppard took a step toward her and touched her shoulder. "You have"—she spun Clara around—"you have a sign on your back, dear..."

Horrified, Clara flailed, reaching for the sign Principal Shep-

pard was struggling to remove. Feeling the paper between her fingers, Clara ripped it off her back. With shaking hands she read the bold, black print.

MY MOM IS A POOR WHORE.

"Why the hell do you shake your head every time I open my mouth?" Alicia seethed as she stared, wide-eyed, at Clara.

Clara had toned out Alicia's droning, so she had no clue what she'd missed, but the anger revived by her daydreamed recollection made it easy to answer. "Why are *you* always such a bitch?" The word slipped out of Clara's mouth before she could stop it. Her shoulders sagged with regret. She knew a one-way yelling match would erupt as a result of her provocation, and her head hurt too much to listen to Alicia's tirade about how everyone was against her, especially Clara.

"A bitch? At least I'm not delusional. You think you're better than us, don't you? You think I don't see through those big blue eyes of yours? You think you're entitled, and you have since you got here." She paused, waiting for Clara to argue.

Clara raised her eyebrows, feigning boredom.

"You're the most tragic out of all of us," Alicia continued. "You think there's nothing wrong with you, that you're unjustly in here. Well, guess what? The judge ordered your admittance; at least we're here willingly. We can admit we're fucked up. And don't think none of us haven't noticed that you *never* have visitors, that *no one* cares that you're in here."

Clara tried to ignore Alicia's derisive words, but the woman's voice filled Clara's head like acid, eroding her defenses. Her anger started taking over, creeping past her carefully constructed barricades and settling among the torrent of thoughts.

"...and all you do is sulk around and act superior to everyone else. You're just as crazy as the rest of us. You're even worse, because you think you're not crazy. I know I have problems; I know I need help. Why the fuck do you think I'm here? But you… you're a psycho, a murd—"

Clara jolted up from her chair. "You want me to kill you, too?" She couldn't help but lash back. The room fell silent and four sets of eyes settled on her. Clara might have at least been somewhat repentant had she not been too busy relishing the way the flush of anger was draining from Alicia's face.

"Clara," Dr. Mallory warned. "We don't threaten each other. This is a safe space."

Clara balked and turned to him. "Are you kidding me?" She pointed to Alicia, who was sitting back, quiet in her chair. "All she does is bully everyone, and you let her."

His eyes narrowed. "Making generalized accusations isn't fair either."

"This is such a joke," Clara muttered and plopped back down.

"Clara," he said, exhaling heavily, "please…"

She rolled her eyes.

He ignored her. "It's your turn to share today." When he paused, she knew he was waiting for her to meet his eyes, but she refused. "Why don't you tell us what you've learned since your admittance"—he scanned her file on his lap—"um…three months ago."

Clara stared around at the three other women. Beth was watching her eagerly, interested to finally hear Clara's story, just like they all had been since the moment she arrived at Pine Springs Hospital. Alicia had wanted to know Clara's story so badly she'd started spreading stories throughout the ward, hoping Clara would refute them and tell everyone the truth.

Little did Alicia know that Clara preferred the whispered rumors over the truth. She liked that people thought she was crazy; she liked that they were scared of her. If the entire hospital thought she'd set her mom's house on fire and that she'd enjoyed watching everyone inside burn to death, that was just fine with her. She wasn't there to make friends, she was only there to serve her court-mandated time. When she had, she would walk away from all of them and never look back.

The doctor cleared his throat again, this time coughing before he said, "Clara…?"

"What?" She finally met his eyes.

"Start with what you've learned since coming to stay with us. What is it that you want for yourself? Share something with us, anyth—"

Suddenly, the door flew open, and Dr. Preston sauntered into the room. And like the flip of a switch, Dr. Mallory's attention was no longer on Clara, but fixated on the six-foot tall brunette woman.

"We have a situation, Dr. Mallory. Can I interrupt your session for a moment?"

Dr. Mallory groaned as he rose from his chair, both hands clamped on the armrests for support. Unsteady, he followed her out of the room, grumbling something as he cleared his throat.

Beth leaned closer to Clara. "A 'situation'?"

Clara ignored Beth and rubbed her hands over her face.

Beth continued to watch her, and Clara could tell questions were bouncing on the tip of her tongue, begging to be asked.

Clara sighed. "What?"

"Did you really set your parent's house on fire?"

Clara's eyes wandered to Beth's. "No, I didn't. In fact, there wasn't even a fire."

Beth looked relieved.

Clara narrowed her eyes. "You should know by now that everything out of Alicia's mouth is a lie. Stop listening to her; she's mean to you, and she's not your friend."

"Fuck you," Alicia said. "It's none of your business—"

"That's enough, ladies," Roberta, the over-weight nurse, said as she stalked into the room. "You're a bunch of rabid panthers today. I could hear you all the way out in the rec room."

"What are *you* doing in here?" Alicia growled from her chair.

"I work here, miss snippy. Come on, group's over." Roberta made a shooing motion to get them up out of their chairs. "You'll continue next week when everything around here has calmed down a bit." When the four women stared at her, showing no signs of moving, Roberta pointed to the open door. "Let's go. NOW."

Alicia's eyes were wild with fear. "But we're not finished yet. We still have over an hour of group left, plus he was late, and—"

"Worried you'll have to much time to consider killing yourself today?" Clara taunted, taking pleasure in the fact that Alicia wouldn't have every part of her day accounted for and would most likely go mad from not keeping busy.

"I hate you," Alicia spat as she pushed her chair back and rushed out of the room.

Roberta glanced between Clara and the empty doorway. "Was that really necessary?"

Clara shrugged and yawned, tired of being cooped up with a bunch of crazy assholes anyway. Pulling herself out of her chair, she headed out the door, leaving Samantha, Roberta, and Beth still inside. The hallway was mostly empty, with the exception of Alicia disappearing around the corner toward the rec room and Devon pushing the laundry cart toward the laundry room. Clara kind of liked the sound of the laundry cart's wheels squeaking on the polished floor. Or, maybe she just liked knowing where Devon was all the time.

He gave her a curt nod before looking away as he passed. He'd kept his distance since the day she arrived, and he seemed to dislike her even though he was clearly attracted to her. For some reason, she didn't mind him rejecting her advances. Maybe it was because playing with him was so much fun or because she knew he was trying to be professional. But either way, his mysterious aversion to her only piqued her interest more.

A shooting pain in the crown of her head made her wince, and her thoughts turned only to sleeping. Her sock-covered feet carried her silently past the rec room and down the next hallway toward her room. Since her roommate had been released a few days ago, Clara had the place all to herself. Her bed was still unmade, her blinds still drawn, and with an "oomph" she crawled under the covers and passed out.

3

The next day was no better. Clara still felt achy and tired. "I hate you," she grumbled as Roberta threw her covers back.

"I don't care. You're here to get better, so you might as well try."

With another grumble, Clara pulled her covers back over her body.

"You think you hate me, now? Miss Clara, if you don't get up, I'll lock Alicia in here with you, and then you'll really hate me."

"Fine!" Clara flung her blankets off, sat up, and turned to let her feet hang over the side of the bed.

"Come on," Roberta said, picking up a wad of Clara's clothes and stuffing them in the laundry basket. "Brush your teeth and get dressed. It's time for breakfast."

Clara cringed as her stomach did a somersault that nearly sent her into convulsions. With the way her insides were feeling, she would rather run a blade across her wrist than eat anything.

"I don't want you falling into that black hole you were in when you first got here. You need to keep eating…for me." Roberta batted her eyelashes.

Only because Roberta was the one faculty member who *would* make Clara's life hell, Clara obeyed.

Fifteen minutes later, Clara was sitting in the white-walled cafeteria, washed in the morning sunlight pouring through the windows and pushing her food around on her plate. She could feel Roberta's eyes boring into the back of her head as the nurse made her rounds through the dining hall. The squeak of the woman's rubber soles on the polished floor practically echoed among the quiet chatter of the other women sitting in clusters at their own tables.

Holding her breath, Clara took a bite of eggs. She immediately regretted it. Food was not settling well with her today. She raised her napkin to her mouth, and as she pretended to cough, she spit the eggs out and wadded up the napkin.

Beatrice, the woman sitting beside her, coughed, but it was Beth who grabbed Clara's attention. Sitting one table over, Beth was watching Clara too closely. With a knowing smile, Beth glanced down at her own plate and pushed her food around the way Clara had done.

Grateful for the woman's silence, Clara winked at her, making Beth's grin grow. As annoying as Beth could be, there was also something about her that was endearing. Clara hadn't found that quality in anyone in a long time. Not since Taylor.

Longing for her best friend brought the sting of tears to Clara's eyes, and she thought of the day Taylor ended their friendship for good.

It was summer break, junior year of high school, and Clara and Taylor had just walked into a deli in downtown Bristow. The moment Clara had stepped inside, she'd felt a combination of white-hot rage and exhilaration. Joanna Rossi, with her long, silky black hair—the hair Clara often dreamt about chopping off—was sitting with a boy in the far corner of the deli. It only took an instant before Joanna's eyes met hers.

Clara enjoyed the look of dread that blanketed the other girl's face. She knew she could turn around and avoid making a scene by leaving, or by simply ignoring Joanna's presence, but Clara wouldn't do that. It would be too easy and not nearly enough fun. Instead, she smiled. She would never *give Joanna the satisfaction of a close call, not now after all of her hard work, after all she'd achieved.*

Taylor pulled on Clara's arm and cast furtive glances at Joanna's table. "We should go."

"We're staying," Clara nearly snarled and nodded for the closest booth.

Taylor lingered by the entrance. "I really don't want to—"

"Stop being such a baby." Clara grabbed Taylor's wrist, tugging her friend toward the booth.

Clara made sure to sit facing Joanna. Weakness wasn't an option when it came to her, *not since the final straw at eighth grade graduation. The power Clara wielded over Joanna now that the tables had been turned was emboldening, and Clara feared that if she let her defenses down for even a moment, that power would be snatched away. All of her hard work—her makeover, her rise in popularity, the boys she'd stolen out from under Joanna's nose—would all have been for nothing, and Clara would be right back where she'd been three years ago.*

"Why do you hate her so much, anyway?" Taylor asked, flattening a napkin in her lap. "It's like you become someone else when you see her. It's—it's sorta creepy."

Clara's eyes shifted from Joanna to Taylor. "Gee, thanks."

Her friend was a round-faced little thing with blonde, wavy hair, brown eyes, and nothing particularly notable about her; in fact, Taylor was even a little boring. But she was loyal and predictable, two traits Clara found immensely valuable.

"Well, it's true. Why can't we, just for once, take the higher

road and leave instead of causing trouble? It's like you like *arguing with her or something. What did she do to you?"*

"Are you serious, Tay? How can you not see what a conniving skank she is? She's always watching, always plotting and planning..." Clara's eyes shot to Joanna, and it gave her immense satisfaction to see Joanna fidget under the weight of her stare. "She's made my life a living hell since I was in elementary school. I'm finally on top; why would I back down now? I won't *let her win."*

"But it's not a game,*" Taylor nearly shrieked. "Look, I know you guys have a past, and I know you have plenty of reasons to hate her, you tell me as much all the time, even if you don't tell me exactly what they are...but don't you think you go a little over the top sometimes? I mean, look at how excited you get when she's around. I don't—"*

"You don't what?" Clara narrowed her eyes at her best friend.

Taylor frowned. "I'm worried about you, that's all."

Clara's glare softened, and a smile curved her lips. "Sorry, Tay. I just...remember how Joanna treated you when you first got here? The way she made fun of you in front of the entire school during your choir performance? I took you in as my friend because no one *should be treated the way Joanna treats people." Clara looked at Joanna, who was tossing her hair over her shoulder and batting her eyes at the boy sitting across the table from her. Clara grinned inwardly, excited by the prospect of another challenge.*

Taylor cleared her throat, recapturing Clara's attention. "See what I mean?" Taylor said, clasping her hands together and resting them on the Formica tabletop. "You're not even paying attention to me, not really."

Clara tilted her head to the side and let out an exasperated sigh. "I'm doing all of this for you as much as I'm doing it for me." She shook her head and lifted her shoulder. "Joanna needs to be put in her place, and I'm willing to do whatever it takes to make sure she feels uneasy around me, just like I felt around her for so many years."

Taylor's brow furrowed. "You—"

"Besides, aside from stealing a few of her boyfriends, I haven't actually done *anything to her since freshman year." She patted Taylor's clasped hands. "I know you don't like confrontation or whatever, but don't you think there are times when standing your ground is more important than running away? She's a bully and deserves to be knocked down a peg or two."*

Taylor bit her lower lip, a sure sign that she was coming around. "Yeah, I guess you're right. It's just...you get sort of...scary."

Clara laughed. "It's just my war face, dummy. Come on, let's order something with way too many calories, and then we can grab Slurpees and watch the guys at the skate park fall on their asses."

A tentative smile spread across Taylor's face, exposing the gap between her front teeth. Apparently content with the idea of fatty food and boys, she scanned the menu. When the waiter approached, Taylor ordered a strawberry milkshake and a cheeseburger with extra cheese, and Clara couldn't help it as her eyes skimmed over Taylor's frumpy clothes and curvy-on-the-cusp-of-chubby body.

"I'll just have a Greek salad and a cup of minestrone soup," Clara said, handing the waiter her menu.

Taylor straightened. "I thought we were ordering food with far too many calories?"

Clara shrugged. "I lost my appetite," she said absently, watching as Joanna and the boy got up from their table and headed toward the exit—toward Clara and Taylor's booth.

Although Joanna was clearly avoiding making eye contact, Clara couldn't help herself. "Hey, Joanna." She nodded toward the tall, blond guy walking next to her. "Who's your friend? Are you going to introduce us?"

The boy's phone rang, and he pulled his cell from his pocket and continued outside while Joanna stopped at the end of Clara's table.

Clara grinned shamelessly. "You know, you might as well..."

Joanna's crystal blue eyes fixed on Clara, and her lips pulled into a satisfied grin. "The fact that you have to steal my *boyfriends instead of finding your own is a joke, Clara." She watched Clara, waiting for her reaction, but Clara had spent years perfecting her Joanna game face, so she simply sat there, looking bored. "Of course,* you *wouldn't care." Joanna smirked. "Like mother, like daughter, only...you're* crazy *and she's just a stupid whore."*

Clara jumped up from her seat, shoving her index finger at Joanna's chest. "Shut your mouth! We are nothing *alike!" Realizing she'd made a bigger scene than she'd intended, Clara swallowed and glanced around at the handful of other deli patrons before narrowing her eyes back on Joanna. "You're such a bitch. You think being mean to people makes you cool? Makes you popular? Well, how does it feel to be the one the rumors are spread about now? You're* nobody. *You're old news. Just remember who did that to you."*

To Clara's relief, Joanna seemed more than affected by her words; her nemesis's eyes even blurred a little. "I was a kid.*" Joanna said, her voice incredulous. "When was the last time I did anything to you?"*

Clara laughed. "Oh, poor Joanna's so innocent. Yeah. Right. Watch your back, Joanna, because payback's a bitch." Clara crossed her arms over her chest, staring Joanna down and loving the thrill of watching the other girl squirm.

Finally, Joanna let out a deep breath and turned on her heel, heading out the door. Clara smiled triumphantly and turned back toward the booth only to find that, at some point during the altercation, Taylor had left, as well.

Beatrice, a woman Clara didn't really know and didn't care to, coughed beside her at the table. The pallid, red-haired woman was halfway finished with her meal when she stood and headed for the juice counter. Glancing around the more-empty-than-usual cafeteria, Clara leaned over and scraped most of her breakfast onto Beatrice's plate, hearing Beth start giggling as she watched.

"Beth," Roberta said.

Clara's attention snapped forward again.

Roberta walked over to Beth's table. "You seem to be enjoying your breakfast this morning." She studied the giggling woman. "What's so funny?"

Beth looked at Clara and then back down at her tray of food, sending Clara's heart into a steady thud. Roberta in a bad mood wasn't something she felt up to dealing with today.

"Um, Clara told Alicia off in group yesterday," Beth said with another giggle. "You should've seen Alicia's face…I—I don't think I've ever seen her so shocked before."

"Really?" Roberta glanced over at Clara and smirked. "Sorry I missed it." She patted Beth on the shoulder and continued her rounds around the room.

As Roberta stepped further and further away from her table, Clara's heartbeat slowed, and she smiled at Beth. After giving her a grateful wink, Clara pushed around the last bit of food on her plate, making it look like she'd at least made as sizeable dent.

4

"What's wrong, munchkin?" Clara asked as she plopped down beside Beth on the red sofa. The instant she did, she regretted it. Her head was pounding, and she was short of breath. The afternoon light filtering in through the windows throughout the rec room was too bright, and the smell of cleaning supplies was too pungent. "I feel like shit," she grumbled, leaning her head back against the overstuffed couch with a groan.

"I don't feel good, either," Beth breathed as she wrapped herself up in a brown, fleece blanket.

Clara's head lulled to the left so she could see the other woman better.

Beth's face was flushed, her bangs were matted to her temples, and her skin looked slick with sweat.

"Did you go see Nurse Hadly?" Clara asked. She would generally brush Beth's health concerns away, but she could tell Beth really was sick, and Clara was feeling especially ill herself.

Beth's rumpled hair swished against the back of the sofa as she nodded. "The door was locked, and the light was out. I think she's off today."

"Do you want me to get you some water or something?"

With a slow shake of her head, Beth said, "No, thank you. I just want to sit here and stay warm."

Clara shrugged and reached for the TV remote, propping her feet up on the battered oak coffee table.

Beth pulled a book out from under her blanket. Its bright blue cover caught Clara's eye, and she raised her eyebrows as a spurt of excitement overshadowed her headache…a little. "You like fairy tales, huh?"

"Yeah," Beth said. "Well, actually I've never *read* any of them, not the real ones, but my grandma sent me this book last week." Her fingers traced the gilt-embossed canvas cover. "She said she saw it and thought of me since I loved Disney movies so much when I was a little girl."

Opening the book to the first story, Beth cleared her throat and began whispering as she read the opening lines of *The Ugly Duckling*. She barely made it through two sentences before she started coughing.

Clara snatched the book out of her hands. "I'll read it to you."

"Oh, um…thanks," Beth whispered. She rested her head against the sofa cushion, letting out a deep sigh as her eyes flitted closed.

Tugging at Beth's blanket, Clara pulled a portion of it over her own shivering body and settled in to read. She hadn't thought about fairy tales since that night—the night she'd lost her prince. The memory was still too painful and infuriating, but secretly, Clara still yearned to prove her theory right. She wanted to prove that there was still truth to the stories everyone thought were mere fairytales.

After a few minutes of reading, Clara quickly fell back into an eager, fluid rhythm. Her voice became lighter, her thoughts less dismal.

"'Ah, you ugly creature, I wish the cat would get you," and his mother said she wished he had never been born. The ducks pecked him, the chickens beat him, and the girl who fed the poultry kicked him with her feet. So at last he ran away…'" Clara twirled her long ponytail around her finger, the anthology propped up on her lap as she flipped through, enthralled. She could feel Beth's toes wiggling beneath the blanket as she listened, coughing every so often.

"That's really annoying," Clara said, looking at Beth and trying to school her growing aggravation.

Beth wore an injured look. "Sorry," she said quietly.

Clara felt bad for the little thing. "Are you sure you don't want to go lie down? You should probably get some sleep or something."

Beth shook her head. "Not yet. I like the way you read…the way you do the voices." A small smile tugged at her mouth. "I'll wait until you're finished."

Clara was happy to hear that. She didn't want to stop reading now, not when they were about to get to the good part; the part where the duckling became the envy of everyone who'd ever mistreated him.

"Have you read this story before?" Beth asked. "You seem to like it a lot."

Clara nodded. "Fairy tales are like my bible," she admitted.

"What do you mean?" Beth started biting her pinky nail, coughing on her hand as she chewed instead of covering her mouth.

Clara shivered. "Stop it," she said and swatted Beth's hand out of her mouth. "Biting your nails isn't an attractive quality. Do you think any of these princesses"—she held up the book of stories—"ever bit *their* fingernails?"

Beth looked at the book in Clara's lap, then up at Clara. "Well…probably not."

"And they always get the prince, right?"

"Well, I suppose…"

"Right, and do you know why?" Clara strummed her fingers on the book impatiently.

Beth shook her head.

"Because there are rules if you want to be a princess like them, Beth, or at least a modern day version of one, and biting your fingernails is against the rules."

"What do you mean, *rules*?"

Clara sighed. "They're more like steps, actually," she said, exasperated. "There are rules to everything, but no one ever thinks to pay much attention to them."

"What *are* the rules?" Beth seemed enthralled, and Clara felt another spurt of enthusiasm.

"If I tell you, you can't tell anyone. It's a secret of mine, and I don't want people like Alicia finding out about my secrets. Do you understand?"

Beth nodded emphatically, looking even more like a little girl than she usually did.

"Well…you know how there are rules whenever you're playing a game? Like, you have to take certain steps to achieve your goal and win the game?"

Beth nodded again.

"It's the same thing in life. Not everyone is born with everything they want, but that doesn't mean we can't fight for it." Clara pointed to the book. "If you're the ugly duckling, you can overcome that, but you have to work hard for it." Clara thought about how hard work and determination had changed her life completely. She'd earned great grades in high school and taken the first scholarship she'd been offered to the University of Colorado in Boulder, finally leaving that hellhole in Oklahoma. Taking *that* step for herself had helped her get away from her mom and Joanna. She'd given herself a fresh start. *She'd* done it for herself.

"It breaks down like this: step one, the underdog can always come out on top." Clara had proven that theory every time she'd stolen Joanna's boyfriend. In the end, Clara'd had it all, and Joanna hadn't been able to hold a candle to Clara's popularity.

"Rule two, there just has to be a transformation."

Beth's eyes widened.

"Like the ugly duckling," Clara said.

Beth sniffled. "But not everyone is a swan."

"Not naturally, no, but there are tons of ways to change that."

Beth cleared her throat. "Is that what you did?"

Clara tried not to be offended by Beth's ignorance. "I had issues in elementary and middle school, and embracing the underlying messages of these stories made everything easier for me."

"Really?"

Clara nodded. "Think about it. Who do you think wrote these?" She waved Beth's impending answer away as the woman glanced down at Hans Christian Andersen's name, written in gold script on the cover. "Yeah, Hans did, but he didn't just make these up. The ideas had to stem from somewhere. I'm sure he had a little sister who was picked on or saw a little orphan girl on the streets back in the day and wrote about her in a way everyone could relate to. These stories were originally social commentaries, his observations of the world around him. He just wrote them in a way people would *want* to read them. It's like subliminal messaging, and most people are too stupid to get it."

"I don't think—"

"For instance," Clara continued. "What's to stop someone from getting a makeover or moving somewhere new to start over, to be someone else? What's to stop them from recreating themselves to become the swan? To become the princess?"

"But"—Beth shook her head—"shouldn't people just be content with who they are?"

Clara glared at her. "Not unless you want to be pathetic your whole life, and you want people like Alicia to pick on you all the time."

"Did someone pick on *you* when you were in elementary school?"

"Of course! Kids are horrible. Especially the rich, pretty ones. But there are things you can do to make things right, to turn them around. Nothing's set in stone, Beth. Everything changes, the hierarchy in high school, your sheets, the government, a giant piece of glass can be broken into tiny shards…can you think of *anything* that never changes at all?"

Beth frowned and shook her head.

"Exactly. So popularity and social status…all of that can change, too. Buy a nicer car, and people will automatically see you differently. It's easy to make things better for yourself."

"What did you do to make things better for *you*?"

Clara let out a harsh laugh. "Everything I could. I stole my mom's clothes so I didn't have to wear my old, ratty ones…and I watched countless videos of how to put on makeup and what to say to boys. I read books, studied movies, and memorized lines from my favorite romances…" Clara let out a deep breath.

"Sounds like a lot of work." Beth started coughing again.

"Yeah, well if you don't put in the work, you stay at the bottom and continue to get pushed around. People are lazy, and they simply accept their lot in life, something I *refuse* to do."

"Well, I think I'd like to try that when I get a little better."

"Yeah?" Clara nudged Beth with her elbow. "I'll help you, and then we'll show them all that you're not the pushover they all think you are."

Beth smiled. "Maybe Alicia will start being nice to me."

Clara smirked. "Oh, she will." Clara leaned over to set the book on the coffee table. Strangely, her time with Beth had helped her shake the growing sickness, and she felt invigorated.

"What's number three?" Beth asked, nestling down further under the blanket.

"What?"

"You said there were three rules."

Clara's eyes narrowed. "Yeah, there's a third one…but it's not as easily attained as the rest."

"Why? What is it?"

Clara glared at Beth. "Something about the princess always getting the prince." Her voice was cold.

"Why doesn't it work?"

"It doesn't matter," Clara spat. "It's not like you have a prince you're trying to catch." Pushing the blanket off her legs, Clara stood up and walked over to the window beside the wall-mounted TV. She gazed down at the snow-covered grounds, enjoying how pristine and icy everything appeared. The tops of the hedges lining the drive were barely visible, and the birds were restricted to leaf-less branches as they played in the sunny afternoon.

Nearly blinded by the glare coming off the snow, Clara closed her eyes. As much as she wanted to never think about him again, she couldn't contain the whirlwind of memories.

Clara had been on her seventh lap around the track, unwinding from a tedious day of classes and keeping up appearances. As she came around the final bend, approaching the water bottle she was using as a mile marker, she knew that once she passed it, she would be done and could shower, put on clean clothes, and head back to her dorm to freshen up before heading out for a night on the town.

She loved being in Boulder; it was so different from Bristow. There were possibilities here. She was finally away from all the drama and could be comfortable in her own skin and focus on her future. Boulder was her fresh start, and college was...promising. There were tons of cute boys and potential Prince Charmings. She loved it.

But while Clara was lost in frivolous thoughts, she misstepped and tripped, landing on the turf with a shooting pain in her ankle. "Shit." A sprained ankle would ruin her plans for the night.

Clara pulled up the spandex of her jogging pants as a shadow was cast over her. She peered up and squinted into the sun, trying to see who was approaching.

"That looked like a bad one," a young man said, his voice low and playful. "Are you alright?"

Clara tried to move her foot, cringing. "I think it's sprained."

He crouched down, his fingers pressing against the tender skin around her ankle. "You training for a marathon?"

Clara shook her head. "No…?"

"I've seen you out here almost every day since the semester started. I thought maybe you were training for something."

"Oh. No, I just like to run." Of course she wouldn't tell him exactly why *she liked to run, that being fit was one of the many things she had to do if she wanted to maintain her allure. "And you"—she craned her neck to see the soccer team running drills in the center of the field behind her —"play soccer?"*

"Yep. I suck, but I love it anyway."

He'd admitted to a weakness, something most men wouldn't do. Clara couldn't hold in her smile. "It's the effort that counts, right?"

He shrugged. "I guess."

Clara couldn't help but admire his shadowed hazel eyes as he looked at her. She was suddenly self-conscious about being so close to him, sweating and smelling like a footlocker.

When she realized his stare was lingering on her, Clara thought she felt the ground shift a little, and her cheeks flushed.

Soccer Boy moved her foot around gently and cleared his throat. "You think you can stand up?" He rose to his feet and held out his hand.

She nodded, "Yeah, I think so."

Bracing her hands on either side of her, Clara balanced on her good foot and tried to rise. She wavered, and big, strong hands clasped her upper arms to steady her. "Thank you," she said, unsure how long she needed to play the injured damsel before he would ask her out.

"No problem," he said, letting go of her arms. "You going to be okay?"

"I think so—"

"Alright, well, I better get back to practice." And with that, he trotted away.

She watched him, dumbfounded. That wasn't what was supposed to happen; he wasn't supposed to just walk away from her. She glanced down at her chest; her cleavage wasn't necessarily voluptuous, but no guy had ever complained about that before. She was wearing her compression pants, which made her thighs and butt look great. Other than the sheen of sweat coating her skin, there was nothing wrong with her.

"Try to watch where you're stepping," Soccer Boy called after her as she limped away.

Thwarted, Clara waved a hand at him without looking back and headed toward the locker room, ignoring the pain of her ankle as best she could. She didn't understand why their interaction hadn't played out the way it should have. There were simple steps to attaining a man's attentions—she had the body, she'd made sure she had the look, and she'd even been the damsel in distress, but not so pathetic that she was crying about it. It had been the perfect scenario, and yet...nothing.

After convincing herself that she wasn't really interested in him anyway and that she really hadn't *tried very hard to lure him in, Clara used her night at home to study instead of sulking, almost completely forgetting about Soccer Boy. She needed to focus on her grades, anyway, especially if she was going to keep her scholarship.*

The next day, Clara was on her way to the library to continue studying for her Chemistry exam when she noticed him—the tall, shaggy-haired soccer player—out of the corner of her eye. He was leaning against one of the stone pillars in front of the library, talking on his cell phone.

As Clara approached the library's glass doors, he ended his call and glanced up.

"Hey," he said, walking up beside her.

Clara met his soft, hazel eyes fanned with dark lashes; she hadn't been able to get those eyes out of her mind. "Hey," she said.

"You have a study group or something?" He stepped in front of her and pointed to the library with his chin. Clara could smell his aftershave and see his barely-there shadow of facial hair.

Shaking her head, she pointed to her messenger bag. "Just need to study before my chemistry test this afternoon."

"Chemistry? So, you're one of the smart ones, then. Do you tutor?"

Clara felt disappointment pull at her features, and her eyes narrowed. She pushed past him. As much as she wanted to shout, "find a different nerd, asshole!" she kept her mouth shut.

He matched her pace, his exposed, athletic arm brushing against hers as he tried to keep up. "Did I...did I say something wrong?"

His skin was warm and soft, but Clara did her best to ignore it. She walked faster. "Of course not," she said as she pulled the heavy glass door open before he could reach for it.

He entered the library right behind her and stopped just as she had, peering around the cavernous study hall, crowded with people. Huge windows filled the room with warmth and light.

"I've gotta study, so if you don't mind..." She scanned the long tables, willing a free seat to come into view.

Soccer Boy pointed to the table furthest to the right. "There are two empty seats right over there, at the end."

Turning around, Clara said, "Look, I'm not smart, okay? I'm just trying to keep my scholarship. I can't help you with your homework or anything like that, so please, just leave me alone."

Before he could respond, Clara headed for the empty seat, and after a few steps, she realized that Soccer Boy had stopped following her. As much as she was relieved her plea had worked, she felt a twinge of anger, too. Of course the bastard only wanted her to help him with his homework. Stupid asshole.

She settled into the hard plastic chair at the crowded table but was no longer in a studying mood. She wanted to call it a day, get gussied up, and go out for a drink...or three. She didn't want to sit inside with a bunch of nerds, pouring over their textbooks with the incessant sound of highlighters gliding over paper, the scratching of diligent note taking, and the irritating throat clearing and sighing.

Drawing in a deep breath for a sigh of her own, Clara pulled out her chemistry book and opened it. She dug the flashcards out from the zipper pocket of her bag. She needed to memorize the elements, including their symbols, their atomic numbers, and their common uses. She started with the first one on her list, Argon, then moved on to Arsenic. Just as she set her "As" notecard aside to start the next element, Soccer Boy pulled out the chair beside her and sat down.

"Mind if I sit with you?" His voice was an enthralling whisper, and she hated herself for the glee it inspired.

Keeping a straight face, she said, "I already told you, Soccer Boy, I can't help you with your damn homework. I have too much to do, and I'm not that smart, I promise." In his silence, she shifted her gaze to him.

He was smiling at her. "You're feisty."

She glared in return, tapping the invisible watch on her wrist.

"Do I look stupid to you?" he asked, whispering closer to her ear this time.

Clara frowned. "Excuse me?" She tried to ignore his warm breath against her ear.

He licked his bottom lip, his smile unwavering. "I'm a law student. Your"—he peered down at her flashcards— "Arsenic *notes won't help me with my Regulation and Public Policy exam."*

Clara couldn't help the heat that spread over her entire body. "Oh."

"I'm Andrew Jensen," he said, offering her his hand.

"Clara Reynolds," she said, accepting it.

Andrew took a bite of a green apple and looked down at her flashcards. "You should be careful...chemistry can be dangerous." He took another bite. "I blew up one too many things in high school. Once I even almost blew my face off and lit my parents' house on fire. I stay away from that stuff now."

Clara tried not to laugh. "You should really chew with your mouth closed."

He only smiled and took another bite, but he did *keep his mouth closed.*

"What did you do?" Clara asked, moving her books over a bit so he could actually fit in the space beside her.

"What? Oh, when I nearly died?" He shrugged. "You know, made household bombs out of Drain-O and aluminum foil...made napalm and lit it on fire. Little did I know it was sticky as shit and hard to put out."

With a tiny giggle, Clara felt herself getting sucked into his every word. "Sounds like you were a troublemaker." Definitely a troublemaker, she thought, but he also seemed like a good boy; he had to be if he was a law student, after all. He had to be a hard worker, sort of like her. Clara liked that.

Andrew shrugged. "So, are you going to freak out again, or can I keep sitting here? Seats are limited, you know..."

Glancing around, Clara shrugged, feigning indifference. "Sure."

Andrew wiped his brow with mock relief. "Good. You had me worried there for a minute."

"Mail!" Roberta called from behind the counter, where she was sitting. The patients lounging around the rec room—playing board games, reading books, and staring at the walls vacantly—scrambled to their feet, scurrying to Roberta like cockroaches to a scrap of food.

Clara didn't move away from the window, only rolled her eyes. They're pathetic, she thought, but a twinge of sadness quickly followed. Pulling a chair in front of the window, she sat down, her legs crossed and pulled up against her chest as she thought about Andrew. She wondered why she didn't think of him more. She liked that she didn't think about what had happened to them at the end very often, but still, she was surprised.

As the rest of the ward filled with chit-chat, Clara couldn't help but feel put-off. Granted, she and her mom had never been close, so there was no reason to ever expect her to write. And Clara hadn't really talked to her at all since moving away, so it wasn't the absence of her mom in her life that was a little heartbreaking. The fact that she never had a mom who cared much about her at all was the kicker. Clara picked at a string hanging from the hem of her gray, oversized sweatshirt, grappling with the encroaching, unwanted emotions.

A sickening rage rushed through her veins. Her mom had been questioned in Clara's trial, so Clara knew she was aware of her situation, of the arrest and the judge's sentence of a long-term stay in a psychiatric ward. Her mom had said, herself, it was best that Clara be locked away.

Well, her mom had always been a selfish bitch. Clara knew she shouldn't be surprised that her mom was completely devoid of any mothering instincts.

"Shut up already," Clara said over her shoulder to the ladies behind her, clamoring and crying for their letters.

"Miss Clara," Roberta called. "You've got a letter."

Clara's eyes widened in surprise but only for an instant. She hadn't received a single letter since she'd arrived at Pine Springs. Resentment and anticipation mixed together in the pit of her stomach. Who would write to her? Andrew? The thought was too much too hope for.

Standing, Clara took unhurried steps toward the nurses' station, her slippers clacking languidly against the polished floor. Her insides were jittery.

Roberta cleared her throat. "You should be excited, darlin'."

Was Roberta mocking her? Clara wasn't sure, and her mood darkened again.

Snatching the letter from between Roberta's ebony fingers, Clara headed back to her chair by the window, ignoring the other women's giggles and tears as they read their letters aloud to one another.

More than curious, Clara flipped the envelope over in her palm, and her fingers tightened, crinkling it in her grasp. It was from the girl's mother, she could tell by the perfect, cursive penmanship.

Unsure whether or not she cared what was written on the pages inside, something made it difficult for Clara to simply toss the letter aside. Blowing out a breath, she tore the envelope open, letting it fall to the ground as she unfolded the white printer paper. A short note was centered on the sheet.

I hope you're happy with yourself. After nearly a year on life support, my Josie is finally at peace. Do you have any remorse about what you've done? Do you care that you've taken a young life from this world? I hope you know I'll do everything in my power to make sure you never get out of there, ever, for my baby and for that nice boy, Andrew.

She's gone?

Peering out the reinforced window and down at the barren oak trees that lined the grounds, Clara wondered if it was remorse or relief that pulsed inside her. Although the day was bright and the sun was shining, she could only see red against a background of darkness. She could only hear her heart pounding in her ears and feel the sweat collecting on her brow and palms. The bubble of hysteria swelling in her chest made it nearly impossible to breathe.

After weeks of being inseparable, of Clara and Andrew going out and about and being seen together by everyone, Clara was convinced she'd finally found her Prince Charming. He was perfect in every way—handsome and smart, successful and funny. Everything was perfect, or at least it should've been.

On the way to Andrew's house, Clara spotted someone who looked a little too similar to Joanna walking in his neighborhood. Way too similar. Clara was unnerved by the thought of Joanna being anywhere near Andrew...anywhere near Clara herself, and the more she thought about Joanna even being in Boulder, the darker her mood became.

Amidst Andrew's channel surfing, he finally muted the TV and turned his attention to Clara. "What's wrong?"

She shook her head and offered him a weak smile.

"Tell me," he said, turning to face her fully. "What's bothering you?"

Clara peered at him, searching his face for answers to the questions she was too scared to ask. "You're not seeing anyone else, are you?"

Andrew frowned. "What? No, why would you ask that?"

Clara shrugged. "I just...we never said we were official, so—"

He took her chin between his fingers and angled her face toward his. "There's no one else. I spend all my time with you... how would I even find the time?"

Clara wasn't stupid. She knew guys could always find time for a fling on the side, but there was truth in Andrew's eyes. Why was she being so pathetic? She needed to show *him why he should be with only her.*

She leaned in and pressed her lips against his, needing him more than she ever had before, wanting to feel euphoria and bliss instead of doubt. His mouth was intoxicating, making her forget about Joanna and flooding her body with reassurance and heat instead of cold uncertainty.

With a grunt, Andrew came up for air, his passion-filled eyes searching hers. "Take off your shirt," he rasped, pulling her bottom lip gently between his teeth. A thrill of excitement ran through her already electrified body.

Without hesitation, she broke their kiss only to remove her clothes and then climbed on top of him, wanting to explore every single inch of his body and feel his hands all over her skin. She wanted to consume him...for him to devour her. *And as if her fairy godmother was watching over her, she was granted her wish.*

Andrew took her readily, need making his grip tighter and his kisses rougher. Clara absorbed every sensation, committing to memory the pressure of his body against hers, the feel of his hot breath on her skin.

And afterward, they lay together, Clara holding him in her arms all night as he slept. There had never been anything in her life so real, so perfect. She felt completed by him in every way. All of her hard work, her determination to be something more than she'd been, had come to fruition. She'd worked so hard and had finally found her Prince Charming, and she knew that nothing short of death would come between them.

But the next night, things seemed to change. Just as Clara finished blow-drying her hair for a date night with Andrew, her cell phone rang. She ran for her purse and fumbled around in the bottomless pit. Finally finding her phone, Clara pressed ACCEPT, and brought it up to her ear. Her smile broadened when she heard Andrew's velvety voice.

"Hey, beautiful." Although upbeat like normal, he sounded somehow different.

"Hey, I was just about to head over."

Clara heard the sound of a door slamming on the other end of the line. "Are you just getting home from work?"

"No." She could hear his car keys jingling. "I'm actually calling to see if you'll take a rain check for tonight."

Clara's breathing grew labored. "Why, what's going on? Is everything okay?"

"Yeah, everything's fine. I just found out a friend of mine is in town. A group of us were going to go out for a few beers," he said, oblivious to her mood change. "That's all."

"Oh." Clara tried not to sound too disappointed that she wasn't included. "Okay, well, maybe we can go out tomorrow night instead."

"Yeah, maybe." His truck roared to life on the other end, and Clara could barely hear him.

*She frowned. "*Maybe*? Do you already have plans tomorrow night?" She felt an invisible weight on her chest.*

"She's only here for a week, visiting her brother, so I think we're trying to get the group together as much as possible."

She? "Well, then why don't we all plan something together?" Clara didn't like the high pitch or the slight waver in her voice, and she hoped he couldn't detect it.

"Sure, I'll talk to the guys tonight, and we'll figure something out."

Flopping down on her bed, Clara kicked off her flats and flung her free hand above her head. "Alright..." She stared up at her blank bedroom walls.

"Sorry, beautiful. I'll make it up to you, I promise."

"You better. Call me when you get home, so I know you're safe, okay?"

"Promise."

"Okay, have fun," she said. "But not too much fun..."

He chuckled. "I won't. Talk to you later."

Pulling her hair back into a ponytail, Clara removed her best jeans and flowy top, replacing them with her favorite pajama ensemble—yoga pants and an over-sized sweatshirt she'd bought her first semester at the University of Colorado. She crawled into her bed, and turned on the TV, flipping through the channels until finally settling on a stand-up comedian who wasn't very funny in hopes that he would make her feel less miserable as she lie there, alone. The longer she watched TV, the more tired she became, and the easier it was to forget about Andrew and the fact that he was out with a girl Clara had never even met.

Around three AM, Clara woke to someone jiggling the locked handle of her dorm room door. Her roommate worked nights, so Clara knew it wasn't her. The knob jiggled again, and then there was a light knock from the other side.

"Clara," Andrew whispered. "Unlock your door..."

Clara jumped out of bed and ran to the door. She eased it open to find her boyfriend propped up against the wooden doorframe.

"Hey, beautiful."

She was beyond happy to see him, and a smile engulfed her face. "Hey, yourself. What are you doing here?"

"I missed you," he said, stumbling inside as she opened the door wider. He was drunk.

"How did you get here, Andrew? You didn't drive, did you?"

Shaking his head, he peered out the window, down at the complex's parking lot. "Nope, Kenny dropped me off."

"Good."

When he turned around, Andrew wrapped his arms around Clara and started kissing her neck. She nearly melted in his arms.

"Did you miss me tonight?" he asked as he trailed kisses from her collarbone up behind her ear.

Steadily and with effort, Clara stepped away from him, causing him to stumble forward. "Why do you smell like perfume?" she asked, trying to keep her emotions in check.

"What?"

"You reek of another woman," she bit out. "Why do you smell like another woman?"

Andrew scrunched his face for a moment "Oh"—his eyebrows rose, and he smiled—"I was dancing with Jo." He shook his head, like that explained everything.

"With who?"

"My friend from Oklahoma I was telling you about." He

sobered, registering the burning fury in her eyes. "It's not like that. Don't get your panties in a twist."

Her eyes narrowed to slits. "Excuse me?"

Andrew hooked one thumb in his pocket and scratched the top of his head with his other hand. "You're seriously going to freak out about this?"

"Of course I am, Andrew!" She turned away from him, trying not to lose it completely. "How would you feel if I sauntered over to your house in the middle of the night with men's cologne pouring off me?"

Andrew heaved a sigh, watching her as she began to pace.

"Look, I'm sorry if I'm over reacting," she said. "But it's not like you to ditch me in the first place, and then you come here, smelling like another woman...a woman I've never even met." Her voice was exasperated, but with great effort, she remained calm.

Moments of silence passed, and Andrew's face was unreadable. Just when Clara was about to scream in frustration, Andrew took a step toward her and gently cupped her face in his hand, stroking her cheek with his thumb. "I wasn't thinking, Clara. I'm sorry, but nothing happened. It's not like that with Jo. She's just a friend."

His sincerity made Clara feel like a fool for doubting him. "Promise?" She hated herself for falling back into the complying, lovesick dimwit she'd once been, but she couldn't help it.

A wolfish grin spread across his face. "I've been thinking about you all night," he said and began trailing gentle kisses down her neck, his hands finding their way beneath her sweatshirt. He apologized, over and over until they were both bleary-eyed and too sore to move.

Everything was Joanna's fault. Andrew leaving her. The Josie woman dying. Clara sentenced to a year in Pine Springs before she could be re-evaluated. It was truly poetic. After years of screwing each other over, Joanna had finally won.

Clara shook her head, wondering how long Joanna had planned it and how she'd found out about Andrew in the first place. Although Clara knew it was borderline paranoia to think her mom had been involved in any way, she couldn't help but wonder if it was a possibility. Or if Andrew…

Bile rose in Clara's throat as reality smacked into her. Had her entire relationship with Andrew been a ruse? Had any of it even been real? Had it all been part of Joanna's elaborate, sadistic plan to get back at her? Questions and memories careened into one another, vying for space; everything began to make sense.

Clara trembled with rage. She fisted the letter in her hand, ready to explode. Her head was throbbing with surmounting emotions, emotions she didn't want to think about, emotions she didn't want to feel. She needed to numb them. She needed something to take the burning anger away…

Hearing the squeaky wheel of the laundry cart down the hall, she glanced over her shoulder in time to see Devon slip into the laundry room.

Determined, she stood and strode after him, away from the chattering girls and complaining orderlies. She could hear the strong but silent Devon whistling a slow, comfortable tune in the laundry room. Pulling her hair from its noose, Clara let the golden tendrils fall around her shoulders and into her face. With a quick rap of her knuckles on the laundry room door, she pushed it open and stuck her head inside. The room was steamy and smelled of detergent and bleach.

The whistling stopped. "Someone there?"

Clara felt a thrill at hearing the deep timbre of his voice. This would be a challenge, she thought, and then smiled with anticipation.

"Want some company?" she said as she stepped inside, clicking the door shut behind her.

Devon cleared his throat. "What are you doing in here?" His

voice was detached, but Clara thought she detected a hint of desire. His features hardened into a mask of aversion.

She knew he was determined to turn her away like he'd done so many times in the past, but what he didn't know was that *she* was determined to get what she wanted this time; she wasn't simply flirting. Something about today felt…promising. Whether it was her sheer resolve to bend him to her will, or her need to be distracted, she was dead-set on making him worship her body. She needed to regain control over her life, the life she'd lost the moment she met Andrew. She was already in hell, so she might as well have as much fun as she could while she was there.

Clara flashed Devon a sultry smile.

"You shouldn't be in here," he said, his body tensing as she stepped closer.

She glanced around the room and lifted her hand to the laundry cart parked beside the door. Running her fingers over the stacks of folded towels, she wondered what Devon's skin would feel like against hers.

"You should go back to the rec room with the others." His voice was strained and impatient, likely a result of the sexual tension flooding the room, she thought.

Clara's smile grew, and she cocked her head to the side. "I should be doing a lot of things…" She noticed his eyes flick from her chest to her lips, so she licked them sensually in a silent offering.

A slight twitch gave Devon's otherwise inscrutable emotions away.

Clara chuckled softly, letting her eyes scan the room as she wondered which corner they could stash themselves away in. "You intrigue me," she admitted.

"Cut the shit, Clara. I already told you, I'm not losing my job over you."

She frowned and walked around the shelves in the center of the room, dividing the machines and the folding station. She strolled toward him, her fingers trailing over the metal shelving as she passed. She felt a thrill of excitement as their gazes met and lingered between the riveted, steel uprights as she walked around the shelves.

"No matter how much you deny it, you know there's an attraction between us. Why are you trying to ignore it? You work long hours…you deserve some fun, too." She stopped a few feet in front of him, leaning against the shelving. "I won't tell anyone, if that's what you're worried about."

Judgment hardened his eyes, and Clara was growing impatient.

"You want me, Devon…admit it."

But Devon's expression was unwavering, and he remained silent, contemplating, his eyes boring into hers.

Undeterred, Clara stepped closer, leaving only a few inches between them.

Devon frowned. "I don't know why I'm even considering this," he muttered as he ran his fingers through his curly, brown hair. When his gaze rose to hers again, his eyes raked over her body with an intense longing he'd never let show before, like he had a hunger he could no longer subdue. "But for some reason I can only picture you…beneath *me.*"

Clara's anger fizzled, and a tranquil heat flowed through her. She exhaled, schooling her smirk so not to upset him, but her triumph made it difficult. He was finally seeing things her way.

Pulling off her sweatshirt, Clara draped it over the laundry cart, knowing her white tank top covered little of her braless chest. Devon's eyes studied the curves of her body like they were an offering meant only for him. She could tell his mind was reeling with possibilities, and she liked it.

Devon dropped the towel he'd been holding and reached for her, gripping her bare arms roughly and pulling her into him.

"Oh," Clara squeaked.

Devon swallowed thickly. "You're gonna get me fired," he groaned. He sucked in a breath as she brought his hand up to cup her breast through the thin material of her tank top. There was something erotic about having such control over a man. It was heady and intoxicating. She closed her eyes and breathed out a keening moan.

Tugging on her arm, he led her into the back of the laundry room, tossed her down on a heap of warm, clean towels, and screwed her senseless until her body trembled with fatigue and her head ached so badly all she could think about was sleep.

5

After another night of being blown off by Andrew, Clara decided she would surprise him by showing up at the club he'd gone to with his friends. Turning her old Volvo onto First Street, where she knew she'd find Sparky's, an old club in downtown Boulder, Clara searched for a place to park, grateful when she found a spot less than a block away, just a few cars past Andrew's truck.

Clara readjusted the strapless top of her dress, fluffed up her hair, pursed her glossed lips, and headed toward the club. After batting eyelashes at the bouncer to no avail, she paid the $10 cover charge and strode inside.

Senses assaulted by bad odors, bright lights, and loud noises, Clara tried to focus on her surroundings. A DJ stood up on the balcony above the dance floor, his turntable illuminated by blue and pink strobe lights. The bar and standing cocktail tables were situated in the back of the warehouse-like space. She spotted some of Andrew's friends clustered to the right of the bar.

Pushing her way past the gyrating bodies that crowded the floor, Clara bumped into one person after another, apologizing at first but soon growing so irritated that all she could do was glare and curse at them. Men were groping women, kissing their necks and grinding against their legs. Women were doing the same, some with men, some dancing with women. Sweat glistened on all of them, and there was a certain euphoria humming in the air that Clara strangely found alluring. For a fleeting moment, Clara wondered why Andrew had never taken her *to a place like this, a place where they could be so close and intimate in public.*

The blue and pink lights continued to flash around the room, bringing faces in and out of focus as Clara waded through the throng of sweating bodies. Dark, shadowed faces flashed around her. Smiling faces. Her *face.*

Joanna stood with Andrew's friends, black hair parted to one side, her eyes narrowed, and a smirk on her face. She looked triumphant.

Clara's stomach roiled, and she squeezed her eyes shut. It wasn't possible. When she opened her eyes again, Joanna was gone.

Horror-struck, Clara felt her legs moving of their own accord as her eyes scoured the dance floor, searching for the one person she never *wanted to see again. She pushed between sweating bodies, not registering the looks the dancers were giving her. She didn't care; her mind was a tornado of puzzle pieces swirling around, and she was trying to reach for them, trying to put it all together.*

Jo…Joanna. Visiting from Oklahoma. Andrew ditching her…

"No," Clara nearly sobbed. Joanna was not *going to take Andrew away from her, she was* not *going to ruin everything. Clara pushed through the crowd, desperate to find Joanna. She would do anything to make her disappear. Anything.*

Clara shrieked as a hand clasped her shoulder and whirled her around.

Andrew stood in front of her, his eyes searching her face and confusion twisting his features. He leaned in, bringing his mouth down to her ear. "What are you doing here? Are you okay?"

Clara could barely hear him as the music reverberated around them.

Andrew pulled back, appraising her. "What's wrong?"

Clara hated how innocent he appeared, and she tore out of his grip, making a beeline for the exit. She couldn't stand the sight of him, not when she felt so vulnerable. What had Joanna told him? What did she plan to do?

Flinging the club door open with all her might, Clara ran to her car, her heels clacking against the pavement.

"Clara, wait a sec!"

She fumbled to find her keys in her purse. Hearing them jangling around inside, she grabbed them and was just about to unlock the door when Andrew's hand wrapped around her wrist.

He pulled her around to face him. "Clara, what the hell happened?" Once again he scanned her body. "What are you doing here?"

Clara scowled. "I came to see you*," she said coolly. "I thought it might be a nice surprise."*

"It is, but you look like you've seen a ghost. Are you okay?" He wasn't acting any differently, at least not yet, but she couldn't be sure it wasn't all for show.

"I'm fine."

Andrew frowned.

"I was hoping to meet your friend Jo..."

His eyes widened. "Oh, well, it's just me and the guys tonight."

She eyed him suspiciously. "Really?"

"Yeah, I told you that."

"You said you were going out with your friends." There'd been no mention of "guys only," and besides, Clara had seen Joanna there. He was lying.

"What's gotten in to you?" he asked, searching her face. Clara could tell he was getting annoyed.

Good. She was fuming. "Why don't we ever come to places like this, Andrew? Are you keeping me a secret or something?"

He blanched. "What? No. Why the hell would you say something like that?"

"Because why come to a club with your friends, and not your girlfriend? Especially if Jo *isn't even with you guys?"*

"Clara, Josh is DJing, that's *why we're here. Why are you acting so crazy?"*

She stilled. Crazy? Clara knew Joanna had said something to him...she'd poisoned his mind against her. "What has she told you?"

"What? Who?" His brow furrowed. "Are you drunk or something?"

She was infuriated now. "Never mind." She needed to take a step back, to think. "I need to go," she said. "I can't do this right now."

"Well, we need to talk about this, Clara. I want you to tell me what's going on. I've never seen you like this before."

Clara bristled. "This is the real me, or didn't she tell you that already?"

Andrew's face was scrunched with feigned confusion, yet again.

"Have fun with your friends," she hissed and climbed into her car.

Jarring herself from sleep, Clara hung over the side of her bed and wretched until it felt like every single morsel of food she'd eaten over the last week was expelled from her body. Her throat was raw and burning, her stomach still churning, and her body quivering and covered with sweat.

She vaguely remembered someone's cool hands on her forehead and a lukewarm rag wiping off the chills that were making her tremble. Her head was throbbing so badly she thought she might be dying.

After a few more futile heaves over the side of the bed, Clara lay back down, lost in a fog of swirling memories.

Pulling into the parking lot outside the gym, Clara searched for Andrew's truck. They'd texted each other a little throughout the day, but they hadn't really talked about the night before, not since she'd sped away. She realized now how outrageous she'd acted and wanted to set the record straight. If Joanna had told him anything, it would no doubt be lies to gain his sympathy. Clara needed to tell him the truth, and she was convinced that once she did, he would understand why she'd been so upset.

She had a couple minutes to find a place to park before he was done with practice. Spotting his truck a few rows down, Clara inched her way toward it, careful not to startle a man and woman walking with their backs to her. The woman giggled and pushed the guy's shoulder, causing him to step into the light of the street lamp.

It was Andrew...with another woman.

Clara focused on the woman. She had long, black hair pulled back in a ponytail that swung back and forth as she walked and laughed.

"No," Clara whimpered. Her stomach lurched, and a painful chill emanated from the base of her spine and raked over her body as reality hit her. It was worse than she'd thought. Andrew wasn't just walking with some woman; he was walking with Joanna.

Seething hatred burned to life. That fucking black hair. Clara's heart seized, and she felt her fingernails gouging into her palms as she squeezed the steering wheel. Joanna hooked her arm through Andrew's before resting her head on his shoulder. Leaning to the side, he kissed the top of her head. He was ruining everything... Joanna was ruining everything...

That arm Joanna was clinging to was the same arm that had been holding Clara against Andrew's body only two nights before. That smile he was flashing her was the smile he reserved for Clara. He *was hers.*

Clara couldn't breathe, and her jaw ached as she clenched it.

All of the reasons she hated Joanna came back to her like rows of playing cards turning over with one quick sweep of the hand, revealing each and every one of the horrible memories Clara had tried so hard to forget.

*This was her Prince...*her *prince. Clara had worked so hard to find him, and he was hers, and they were happy...*

A piercing scream filled the car and sent Clara into action. Pressing the gas petal to the floor, she felt a sense of liberation wash over her as Joanna glanced back, her eyes filled with terror.

"Josie, look out!"

Although Clara heard his voice, she was too enveloped by the sound of the revving engine and the sight of Joanna's pretty little body hitting the Volvo with a solid thud. She was pinned against Andrew's truck, hopefully dead, and would never be able to hurt Clara again.

The tension left Clara's body, and a smile tugged at her lips. She was finally rid of Joanna.

Peeling her eyes open, Clara focused on her surroundings. The walls of her room were white, barren, the blinds on the window behind her were drawn, and the air smelled of vomit and sweat.

With a groan, Clara sat up, the ache in her head was duller than before, but it was still there. She felt different, lighter somehow. Glancing around the room, she noticed that it was in complete disarray. Her desk chair was on the opposite side of the room from the desk, her bedside table was moved further away from the bed, and the books that been stacked on her desk had fallen on the floor; a mound of white rags, mostly stained with yellow and green, were piled in their place. There was puke on the side of her bed and a small garbage can against the wall filled with more vomit.

Clara's head lulled back and she immediately regretting the motion. Righting herself, she leaned forward, her hair swung into her face, a hard, clumpy mass of it brushed up against her jaw. She froze. Pulling at the strands with her fingertips, she cringed. Vomit was matted in her hair, and she stank horribly.

Gag reflexes kicking in, she ran for the bedroom door, flung it open, and ran down the hall and into the bathroom. She made it to the toilet in time to empty what looked like water into the toilet bowl. Although there was nothing left in her stomach, she continued dry heaving, unable to stop. She felt like her insides were tearing apart, and her muscles were fatigued, barely able to support her weight.

Trembling and using the wall for balance, Clara inched her way toward the closest shower stall. She turned the nozzle with all her might until, finally, water starting streaming from the showerhead. Twisting the knob all the way to the left, she waited for it to heat from cold to warm to near scorching before stepping, fully clothed, under the falling water. She didn't have the strength, nor the energy, to strip out of her soiled tank top and pajama pants.

Although steam filled the air around her, soothing her raw throat and prickling skin, her bones felt brittle with cold. Huddling in the corner, she sat on the tiled floor in a haze of heat and weariness. Beyond the sound of water pouring ceaselessly over her, Clara heard Roberta's voice echoing in her mind. She felt the pressure of fingers and the discomfort of her muscles as they strained and moved. She felt the roughness of terrycloth against her skin and the biting cold as she was rushed out of the bathroom.

Words bounced around in her mind, but her eyelids were too heavy to open, her mind too numb to process.

"...bed...warm...sick...dead...careful..."

Teeth chattering and body convulsing, Clara felt a soft pressure cover her, comforting her, and something malleable cradled her head.

"Sleep," was the last thing she heard before her mind grayed and her thoughts were lost in darkness.

6

A crash and screaming woke Clara from a deep sleep. Her mind had been dormant, warm and safe in the fissures of her consciousness. But the crashing sound…it riled her awareness, and the cool air lapped at her exposed cheeks and her nose.

Annoyed, she sat up in bed. Her room was dark, and she glanced at the digital clock on her nightstand. 7:46 PM. Her stomach gurgled with hunger, and her mouth was stale and dry. How long had she been asleep?

Peering around her tidied room, Clara was confused. She remembered piles of rags and the stench of vomit. Now, her room was clean; he putrid smell was gone, and the rags and vomit-filled garbage can were nowhere in sight. All that remained was an empty wastebasket on the floor beside her bed, and a mountain of blankets covering her.

She remembered Roberta's voice and the warmth of the shower. Clara shivered at the memory. She'd been so cold, so tired. She'd thought she was dying.

A clatter in the hallway startled her, and she threw the covers back and stepped onto the cold floor. Removing a clean sweatshirt from the bottom drawer of her dresser, Clara pulled it over her head before tugging on a clean pair of jeans.

Her head was still filled with cobwebs, and she rubbed her temple with one hand as she opened the door to the hallway with the other. Maybe some food would help…

Stepping out into the empty hallway, she peered down at the bedrooms to the right. All the doors were closed. She peered to the left. The light of the television flickered in the darkened rec room, sparking a feeling of unease.

Where was everyone? Clara couldn't hear chatter coming from the rec room, and it was Sunday, so there shouldn't have been any group sessions. At least, she thought it was Sunday. Maybe everyone was in the cafeteria for dinner?

A loud crash startled her. It was coming from inside Alicia's room, directly across from hers. Clara took a tentative step out into the hall. Another crash, closely followed by a bone-chilling scream reverberated through Alicia's door.

"Alicia?" Clara rasped, her voice hoarse from disuse. Clearing her throat, she tried again. "Alicia?"

But there was no answer, only the sound of more crashing and screaming.

Hesitantly, Clara reached for the handle. The door was locked.

BANG. Clara jumped back, her hand clasping over her mouth as she tried to control her breathing. BANG. The door rattled and the handle jiggled as what sounded like snarls and growling emanated from the other side. BANG. BANG.

Fingers wrapped around Clara's upper arm, and she spun around with a shriek. Roberta stood there, eyes wide with alarm. "That door stays shut."

Clara exhaled a shaky breath and let Roberta lead her down the hallway toward the rec room.

"What happened? What's wrong with her?" Clara asked, shocked and shaking.

Roberta glanced down at her watch, and then up at Clara. "You've been asleep for almost three days. A lot has happened." She stopped outside of Samantha's room and glanced at Clara. "Wait here for a moment." Slowly, Roberta opened Samantha's door, poked her head inside, and then entered fully before closing the door behind her.

Clara peered around the rec room. Most of the lights were off, and except for Greta, an orderly who was on the phone at the nurses' station, no one was in there. A pile of blankets were folded tidily on the couch as usual, but as far as Clara could tell, everyone else was gone. In their rooms?

Clara turned back around, her eyes sweeping over all ten of the closed bedroom doors on either side of the hall. Was everyone in their rooms, sick like she'd been? The thought brought on a new wave of dread.

When Clara's eyes landed on Beth's door, she swallowed. There was a large X taped on it. After a few tentative steps, Clara pressed her ear to the door, held her breath, and listened. There was no sound. Beth wasn't humming, like she often did; she wasn't talking to herself or screaming and throwing things like Alicia was doing. It was completely quiet.

Clara tapped on the door gently. "Beth?" There was still no sound. Staring at the handle as if it might burn her, Clara reached for it to find that, unlike Alicia's, it wasn't locked. Throat dry and heart pounding, she turned the knob and inched the door open.

Beth's room was dark and reeked of the foul stench of bile. Through the dim glow of the moonlight shining through the window, Clara could see Beth's silhouette on the bed.

"Beth," she breathed, willing the meek woman to answer.

The light flicked on, and Clara screamed. Beth was gray and covered in vomit.

She was dead.

"I told you to stay in the hallway," Roberta reprimanded,

pulling Clara out of the room and switching off the light before she closed the door behind them. "There *was* a reason, you know."

"She's dead," Clara gasped. She couldn't tear her eyes away from Beth's closed door.

"I know," Roberta said, patting Clara's shoulder as she walked her toward the nurses' station. "Most of them are."

Clara looked back at the doors, realizing how many of them had X's on them. "But I'm—you're…"

"You were sick, but you got better. Don't ask me how," she said as she wrote something in a file. "I have no idea how you recovered while everyone else is either dead or more insane than when they got here."

"But, *you* seem fine."

"I was sick too, but it passed quickly. I came into work two days ago and found you in the shower, covered in vomit, and some of the others were already dead from whatever the hell this virus is." She paused, then added, "Alicia killed Devon and Beatrice."

Clara blanched. "Why didn't the police—"

"Greta and I called them hundreds of times, but they never came. The last time we tried to get through to anyone, the phone just rang and rang." She set the file on the counter.

Clara couldn't even blink, she was so overwhelmed. "What about Dr. Mallory and—"

"I haven't been able to get a hold of any of them, either. It's just Greta and me for now, until either someone comes to help us or…" She shrugged. "Who the hell knows." Roberta's exhaustion was evident. "What happened here and what little I've seen on the news is all I have to go off of." She turned on the stereo they used as a PA system and pressed RADIO. "You should listen to it. I have to go get Samantha some clean sheets. I'm running low on everything…" Roberta continued to mutter to herself as she passed through the rec room and down another hallway.

Clara turned the volume up on the radio.

…is at war, yet our enemy is not one we can fight openly. Our enemy has swept through every nation, attacking discretely, killing indiscriminately. We lost thousands before we even knew we were under attack. Many have already fallen, and many more will fall. But we cannot give up the fight.

Clara wrapped her arms around herself, dread filling every ounce of her as she prepared for what she might hear next. She fingered the backs of her sleeves, drawing her arms tighter around herself.

Over the past century, through technological achievements, we made our world smaller. We made the time it takes to communicate across oceans instantaneous, and the time it takes to travel those same routes nearly as fast. We made our world smaller, and in doing so, we sowed the seeds of our own destruction: a global pandemic.

I regret to tell you that as of midnight on the 10th of December, over eighty percent of the world's population has reported or is assumed dead. It is estimated that the death toll will continue to climb. This news is devastating, I know, but all is not lost.

Some of us are surviving. This is how we will fight our enemy—by not giving up, by being resilient and resourceful, by surviving. We are not a species that will go out quietly, so I task those of you who are still alive with one essential purpose: live.

Survive.

Thrive.

If you believe in a higher power, ask for guidance. If you don't, believe in your fellow man. You, the survivors, have the chance to start over, to build anew. Learn from our mistakes. Let the world remain big.

And most importantly, live.

God bless you, my beloved citizens of this great nation. God bless you, and goodnight.

Hearing another crash from down the hall, Clara started trembling. She couldn't help it. She didn't care if it meant she was weak and pathetic. She didn't want to die. She didn't want to lose herself to complete madness or get sick again. She didn't want to turn into whatever Alicia had become. She'd killed Devon. Clara had been with him only days earlier, and now he was dead.

Absently, she walked toward the window, her mind racing with destructive, fearful thoughts of what might happen next.

Hurried footsteps bounded down the hall, too heavy to be Roberta's. Cautiously, Clara turned from the reinforced window as a man rushed into the room.

When his eyes met hers, he straightened. "The nurse sent me in here…are you Clara?" He was holding a shotgun at his side, and his chest was heaving.

Reluctantly, she nodded.

"I need morphine and antibiotics. She said you'd know where I could find them."

Clara continued to stare blankly at him. Who was he?

Taking an assertive step toward her, he inhaled deeply and pointed out toward the road. "There's a man dying out there," he said slowly. "I need meds."

Clara nodded and showed him to Nurse Hadly's office down the hall. As she suspected, the door was locked. "I don't have a key—"

He kicked open the door like it was made of cardboard.

Clara flicked on the light and couldn't take her eyes off of the stranger while he rummaged through the cabinets. He embodied strength and determination, and while she thought she should distrust this stranger, a man who'd wandered into a psychiatric ward, pleading for help and carrying a shotgun, she could only admire him. There was an air about him that made her skin tingle with excitement.

He would keep her safe, she realized. She just had to make sure that she stayed with him, no matter what. Maybe *he* was her real Prince Charming.

This concludes the fifth installment of *The Ending Beginnings*. Clara is also a supporting character throughout The Ending Series: (1) *After The Ending,* (2) *Into The Fire*, and (3) *Out Of The Ashes* (August 2014).

JAKE AND CLARA

VOLUME SIX

1

JAKE

Jake sat on an overstuffed couch in the hospital's rec room, the stark furniture and barren walls brightened by the muted, flashing television. The President's address looped on the radio at the nurses' station behind him, and the more the words sank in, the more his mind reeled. A global pandemic? Start over? Build anew? Was that even *possible*? Amidst his chaotic mind chatter, Jake wondered what the hell he was going to do next.

Rising from the couch, he took three steps toward one of the barred windows across from him, braced his hands against the wall on either side, and let out a long exhale. He stared out at the crashed Cadillac and the few buildings that were visible through the trees across the road. Despite the fact that the city was enshrouded in midnight, it was so changed. It was desolate, like living in the country, but in a more unnatural way. There was no one catching a late night cab…there was no traffic. Street lamps illuminated the haphazardly parked cars on the snow-covered pavement, and a lone, scraggly terrier trotted down the sidewalk, a leash dragging in the snow behind him. The dog stopped and sniffed around the back of the Cadillac, no doubt searching for the remnants of the chips Kyle had left behind, before trotting out of sight.

Choked sobs came from the cafeteria down the hall, breaking Jake's concentration. The nurse, Roberta, hadn't been able to calm Kyle down since the kid realized his father was dead, and it was beginning to grate on Jake's nerves.

As much as he thought he should care about the situation he was in—the disease, the billions dead, the pandemonium—he couldn't, not really. The memory of Becca, struggling as she took her final breath, was too fresh in his mind, too raw. She was gone; Gabe took her away from him.

Jake's hands clenched into fists. He needed to stay focused. He needed to get to Peterson Air Force Base. He needed to find Gabe…to *hurt* Gabe. Emotions boiling, Jake let his hate and anger fuel him into action. He let out a resolute breath and pushed away from the window.

But as suddenly as Jake turned around, he stopped. Clara, the blonde-haired woman whose blue eyes were too assessing, stood in front of him.

Her head was tilted, her lips pursed, and her gaze flicked over his body. "Are you alright?" she asked, her voice light and curious.

Giving her a curt nod, Jake brushed past her with the intention of heading toward the cafeteria.

Clara reached out to him, her hand lightly clasping his biceps.

Body tensing under her touch, Jake froze, looking down at her pale, delicate hand, then into her penetrating eyes.

"It was nice that you tried to help that man," she said, and a small smile pulled at her lips.

Jake made a derisive noise. "Yeah, well, apparently it wasn't enough."

Her brow furrowed, and she let go of his arm. "You did what you could."

Nodding, he started to take another step.

"You're leaving, aren't you?"

Jake frowned and paused again, wondering why she cared one way or the other. "I never should've stopped in the first place."

"No?" Clara's soft voice turned sharp, and she walked to the window Jake had been staring out of only moments before.

She was scared, he realized. *He* should be scared. "You'll be alright here," he said, his voice carrying a weak attempt at comfort.

Clara muttered something he couldn't hear.

He tried again. "You have food…Roberta and the other nurse…"

But Clara seemed unfazed by this words, and she turned to face him. "If it's so safe here, then why won't you stay? Why leave three helpless women and a child alone?"

Jake shook his head, uncertain why he felt the need to explain *anything* to this woman. "There are things I have to deal with."

After a few impatient steps, Clara was directly in front of him. "Take me with you, please?" Her eyebrows lifted and drew together.

"No," he said. "That's not going to happen." He suddenly needed to get out of the room as soon as possible.

"Please." Like a blade, the word cut into him, threatening to sever his last shred of decency. "Please," she whispered.

Unable to resist, Jake turned around.

Clara's eyes were even more pleading than her voice, they were shimmering, and her chest was heaving. "Please," she repeated. "You *have* to take me with you. I can't stay here. You don't understand, I'll die if I stay here…"

No. The word was on the tip of his tongue, but it felt leaden and uncooperative. "I have to go to Peterson, alone," he reminded himself. "I have to go."

"What's in Peterson?" she asked, so close that her presence was distracting him. When he didn't answer her, she continued, "Is it safe there? We need to leave…to go somewhere safe. Please take me somewhere safe, Jake. I can't bear to be here—in this place, in this city—any longer."

Slowly, Jake's eyes shifted to hers, his mind feeling muddled. Words tried to form, and he tried to shake his head, to refuse her pleas, but he couldn't. There was something about her…something unsettling that made him want to walk away and never look back. But another part of him wanted to give into her…to take her with him…to leave Colorado Springs and find somewhere safe…

Clara reached out to touch his arm again, and Jake flinched away.

Straightening, she seemed to collect herself in a single, fortifying breath. Then, when her eyes met his, it was like they were piercing into his soul. "Please."

2

CLARA

"I just need to grab a few things from my house," Jake said, his voice gruff.

As far as Clara could tell, he hadn't spared her a single glance for over an hour, not since they'd climbed into his Jeep back in Colorado Springs and sped away from the hospital for good. Jake's intense focus on the road ahead had only increased since leaving the eerily desolate, looted city behind.

"Okay," Clara said softly. She allowed herself a quick peek at him out of the corner of her eye. One of his elbows was propped on the door as he drove, his head leaned against his upraised hand, just as it had been since he first pulled away from Pine Springs Hospital. "Do you want to rest for a little bit? Maybe stay—"

"No." Jake sounded exhausted…or irritated…or both. His fingers tightened audibly around the steering wheel.

Clara had been casting discrete glances in his direction since they'd been on the road, struggling to understand why his mood had darkened so much. They'd barely interacted at all, other than breathing the same air; there was nothing she could've done to upset him, at least nothing she could think of.

"If you're sorry about leaving that little boy behind with

Roberta, don't be. She'll take good care of him." Clara waited for some sort of reaction from Jake as he guided the Jeep off a frontage road and onto a dirt driveway that disappeared over a slight hill.

Jake raised one shoulder in a minimal shrug. "He's better off with the nurse than he is with me."

Blatantly this time, Clara eyed him. "Is it the kid's dad that's bothering you—that he died?"

Finally, Jake tore his gaze from the windshield and looked at her. In the darkness, his eyes seemed empty. "No. I'm fine."

Even with questions burning on her tongue, Clara decided it was best to let the topic go. The last thing she wanted to do was upset her Prince Charming before they'd even had the chance to get to know one another. At the rate they were going, it would be a long time before *that* happened, Clara thought bitterly.

She wanted to express how grateful she was to him for bringing her along, but he clearly wasn't in the most receptive mood. Back in the hospital, she'd seen his resolve, seen the way his eyes had burned with determination to do something reckless, and a desperate fear had ignited inside of her. Clara'd all but willed him to take pity on her, to abandon his suicide mission—whatever it was—and take her somewhere safe; she'd wanted to be with him with every fiber of her being.

Although she knew what her own reasons were for wanting to leave with Jake—she was drawn to this alluring, protective man who she would willingly spend the rest of her life with—she was clueless as to *his* reasons for changing his mind and allowing her to tag along. He didn't seem to care that he'd found her in a psychiatric hospital; in fact, he hadn't asked her a single question about it. To Clara, the fact that he'd been able to look past *that* proved there was something real and intense budding between them. They were meant to be together, and she just needed to hold on to that.

She almost smiled. What an interesting story they'd have to share with their children one day…

Clara couldn't dismiss her curiosity about *his* past though, especially if his day had been anything like hers, filled with crazy murderers locked behind metal doors and rooms housing cold, dead bodies. If that was the case, it was possible that the man sitting beside her wasn't the man he'd been yesterday. After all, he'd wanted to go to Peterson Air Force Base so badly that he'd almost refused her plea. It was her obvious fear, she thought. Her fear mixed with their simmering attraction had finally won him over.

Clara smiled inwardly. Her path had crossed with Jake's for a reason, and now this tall, dark, and handsome stranger was taking her away from the hell she'd woken up in. It was like her own fairy tale was being written, jumping off the page, and becoming her reality, and despite her Prince Charming's grim mood, her body was humming with giddiness. He'd proved just how noble he was when he tried to save Kyle's father, even if he and Roberta had failed, and he'd saved *her* by bringing her with him, despite his initial reservations. No, Jake was the real thing, nothing like Andrew. Jake had proved he was a man of good conscience, that he was valiant, even.

Joanna could have Andrew and his mind games.

Silently, Clara chided herself for letting her thoughts run away from her. She knew it was stupid to believe in fairy tales, especially after how much trouble they'd gotten her into. But the little girl bottled up inside her still hoped, with all her might, that she could still have a shot at her own happy ending.

From the corner of her eye, Clara studied Jake's profile. Once again, his gaze was fixated intently on what lie beyond the windshield. Strength radiated off of him in nerve-settling waves, making her feel grounded and safe.

Staring out the passenger side window, Clara watched as the tree-lined horizon brightened with the subtle glowing hue of sunrise. After a few more bumps in the road, the Jeep crawled to a stop before a small farm house, just behind what Clara assumed was a snow-blanketed sedan.

Her gaze settled on the car. It looked like it hadn't been moved in days. Whose was it? When Clara turned to ask Jake, his eyes were no longer empty, but illuminated by the dash lights; they were dark pools of pain.

Clara's stomach turned sour. She thought he was probably thirty or so, which meant he could have a wife…and children. Why had she not considered the possibility sooner? With a minimal sense of guilt, Clara hoped that maybe his family was dead, just like everyone else seemed to be.

Taking a deep breath, she glanced around at her surroundings while Jake sat, unmoving, beside her. There were pine trees with snow-laden branches littering the land, and she could make out what appeared to be a separate, rundown garage behind the house; it was so old, it looked close to crumbling. No wonder Jake had seemed reticent to come home, Clara thought. The place was depressing. Although the house seemed charming enough, snuggled in among frozen trees and a few inches of snow, the porch light revealed pieces of pale paint curling off the wood siding, giving Clara the impression that Jake's past wasn't one of privilege, but one of hardship and struggle.

A small smile curved her lips. It was just one more thing they had in common.

3

CLARA

Hot, stinking breaths heaved against the left side of her face, dissolving what few pleasant thoughts she had left. Dogs. Clara didn't do *dogs*. Cooper was propped up on the center console, separating her and Jake.

In silence, Jake stared at the house, completely oblivious as the Husky licked the side of her face, making her cringe, his wet nose cold against her skin. Letting out an annoyed breath, she turned away from him and tried to school her revulsion.

"Are you going inside?" Clara asked, her tone harsher than she'd intended. She wasn't sure why Jake had needed to come back to this place, but she hoped they wouldn't stay long. The thought of being in a house—a *home*—he might've shared with another woman made her heart seize and her blood burn.

As if her words had stirred Jake into action, he opened his door and climbed out of the Jeep before Clara could even remove her seatbelt. Cooper leapt into the driver seat, his bushy tail swatting her in the face before he, too, jumped out of the Jeep and began sniffing around in the snow.

Reaching for her own door handle, Clara briefly met Jake's eyes from where he stood at the open door. She stilled. The way he was staring at her—inscrutable emotions shadowing his eyes and tensing his expression—made her feel uncomfortable, almost unwanted. She bristled.

"I'll be back in a minute," he said. "You should wait out here."

Clara didn't know who might be waiting for him inside, but she wasn't about to give him leeway to change his mind about her. "Do you mind if I come in to pee?" she asked. She cast her eyes downward, hoping to look timid. "I won't get in your way."

After a frustratingly long moment, Jake nodded and shut the driver side door.

Opening her own, Clara slid out of the passenger seat. As soon as her feet crunched down into the slushy snow and a frigid wind gusted past, she questioned her decision to leave the warm confines of the Jeep. Shivering, Clara yanked her scarf out of the backseat and wrapped herself up. She would learn nothing about Jake by waiting for him; she *needed* to go inside.

Brushing stray bits of dog hair off her black peacoat with one hand, Clara shut the door with the other and followed after Jake. She found it increasingly difficult to walk in the snow. How long had it been since she'd gone outside? Two weeks? Three? Being locked in the hospital hadn't afforded her much leisure time to be out and about.

Jake, however, trudged through the snow easily, and his footsteps sounded heavy as he walked up onto the porch and stopped before the front door. He fumbled to fit his key into the lock. He was anxious, Clara realized. Something about this place unnerved him, and the realization made her uneasy, too.

When Jake finally managed to push the door open, Cooper trotted inside. Jake, however, remained at the threshold, staring into the darkness as if it housed all his demons and childhood nightmares. Clara stood behind him, waiting, wondering. After a long, deep breath, Jake took a hesitant step into the house, Clara following tentatively behind.

She knew why *she* was reluctant to be there, but was wary

about why *he* was. "Is it safe?" she asked as she entered what appeared to be a haphazardly decorated living room washed in predawn light. There was a sharp, acrid scent in the air that she couldn't place.

Jake flicked on the light switch beside the door, and the overhead light flared to life, but he stood rigid, motionless.

Taking a timid step toward him, Clara peered over Jake's shoulder and gasped. There was a large blood stain and what appeared to be dried vomit on the hardwood floor across the room, near a hallway. "Oh my God," she breathed. Her hand flew to her mouth. "What happened?"

Cooper began sniffing around the blood and vomit.

"Leave it, Coop," Jake ordered, and the dog lifted his eyes to his master's before whining and retreating down a dark hallway.

Clara could only imagine the horrifying scene that had played out in this room, and she wanted nothing more than to comfort Jake…even if she was relieved to learn whoever else had lived there was apparently dead. "What happened?" she repeated, slowly reaching for Jake's shoulder.

Jake stepped out of her reach. "The bathroom's in there," he said, pointing to a closed door in the mouth of the hallway before following after Cooper. A light flicked on further down the hallway, and Clara could hear Jake rummaging around in what she assumed was probably his bedroom.

Questions mounting and bitterness sprouting from his disregard for her concern, Clara shifted her stare back down to the blood on the floor and tried to let the fact that Jake had completely ignored her roll off her back. He was obviously still coping; she would give him time to come around.

Clara listened to Jake moving around in the room down the hall while she studied the stark living room, devouring every single detail from the scant décor to furniture he'd no doubt bought at a garage sale or a thrift shop. Her gaze landed on a brown leather sectional that rested beneath a picture window, and a small, black purse—its contents sprawling out over the cushions—that was discarded there. Her eyes narrowed.

Forcing herself to look away, Clara peered around at the walls, but there was nothing of interest on them aside from three patches of paint coloring the space between the front door and the large window—one mocha, one taupe, and one that was more of a sage. There weren't any pictures to scrutinize, nor any artwork or sports memorabilia to indicate his hobbies and interests…or *hers.* In fact, the room was lacking any sort of feminine touch.

Honing in on a desk situated against one of the walls across from her, Clara walked toward it; its old-fashioned charm and messiness stood out in the bachelor-esque space. Papers were strewn around on the desktop, a couple nursing textbooks were stacked to one side, and highlighters and pencils were scattered among the crumpled papers instead of inside the empty "Got Coffee?" mug that held only a single pen. The desk seemed to be the only part of the house that wasn't meticulous—other than the blood and vomit she'd bypassed—and the only thing that had much character at all.

Nursing books? Clara looked behind her at the purse on the couch, a Coach knockoff. Jake had *definitely* had a woman in his life, and based on all of the evidence, Clara guessed the desk was hers.

Just as Clara looked down at the desk to study what was written on the papers—to look for a name or study the style of penmanship—Cooper scampered into the room, his nails clacking on the hardwood, making her jump.

"Stupid mutt," Clara muttered. He trotted into the kitchen, where a half-filled food bowl awaited him beside a round dining table. Wondering if they could leave the dog behind, Clara watched as Cooper scarfed down his food. She could hear the crunch of dried kibble and the sound of the bowl clanging against the wall with each impatient bite. She wasn't sure why the dog's mere presence annoyed her so much, but it did. She rolled her eyes.

Hurrying back up the hallway, Jake entered the living room with two large duffel bags slung over his shoulders. "I need to grab a few more things from the garage." His eyes darted to Clara's, and she blushed, wondering if he could tell she'd been snooping. "I'll be right back," he said, dropping the bags near the front door. "There's food in the cupboards." He strode back into the hallway, opened a door that revealed a closet, and pulled out a canvas bag filled with more bags. "Fill these with food that won't spoil," he said, thrusting them at her. "There are more paper bags underneath the sink if you need them." With that, he headed through the kitchen and out a side door, leaving Clara standing by the closet with the canvas bags balled up in her arms.

She definitely wanted Jake to think she was useful, so she went to work, filling the bags with as much food as possible. After stocking them with granola bars, beef jerky, crackers, an almost empty bag of trail mix, a few plastic cups, bowls and spoons, cans of soup, and several bags of chips, Clara grabbed the few apples and oranges that were sitting in a fruit bowl on the counter, stuck them in one of the bags, and left everything on the kitchen table. With a sigh, she headed into the bathroom since she'd used it as her excuse for following him into the house to begin with.

The moment she flicked on the bathroom light, Clara's eyes found and lingered on the two toothbrushes in the holder. Closing and locking the bathroom door behind her, she tried not to feel angry or hurt, but it was impossible. She pictured Jake standing in the tight confines of the bathroom, his arm brushing against a woman's as he stood beside her…washing up before they crawled in bed together for the night.

Unbidden, an image of Joanna flashed through Clara's mind, and she momentarily saw red. Realizing there was no possible way Joanna could've known Jake, that she could've been in *any* part of his life, Clara rolled her eyes at her own ridiculousness and went about her business.

When she was finished, she washed her hands and face, then

took a long, scrutinizing look at herself in the mirror. She stared into her shadowed, blue eyes, wondering if she might look like the woman from Jake's past. She squinted and turned her head to the side, examining her jawline and pointed nose. She wondered what Jake thought of her appearance as she ran her fingers through her long, blonde hair. Was he helping her because she looked like the other woman? Clara realized that must be it. Why else would he keep his distance but be unable to let her go at the same time?

It was all starting to make sense—the conflicted cast to Jake's eyes, his hesitation. Clara wondered what else might be storming behind his intense gaze and quiet manner.

With a sigh and a promise that, one day soon, she would ask Jake all of her questions, Clara flicked off the bathroom light and opened the door. The living room was silent, meaning Jake was still in the garage. Unable to resist the temptation, Clara took the opportunity to explore the rest of the house.

She took a few quick steps further down the hall and stopped in the doorway to the room Jake had been banging around in earlier. Switching on the light, she noted that the bedroom was in disarray, but after all the drawer-slamming she'd heard, she wasn't surprised. What *did* surprise her—and fill her with relief—was the lack of anything feminine in the small space. The dresser drawers were open, but all Clara saw were white t-shirts and a lot of neutral-colored long sleeve shirts. There were no pictures or jewelry boxes resting on top of the dresser, no photos hanging on the walls or decorative pillows on the bed, and the nightstand had only a glass of water and an alarm clock. There was nothing to make Clara think that Jake had shared this room with a woman.

Her heart lightened.

Turning off the light, she backtracked up the hall, stopping in a different doorway. With another flick of a switch, the room was illuminated, and Clara finally began to understand. Jake hadn't lived with a spouse, but perhaps a roommate or sister. The bedroom was messy but feminine. A Queen bed was situated in one corner, a comforter balled up on top, and textbooks and tissues were scattered on the floor. Framed, scenic photographs, brightly colored painted canvases, and corkboards cluttered with scraps of paper and magazine cut outs decorated the walls around the room.

"You shouldn't be in here," Jake said from behind her.

Clara startled. "Is this your sister's room?" she asked, standing in the center. She hadn't even realized she'd entered it.

Jake stared at Clara, giving her a quick nod before turning and leaving the room. "Come on," he said from the hallway. "It's time to go."

She could tell he was trying to control his temper. The chill in his voice sounded more like hurt and sadness than anger, and she suddenly felt horrible for snooping—relieved the woman was his sister, but horrible, too.

Hurrying after him, Clara entered the living room.

Jake wasted no time in handing her a few of the food bags and nodding to the open front door. "We'll put as much as we can in the back of the Jeep, but it's getting full."

Clara lugged one of the bags up onto her shoulder. "Can I help you pack anything else?"

Jake shook his head. "I've already put as much fuel as I could find in the back." He scanned the living room and kitchen. "We should have enough food to last until we get to Indiana."

"What's in Indiana?" Clara asked, heaving another bag of food onto her other shoulder.

As Jake stared at her, his face softened, just a little. "A safe place, I hope."

4

JAKE

It was still night as Jake drove through the flatlands of the Missouri countryside, Cooper curled up in the back of the Jeep and Clara asleep in the passenger seat. Only the static of the radio interrupted his renegade thoughts now and again.

How had it come to this, making a mad dash for Joe's with a stranger? He still wasn't clear on how many days had passed since his sister killed herself. The blood stains on the floor had been the only trace of Becca…the only sign that his worst nightmare had actually been reality. Now he was driving away from Colorado—away from Gabe—and Jake knew he'd never discover the truth. He'd never know *why* any of it had happened. He wasn't even sure if Gabe was still alive. He wasn't even sure if he cared.

Glancing over at Clara, Jake felt lost. Her head rested against the window, and she looked almost angelic in her sleep, but he was still wary. He hated himself for letting her convince him to abandon his vendetta against Gabe, but for some reason, he couldn't help it. Getting Clara away from Colorado weighed on his mind…consumed him. He *had* to do it.

Jake took a deep breath. He knew, without a doubt, that Clara was trouble. From the first moment she peered at him with her big, blue eyes back in the hospital, looking both frightened and hopeful, he'd known. He'd found her in a psychiatric ward, for God's sake. He'd had a plan; he'd been determined. So how had he veered so completely off track? He had his own problems to worry about, and he needed space, not someone else to look after.

Jake's only solace in abandoning his original plan was that he was honoring his sister's dying plea by leaving Colorado Springs. At the thought, Jake felt the tiniest spark of hope; he might even get to see Joe.

Shaking his head, Jake scrubbed one hand over his face. Regardless of whether or not he would get to see the old man, Jake definitely shouldn't have said yes to Clara. He may not have understood *why* he'd agreed to help her, but he had, and now he needed to figure out what to do with it.

With a loud yawn, Cooper stretched in the backseat and perched his front paws up on the center console. Jake patted the dog's head absentmindedly, glancing into the rearview mirror to see if there were any other drivers on the road behind him. It had been over an hour since he'd passed another car, and almost an entire day before that. He and Clara had only stopped in a town once, to use the bathroom and syphon more fuel. They'd watched three men run into a department store, closely followed by the sounds of gunshots and shouting, and from then on, he'd stayed away from heavily populated areas. People weren't just dying of a virus; they were losing their goddamn minds, and much to Clara's dismay, bathroom stops had become road-side only.

On the radio, the same broadcast looped over the airwaves for the umpteenth time, intermingled with more static and silence, and their dire situation became more and more apparent. Other than Clara and his dog, Jake was completely alone. He could only hope that reclusive Joe was still alive and uninfected. As he considered the alternative, Jake swallowed back the emotion balling up in his throat.

Clara stirred and stretched in the seat beside him. "How long have I been asleep?"

Jake glanced at the clock on the dashboard. "About four hours."

Raising his head, Cooper licked Clara's cheek, making her cringe. She clearly didn't like dogs, and for some reason, the fact that she was trying to hide it made Jake want to smile.

Hesitantly, Clara reached for Jake's forearm. "Do you want me to drive for a little while? You should probably get some rest…"

Although exhaustion had settled in his bones and had been weighing heavy on his mind for hours, Jake didn't feel comfortable with that scenario. He wasn't sure how comfortable he felt with Clara touching him, either. Looking at her, he shook his head. "I'll be fine."

Clara smiled, a sympathetic light he didn't quite understand filling her eyes. "Are you sure?"

He looked back out at the road, and Clara removed her hand from his arm.

"There's no more snow," she said as she peered out the window, her gaze fixed on the SUV stopped in the opposite lane as they drove passed it.

Jake noticed the outline of the dead driver. "Not since we crossed the state line," he said.

Clara cleared her throat then looked at him. "Do you mind if we pull over somewhere soon so I can go to the bathroom?" she asked, suddenly fidgeting in her seat; he noticed that her ankles were crossed and that she was biting her lip.

Jake fought his amusement. "Sure." Although Clara's fluttering lashes and demure smiles were lost upon him, she was entertaining at times, making him feel somewhat better about having her around. He rubbed his face, his mind feeling a bit hazy. He needed to get some air. "I have to refill the gas cans anyway."

After a few more miles, Jake pulled off Interstate 60 and into a small, historic-looking town—population 11,169, according to the sign. The less people they had the chance of running into, the better, and Jake didn't know how many more opportunities he would have to scavenge fuel.

The off-ramp spat them out next to a small shopping center at the end of a brick home and bare tree-lined suburbia. With no other cars or people in sight, Jake turned into the plaza entrance nearest a giant, unlit Shell sign and headed for the gas station situated kitty-corner to a small grocery store. Driving between the buildings when possible, Jake tried to stay out of plain sight and hoped the rumbling sound of the Jeep's engine didn't attract any unwanted attention.

Once in the alleyway between the grocery store and a fence lined with leafless trees, Jake parked the Jeep. "Wait here. I'm going to check everything out."

He looked back at Cooper, scratching the dog underneath his chin, but spoke to Clara. "Do your business by the Jeep, but make sure he stays with you and get back inside and lock the doors when you're finished." Jake peered out at the parking lot. Without snow covering the ground and tire tracks to analyze, it was difficult to tell if anyone had been around in a while. The few cars in the lot looked like they hadn't been moved in days; they were dirty with what Jake assumed was recently melted snow, but there was no way to be certain. All the storefronts were dark and looked empty, and they weren't broken, making Jake feel slightly better.

"Keep the engine running, just in case," he said, giving Cooper's ear a quick, gentle tug.

Reaching between the center console and his seat for his handgun, Jake tentatively opened his door and climbed out. He popped the collar of his brown military style jacket to shield his neck from the cold and headed toward the edge of the fence, hoping to catch a clearer glimpse of the gas station beyond. It was quiet except for the sound of the gusting wind, and the air was so cold it burned his ears and the inside of his nose.

Glancing around furtively, Jake headed toward the grocery store. After scanning inside, seeing no movement, and deeming the coast clear, at least as far as he could tell, Jake headed back to the Jeep and grabbed two fuel cans and ten feet of tubing before setting off for the gas station to syphon as much fuel from the reservoirs as possible.

After a few minutes of fumbling with numb fingers, Jake crouched beside the cans as they filled, impatiently waiting. He regretted not grabbing any gloves from his house. But then, he'd been regretting a lot of things…

Whining recaptured his attention, and Jake looked up to find Cooper and Clara standing in front of the Jeep, waiting for him. He shook his head. He'd wanted to leave her behind with Roberta, but for some reason he couldn't. He'd told her to wait in the Jeep when they were at his house, but she didn't want to. He told her to wait for him in the Jeep with Cooper, but they both stood there, out in the open, watching him. Jesus Christ, Jake thought. She was going to get him killed.

Cooper whined again, his tail wagging as he fidgeted in place. Jake held out his hand, commanding the Husky to stay put, and when the gas cans were full, he removed the tubing and screwed the lids on tight before heading back to the Jeep.

Clara watched him, her eyes narrowed like she was trying to read the depths of his soul. He'd caught her watching him before, and he didn't like it; he appreciated not knowing much about her, and her not knowing much about him. Everything would be easier that way, he kept telling himself.

"You should be inside the Jeep," he grumbled and brushed past her as he headed for the back of the car.

"I know, but…" Clara said, trailing off.

Jake heaved the large gas cans into the back.

"Jake," Clara whisper-screeched.

He looked up to see two people in white down jackets and gray beanies walking away from the grocery store. One of them was carrying a shotgun at their side, the other, two bags that Jake assumed were filled with groceries.

Jake shut the back of the Jeep slowly, quietly, and pulled the handgun out from his waistband. "Get inside," he whispered vehemently, and motioned for Cooper to be quiet.

Without hesitation, she moved to do as he said, but a gust of wind slammed the door shut, catching the duo's attention. They stopped and peered around.

Straightening, Jake clicked off the safety of his gun as two heads turned his way; an older, bearded man and a middle-aged woman stared back at him. The man, who had the shotgun clutched in his right hand, studied Jake, but he made no move to raise his gun. The woman looked frightened as she clutched the two grocery bags in her arms, her gaze skirting between Jake and the man beside her.

"We're just here to get some fuel," Jake said, and he relaxed his grip on his pistol. "We don't want any trouble."

The older man's eyes shifted from Jake to Clara in the Jeep, studying them both. He turned to the woman beside him, murmured something, and after squeezing her hand as she reached out and gripped his arm, he looked back at Jake like he was waiting for reassurance.

Unwilling to put his gun away, Jake only nodded.

Glancing at his companion, the old man nodded to her before starting toward Jake, who did the same. They met in the middle, stopping a few feet from one another.

"Where are you from, son?" The man asked, his voice gravelly.

"Colorado, headed to Indiana. We only stopped for fuel."

The man's eyes darted to the Jeep once more. "Is that your girl?"

"No," Jake said easily. "She had nowhere to go…"

The man's eyes found Jake's again, and Jake couldn't help but feel like the man was waiting for Jake's expression to give something away. But the old man surprised Jake when he said, "You look like you could use some rest, and I'd be interested to learn what the rest of the country looks like right about now." He pointed over his shoulder. "My wife and I live in that neighborhood over there. You're welcome to stay the night, to get some sleep and have something warm to eat before you get back on the road."

Although Jake was apprehensive about the old man's intentions and skeptical of his immediate trust, the fear in his wife's eyes confirmed that she was just as leery as Jake was, making him feel a little more at ease. Besides, Jake was just as curious to learn what the couple had to say, and he knew he needed to rest if he and Clara were going to make it to Joe's in one piece.

"That's kind of you," Jake said, accepting the man's offer with a nod.

The old man mirrored Jake's gesture and started back toward his wife. Jake watched them for a moment. The man mumbled something as he wrapped his arm around the woman's shoulders, and soon they were walking briskly back toward the neighborhood, using the sidewalks and tree coverings to help them stay out of view.

Realizing he was shaking from the cold, Jake retreated to the Jeep and filled Clara in on his brief conversation with the man.

"Are you sure it's safe?" she asked.

Jake shook his head. "But we could use the rest and some real food."

When Clara's concern didn't lessen, he added, "The woman he's with is just as suspicious of us as we are of them. If she's scared…that's a good thing."

"Why is that a good thing?"

Jake put the Jeep in gear. "Because it means she's not insane."

Clara scowled. "What about the man?"

Not taking his eyes off the road as he drove out of the plaza, Jake tried to reassure her the best he could. "He seemed fine. Besides, we still have a long drive ahead of us, and they might know something that we should know, too."

5

JAKE

In a heavy silence, Jake guided the Jeep through the neighborhood, following the man and woman. Cars lined the street, but Jake couldn't help but notice that only two of the brick homes on the entire block had smoke billowing from their chimneys, one of them apparently belonging to the couple.

As the man and woman entered a two story home, Jake brought the Jeep to a stop at the curb directly in front of the house and turned the engine off. He reached into one of the duffel bags and pulled out a black-handled hunting knife. Handing it to Clara, he said, "In case I read these people wrong."

She pulled the knife out of its sheath and her eyes widened. It was small but serrated and menacing. Jake had no clue if she could or would use it, but he couldn't send her inside empty handed. Risking his own life blindly was one thing, but hers… Although he didn't necessarily want her there, he couldn't ignore her safety, either.

He was about to offer her an escape plan should something happen, but he hesitated. She'd proven multiple times that she didn't really listen to him, so he decided not to waste his breath. "Just get out of there if anything goes wrong, okay?"

Clara blinked and shook her head. "But…what about you?"

"I'll be fine," he promised. And, recalling the past few days of near-death experiences—specifically, the bullet that should still be in his chest—Jake thought it was probably a promise he would strangely be able to keep. Or maybe it was just that he didn't really care… "Just make sure you get yourself out of here if things go south."

Her brow lifted before she nodded and shoved the knife into her coat pocket.

Leaving Cooper in the Jeep, Jake peered up and down the street before he and Clara headed over to the house and up the steps; the front door creaked opened before they could even knock.

The older man poked his head out of the house and surveyed the sidewalks and road. Jake could smell smoke from a fire, and the warmth from inside grazed his face.

"Come on in," the man said with a welcoming smile.

Noticing the man had come to the door without a weapon of any kind, Jake hesitated. Although *Jake* knew that he and Clara were harmless enough, the man didn't know that, and it struck him as a bit odd that the old man wasn't being more cautious.

Jake's reluctance must have given him away, because the old man shook his head and pointed to his temple. "Don't ask me how I know, but I do…you're a good guy, and we have nothing to fear from you."

As strange and nonchalant as that sounded, the honesty and kindness in the man's light brown eyes persuaded Jake to believe him. And the way the man's gaze narrowed with uncertainty on Clara set Jake even further at ease. It looked like *he* didn't trust her completely, either. That, alone, told Jake he could trust the old man.

With a nod, Jake stepped inside the house, Clara following in after him. The scent of cigars mingled with the smell of the fire.

"My name's Dale," the old man said. He gestured to a coat rack behind the door, and Jake and Clara removed their jackets and scarves.

Relieved of his outerwear, Jake offered Dale his hand. "I'm Jake."

"I'm Clara." She extended her hand to Dale, as well.

Dale eyed her again before smiling and pointing over his shoulder into the living room. "Come on, my wife, Linda, has some chicken soup on the stove, and we just picked up some rolls over at the store."

The three of them left the entryway and entered a narrow living room. Jake surveyed the home, conscientious of their surroundings. The house was small with a staircase to the right of the entryway leading up to what he assumed were the bedrooms on the second floor. The living room was filled with colonial furniture and accented with floral and lace-trimmed pillows, just what he would expect to find in an older couple's home, and velour drapes were drawn over every window. If not for the blaze of the fire in the brick hearth in the living room and the candles lit on the dining room table in the next room over, the house would've been completely dark.

"I hope neither of you are claustrophobic," Dale joked, ushering them through the living room and toward the rectangular dining room table. "We try to keep a low profile…keep everything closed up so nobody notices we're here."

Jake glanced over at the roaring fire, thinking of the smoke he'd seen rising from the chimney.

"Some days it's cold enough to chance it," Dale said in answer.

Linda set a tea kettle and mugs on the table, her eyes still held suspicion, but she ventured a warm smile nonetheless.

"You'll have to forgive my wife's reserve," Dale said as he pulled out a chair for himself and sat down.

Jake stood in the living room, Clara directly beside him. Her hand wrapped around his forearm, and Jake looked down at her, but she didn't seem to notice.

"You're the first *normal* folks we've seen in a few days," Linda offered.

"Dear, this is Jake and Clara. They're from Colorado." He met his wife's worried eyes and gave her a reassuring smile before turning his attention back to Jake. He gestured toward the other chairs at the table "Please, have a seat, and get comfortable."

Linda retreated to the kitchen and returned with a pot of coffee. "Coffee or tea?" she asked, holding up the coffee pot.

"Or would you care for something a bit stronger?" Dale said with a smirk and pointed to a bottle of Scotch at the far end of the table.

Jake grinned and stepped out of Clara's hold and toward the table.

"Pour him a glass of Scotch, please, my dear."

Jake pulled a chair out at the head of the table and sat down, the tension in his body quickly subsiding. "Thank you," he said, glad to be putting something inside him that would calm the unease he'd been feeling ever since Becca fell ill. He accepted a highball glass from Linda and nodded his thanks.

Slowly, Clara approached the table, pulled out the chair to the left of Jake's, and sat down.

"What would you like to drink, dear?" Linda raised her eyebrows and smiled warmly.

Clara clasped her hands in front of her. "Uh, tea, please."

Jake could feel Clara's ever-present gaze as it settled on him, but he kept his focus on Dale. "Other than the President's address, there's been no word on the radio all day," he said, running his hand over his short hair. "You have any idea how bad things have gotten?"

Dale shook his head and laughed bitterly before holding up his coffee mug. "To sanity," he said dryly.

Standing beside him, Linda sighed and brought her tea mug up to clank against the rest of theirs before sitting in the chair beside her husband.

With a long contemplative exhale, Dale continued, "There's been some chatter on the radio waves every once in a while, but I can't understand much of it."

"What sort of chatter?" Clara asked.

Jake watched her as she carefully sipped the hot liquid from her mug, but when her eyes shifted to his, he looked away. The last thing he wanted was to encourage any sort of familiarity between them—not until he could get his brain working right and he felt in control of his life again.

Dale poured a bit of Scotch into his coffee. The moment he took a sip, he seemed to relax a little. "It's difficult to make out. Pretty sure it's military because a lot of what they're saying to one another is in code. The most I could get out of it was a small band of survivors at Fort Knox."

"More survivors," Jake thought aloud as a sudden, hopeful thought popped into his mind. Kentucky wasn't too far off course to Indiana, and military personnel would be able to care for Clara. He could leave her with them, then be on his way.

"Yes, it would seem so," Dale said thoughtfully. "But other than the young man down the street, we've seen no other sane people in days. Luckily, we've been pretty well left alone in our neck of the woods, but I'm not sure how long that'll last. People are going to get desperate, especially if winter worsens."

Linda cleared her throat and stood. She smiled at Clara. "Do you mind helping me dish up supper in the kitchen, Clara?"

Clara's gazed skipped to Jake's. He wasn't sure if she was asking his permission or if she wanted him to protest, but when he nodded, Clara rose from her seat. She followed Linda to the kitchen, glancing back at Jake and Dale before passing through the doorway and out of sight.

"Be careful with that one," Dale warned quietly. "I can't put my finger on it, but something's not right about her."

Jake stared into Dale's warm eyes and nodded. He didn't need the old man to elaborate; he knew Clara was trouble. Leaning back in his chair, Jake rubbed his hands over his face and let out an exhausted exhale. "The roads have been deserted for a good day or so. I stopped driving into cities and towns as much as possible, because unlike the roads, the cities aren't deserted, and most of the people who're left…" He shook his head. "Best to avoid them."

Dale took another sip of his spiked coffee. "Mark, the man down the street, watched his girlfriend and best friend get shot dead in Branson. Apparently home was the only place he could think to go. He drove like a bat out of hell getting back, ran into my truck when he spun out coming around the corner. He was shaken up pretty bad, and he hasn't come out of his house since. That poor boy's going to die in there."

Jake stared into the kitchen, listening to the sounds of Linda and Clara milling around. "So this virus nearly kills everyone and turns most of the survivors into crazed lunatics…" He shook his head and took a gulp of his Scotch. "I don't get it."

"The end of days," Dale said as he stared into his mug. "I've always let my wife go to church and believe whatever she likes. I've never said much about it one way or the other. But I have to admit, I'm starting to regret not opening up the good book more than a few times in my life, especially over the past week." He took another sip from his cup. "It makes me wonder if I shot myself in the foot not going to Sunday mass and reading what I thought was wish-wash filling the pages…it's like I'm missing out on the bigger picture."

Jake had no desire to get into a theological debate over the virus and whether or not God had anything to do with it. Finishing his Scotch, he reveled in the wake of warmth the liquor left behind as it coated his insides. He felt a little lighter. "I appreciate you letting us rest here, Dale, I really do. We'll be gone first thing in the morning."

Dale poured Jake another glass of Scotch. "It's nice to have visitors. Who knows if we'll ever have any again."

Rotating his glass on the table, Jake thought about tomorrow and the day after that. The idea of spending who knew how long with Clara, facing who knew what together, was bothersome. It wasn't that she'd done anything to upset him, at least nothing he could put his finger on, he just didn't want the responsibility of looking after her, and he didn't like how she made him question his instincts every time she opened her mouth.

"So," Jake said, breaking the silence. "Do you think heading to Fort Knox is a good idea?"

Dale shrugged. "Sounds that way. But I don't think we'll be going there any time soon." Dale smiled, but it didn't touch his eyes. "I'm not a big fan of the military. It's just engrained in me, I guess. I was bitter when they rejected me," he said, lost in a memory. "They said asthma was one of those make-you-or-break-you deals. I refused to support them for years after that. In fact, I met Linda in a picket line speaking out against the conditions and treatment of soldiers." He downed the last of his coffee and Scotch concoction. "I was young and stupid for most of my life it seems. There's nothing like a global outbreak to put things in perspective."

Unable to stomach sitting there, rehashing all their regrets, Jake stood. "I should go check on my dog," he said. "I'll be back in a bit."

Dale nodded, seeming to understand Jake's withdrawal. "You're welcome to bring the dog in; it can sleep in the entryway. It's gonna be a cold one tonight…might even get some snow."

"Thank you," Jake said and retrieved his jacket, then headed out the front door. He was grateful Dale was so kind…and trusting. But he also worried for the old man and his wife; that trust might be their downfall.

After letting Cooper out to get some exercise and do his business, Jake led him back into the house. Closing the door, he told the Husky to lie down in the entryway, then removed his jacket once more. When he walked into the living room, Jake noticed that

Clara and Linda were sitting down at the table, deep in conversation, Dale watching them blandly.

Jake paused, listening.

"And how long have you known each other?" Linda said with an inquisitive smile.

Clara smiled back before slurping broth from her spoon. "It's been a while, now."

"Well, it sounds like you two are perfect for each other, like he's your own knight and shining armor."

Absently tearing a piece of bread in half, Clara's smile broadened. "I know. I don't know what I would've done without him. I was barely recovered from the flu, and he was the first sane person I'd seen…it's like it was meant to be."

Clara's omission of the complete truth and her sudden animation bothered Jake, and he definitely didn't like the way she'd twisted everything into a damn fairy tale in her head. Continuing forward, he made sure his footsteps were loud and heavy, wanting the conversation to end.

Fort Knox was looking more and more convenient by the minute.

6

CLARA

It had been almost an entire day since Clara had left Dale and Linda's house with Jake, and he'd barely said a single word to her the entire time they'd been on the road. Jake wasn't a talkative man to begin with, but he'd become even more tightlipped than before. Alternating between reading a magazine and sleeping hadn't distracted Clara like she'd hoped, and her curiosity and frustration was growing in leaps and bounds.

Eyes skirting over to Jake, she appreciated the golden sheen the sinking sun cast over his contemplative face. "What's wrong?" she asked, her tone soft and concerned. "You've been quiet all day. Did I do something—"

"I'm fine," he said.

She bristled. He said that simple phrase way too often for her liking. "You don't *seem* fine," she said, this time her tone was terse and impatient. "If you don't tell me what's wrong, then I can't help you…"

Jake looked away from the road to glare at her, catching her off guard. "I said 'I'm fine'."

Sharp irritation smoldered inside her as he returned his eyes to the road. "Will you at least tell me where we're going?" she asked.

"Or is it a secret?" If he was going to give her attitude, then she was perfectly capable of dishing it right back at him.

Resting his elbow on the door, Jake rubbed his forehead. "We're stopping at Fort Knox. Dale said there are survivors there, and I could use a break from driving."

"Oh." She wasn't sure if she was relieved to be stopping or a little let down by the idea. Stopping meant that, once again, she wouldn't be spending quality time with him—alone.

Clara ran her fingers through her hair and heaved a sigh. She'd had a restless night at Dale and Linda's with Jake sleeping on the couch downstairs and her futile attempt to sleep in the guest room upstairs. She hadn't liked not having him close, and she felt like the night of separation had made Jake more irritable and impatient with her. So now, his distance, whatever the cause, was putting a wedge between them. What damage would another night like that cause? She didn't want to lose him when they were just getting started…before they could explore a future together she knew they were destined to have.

"But…" Clara hedged. "What if they're not the good kind of survivors?" Innocence dripped from her voice, she made sure of that. She hoped that by playing the demure damsel role he might revert back to her protective Prince Charming. So, she watched Jake's reaction carefully and held in a victorious smile as a fleeting look of concern shadowed his rich, brown eyes and momentarily relaxed the hard set of his features.

Clearing his throat, Jake changed lanes and took the Fort Knox exit. "I'm sure it'll be fine."

That was it? That was all the reassurance he was going to give her? Her dejection solidified. "Well, as long as you're sure," she said with a sneer. She couldn't help the growing suspicion that there was something else going on, something he didn't want her to know. Whatever *it* was, it was pissing her off, and she was determined to figure it out. She needed Jake—she *wanted* him—and goddammit, they'd come this far together; she was going to have him.

Clara wanted to scream, but she folded her arms over her chest and made a point to turn her attention out her window, away from him.

"It'll be good for us to get out of the Jeep and stretch our legs," he said.

She detected a note of apology in his voice, and her mood immediately brightened a little at his effort. "But don't you want to get to Joe's? Isn't Kentucky out of our way? We're only a day away from Indiana."

Jake glanced down at the folded map on his lap. "Not too far out of our way," he said and turned onto a frontage road, his focus back on the journey instead of on her.

Of course it was.

As they drove on in silence, Clara scanned the landscape surrounding them. Whatever area they were passing through was lined with withered fields and barbed wire fences, nothing that was particularly memorable.

"Who do you think will be there?" Clara asked. She spotted what appeared to be a book lying on the pavement, and she straightened in her seat. As they drew nearer, she noticed the gold embossed vines on the cover and wondered if it was a book of fairy tales or—

With barely a thump, the Jeep drove over the book. Clara glowered at Jake only to find that he was completely oblivious. Feeling another beat of annoyance, she returned her gaze out the window.

Steadying her voice, she ventured to start another conversation, "Do you think there will be a lot of people—survivors, I mean?" When Jake didn't answer her again, she shifted in her seat to look at him again, expectant.

He glanced in the rearview mirror, his eyes jetting to her then back out at the road in front of them. "I don't know, Clara. Maybe." He was clearly distracted.

Turning back to the passenger window, Clara rolled her eyes. Never mind, she thought. She'd just wait and see.

The nearer the Jeep drew to the military base, the more thankful Clara was that they were stopping to take a break. She was trying to be agreeable; she was holding her tongue and doing her best to keep her emotions at bay—two things she'd never been very good at—but Jake was being difficult. They could stand to put some space between them; she needed to clear her head, at least for a little while.

From the corner of her eye, Clara noticed Jake yawn and rub the back of his neck. Unsure why she hadn't thought of it before, she wondered if, like her, he hadn't slept well. It was certainly possible that he didn't like the thought of her being so far away from him, either. Maybe he'd been worried about her all night and was moody as a result of it. Yes, that would make perfect sense.

Clara settled in, feeling a bit lighter.

The tension filling the Jeep seemed to dissolve as they pulled through the main gate of the Fort Knox military base, the entrance flanked by two massive tanks. Slowly, they made their way around the base, Clara watching Jake as his gaze flicked ceaselessly around them.

For minutes, they found no sign of survivors. Everything was stark and dead, completely consumed by winter's brutality. They drove past the gold vault surrounded by the chain-link fence and continued on, soon passing a couple abandoned warehouses. As they rounded a group of office buildings with broken windows, one of which appeared to have caught fire and had soot decorating the side of it, Clara noticed movement a dozen yards ahead.

Squinting, she could just make out a man in fatigues—a soldier, she assumed—standing beside a Hummer in front of an auto mechanic shop. He was smoking a cigarette, his left foot propped up on the back tire of the massive vehicle. When he noticed the Jeep coming up the road, the man's easy expression faltered, and he stiffened, immediately picking up a rifle that had been leaning against the Hummer's fender.

Jake slowed the Jeep, and Clara's heart drummed wildly in her chest at the sight of the giant gun in the man's hands.

The soldier eyed them for a moment, his cigarette hanging out of the corner of his mouth, then waved them onward.

Jake nodded cordially at the soldier as he approached and stopped the Jeep at the mouth of a small parking lot. Clara rolled down her window as he walked over to them.

"Well, look what we got here," the solider said, his voice gruff. "Survivors." He must've noticed Clara staring at the rifle in his hand because he said, "Just for precaution, darlin'" and he nodded down at it and gave her a playful wink—there was something about the way his eyes latched onto her that made her skin prick with annoyance…and a muted sort of fear.

"We heard there were survivors on base," Jake said, offering a reason for their unexpected arrival. "We thought we'd check it out."

"Did ya now?" The soldier chuckled and shook his head. "Well, alrighty then." His eyebrows rose, and he winked at Clara, again. "You'll want to head north toward the barracks. My commanding officer's there. He's the one you need to talk to."

"Thanks," Jake said, and Clara wondered if he had noticed the way the soldier was looking at her.

As they pulled away, Clara couldn't help but turn around. The soldier stood on the side of the road with the gun draped across his shoulders and a grin that lingered too long on his face. She was grateful when the Jeep rounded a bend and he disappeared from sight.

"I don't like him," she muttered, earning a questioning look from Jake. She turned around again, grateful that no one was following behind them.

Hearing movement beside her, Clara looked over at Jake. He

pulled a handgun from between the center console and his seat and slid it into the back of his pants, pulling his thermal shirt over it.

"What's that for?" she asked, dread washing over her.

"Just in case," he said calmly, and he pointed over his shoulder into the backseat. "Grab the two knives and shotgun in the duffel next to Cooper and shove them underneath my seat."

Clara whined and grunted as she climbed into the back, trading places momentarily with Cooper. "Why are we hiding them? Won't they find them under the seat, anyway?"

"If they search the Jeep, they will, but it's better to stash them out of sight than to leave them out in the open, inviting them to search us. We don't want them to get the wrong idea." He snapped his fingers. "In the back, Coop."

When Clara was finished, she crawled back into the front seat and smoothed her rumpled sweatshirt, trying to look as un-mussed as possible. "If you don't trust them, why are we going in?"

Jake glanced into the rearview mirror. "I don't trust anyone; that doesn't mean anything."

A few heartbeats later, the barracks came into view. Two more soldiers were standing outside the building, apparently waiting for them.

"He must've radioed them," Clara thought aloud.

A moderately attractive, older man with salt and pepper hair stood on the curb, a welcoming grin on his face, a handgun holster around his waist, and his hands resting easily on his hips. He was dressed in fatigues, as was the younger, well-built soldier standing beside him. The younger man had a blond buzz cut, which Clara randomly thought she might like to run her fingers through, but then she noticed the rifle at his side and her thoughts turned less agreeable.

The fact that everyone was armed was troublesome, but then, the world *had* ended for the most part, and the soldiers were probably as skeptical about strangers as she and Jake were.

Bringing the Jeep to a stop, Jake said, "Let me do the talking."

The older soldier started around the car toward the driver side window. His minion stayed on the curb, his face twisted into a scowl.

As Jake rolled down his window to speak to the approaching soldier, Clara continued to stare at the intense, glowering man. He was big and strong and had a scar over his right eyebrow, and even though he glared at them, his gaze didn't waver, his eyebrows didn't twitch…he hadn't seemed to even notice Clara at all, not like the first soldier they'd talked to. She grew equal parts thwarted and intrigued.

Unbidden, her fingers moved to the door panel, and she cranked the window down slowly. Look at me, she thought. Look at me and *see* me.

His gaze darted to her—to her lips—and then narrowed on her eyes. Some emotion roiled in their dark depths before he looked away again, refocusing on Jake.

Uncertain if it was just luck or the fact that she'd distracted him by rolling down the window, Clara felt triumphant and had to hold back a smile.

"The name's Jones, *Captain* Jones, and that grunt over there is my right hand, Bennington. And you've already met Taylor, down the road."

Jake nodded to Bennington through the windshield, then held out his right hand to Jones. "Jake Vaughn," he offered.

Jones accepted Jake's handshake through the window frame and looked at Clara. "And who's this?"

"This is Clara," Jake said, looking over at her, completely missing Jones's toothy grin. "We met in Colorado…she needed a place to go."

That's his explanation? Clara held her breath a moment while she counted to three, waiting for her mounting fury to subside. To distract herself, she soaked up Jones's attention as it hung on her a moment longer than it probably should have. She was suddenly desperate to make Jake jealous.

Jones smiled at Jake. "You're a good man, taking in a woman in need. I like you already." He patted Jake on the shoulder. "What brings you two to Fort Knox?"

"We got word that there were survivors here," Jake said.

"I see." Jones eyed them both a moment, and Clara wondered what exactly he was thinking as his lips quirked up on one side.

"We haven't seen many people since we left Missouri," Jake explained. "We thought you all might have a little insight into what the hell's going on."

"Missouri," Jones scoffed. "Now that's as barren a place as any." He was joking and smiling with Jake, but there was something too big about his smile, something off about the tension around his eyes. "We don't know much of what's going on, at least, not outside of our little paradise."

Clara tried not to let her disgust register on her face as she scanned her surroundings. It was *far* from a paradise.

"Anyway,"—Jones's palm hit the window frame with a loud clap—"you folks should come in all the same." His gaze shifted from Jake to Clara again, studying her face. "We could probably learn a thing or two from one another…"

Although Clara felt a prick of unease in the back of her mind as Jones's eyes lingered on her for a heartbeat too long, she also felt a thrilling sort of challenge. She wasn't about to let some *man* frighten her off, especially not when she had Jake to protect her. Besides, she thought, it would be good for him to have a bit of competition. Maybe he'd stop taking her for granted and own up to his feelings…maybe he'd even express them a little.

7

CLARA

Standing beside Jake, Clara stared up at the barracks; they were outdated and boxy and gray, looking more like a prison than a command post. *Definitely* not her idea of a paradise, but she was happy to be out of the Jeep and the only woman standing amongst three strapping men whose attention—mostly—was focused on her.

Although Jake had seemed reticent to park and go inside—probably because he didn't like the way Jones had been looking at her, though Jake would never admit it—Clara had implored him to take a break and go inside; she insisted he needed to—for their safety—and it hadn't taken long before he'd given in, leaving her to feel triumphant…again.

"This way," Jones said as he motioned them toward the entrance. When Clara's eyes met Jones's, he sent her a quick wink before turning to head inside.

Without thinking, she reached out and laced her fingers through Jake's. His hand flexed in hers, but he didn't pull away, and the nagging uncertainty she'd been feeling around him all day instantly dissolved. She felt validated, hopeful even, knowing that her dedication to their relationship, her determination, was starting to pay off. Jake would be putty in the palm of her hand by the end of the day.

Together, they followed Jones through a large glass door that Bennington was holding open for them. They entered what appeared to be a rec room. A large, brick fireplace was inset in the far wall, couches and recliners were scattered around the open space, and a pool table was situated in the far left corner, alongside an air hockey and foosball table.

"This is the common room," Jones said before he quickly headed through the space toward a set of open metal doors. The soles of his shoes squeaked on the polished cement flooring. "Originally, this building was used for civilian barracks, but we decided to convert it into our makeshift command post since there's just a few of us left. We make do just fine here."

Clara thought the light, almost melodic tone of Jones's voice was odd, given that a little over a week ago the base had been teeming with people, but now, it was more or less empty.

"How many of you are left?" Jake asked as he and Clara entered a vacuous cafeteria behind Jones and Bennington.

Jones stopped and looked back at them, his eyes boring into Clara's before they rested on Jake. "There are six of us," he said, his voice suddenly flat.

Briefly, Clara's gaze met Bennington's before she shifted his attention away from her, leaving Clara to wonder how long he'd been staring at her. She tried to ignore her annoying mind chatter, telling her she should be fearful of this place—of these men—but she mostly felt compelled to learn more about them, to see what would unfold between Jake and the soldiers whose gazes lingered on her longer than they probably should.

"The kitchen's back there," Jones continued, "and there are bathrooms over there…"

Clara let Jones's time-worn voice fade into the background as unwanted memories of her time at Pine Springs Hospital crept into her mind. *This* cafeteria was well lit with natural, dying sunlight that shone through the large, naked windows. But with its polished floors and white walls, it resembled the hospital's cafeteria too much, the only notable difference being the unbarred windows. *That* particular fate—the one where she was a prisoner trapped within a world of clinical crazies and cut off from life, from men—made her skin crawl more than any of the leering eyes she felt on her.

"Come on," Jones said, his voice suddenly booming. "I'm assuming you'd like some rest. I'll show you to your sleeping quarters where you can put your things." He turned and headed back out the open metal doors. "Our accommodations are nothing fancy, of course, but then, we're simple men."

"I'm not sure we'll need to stay the night," Jake said as he followed Bennington and Jones back out into the common room. Clara jogged to catch up, and when she reached Jake, she interlaced her fingers with his once more.

"You won't stay, huh?" Jones said. It didn't sound like a real question, more of a "we'll see about that" sort of comment. Clara's eyebrows rose.

"We need to get back on the road, soon," Jake explained.

Clara stopped in her tracks. "I think we should stay," she said, her eyes imploring him to give in. "You need rest, we *both* need rest."

Jake frowned at her.

"You need to take a break, Jake. You said yourself we needed to stretch our legs a bit." She let her words sink in, her eyes locked on his. "We should stay here."

Jaw clenching, Jake said, "We'll see," on a heavy exhale.

Which means yes, Clara knew. She allowed herself a satisfied smile this time, but when her stare met Jones's, Clara had a feeling her smile wasn't as bright as his was intrigued.

Jake cleared his throat, drawing Clara and Jones's attention back to the moment.

Clara was pleased to see the hard set of Jake's jaw.

Jones and Bennington continued onward, Clara and Jake following behind them toward a dark and uninviting hallway with offshooting corridors.

Noticing a pair of beat up doors near the mouth of the hallway, Clara froze, leaving the others to continue forward without her. Something malevolent lurked in the rooms beyond, she could feel it prickling the backs of her arms and neck.

A rough hand gripped her upper arm. "That's just some old storage rooms," Jones said, his blue eyes boring into hers. "There's no need for you to go poking around in there." His eyes flicked to her mouth, and he licked his lips.

Clara smiled, wondering what she might get away with if she'd met this man in another life. "I wouldn't dream of it," she said deliberately and glanced down at his fingers. "Let go of my arm, please."

Jones's thumb brushed over her arm as he considered something, then he released her. "My apologies," he said, inclining his head.

Clearing his throat, he strode over to join Bennington and Jake as Bennington opened a dormitory door down the hall. "This will be your room," Jones said. "Should you decide to stay, of course." Jake opened his mouth to say something, but Jones spoke over him. "Now, let's have a drink, shall we?"

Clara listened to their retreating footsteps as she lingered in the shadows a moment longer, wondering what was really in the storage rooms that were clearly off limits.

"Clara?" Jake called from the common room. She thought she could hear a hint of concern in his voice.

This place was good for them, she thought happily. If nothing else, it kept Jake on his toes. "I'm coming!" she chirped, offering one final glance at the closed and presumably locked doors that housed some deep, dark secret.

As Clara hurried into the common room, a slender, red-haired woman walked in through the main doors from outside. And Clara was pretty sure her heart skipped a beat. Where had she come from? Clara wasn't sure how she felt about that.

Jones pulled the red head into his arms, causing her to shriek and drop the folded towels she'd been carrying on the floor.

Clara watched the woman's timid gaze shift between Jones and the towels. "I'm sorry," she said so quietly that Clara could barely hear her. "I didn't—"

"Not to worry, my dear." Jones's arm tightened around the woman's shoulders, and he pulled her closer to him, his nail beds turning white as his fingertips dug into her upper arm. "I want you to meet our guests." He turned his attention to Jake. "This, here, is my girl, Summer." His eyes glinted with warning. "Summer," Jones continued, "these are our guests, Jake and Clara."

Summer was no great beauty, but she was pretty enough, and Clara liked that Jones was marking his territory. After all, she didn't want Jake getting any ideas.

"Aren't you going to welcome our guests?" Jones asked the trembling woman in his arms.

Summer cringed, then smiled, her hazel eyes skirting over Jake and Clara quickly before settling on the polished cement floor. "Yes, of course," she said, clearing her throat. "It's nice to meet you both."

Jake's gaze loitered on Summer longer than Clara liked, and she felt her fingernails digging into her palms as she clenched her fists. Automatically, she reached out and took Jake's hand again.

Summer's eyes lifted briefly from the floor up to Clara and then to Jake.

As Clara glowered at Summer, conveying warning and her ownership of the rugged man beside her, she felt less threatened. At first glance, Summer *was* pretty, but she was also meek, which was more than annoying; it was pathetic. Plus, Summer's nose was too small for her face, and the dark circles under her eyes made her appear tired and sickly. In fact, Clara thought the woman resembled a faded, wet blanket, and she suddenly felt much better. Even if Jake had felt any interest in her, it would dissolve quickly enough.

Jones closed his eyes and inhaled the scent of Summer's hair, taking no great pains to hide his enchantment with her. "Actually, why don't we skip that drink and call it a night," he drawled, his eyes opening and a hungry gaze fixed on Summer's mouth. "We'll have the ladies cook us a big breakfast tomorrow and then we can decide what happens next. I'm sure you could use some rest." Jones looked at Jake, who only nodded in reply, and without another word, the older man led Summer out of the room and down the hall toward the mysterious storage area. With a final glare in Jake and Clara's direction, Bennington disappeared out the front door, leaving them to themselves.

"We should go before—"

"I told you I want to stay," Clara said over him.

He glowered at her. "Why the hell—"

She took his hand in hers. "You need a driving break, and I want a good night's sleep." With him…in bed beside her, she didn't say.

Jake studied her a moment, his brown eyes more luminous, more alive and wanting than she'd ever seen them as they flicked from her lips back up to her eyes.

Jake shook his head, his face scrunched as if he were in pain.

"See, you *do* need rest…I *want* to stay, Jake," she repeated, willing him to agree. She hoped that once again he'd see the same emotion in her that had influenced him to change his mind back at the hospital.

With another shake of his head and a despondent sigh, Jake conceded. "I don't know why the hell I'm agreeing to this," he muttered. "Go into your room," he told her.

Our room, Clara wanted to correct, but she was too excited by this tone.

"Lock the door behind you, and don't open it for anyone but me."

"Wait, what?" Clara's excitement vanquished, and she frantically searched Jake's insistent gaze for answers. "Why? What are you going to do?"

Jake scanned the common room. "I'm going to figure out what the hell's going on around here." He looked at her. "And *tomorrow*, I'm leaving with or without you."

8

JAKE

Jake had done it again. He'd given in to Clara's pleas and made a slew of stupid-ass decisions. What the hell was it about her that had him so mixed up all the time? And why the hell had an image of them, lying in bed together, flitted into his mind?

Jake ran a hand over his head. Dropping her off at Fort Knox had seemed like a good idea; in fact, it had sounded like an increasingly *great* idea the longer he was around her, feeling muddled and anxious. But from the moment he first noticed the soldiers' ogling looks, Jake had been unable to shake a sense of irrefutable dread. Now, he was in an unfamiliar place with armed soldiers—possibly six of them—and the woman, Summer, who'd clearly been mistreated, probably abused in more ways than he'd ever know. None of which was anything he was qualified to deal with. But he also couldn't do *nothing*.

After a night without an ounce of sleep, Jake sat at one of the cafeteria tables, waiting for Clara to get dressed and join him. By the time he and Cooper had returned from their reconnaissance of the base, the sun was already on the rise, and Jake was too anxious to sleep. He was going to leave today. He just needed to figure out if he was going alone. He needed to be strategic in getting Summer out of there, so not to get them all killed. Six soldiers against a single, untrained, and mostly unarmed man didn't make for a promising outcome. Unless… Realizing he'd only seen three men, Jake wondered if Jones had been bluffing, or perhaps stretching the truth.

Jake scrubbed his hands over his face. Regardless, his weapons had been confiscated from the Jeep, so all he had left was his pistol.

Elbows on the table, he rested his head in his hands and exhaled deeply.

"Look who decided to come back," Clara said curtly.

Jake looked up at her as she strode into the cafeteria, her gaze pinning him in place.

With a huff, she sat across the table from him and crossed her arms over her chest. "Where were you last night? I was expecting you to at least check on me, or—"

"We're leaving," Jake said quietly so not to be overheard. "And we're taking Summer with us. I—"

"Jake!" Clara stood, anger burning in her bright blue eyes.

He glared at her, keeping his tone flat and deliberate. "I'm not leaving her here to be raped and beaten more than she already has been."

Clara shook her head, and her nostrils flared a little. "It's not your job to protect *her*," she nearly snarled. "You're supposed to protect *me*."

Jake's patience was beyond thinning. "You're—"

"There you are," Jones said.

Jake's attention snapped to the cafeteria doors as Jones walked through, stretching audibly. Summer was shuffling lazily behind him, almost stumbling, like she was drunk.

In spite of the fact that Jake had never murdered anyone, he had to resist the temptation to pull out his pistol and shoot Jones right then and there for the apparent liberties he had taken with the dazed woman who had to grab onto him so not to fall over.

Chuckling as he righted Summer, Jones glanced between Jake and Clara. "Lover's spat?"

Clara smoothed her expression. "I think we just need some breakfast." Jake didn't miss the glare she fixed on him, it was all but screaming.

"Yes. Breakfast…" Jones turned to Summer, about to say something when approaching footsteps echoed from the common room. "Oh, there's my boy," Jones said as Bennington strode in, his gaze immediately fixing on Jake.

Jake wasn't sure why Bennington was glaring daggers in his direction, but it only increased his resolve to get away from the base as soon as possible.

Jones slapped his friend on the shoulder and nudged Summer. "Why don't you go rouse your lovely Miss Tanya and Taylor's little chickpea so the women can whip us up some breakfast?" he said, then he turned to Clara. "You don't mind helping, do you?"

Jake struggled to keep any telling emotions from altering his placid expression.

"I have some questions for Jake in the meantime." Like clockwork, another false smile broadened Jones's lips.

A smoker's cough emanated from the other room. "I hope you're not starting the party without us," a lazy voice said from the doorway. Jake glanced over to find another sorry excuse for a man, Taylor, standing at the cafeteria entrance, a rifle in his hand and a tall woman with disheveled, dirty-blonde hair leaning against the door frame beside him. She had a smear of what looked like blood on her arm.

At least three women, Jake thought. His body tensed, anger roiling inside him so violently that he had to clench his hands to keep them from shaking.

"Perfect timing," Jones said. He was all smiles and hospitality as he pointed his chin at his comrade. His focus shifted to the woman standing in the doorway. "Stacey, would you be a darlin' and whip us up something to eat? Our guests are hungry."

"When we're finished," Taylor said, a sadistic grin encompassing his face. "I was just taking a cigarette break." He smacked Stacey on the ass before grabbing her hand and yanking her behind him as he strode away from the cafeteria.

As soon as they were gone, Jones turned his attention back to Clara and Jake, his face a mask of patience, but the tightness of his smile made Jake think that Jones was fighting to stay in control of his temper.

Surprisingly, Jones shrugged. "Young love, what can do you do?" He turned to Summer, still wobbling beside him. "Make breakfast," he ordered, all false kindness gone. As if he'd realized his façade was cracking, he leaned over and kissed her cheek, though she didn't seem to register it at all. Jones glared over at Bennington. "Don't you have a job you're supposed to be doing?"

Bennington's eyes narrowed infinitesimally before he turned and headed out a separate pair of doors that lead to what looked like a quad outside.

Jake stiffened. He could feel Clara's eyes boring into him, but he didn't care. His attention was on the soldiers, sizing them and trying to formulate a plan.

With a huff, Clara approached Summer and pointed toward the kitchen. "I'll help you," she bit out.

"Perfect," Jones said, and once again he was focused on Jake. "Let's take a walk while we wait."

With a steadying breath, Jake followed Jones through the same glass double doors that Bennington had exited. Jake wondered if this wasn't the perfect opportunity to shift the odds a bit more in his favor; he could take out Jones, leaving only Taylor and Bennington to deal with…assuming he was right in thinking it was the three soldiers and the three women that made up the six members of the group that Jones had referred to.

Jake's gun was still at the small of his back if he needed it, easing his mind a little as he followed Jones.

Cooper rose from his curled position in a patch of sunlight and followed after them. As the duo and dog stepped out into a quad behind the barracks, the morning sun was nearly blinding.

"So, Bennington's sort of a night owl," Jones said. Jake could tell by the man's tone that he was fishing. "Says he saw you out and about last night…late…"

Jake tried to remain unfazed as his dread thickened. He'd been so careful…

Feigning indifference, he focused on the red graffiti tagged on the brick and wood-slatted buildings that flanked either side of the quad. "Did he," Jake said; it wasn't a question. "Guess I couldn't sleep."

Jones stiffened as Cooper scampered past them, then let out a steadying breath. Jake couldn't help but wonder if Jones was afraid of dogs.

After another deep breath, Jones placed his hands on his hips and said, "I figured as much…told him you and that tart of yours probably had a little tiff."

They walked between two buildings and headed toward a patch of woods that fanned out around the northern perimeter of the base. The farther away they walked from the barracks, the better his chances were of killing Jones without the others immediately catching on.

Jones chuckled. "She sure does seem like a firecracker."

"You could say that," Jake said dryly.

"I always liked blondes," Jones said wistfully, then shrugged. "But Summer's a good girl."

"Yeah, it seems like you've got yourself a nice set up here," Jake said, awaiting Jones's reaction.

"That we do." They walked deeper into the woods, the pines thickening around them. "Especially now that it's just me and the boys running things." Unexpectedly, Jones halted. "Which is why you and I should clear up a few things."

Jake glanced around, his voice bored. "And what's that?" He took a few steps away from Jones, keeping his distance from the other man, ready to pull the cool metal gun from his waistband if Jones made even the slightest wrong move. Part of him *wanted* Jones to try something…to give Jake an excuse to get rid of such a worthless piece of shit.

"We've got a certain way of doing things around here, a pecking order if you will. Now, I told the men I thought it would be fine to check you folks out and see if we all might be a good fit—you sort of remind me of myself when I was a lad. But"—Jones shook his heads —"I can't have you snooping around and causing problems for us." Jones's easy, light tone didn't make his meaning any less threatening.

"Causing problems?"

"It's what you don't say that worries me, son." Jones crossed his arms over his chest again and eyed Jake carefully. "*Do* I have to worry about you, Jake?"

Jake shook his head. "Clara and I will be leaving after breakfast. You won't have to worry about us at all."

"Really?" Jones didn't seem surprised. "Well, I think you should stay…or that *she* should stay."

Jake let out a single, humorless laugh. "I bet you do. But she's coming with me."

Jones's eyes narrowed. "I'm sorry you feel that way, Mr. Vaughn. I really am…" Jones turned and walked away, his hands shoved in his pockets, and he began to whistle.

Sensing that he was running out of time, Jake reached behind him, his fingers clamped around the hilt of the pistol, ready to draw and shoot, when he heard a rumbling voice floating on the air around him. The hair on the back of Jake's neck rose.

"You shouldn't have come," Bennington said, his voice rumbling from somewhere within the trees. Jake couldn't see him.

And before Jake knew what was happening, he felt a searing pain in his back and fire in his chest as a knife blade sank deep. He tried to move, tried to turn, tried to fight.

Bennington yanked the knife free and drove it home again, the blade lodging in the base of Jake's spine. He fell to his knees, and pain and darkness washed over him.

9

JAKE

Jake started awake. At first, all he could feel were the jagged rocks littering the ground beneath him, but feeling slowly returned to his stiff body. His bones felt frozen through and through. As he stirred, a smarting pain shot up his spine, and he winced. He struggled to remember where he was, why he was in pain, and what he was doing on the cold, hard ground. He blinked, too groggy to remember what had happened.

Distant howling roused him from confusion, and he peered out into the winter-ravaged forest surrounding him. As he scanned the gray, pre-dawn light that enshrouded the forest, his blurred memories sharpened, coming into focus.

The forest was familiar. Jake was lying in the same woods he'd been walking in…with Jones hours, maybe even days, ago.

He tried to move again, but a familiar yip and a bark resounded through the crisp air and Jake froze. His confusion gave way to understanding and then…rage. He was lying in the very place he'd been standing the moment Bennington had suddenly appeared, vicious and intent. He was lying exactly where he'd fallen after the bastard had stabbed him. The fleeting thought of how the soldier seemed to have appeared out of nowhere was unsettling.

Climbing to his feet, Jake faltered and lurched forward, cursing as he fell back onto the ground and another jolt of pain shot through his back. He reached his arm behind him, his fingers finding the hilt of the knife still protruding from his lower back.

"Bennington!" he bellowed. "You son of a bitch!" Twisting his arm further back, Jake groaned as he wrapped his fingers around the knife's handle. Awkwardly, he struggled to pull the blade from the base of his spine as he let out a roar, his anger masking the searing pain.

The wound burned and ached, but only for a few seconds. Chest heaving, Jake tried to process what was happening to him as he brought the combat knife around, eyeing the bloody blade. How had he survived? He remembered the bullet wound. How had he survived, *again*? He squeezed the knife's cool, metal handle and took a deep, fortifying breath.

Forcing himself to stand, Jake used the nearest tree for leverage and climbed to his feet. His body creaked and protested as his joints worked for the first time in…he didn't even know how long. Irate, he threw the combat knife and it hit the ground with a muffled thud a few yards away. He instantly regretted his decision. He would need a weapon, something to protect himself with when he ran into Bennington and the others again.

Jake heard howling again and realized he needed to find Cooper before the lunatics back at base did something horrible to him. Or maybe they already had.

Taking an uneasy step toward the knife, Jake felt something hard beneath his right boot. He glanced down, spotting a metal object partially covered with withered leaves. It was a pistol—*his* pistol. Jerkily, he bent down and picked the gun up, the movement less excruciating than it was a few moments before.

Resolved to find Cooper, Jake checked the ammo. Satisfied the clip was still full, he held the pistol at his side and strode toward the distant barking.

"Cooper!" he called, hoping his ears weren't deceiving him.

Like he'd only been patrolling the woods nearby, Cooper came bounding through the trees, barking excitedly as his tail whipped back and forth.

Jake squatted to rumple the dog's scruff, the Husky licking his face and hands ecstatically. In the violet dawn, Jake noticed blood crusted on Cooper's white muzzle.

"What'd he do to you, Coop?" Jake murmured as he searched the dog's body for wounds. He could find none, only patches of dried blood Jake assumed belonged to someone else.

With a quick jerk, Cooper pulled away from him, whining and panting and wagging his tail as he took a few anxious steps back in the direction he'd come from. The dog gazed back at his master, clearly wanting him to follow.

"I'm comin'." The handgun still at this side, Jake followed Cooper deeper into the trees.

With another burst of energy, Cooper trotted up to a sprawling hickory tree, barking and jumping at the base as if a toy had gotten stuck up in its outreaching limbs. But Jake's eyes lingered on the blood staining the forest floor. After taking in the red-stained ground cover, he glanced up into the tree. Someone was up there.

In the first golden rays of sunlight, Jake noticed the outline of a person bracing himself between the trunk and a gnarled branch.

It was Bennington. He wasn't dead, but he might as well have been. His face was mauled, barely recognizable, and his throat hissed with each shallow breath. Glancing back at the copious amounts of blood covering the ground, Jake wondered if the soldier had any blood left to lose; it was only a matter of time before he took his final breath.

Standing on hind legs with front paws braced against the tree, Cooper yipped again, trying ineffectually to get to the dying man.

"Cooper," Jake grumbled. "Sit."

The dog looked back at him, almost pleading, but sat down obediently with his head cocked to the side.

At the sound of Jake's voice, Bennington's eyes opened to slits.

"You were…dead. I—I…killed…you." he choked out, each word more of a struggle than the last.

Ignoring him, Jake glanced down at Cooper. "You did this?"

The Husky yipped, and out of the corner of his eye, Jake saw Bennington wince.

"Why'd you try to kill me?" Jake asked coolly as he looked back up at the soldier. "Why'd you stab me in the back like a coward?"

Bennington tried to speak, but all that came out was an incomprehensible gurgle.

"Never mind," Jake said, knowing Bennington was the least of his problems. Jones and Taylor were more than likely holed-up in the barracks or still searching for Bennington since he'd clearly never made it back to the barracks, and Jake still had Clara and the three other women to worry about.

A sudden burst of panic gripped him. What had the men done to the women—to Clara—since he'd been gone?

When Jake's eyes shifted back to Bennington, the man's head had lolled to the side and his arms were no longer wrapped around his middle, instead hanging at his sides. Dead or just unconscious, Jake didn't care. He was too exhausted and Bennington clearly wasn't a threat…not anymore.

Although his pain had dissipated, Jake's limbs were heavy and his muscles ached. And despite his intentions to head back to the barracks, his body wanted to rest a bit longer.

Feet dragging, he searched for a hidden place to sit down for a minute, a place Jones or Taylor wouldn't stumble upon him. A bed of fallen pine needles and withered leaves collected beneath the low hanging branches of an evergreen seemed as good a place as any, and Jake lowered himself to the ground and situated himself against the base of the tree. Cooper, clearly equally exhausted, curled up beside him, his tail thumping casually.

Jake let out a deep breath and scrubbed his face. "Don't wander off, Coop, and stay quiet," he said. The dog's ears angled back as he tail thumped a bit faster. "We're just resting for a minute…" But in the midst of rallying himself to get up and head back to the barracks, the world around him faded to darkness, and Jake fell asleep.

10

CLARA

Two days. It had been *two* days—well, forty-seven hours—since Clara had seen Jake or Cooper, or even Bennington, for that matter, and Clara was freaking out. Unable to sleep, she sat at the cafeteria table, the last place she'd seen Jake before she'd stormed away from him.

Jones had told her that Jake had left her behind, but she knew he wouldn't have done that. Not after all they'd been through. He'd said he wanted to get her out of there, hadn't he?

His Jeep *was* gone; she'd gone to check the instant Jones told her that he'd taken off. But, Jake was coming back, he had to. This was all part of his plan. He'd wanted to take *all* the women away; he wouldn't *leave* them all instead.

She'd been snippy and moody with him, though. Of course, she'd thought he deserved it at the time, but when it came to Jake, Clara knew she was irrational sometimes; she couldn't help it. But she also needed to remember that he'd been through a lot with his sister dying…he'd been doing all the driving…all the planning. He'd clearly been exhausted, and Clara regretted not giving him more space and less attitude. What if he *had* left her behind?

Clara squeezed her eyes shut and ran her fingers through her hair in an attempt to clear her head. Once again she'd let her emotions get her into trouble at her heart's expense. She'd probably pissed Jake off, or even scared him away. She wanted to believe that their connection was enough to keep them together, regardless of the tension that often simmered between them. But all of that was hardly comforting when he was nowhere to be found.

"Are you alright?" Tanya asked. When Bennington didn't come back, Tanya had come out of his room…and she hadn't gone back in since. She let her mousey-brown hair hang in her face as she sat down beside Clara.

Clara's regret and concern for Jake turned to annoyance. Tanya and the others were pathetic. *She'd* been without Jake for two days, and none of the other men had touched her. They'd wanted to, she could see it in Taylor's eyes, in Jones's, but they hadn't put a finger on her.

"Clara?"

Clara waved Tanya's question away, focusing on the fading bruise that highlighted the woman's right eye. "You shouldn't let them hit you."

Tanya cleared her throat. "Are you worried about your friend…Jake?"

Clara glared at her, irritation turning to resentment. "We're more than *friends*," she bit out. "And yes, I'm worried about him. He wouldn't have just left me here." She realized the truth in her words the moment she uttered them. She straightened. "Something must've happened to him."

Tanya glanced to the doorway as if to make sure no one was watching them. "If he fought back, they would've killed him." Tanya swallowed thickly. "That's what they do…they probably killed him anyway."

Clara rose, the metal feet of her chair screeching against the polished floor. "He's *not* dead," she seethed. "He protects me."

When she realized her head was shaking, she took deep breaths to calm herself down. "He *can't* be dead."

Tanya only looked at her, sympathy filling her eyes. "I hope you're right," she said quietly. "I really hope you're right."

As Clara felt the need to hit someone, her vision became splotchy and her fists clenched. "Shut up!" she shouted, banging her fist on the tabletop. "You don't know what he's capable of. He tried to save a boy and his father…he rescued me. He wouldn't leave me behind. He would *never* leave me behind."

"Leaving you is different than dy—"

"Don't say it," Clara warned. Tanya looked like a drowned rat, wearing clothes that were too large for her emaciated frame. "He's not as pathetic as you are," Clara said. "He can defend himself."

Tanya recoiled.

Smoothing her sweatshirt, Clara sat back down and scooted her chair closer to the table. "I'm sorry," she whispered as she tried to reel in her emotions. "It's just…you don't understand. You don't know Jake. We're meant to be together, and Jones or Taylor or Bennington won't change that—not after all we've been through."

A wistful sigh escaped Tanya. "I used to have someone I felt that way about."

Clara eyed her. She had a hard time picturing Tanya in any state other than a despondent heap of patheticness. "Why do you let them touch you?" she asked without thinking.

Tanya blanched and pulled her sleeves down over her bruised hands.

Clara felt disgusted. "Don't you even put up a fight?"

"I used to." Tanya stared blankly at the tabletop. "But it's pointless now."

"They'll *never* touch me," Clara spat. "Jake would kill them. *I* would kill them."

"Then you're not as smart as I thought you were," Tanya said.

It was Clara who blanched this time. "Excuse me?"

"You're no different from any of us."

Eyes narrowed, Clara said, "They will *not* touch me."

"And how can you be so sure?"

"I just…know." Clara felt her brow furrow. She wasn't exactly sure how she knew, but she did.

"Really? And if they *did* decide to do something, do you think it would be easy to overpower a crazed man? *Three* crazed men?" Tanya rose from her chair. "You're stupid if you think you're stronger than them. Don't you dare judge me!"

Clara felt the color drain from her face, and remorse filled her. Regardless of how much she believed the men wouldn't touch her, she knew it would be difficult to stop them if they tried. "You're right," she said. "I shouldn't have said that. I know I haven't—"

"No," Tanya said bitterly, "you haven't." She sat back down. "Can we please talk about something else. My sister's"—she swallowed—"*indisposed* at the moment, and Stacey's with Taylor. I don't want to go back to his bedroom…to wait."

Clara eyed her. She was reluctant to ask, but couldn't help herself. "Wait for what?"

"For Bennington to come back," she said.

A long, depressing silence hung between them for a few breaths, then a few more. "I won't let them touch you anymore," Clara swore. "We'll figure something out."

Tanya shrugged. "If I'm lucky, your Jake killed Bennington, and that's one less problem we have to deal with."

Clara liked the pleasure that thought provoked. "When Jake gets back"—Clara eyed Tanya—"and he *will* come back, he'll take care of Jones and Taylor, I promise you that. He's probably somewhere coming up with a plan right now…he said so himself before —well, before he disappeared."

"You think so?" The hopeful lilt of Tanya's voice was nearly heartbreaking.

Clara nodded. "I do." She wrapped her arm around the slender woman's shoulders.

Tanya flinched at the gesture, but when Clara showed no sign of intending to hurt her, Tanya's eyes filled with tears, and she started to cry.

Clara held Tanya more tightly against her. "I really do," she said. Fairy tales always had a way of working themselves out. She just needed to remember that. "We'll make them pay for what they've done to you," she whispered. "It always works out that way…"

11

CLARA

The next day, Clara found herself once again sitting at a cafeteria table with Tanya. They'd been up all night, exchanging stories about what had happened over the past couple weeks. Tanya, slowly but surely, filling Clara in on life at the base.

At first, when people started dying, there'd been order and safety. The ranking officers quarantined the sick and made sure everyone was taken care of…protected against those who started going mad.

"My husband didn't last long…he was one of the first to go, in fact. I was destroyed, utterly lost to sadness…until one day, Summer brought me out of it. She told me how lucky we were to have one another…" Tanya stared out the glass double doors into the baleful afternoon. "But by the time I snapped out of my depression, things had gotten so much worse. The officer in charge had died, and Jones had taken it upon himself to make some changes. He was suddenly in charge, but I'd never seen him until he started ordering the remaining few people around. He brought in Taylor and Bennington the next day, they were stationed on a different area of the base, at least that's what I was told."

Clara sighed heavily and strummed her fingers on the tabletop.

"You probably shouldn't be telling me this," she said absently, sort of bored in fact. "He'll probably punish you."

When Tanya said nothing, Clara looked at her.

Tanya shrugged, an action that had become her answer to everything. "I'm not sure I care anymore. What could be worse than this?"

Clara felt herself getting frustrated with the diminutive woman once more. "Death," she said. "*Death* would be worse. Don't you want revenge? Don't you want them to pay for what they've done? If you're dead, they win. Can't you see that?"

Tanya shrugged again. "I'm not sure revenge is all that important when you're already dead inside."

Clara rolled her eyes. "Right."

Hearing heavy footsteps in the common room, Clara and Tanya turned toward the cafeteria entrance. Taylor walked in, a cigarette hanging out of his mouth, and Clara cringed. His eyelids were lust-heavy, and his face rosy from exertion. Smiling, he winked at Clara and Tanya before striding over to an industrial-sized coffee pot plugged into a generator.

Upon finding the coffee pot empty, he shoved it back into its holder and turned to them, glaring at Tanya. "With Bennington out, the least you could do is make some fucking coffee," he said, taking two intimidating steps toward them. "Is that expecting too much? Every time I walk in here, the two of you are sitting there, not doing a damn fucking thing."

Flinching, Tanya rose and scampered into the kitchen, Taylor eyeing her as she left. Clara could hear Tanya fumbling around noisily in the other room, the clanging and banging around only heightening Clara's already unsettled nerves.

"You," Taylor said, drawing Clara's gaze up to meet his. His heated stare raked over her, almost palpable, before his filmy eyes settled on her lips.

"Where's Jake?" she blurted, ignoring her bubbling panic.

Taylor blew out a puff of smoke and made a pouty face. "Don't you worry about him, love." His usual, sadistic grin spread his lips. "You know, everything's changed since you got here." He sounded amused, rather than accusatory, making Clara instantly bristle. He took a step closer, closing the distance between them. "Suddenly Jones wants you left alone—a woman he'd normally take into his room and bend over his dresser."

Rage boiled in Clara's blood. "None of you will *ever* touch me, so get the idea out of your head," she demanded.

"You've got a big mouth." He put his cigarette out on the table top, and his eyes locked on hers.

"And you've got stinky breath. What's your point?"

His smile faltered. "*Too* big a mouth for your own good," he growled.

Clara raised one eyebrow in defiance, trying to ignore Taylor's sweat-sheened skin and his glassy eyes that were zeroed in on her.

Before she could finish swallowing, his fingers wrapped around her throat. "You don't want to know what I'll do to you." His voice was throaty and eager, and his grip tightened.

Clara fought back panic, fought the urge to gasp for air. A distant part of herself told her to stand her ground. "Let. Go." She struggled to say the words, glaring into his wild, green eyes.

"Taylor," Jones said as he marched into the cafeteria, scanning the room. "Let her go. We've got company."

Clara gasped for breath the moment he dropped his hand, and she clutched her throat.

Tanya strode out of the kitchen with all the fixings to make more coffee. "You," Jones said, pointing to her. "Get to your room. Now." He turned to Clara, considering her for a moment before simply walking past her toward the hallway. "It's a group this time."

Taylor groaned. "Shit." He glared at Clara one last time, then followed after Jones. "We should just kill them before they get a chance to—"

"Not yet," Jones interrupted. "We're out numbered…and

they're military."

Taylor grumbled something as he passed through the doorway, leaving Clara and Tanya standing alone in the cafeteria once more.

"Come on," Clara said, her breathing still a little unsteady as she motioned Tanya toward her. "It sounds like they'll be preoccupied for a while. I need a minute to think, to figure out how to get this new group to help us without getting killed by Taylor or Jones in the process."

Tanya accepted Clara's outreached hand. As they walked into the common room, a slew of people shuffled in from outside. A tall, dark-skinned man with a handsome face and a kind smile nodded to Clara and Tanya, followed closely by a man in a Red Sox baseball cap, who stumbled through the threshold like he was drunk.

Great. Clara rolled her eyes and moved to push past them with Tanya in tow when she froze, dead in her tracks. A woman stood before her…long, jet-black hair and jewel-like, blue-green eyes.

Joanna.

Red. Red and black splotches floated around Clara's vision, and her heartbeat thudded in her ears. A hot flash of rage flared through her, and her jaw ached as she clenched her teeth to stifle the scream welling in her throat.

"…okay?"

Clara jumped at the sensation of cold fingertips against the back of her hand.

"Are you okay?" the woman repeated.

Clara blinked, hoping it was a nightmare she would wake up from, that she was still sitting in the Jeep with Jake—her Prince Charming, who had saved her life. But it wasn't a nightmare. Her Prince Charming was gone, and a woman whose eyes were unnaturally bright stared back at her. Joanna was haunting her. Clara almost couldn't breathe. "Joanna."

The woman shook her head, her brow furrowed. "My name's Zoe."

12

JAKE

Jake woke to Cooper's tongue lapping at his cheek and dog breath assaulting his nostrils. "Jesus, Coop." He nudged the dog aside. "We need to brush your teeth."

The dog whimpered.

"What is it?" Jake grumbled climbing to his feet. He felt rested—a hundred times better—and he wondered how long he'd been asleep for this time. Gray clouds filled the sky once more, covering the sun, and a cold breeze rushed him from behind. It carried a scream.

Jake stiffened, and Cooper took a few anxious steps forward.

"Easy," Jake murmured, and the Husky glanced back at him, waiting for a command. But hearing another scream, the pair were sprinting toward the cry for help.

"Go to hell!" a shrill voice spat as Jake and Cooper lurched to a stop at the edge of the clearing. He didn't recognize the raven-haired woman struggling to free herself from Taylor's grasp. "No!" she sobbed, fighting against him.

Jake's body heated with rage, and his stomach churned with disgust. "Let go of her, Taylor," he ordered.

Taylor's hold loosened, and he glared back at Jake as the woman scrambled out of his grasp.

Jake returned the bastard's glare, wanting to shoot him between the eyes and be done with it.

"What the hell are *you* doing here, Vaughn?" Taylor said, a smirk stretching across his face.

Jake ignored him and focused on the woman cowering beside a tree, her chest heaving and her chin trembling as she wiped the tears from her dirt-streaked face. She was scared, but there was a fierce determination in her eyes.

Her eyes…

"I thought you were dead," Taylor prompted, but Jake continued to ignore him.

He vaguely registered nodding to Cooper, before the Husky ran over to the woman. All Jake could do was stare at her—at her *teal* eyes.

It wasn't possible. What Becca had said couldn't have been…a prediction?

Taylor chortled, and Jake forced himself to refocus on the soldier leering at the woman on the ground.

"You're a piece of shit, Taylor," Jake said and raised his pistol, aiming it at Taylor's chest.

"Whatcha gonna do with that gun, Jake?" Taylor sounded more amused than concerned.

No matter how crazy he was, Jake knew Taylor wasn't stupid. He could see his finger's twitching nervously at his side, itching to grab his own gun.

"I don't think you have it in ya to kill someone, Jake." He took a step forward.

"There's a lot you don't know about me," Jake countered and risked another glance in the woman's direction.

"I should've known we couldn't get rid of you that easy." Taylor spat on the ground in front of him, his tone hardening. "You've been causing problems since you got here."

In the blink of an eye, Taylor's gun was drawn and the woman was screaming. Jake pulled the trigger without hesitation, putting a bullet in Taylor's chest.

Taylor dropped to the ground.

Taking a step forward, Jake studied the dead man. Two dead. One to go.

And as if Jones had been the last in a line-up, ready for his execution, he strode through the trees, slow and confident. "Well, well. I thought you were dead," he said conversationally.

Jake's eyes shifted between Jones and the black-haired woman, his mind half spinning. "I've been hearing that a lot lately." He couldn't help but assess her wounds. *"She'll die because of you, Jake. The woman with the long black hair and teal eyes…You'll save her, but she'll die because of you."* Jake shook his head, refusing to believe there was any truth in his sister's final words.

"What did you do to my man?" Jones asked, kneeling down beside Taylor's body. He placed his fingers on the dead man's throat. "You son of a bitch," he bit out. "You killed him." He shot up to his feet. "Did you kill Bennington, too?"

"That's what I tend to do when people are trying to kill me," Jake answered dryly.

Jones's mouth twisted into an ugly sneer. "It's like you're *trying* to piss me off." He reached for his gun, but Jake was quicker. He pulled the trigger, and Jones fell.

Out of the corner of his eye, Jake noticed the woman start to run away, but for some reason, when she looked back at him, she hesitated. Keep running, Jake wanted to yell, but a loud crack startled him as Jones pulled the trigger of his gun.

A bullet hit Jake in the shoulder, and he dropped to his knees in sudden agony. "Shit," he rasped. He wasn't sure he could die all over again.

Jones cursed in pain of his own, immediately followed by yelling and snarling and barking as Cooper attacked him.

Unaffected by Jones's cries and pleas, Jake rallied himself to stand, to ignore the woman watching him. After a few long moments, he was on his feet, trying—and failing—not to jostle his injured shoulder. "Cooper," he finally called, feeling a little woozy and unsteady on his feet.

Cooper relented, but as Jake struggled to control his breathing, Jones's movements caught his attention.

Jones was reaching for a pistol lying on the ground just out of reach.

With shaking muscles, Jake took aim and shot Jones once, and then again, ensuring he was really dead before nearly collapsing against a tree.

Sobbing and face red and swollen, the woman limped over to Jake. "Oh my God," she rasped, her hands hovering over his body as she examined him for more wounds.

Jake felt lost in the intensity of her eyes, shimmering pools of emotions he struggled to look away from. *"She'll die because of you, Jake. The woman with the long black hair and teal eyes... You'll save her, but she'll die because of you."*

There was no way his sister could've predicted the future, that Becca could possibly have known he would meet this woman. There was no way she could've known that he would have to save her. It was a coincidence.

The woman fussed over him, taking off her long sleeve shirt and using it to put pressure on the bloody hole in his shoulder. "What can I do?" she implored, her eyes meeting his.

Unable to process what was happening, Jake straightened. "Nothing," he bit out and pushed her away. There was nothing she could do, unless she could bring back his dead sister to ask her what the hell was going on.

Jake wasn't certain of much anymore, but he was certain of one thing—this woman would *not* die because of him.

This concludes the sixth and final installment of *The Ending Beginnings.*

Carlos, Mandy, Vanessa, Clara, and Jake are also supporting characters throughout The Ending Series:
(1) *After The Ending,* (2) *Into The Fire*, (3) *Out Of The Ashes*, and (4) *Before The Dawn.*

Reviews are always appreciated.
They help indie authors like us sell books (and keep writing them!). Thanks!

OTHER NOVELS BY THE LINDSEYS

THE ENDING SERIES

The Ending Beginnings: Omnibus Edition

After The Ending

Into The Fire

Out Of The Ashes

Before The Dawn

World Before: A Collection of Stories

NOVELS BY LINDSEY POGUE

A SARATOGA FALLS LOVE STORY

Whatever It Takes

Nothing But Trouble

Told You So

FORGOTTEN LANDS

Dust And Shadow

Borne of Sand and Scorn

Wither and Ruin (TBR)

Borne of Earth and Ember (TBR)

NOVELS BY LINDSEY FAIRLEIGH

ECHO TRILOGY

Echo in time

Resonance

Time Anomaly

Dissonance

Ricochet Through Time

KAT DUBOIS CHRONICLES

Ink Witch

Outcast

Underground

Soul Eater

Judgement

Afterlife

ATLANTIS LEGACY

Sacrifice of the Sinners

Legacy of the Lost

ABOUT AUTHOR LINDSEY POGUE

Lindsey Pogue has always been a sucker for a good love story. She completed her first new adult manuscript in high school and has been writing tales of love and friendship, history and adventure ever since. When she's not chatting with readers, plotting her next storyline, or dreaming up new, brooding characters, Lindsey's generally wrapped in blankets watching her favorite action flicks with her own leading man. They live in the Napa Valley with their rescue cat, Beast. You can follow Lindsey's writing shenanigans on social media and online at www.lindseypogue.com.

ABOUT AUTHOR LINDSEY FAIRLEIGH

Lindsey Fairleigh lives her life with one foot in a book—as long as that book transports her to a magical world or bends the rules of science. Her novels, from post-apocalyptic to time travel and historical fantasy, always offer up a hearty dose of unreality, along with plenty of adventure and romance. When she's not working on her next novel, Lindsey spends her time trying out new recipes in the kitchen, walking through the woods, or planning her future farm. She lives in the Pacific Northwest with her two rather confused cats. You can find out more at www.lindseyfairleigh.com.

Made in the USA
Middletown, DE
15 January 2019